T0063402

Praise for *Amiable with Big Teeth*
and Claude McKay

"This is a major discovery. It dramatically expands the canon of novels written by Harlem Renaissance writers. More important, because it was written in the second half of the period, it shows that the renaissance continued to be vibrant and creative and turned its focus to international issues—in this case the tensions between Communists, on the one hand, and black nationalists, on the other, for the hearts and minds of black Americans."

—Henry Louis Gates, Jr.

"Claude McKay is such a romantic, questing figure in American literature that he belongs as much to the Lost Generation as he does to the Harlem Renaissance. The dramatic work of his expatriate youth is celebrated, but much less attention has been paid to what he wrote after he returned to New York in the mid-1930s. Indeed, his autobiography, a monumental survey of Harlem, and his occasional pieces were all we knew of his late work. Now two brilliant scholars have discovered McKay's last novel and thereby changed our picture of his closing years. *Amiable with Big Teeth* also tells us a lot about how black people around the globe responded to the invasion of Ethiopia and the specter of fascism. McKay is always interesting and always heartbreaking, he is so original and desperate and brave."   —Darryl Pinckney

"As a creative work and a historical document, *Amiable with Big Teeth* is nothing short of a master key into a world where the intersection of race and global revolutionary politics plays out in the lives of characters who are as dynamic and fully realized as the novel itself. . . . For today's audience, McKay's last novel should make for fascinating and timely reading as Americans enter an era in which solidarity-building across racial identities and national borders feels more necessary, and perhaps more difficult to achieve, than ever."   —*The Atlantic*

"McKay (1889–1948) has long been considered one of the great authors of the Harlem Renaissance. . . . Scholars and admirers now have a new piece of the oeuvre to admire. . . . *Amiable with Big Teeth* lives up to McKay's reputation."   —*Time*

"A satire of the political activists and intelligentsia of 1930s Harlem, it is a capstone to the literary career of McKay (1889–1948), considered one of the pillars of the Harlem Renaissance."
                                                                                                                                  —*Newsday*

"As a roman à clef written just a few years after the period it covers, *Amiable with Big Teeth* reflects that era with an intimacy impossible to capture in a later time—a miraculous feat for a book discovered seven decades later. . . . It inevitably recasts the narrative of Claude McKay's later years—altering our understanding of a novelist who seemingly wrote his last novel fifteen years before his death—and it's a satisfying rewrite."   —*Paste*

"To read *Amiable* today is to discover a lost world that, with its internecine struggles over race and class in New York and elsewhere, may seem equally alien and visceral. . . . The novel is an essential window into an overlooked era, when turmoil in Europe and the Depression at home didn't stop Harlem's brightest lights from carrying on with their work."   —*The Village Voice*

AMIABLE WITH BIG TEETH

CLAUDE MCKAY (1889–1948) was raised in the parish of Clarendon, Jamaica, the youngest of eleven children of the peasant farmers Thomas and Ann McKay. While still a teenager he began to publish poems in newspapers such as the Kingston *Daily Gleaner* and the Jamaica *Times*, some of which were collected in his two groundbreaking books of dialect poetry in traditional verse forms, *Songs of Jamaica* and *Constab Ballads* (1912). He moved to the United States to study agriculture but soon settled in New York, where he established himself within the literary scene, placing poems in avant-garde periodicals such as *The Seven Arts* and *Pearson's*, and above all with Max Eastman's influential socialist magazine *The Liberator*, where McKay came to serve on the editorial staff. His poetry collection *Harlem Shadows* (1922) is often described (along with Jean Toomer's *Cane* and James Weldon Johnson's anthology *The Book of American Negro Poetry*) as one of the key publications that kicked off the surge of artistic activity among African Americans that would come to be known as the Harlem Renaissance. Ironically, McKay would spend almost the entire next decade away from the United States. After traveling to Moscow in 1922 (where he spoke as an unofficial delegate at the Fourth Congress of the Communist International), McKay settled in France, where he wrote his first novel, the bestseller *Home to Harlem* (1928), and began work on his second, *Banjo* (1929), which he completed while voyaging in Spain and Morocco. He eventually took up residence in Tangier, where he lived from 1930 to 1934 and completed a book of short stories, *Gingertown* (1932), and another novel, *Banana Bottom* (1933). In 1934, McKay returned to the United States, where he struggled to find employment before joining the New York branch of the Federal Writers' Project, which allowed him to complete his autobiography, *A Long Way from Home* (1937).

The last book McKay was able to publish in his lifetime was a study of black life in New York, *Harlem: Negro Metropolis* (1940). Despite a succession of serious health problems beginning in 1941, he continued to write poetry and composed *Amiable with Big Teeth* under contract with E. P. Dutton (which had previously published *Harlem: Negro Metropolis*), although in the end Dutton declined the novel. McKay became involved in the activities of Friendship House, a Catholic-sponsored community center in Harlem. By 1944 McKay had formally converted to Catholicism and moved to Chicago, where he spent the remainder of his life teaching classes at the Catholic Youth Organization.

JEAN-CHRISTOPHE CLOUTIER is an assistant professor of English at the University of Pennsylvania. He received his PhD from Columbia University, where he also interned as an archivist and processed the papers of Samuel Roth, Erica Jong, and Barney Rosset. He is the editor of the original French writings of Jack Kerouac, *La vie est d'hommage* (2016), and translator of Kerouac's two French novellas, "The Night Is My Woman" (*La nuit est ma femme*) and "On the Road: Old Bull in the Bowery" (*Sur le chemin*), in *The Unknown Kerouac: Rare, Unpublished & Newly Translated Writings* (2016), where his Translator's Note also appears. He contributed the essay on the 1948 "Harlem Is Nowhere" collaboration between Ralph Ellison and Gordon Parks for *Invisible Man: Gordon Parks and Ralph Ellison in Harlem* (2016). His work has been featured in *The New York Times*, *The Chronicle of Higher Education*, *The Huffington Post*, *BOMB* magazine, *Le Monde*, *Maclean's*, and several other media outlets. Cloutier's articles, reviews, and translations have also appeared in *Modernism/modernity*, *Novel*, *Cinema Journal*, *Public Books*, *A Time for the Humanities*, and elsewhere.

BRENT HAYES EDWARDS is a professor in the Department of English and Comparative Literature at Columbia University, where he is also affiliated with the Center for Jazz Studies and the Institute for Comparative Literature and Society. He is the author of *The Practice of Diaspora: Literature, Translation, and the Rise of Black Internationalism* (2003), which was awarded the John Hope Franklin Prize of the American Studies Association and the Gilbert Chinard Prize of the Society for French Historical Studies, and was a runner-up for the James Russell Lowell Prize of the Modern Language Association. With Robert G. O'Meally and Farah Jasmine Griffin, he coedited the collection *Uptown Conversation: The New Jazz Studies* (2004). Edwards was appointed the Harlem Renaissance period editor for the revised third edition of *The Norton Anthology of African American Literature* (2014), and he has also prepared scholarly editions of classic works by W. E. B. Du Bois, Frederick Douglass, and Joseph Conrad. His most recent work includes *Epistrophies: Jazz and the Literary Imagination* (2017) and his translation of Michel Leiris's 1934 *Phantom Africa* (2017), for which Edwards was awarded a 2012 PEN/Heim Translation Fund Grant.

Claude McKay, July 25, 1941. Photograph by Carl Van Vechten /
The Van Vechten Trust / Beinecke Library, Yale.

CLAUDE MCKAY

Amiable with Big Teeth

A NOVEL OF THE LOVE AFFAIR
BETWEEN THE COMMUNISTS AND
THE POOR BLACK SHEEP
OF HARLEM

Edited with an Introduction by
JEAN-CHRISTOPHE CLOUTIER
and
BRENT HAYES EDWARDS

PENGUIN BOOKS

PENGUIN BOOKS

An imprint of Penguin Random House LLC
375 Hudson Street
New York, New York 10014
penguin.com

Copyright © 2017 by the Literary Estate for the Works of Claude McKay
Introduction and notes copyright © 2017 by Jean-Christophe Cloutier
and Brent Hayes Edwards
Penguin supports copyright. Copyright fuels creativity, encourages diverse voices,
promotes free speech, and creates a vibrant culture. Thank you for buying an authorized
edition of this book and for complying with copyright laws by not reproducing, scanning,
or distributing any part of it in any form without permission. You are supporting writers
and allowing Penguin to continue to publish books for every reader.

Excerpts from letters by Claude McKay to Carl Cowl on July 28, 1947; to Max Eastman on
March 22, 1941 and July 28, 1941; to Mr. Kohn on March 23, 1942; to Catherine Latimer
on February 19, 1941; to Ruth Raphael on January 21, 1942; to Simon Williamson on May
29, 1941; to Max Eastman on August 6, 1941; and to John Macrae on August 8, 1941, are
used with the permission of the Literary Estate for the Works of Claude McKay.

Excerpts from letters from Max Eastman to Claude McKay
reprinted by permission of the Yvette and Max Eastman Estate.

ISBN 9780143107316 (hardcover)
ISBN 9780143132219 (paperback)

Set in Sabon LT Std

146028962

Contents

Introduction

Habent sua fata libelli[1]

—Terentianus Maurus

In 1940, after publishers rejected the Irish writer Flann O'Brien's manuscript of *The Third Policeman*, published posthumously in 1967 and now considered a masterpiece, O'Brien put it away in a drawer, pretended to friends that it had been lost, and never spoke of it again. A year later, around July or August of 1941, E. P. Dutton declined to publish Claude McKay's *Amiable with Big Teeth*. Like O'Brien, McKay seems to have never again mentioned his novel, or at least the archive bears no such trace; but unlike the Irish novelist, McKay did not control the destiny of his own manuscript. That task, in a strange twist of fate, fell to Samuel Roth, a convicted pornographer and reputed literary "pirate"—a misleading epithet that haunted the independent, infamous New York–based publisher for his entire career.[2] Hidden in Roth's files, the manuscript lingered, deracinated from its original provenance.

The discovery of an unpublished and previously unknown manuscript by a major modern writer is a rare occurrence. While the collections of important literary figures are often mined for juvenilia, ephemera, undisclosed or unfinished projects—one thinks of recent publications drawn from the papers of Vladimir Nabokov (*The Original of Laura*), Ralph Ellison (*Three Days Before the Shooting*), Jack Kerouac (*La vie est d'hommage*; *The*

Unknown Kerouac), Harper Lee (*Go Set a Watchman*), and David Foster Wallace (*The Pale King*), for instance—it is not often that there appears a complete and corrected typescript by a well-known twentieth-century novelist.[3] Thus the publication of McKay's long-lost *Amiable with Big Teeth* is a cause for celebration as well as a monumental literary event.

The novel is as vibrant and accomplished as McKay's other celebrated works of long fiction, *Home to Harlem* (1928), *Banjo* (1929), and *Banana Bottom* (1933). But *Amiable with Big Teeth*, with its piquant burlesque of political machinations in Harlem during the mid-1930s in response to the Italian invasion of Ethiopia, is an eye-opening addition to McKay's body of work, taking up new and different themes and greatly expanding our understanding of his concerns in the final decade of his life. McKay, who spoke as an unofficial representative of the "American Negro" at the 1922 Fourth Congress of the Communist International in Moscow and interacted with many of the key leftist intellectuals of the era in the United States and Europe (including Trotsky, George Bernard Shaw, W. E. B. Du Bois, Frank Harris, Max Eastman, Louise Bryant, and John Reed), is widely recognized as one of the most important literary and political writers of the interwar period. *Amiable with Big Teeth* gives us for the first time McKay's fictional take on the tumult of the 1930s, including the Popular Front and the rise of fascism.

The last book McKay saw published in his lifetime was his ambitious nonfictional work *Harlem: Negro Metropolis*, which was released by E. P. Dutton in 1940. In his biography *Claude McKay: Rebel Sojourner in the Harlem Renaissance*, Wayne Cooper notes that McKay "tried also to publish at least one more book-length manuscript."[4] In fact, he worked on multiple book projects in his final years, including a sonnet collection he called "The Cycle" (composed around 1943), a manuscript of his "Selected Poems," and a memoir of his childhood called *My Green Hills of Jamaica* (written in 1946).[5] Some sources describe the short, possibly incomplete novel *Harlem Glory* as McKay's "final" attempt at fiction. But evidence in McKay's correspondence proves that he composed *Harlem Glory* around 1936–37, before he wrote *Harlem: Negro Metropolis.*[6]

There have been hints that McKay was also working on a novel in the last years of his life. Many years after his passing, the writer's last agent, Carl Cowl, became aware of the existence of a book manuscript McKay had supposedly written in the 1940s. In a letter to the French literary critic Jean Wagner in early 1970, Cowl mentions that Dutton claimed to have paid McKay $475 as an advance on a novel titled "God's Black Sheep" that the publisher ended up rejecting.[7] The phrase clearly echoes the subtitle of *Amiable with Big Teeth: A Novel of the Love Affair Between the Communists and the Poor Black Sheep of Harlem*, and the formulations "God's black sheep" and "poor black sheep" also appear repeatedly in the body of the text, especially in Reverend Zebulon Trawl's sermon in Chapter 10. In fact, "God's Black Sheep" was the title under which McKay initially submitted the novel to Dutton.[8] But Cowl never found a copy of the manuscript, for reasons we explain below.

In February 1934, McKay returned to New York nearly penniless after almost twelve years living as an expatriate in France, Spain, and Morocco.[9] His financial struggles continued, as literary opportunities in the city had dried up with the advent of the Great Depression, but McKay kept writing, starting work, for example, on the autobiographical manuscript that would be published as *A Long Way from Home* in 1937. Still, as Cooper points out, the autobiography is "only partially indicative of how completely involved he had become in the social and political controversies that dominated the American literary scene in the 1930s."[10]

Upon his return, McKay quickly immersed himself in the Harlem arts scene, which remained energetic despite the bleak economy. McKay grew close to a number of visual artists linked to the attempts to found a Harlem Artists' Guild in 1935, especially the painters Romare Bearden and Jacob Lawrence, who both had studios in the building at 33 West 125th Street, where McKay would live for a couple of years at the end of the decade.[11] But he was especially active in the Harlem literary scene. McKay tried to found a literary journal called *Bambara* in 1936 and was at the center of the effort to establish a Negro Writers' Guild the next year, which brought together some of the most talented younger writers and an eclectic group of leading literary lights from the 1920s, including Countee Cullen, James Weldon Johnson, Arthur Schomburg, Jessie Fauset, and Richard Bruce Nugent.[12]

The most important institution in McKay's life in this period, however, was the Federal Writers' Project (FWP), which provided a crucial "refuge from destitution" (to adopt Cooper's phrase) by employing McKay on its "Negroes in New York" project from the spring of 1936 through the end of 1939.[13] His colleagues at the FWP offices in the Port Authority Building on lower Eighth Avenue included many of the most talented black writers in the city, such as Dorothy West, Abram Hill, Richard Wright, Ralph Ellison, J. A. Rogers, Richard Bruce Nugent, Simon Williamson, Waring Cuney, and Ted Poston. The FWP team undertook an ambitious project collecting resources for the study of black New York. McKay himself wrote essays on topics as various as "Negro Artists in New York," "Negroes from New York in the US Diplomatic Service," "Group Life and Literature," and "On the First Negroes Coming to America," and conducted interviews with artists including Augusta Savage, Romare Bearden, and Beauford Delaney.[14] The FWP was invaluable not only in providing McKay a regular paycheck but also in supporting his own work, since, as he himself put it, the "special research work" of the project—which mainly involved biographical sketches and interviews of significant Harlem personalities, and short overview essays on major themes in African American history— gave the writers a range of resources that were "of intrinsic value to those of us who were writing about Negro life in our off-project time."[15]

If the resources of the FWP were instrumental for McKay's work on *Harlem: Negro Metropolis* (a book that included detailed discussions of black luminaries such as Marcus Garvey, Casper Holstein, Father Divine, A. Philip Randolph, and Sufi Abdul Hamid, for which McKay drew on FWP materials to supplement his own firsthand impressions), they proved equally crucial for *Amiable with Big Teeth*. A number of Harlem personalities (including Hamid and the infamous black fighter pilot Hubert Fauntleroy Julian) are depicted by name in McKay's novel, and a number of fictional scenes echo historical episodes and information in the FWP archive.

Perhaps the most striking example is the extraordinary section of *Amiable with Big Teeth* devoted to a portrait of a nightclub in Harlem called the Merry-Go-Round, the "largest and bawdiest bar in Lenox Avenue," where young men "had charcoaled and elongated their eyebrows and rouged their cheeks like the girls" (p. 147). The eponymous Chapter 13, set in the streets outside the Merry-Go-Round during an anti-Italian protest—remarkably reminiscent of actual events, such as the demonstration that erupted in violence in July 1936 in front of the Bella Restaurant at 329 Lenox Avenue between 126th and 127th Streets[16]—describes the goings-on in the Merry-Go-Round in a manner that seems informed not only by McKay's knowledge of Harlem nightlife but also of specific FWP materials such as Wilbur Young's rich biographical piece on Gladys Bentley, the legendary cross-dressing lesbian singer who thrilled and scandalized audiences at Harlem spots such as Hansberry's Clam House (on 133rd Street) and the Ubangi Club (on Seventh Avenue at 131st Street), with its "chorus of singing, dancing, be-ribboned and be-rouged 'pansies.'"[17]

Amiable with Big Teeth is set in the mid-1930s during what became known as the "Italo-Abyssinian crisis," which erupted in October 1935 when Mussolini's forces invaded Ethiopia. McKay's novel is above all concerned with efforts among the Harlem intelligentsia to organize support for the defense of Ethiopia. The FWP collected a good deal of material on this topic, with a richness of detail that would have been very difficult to obtain elsewhere only a few short years after the events. Indeed, McKay's *Harlem: Negro Metropolis* was one of the first books to include substantial historical coverage of the crisis.[18]

If *Amiable with Big Teeth* might then be described as an elaboration of this thread in *Harlem: Negro Metropolis*, McKay's novel takes a notably different approach from his opinionated nonfiction study.[19] *Amiable with Big Teeth* is a satirical yet sentimental political novel full of earnest pleas and impassioned rhetoric, public grandstanding and nefarious backroom imposture, savvy diplomacy and dimwit romance. Set in the turbulent Harlem of 1936, the novel immerses the reader in the concerns, anxieties, hopes, and dreams at the heart of black America during a period when (to quote the opening of Chapter 4) the "tides of Italy's war in Ethiopia had swept up out of Africa and across the Atlantic to beat against the shores of America and strangely to agitate the unheroic existence of Aframericans" (p. 27).

Biographer Wayne Cooper suggests that the importance of McKay's articles and correspondence from the late 1930s has not been fully appreciated: "In a real sense they represent the culmination of his writing career, a summing up of his concerns as a creative writer. As such they form a logical sequel to his earlier preoccupations as a poet and novelist."[20] Something similar might be said about *Amiable with Big Teeth*. From this perspective it makes perfect sense that the author of *Home to Harlem* and *Banjo* would have been drawn to the Italo-Ethiopian crisis as a potential topic for fiction. McKay was himself directly embroiled in the debates in Harlem around the Popular Front, Communism, and the rise of fascism, first of all. And the Italian invasion of Ethiopia—even more than the Spanish Civil War, the 1936 Olympics in Berlin, or the second Joe Louis–Max Schmeling fight in June 1938—was arguably *the* single event in the period that most powerfully inflamed the imagination of blacks throughout the world, as an attack on the very principle of black sovereignty at a time when the great majority of peoples of the African diaspora lived under colonial domination. "Almost overnight," as the great historian John Hope Franklin famously observed, "even the most provincial among the American Negroes became international-minded."[21] As a result, the very word "Ethiopia" came to seem "confluent" with the notion of Africa: it "became a most ancient point of reference—a term signifying historicity and racial dignity in ways the term 'Negro' could not match."[22] McKay himself hints at this unparalleled symbolic resonance in *Harlem: Negro Metropolis*, reflecting on the depth of sentiment in the African American response to the Italian invasion:

> To the emotional masses of the American Negro church the Ethiopia of today is the wonderful Ethiopia of the Bible. In a religious sense it is far more real to them than the West African lands, from which it is assumed that most of the ancestors of Aframericans came. They were happy that the emperor had escaped alive. As an ex-ruler he remained a symbol of authority over the Negro state of their imagination.[23]

One of McKay's coworkers on the FWP, Roi Ottley, observed a couple of years later that "from the beginning the

Ethiopian crisis became a fundamental question in Negro life. It was all but impossible for Negro leaders to remain neutral, and the position they took toward the conflict became a fundamental test. The survival of the black nation became the topic of angry debate in pool-rooms, barber shops, and taverns."[24] Historian William Scott puts it in equally emphatic terms:

> [T]he pro-Ethiopian crusade of African-Americans represents an extraordinary episode in modern U.S. black history. A mass impulse, its scope was broad and its force intense, exceeding in size and vigor all other contemporary black freedom protests. In magnitude and might, no other black-rights agitation of the interwar years paralleled the scale and depth of African-Americans' pro-Abyssinian remonstrations.[25]

In the literature of the period, perhaps the most obvious parallel to McKay's *Amiable with Big Teeth* are the Ethiopian-themed serial novels George Schuyler published under multiple pseudonyms between 1936 and 1939 in the *Pittsburgh Courier*. But Schuyler's "Ethiopian" work is only one strand of his prolific exploration of the possibilities of black pulp fiction, which includes nearly three dozen stories set everywhere from Harlem to the Mississippi Delta to "the African bush."[26] Schuyler's work in this vein tends to involve lurid tales of "international intrigue" with elements of science fiction: even when they allude to contemporary events, it is usually in the service of vindicationist Pan-African fantasy, as in "Revolt in Ethiopia: A Tale of Black Insurrection Against Italian Imperialism" (1938–39), in which—to quote editor Robert A. Hill's plot summary—"a wealthy young black American on a cruise gets involved with a beautiful Ethiopian princess seeking a hidden treasure needed to finance Ethiopia's war against Italian occupation."[27] In contrast, despite its own sensationalist elements, *Amiable with Big Teeth* is much less concerned with fantasy and much more framed as a caustic, even overtly polemical, depiction of the complex Harlem political landscape in the mid-1930s as it shifted in the shadow of international events. In his own words, McKay was writing "a novel of ideas"[28] and intentionally "breaking with [his] former performance in fiction" in order to craft "a contemporary historical tale of local conflict with an ethical basis."[29]

In this respect, it is striking how many plot points and characters in *Amiable with Big Teeth* are derived from historical antecedents, starting with the Princess Benebe hoax at the heart of the novel (see Chapter 16). Among the many hustlers, impostors, and frauds that sprouted in Harlem during the mid-1930s,[30] one of the most famous was a certain Princess Tamanya, purported to be an Ethiopian princess and the first cousin of Emperor Haile Selassie. In the summer of 1935, Princess Tamanya summoned journalists to a sumptuous suite in the Broadway Central Hotel to give an impromptu press conference about the plight of her nation. It was later revealed that Princess Tamanya was in fact Miss Islin Harvey, a local girl who had been put up to the stunt by the notorious black promoter and PR wizard Chappy Gardner, a man once referred to as "the black P. T. Barnum," and an eventual member of the Negro Writers' Guild in 1937.[31] Although McKay transposes the fictional version of the fraudulent Ethiopian Princess Benebe into a somewhat different context in *Amiable with Big Teeth*—making the masquerade the work of the villain Maxim Tasan, a white Communist infiltrator, rather than a black entrepreneur—he draws directly on many of the details of the Tamanya story as it actually took place at the time.

Although there does not appear to be a single historical source for the novel's villain, Maxim Tasan, the character's name seems to be in part an allusion to the prominent Soviet diplomat Maxim Litvinov, who, starting in 1930, served as the People's Commissar for Foreign Affairs. Litvinov represented the Soviet Union in the League of Nations between 1934 and 1938; indeed, during the Italo-Ethiopian crisis he was the chairman of the League of Nations Council.[32] He visited New York in 1933 on his way to Washington, DC, where he met with President Roosevelt and successfully persuaded the United States to recognize the legitimacy of the Soviet government, and his comments on US race relations—during his visit, Litvinov declared, "White workers cannot free themselves so long as a Negro nation is enslaved in the Black Belt of the South"— were reported widely in left-leaning black newspapers.[33]

It is perhaps not a coincidence, either, that when he first returned to New York in 1934, McKay was represented by a particularly repugnant and ineffective literary agent named Maxim Lieber.[34] This second Maxim was not only a member of the Communist Party of the United States, but also a key player in a Soviet espionage ring in New York. Lieber's role as a spy was not revealed until years later, during the Alger Hiss affair at the end of the 1940s.[35] Biographer Wayne Cooper conjectures that while McKay may have been aware of Lieber's party membership, he "certainly had no knowledge of Lieber's employment as a Soviet agent."[36] Intriguingly, however, there is evidence that McKay did have knowledge of Soviet espionage in the period. In an article published in the *New York Amsterdam News* in May 1939, McKay contended that "if Negroes do not assert their independence, radicals will use them precisely as any other political party," adding that "there are significant angles of the radical approach towards the Negro which are known to initiates only." He proceeded to divulge what he described as "information received some time ago" in support of his claim:

> I was told that some five years ago the Russian Communist Party dispatched a secret agent to America to gather material facts and to report on the economic status and the political

possibility of the American Negro. Incognito the Russian comrade visited Harlem and other Negro communities, made a
survey of living conditions among the common people and in-
terviewed some of the leading Negroes, who were not aware of
his identity. Upon the completion of his study the Russian recommended to the American Communist Party that Negroes
should be organized as an autonomous cultural group, similar
to the various language groups, with their own leaders, clubs,
publications, etc. But the local Communist hierarchy objected,
saying that Negroes would resent organization along such
lines.

However, there was a minority of colored comrades, who
supported the Russian's viewpoint.[37]

Whether or not Lieber was the "secret agent" in question, it is
a tantalizing archival tidbit, suggesting that in concocting
Maxim Tasan, McKay was transposing elements of the historical record, alluding to fact (and perhaps both to Litvinov and
Lieber) while warping and reworking it in the interest of a
polemical interpretation of the Communist influence in 1930s
Harlem.[38]

The Ethiopian envoy in the novel, Lij Alamaya, functions as
a similar sort of composite of historical reference points. Less
than a year after McKay returned to the United States, he witnessed firsthand the upsurge of concern in Harlem for the
Ethiopian cause. In the late 1930s, he became personally acquainted with the most prominent Ethiopian emissary in New
York, Dr. Malaku Bayen, who was Haile Selassie's cousin and
personal physician. Bayen had attended medical school at
Howard University in Washington, DC, where he met his African American wife, the former Dorothy Hadley. Due to the
military crisis in Ethiopia, Bayen returned home in June 1935,
but fled with the emperor to London in the wake of the Italian invasion. And in September 1936 Bayen was dispatched

back to the United States to serve as a "Special Envoy for the Western Hemisphere," charged with raising funds to support the Ethiopian struggle for independence.[39] On September 28, Bayen gave a rousing speech to an audience of two thousand at Rockland Palace in Harlem, where he proclaimed that "our soldiers will never cease fighting until the enemy is driven from our soil."[40] He worked closely with the United Aid for Ethiopia, one of the most important Harlem organizations, but gravitated away from it when "members of the American Communist Party took sharp interest in the United Aid and attempted to transform it into a Communist front."[41] In August 1937, Bayen founded a new aid organization called the Ethiopian World Federation, appointing a respected Methodist minister, the Reverend Lorenzo H. King, as the organization's president.[42] McKay not only discusses Bayen in *Harlem: Negro Metropolis*, but also includes a photo of him at an event in Harlem (which Bayen allowed him to use free of charge).[43]

In fact, however, Bayen was the second Ethiopian envoy to be sent to Harlem during the crisis. The opening scene of *Amiable with Big Teeth* is a thinly veiled depiction of a monumental rally held in December 1935 at the Abyssinian Baptist Church by the Provisional Committee for the Defense of Ethiopia, one of the first aid organizations. Lij Tasfaye Zaphiro, a young functionary who had been a member of the Ethiopian delegation in London, had come to New York that month, and he was one of the featured speakers at the rally, which attracted an audience of nearly four thousand.[44] In fact, it was Zaphiro, working in collaboration with African American supporters including the Reverend William Lloyd Imes, the pastor of the prestigious St. James Presbyterian Church, and Philip M. Savory, an insurance executive who was co-owner of the *New York Amsterdam News*, who went on to found the United Aid for Ethiopia (the same organization that would later support Bayen in his fund-raising efforts in the fall of 1936).[45]

Initially Zaphiro also drew support from the Committee on the Ethiopian Crisis, the most important white-run aid organization, which was directed by John Shaw, a naturalized American born in the United Kingdom who ran an import-export business with significant commercial ties to Ethiopia.[46] Largely due to those ties, Shaw was subsequently appointed as the honorary Ethiopian consul in the United States, and as such he began to attempt to consolidate the Ethiopian aid effort (which had been scattered among a confusing plethora of overlapping organizations) under the umbrella of yet another newly formed group, the American Aid for Ethiopia.[47] Unconvinced of the need for African American–run Ethiopian aid initiatives, Shaw came to distrust Zaphiro and the United Aid for Ethiopia in particular. In March 1936, questions were raised about Zaphiro's credentials as an official envoy of the Ethiopian government, and Shaw was instrumental in bringing about Zaphiro's abrupt recall to London.[48] His departure was met with consternation in the black press; as one newspaperman wrote a few months later in the *Chicago Defender*, for instance: "Black America accepted the slender, lemon-colored youth with the pronounced Oxford accent and regal bearing with open arms. Although he carried no papers, no letters of introduction, nor anything to officially stand him in good stead when called upon to prove his status, the public was willing to take him at his word."[49] But Shaw saw to it that the young Ethiopian envoy was discredited, thereby undermining the black-led United Aid for Ethiopia at the same time. This is to say that in *Amiable with Big Teeth*, with Maxim Tasan's elaborate scheme to destroy the credibility of Lij Tekla Alamaya (and thereby to destabilize the black-run Hands to Ethiopia), McKay again transposes and refashions a historical episode in the service of the novel's critique of Communist intervention in Harlem politics.

Another man who was pivotal in the founding of the United Aid for Ethiopia was Willis N. Huggins, an African American high school teacher, bibliophile, and historian who became deeply involved in the effort to support the Abyssinian cause, even traveling to Geneva in the summer of 1935 to deliver a petition to the League of Nations.[50] Months before Zaphiro's arrival in the United States, as the scope of Italian imperialist designs on Ethiopia was beginning to become apparent, Huggins was one of the first to plan an organized African American response through the Provisional Committee for the Defense of Ethiopia. On a rainy night in early March 1935, he was one of six speakers at a packed inaugural meeting of the Provisional Committee at the Abyssinian Baptist Church.[51] In December, Huggins also spoke at the Abyssinian gathering where Zaphiro was first introduced to the Harlem public.[52] From the beginning, Huggins insisted on the symbolic importance of Ethiopian independence to peoples of African descent around the globe, warning in the wake of Italy's victory that "with the fall of Addis Ababa comes the fall of the black world."[53]

In *Amiable with Big Teeth*, the memorable character of Professor Koazhy seems to be yet another hybrid figure loosely based on Huggins as well as another black bibliophile and independent historian, Charles C. Seifert (who, like Koazhy in the novel, assumed the title of "Professor" even though he held no official degree). McKay knew both men personally: he thanks Huggins in the acknowledgments of *Harlem: Negro Metropolis* (just as Huggins thanks McKay in his 1937 book *Introduction to African Civilizations*),[54] and the two men appeared together at various public events in Harlem, such as the December 1938 panel held at the 135th Street Library, where they discussed "Anti-Semitism and the Negro."[55] McKay was acquainted with Seifert, too, through the thriving networks of black independent historians and bibliophiles in Harlem. Four years earlier, at a time when he was unemployed and homeless, McKay supported himself for a few months toward the end of

1934 by working as a sort of research assistant for Seifert in exchange for room and board, helping him "shape up and write his researches" on ancient African history.[56] McKay was disdainful of the work itself, complaining to his friend Max Eastman that "the old fool" Seifert was "always butting in on me with senile talk about ancient African glory."[57]

But in *Amiable with Big Teeth*, the portrayal of Professor Koazhy is largely sympathetic. Most notably, in the novel's almost comically melodramatic conclusion, the duplicitous Maxim Tasan meets his doom during the ritual sacrifice performed during the gala of the Society of African Leopard Men at the hands of Koazhy's Senegambians. In McKay's fiction, in other words, the avenging force that finally defeats the Communist menace emerges from what is seemingly the most unlikely of sources: the circuit of black bibliophiles and independent historians like Huggins and Seifert who, while often dismissed in their time and largely forgotten since, were crucial in the emergence of organized black radicalism throughout the twentieth century.[58]

Even as the novel's denouement alludes to actual historical controversies involving tales of "leopard men" and human sacrifice in colonial Africa,[59] it is important to recognize that the Senegambians are not some mystical cohort dedicated to "primitive" ritual. Instead, they are an autonomous, underground diasporic fraternity involving African Americans as well as Africans (such as Diup Wuluff)—at once a sort of voluntary study group (at the end of Chapter 1, Koazhy is called a "historical mentor" to the Senegambians, who are described as his "students"), a political and even martial organization (ready to rumble in street fights when necessary, as in the conflict in front of Reverend Trawl's church in Chapter 10), and a sort of secret society. So, in the novel, the force of retribution is ultimately rooted in an impulse toward diasporic solidarity, historical documentation, collective study, and political

liberation that is generated out of some deep, possibly fundamental wellspring in black life, in a manner that at once provides
the momentum behind African American institution-building
and exists somehow beyond or outside formal institutions.

While considering the stakes of the historical transpositions
woven into *Amiable with Big Teeth*, one might also ask about
the origins of McKay's suspicions of the Communist Party,
which prove so central to the plot of the novel. In this respect it
is helpful to turn to the many articles and editorials on politics
and current events that McKay began publishing in the late
1930s. He penned a regular column in the *New York Amsterdam News* for two months in the spring of 1939, and wrote a
steady string of pieces for journals including the *New Leader*,
Opportunity, the *American Mercury*, and *Common Sense*.[60]
Major themes include not only the aftermath of the Italo-
Ethiopian crisis and the Spanish Civil War, but also and more
broadly the implications of the Popular Front, the threat of fascism in Europe, and Harlem politics (especially anti-Semitism
among African Americans).[61] Even as he took up this wide
range of contemporary issues, McKay also became involved
with the journal *The African: Journal of African Affairs*, founded
in October 1937 by the Universal Ethiopian Students Association. As Wayne Cooper describes it, *African* "sought to expose
the injustices committed by European imperialism in Africa, to
inform readers about black problems in the United States, and
to encourage American blacks to see their problems in a broad,
international perspective. It also sought to keep alive the strong
black interest in the fate of Ethiopia."[62] McKay not only published a piece in the journal (a fascinating essay about Tangier),[63] but at one point he was even in negotiations with the
group to take over the editorship, in what was planned as a
collaboration with poet Countee Cullen.[64]

It is in these articles and editorials that McKay first begins
to articulate what becomes the increasingly fervent anti-

Communist stance that is a key feature of his late career, as evidenced by *Harlem: Negro Metropolis*, *Amiable with Big Teeth*, and many of the poems in his 1943 "Cycle" sequence. The rhetorical tone in these articles is often as heated and hyperbolic as some of the more polemical passages in the novel. In one 1939 piece in the *New Leader*, for instance, in which McKay discusses "the danger of Negroes coming under the control of Moscow-dominated Communists exploiting their grievances"—which of course is the main theme of *Amiable with Big Teeth* as well—McKay goes so far as to declare that "the Communist dictatorship is a greater danger to humanity than the Nazi dictatorship."[65] In *Harlem: Negro Metropolis*, he complains that in the late 1930s "Harlem was overrun with white Communists who promoted themselves as the only leaders of the Negroes. They were converting a few Negroes into Bolshevik propagandists, but they were actually doing nothing to help alleviate the social misery of Negroes."[66] It is logical, then, that in writing *Amiable with Big Teeth*, McKay would set this theme in the context of pro-Ethiopian activism, since it was during the Italo-Ethiopian crisis that McKay had first inveighed against the pattern of Communist intervention.

McKay's mistrust of Communism emerged as a principled response to what he observed in the political currents of his time, rather than a knee-jerk rejection of Marxism or a simple retreat from his previous affiliation with political radicalism in many forms, including the Comintern itself (in his 1922 visit to Moscow). Throughout his career, he was consistent in his discomfort with groupthink of any sort: "I am intellectually independent and not specifically labeled with any 'ism,'" as he put it in one 1937 article.[67] At the same time, McKay was equally consistent in his commitment to social and economic justice, and as late as the fall of 1938 he explicitly praised the Communist Party for its role in labor relations in the United States, writing in one article that "it must be admitted that more than any other group the Communists should be credited with the effective organizing of the unemployed and relief workers." What he rejected, McKay explained, was not the principles of unionism or Marxism itself, but instead the "basic political ideology" of Communism: "I reject absolutely the idea of government by dictatorship, which is the pillar of political Communism." While critical of the Popular Front, which he considered a "smoke screen," McKay was above all worried that black political organizations would be manipulated for purely propagandistic ends: "As a member of this group and also as a radical thinker, I am specially concerned about its future and the danger of its being maneuvered through high-powered propaganda into the morass of Communist opportunism."[68] Or as he rephrased his objection in *Harlem: Negro Metropolis*, "the Communists were out to exploit all the social disadvantages of the Negro minority for propaganda effect, but they were little interested in practical efforts to ameliorate the social conditions of that minority."[69]

As mentioned earlier, the novel's original title, "God's Black Sheep," is plucked from the sermon given by Reverend Zebulon Trawl in Chapter 10, in which he deploys variants of the phrase, at times to plead with the Lord to provide "guidance" for "thy poor black sheep," and later to demarcate the color line among the Lord's herd, underscoring black vulnerability: "Lord, the white ones have swarmed up here like hornets and peckawoods to sting and peck at God's black sheep. What have we done for the white people to invade us in this high reservation to frighten and stampede thy black sheep?" (p. 110). But the phrase also captures the way McKay felt by the end of the 1930s about the "gullible" black intellectuals who had fallen under the Comintern's spell. As he had written in *Harlem: Negro Metropolis*: "While many of their outstanding white colleagues wisely ran to save themselves when the

Communists ripped off their masks and flashed daggers, the Negroes stood emotionally fixed like the boy on the burning deck."[70]

The novel's revised title, *Amiable with Big Teeth*, likewise resonates with Reverend Trawl's sermon, but adds another layer of metaphor. The new phrase, which might at first seem obscure or even cryptic, is at its base a variation on the biblical warning against false prophets (i.e., the wolf in sheep's clothing).[71] "Harlem is the stamping ground of false prophets," Trawl proclaims. "The racketeers of Satan are posing as angels to deceive your black sheep and lead them astray" (p. 110). (Reading this passage, it is hard not to notice that "Tasan" is an anagram of "Satan.") There are echoes of this sort of metaphor in a number of McKay's articles and editorials in the late 1930s, where they serve as a figure for his fear that African Americans were being "dangerously misled" by Communist activists in the Popular Front.[72] For McKay, this fear was exacerbated by his sense that the "Negro world" was especially vulnerable to such manipulation, given its limited resources and its weakness due to the ravages of racial segregation and economic exploitation. As he writes in *Harlem: Negro Metropolis*: "The white world is wide and complex as its boundaries are elastic. A savage onslaught of propaganda is not so powerful and effective as it may be in the Negro world, where all strata are close-packed and the propagandists can leap to action like wolves in an overcrowded sheepfold."[73]

One of McKay's 1939 articles in the *New Leader* may come closest to the title of the novel in describing the Communist threat:

But the Communist hyena disguised as shepherd dog is the sinister enemy that works havoc in the sheepfold under cover of darkness. He is assiduous in unhappy Harlem, often prowling behind the scenes, ready to pounce upon every social issue and convert it into an empty slogan and seeking by any means to discredit the wary individuals and groups that keep him out.[74]

In *Amiable* itself, two of the novel's major characters, Dorsey Flagg and Lij Alamaya, do employ the word "hyena" in reference to Communists or Stalinites: "I have to use my head against the Stalinite hyena," says Flagg (p. 187), and when Lij Alamaya is shown evidence that Maxim Tasan is responsible for the theft of his official letter from the Emperor, he punches Tasan in disgust and cries out, "I'm getting out of this hyena's lair" (p. 218). But although McKay makes recourse to similar metaphors on numerous occasions in his articles and poems,[75] there does not seem to be an instance where he employs the exact phrasing ("amiable with big teeth") that provides the vivid and arresting title of the novel.

Harlem: Negro Metropolis was published in October 1940. That winter, just after the new year, McKay received a letter from his publisher, E. P. Dutton, acknowledging a letter McKay had sent on January 4 to request an appointment to discuss "a novel which you have in mind."[76] McKay met with John Macrae, the president of Dutton, to discuss his plans for the new work. Dutton ended up giving McKay an advance of $350 for the novel, paid in weekly installments of $25, and later even agreed to grant him an additional $125, "on account of royalties to be earned," to support his writing progress.[77] McKay moved out of New York, staying at the home of Clyde Wells, a friend in the remote town of North Wayne, Maine, in order to work on the book, planning to live on the advance while he was writing.[78] Toward the end of February, McKay wrote to Catherine Latimer, the librarian at the Harlem branch of the New York Public Library that would become the Schomburg Center, apologizing that he had been slow to reply to a letter she had sent him because he "was fully occupied with literary negotiations and practical matters prior to leaving New York, besides being in the midst of packing." He explained that he had gone to Maine "to do some important work" and preferred to be isolated, living in a small farmhouse located a dozen miles from the nearest town, "up here where it is cold and bracing."[79]

Interestingly, the agreement McKay had made with Dutton president Macrae stipulated that McKay should "keep in full harmony and in direct contact with Mr. Max Eastman so that you would have his valuable advice in the writing of your proposed novel."[80] It seems that Eastman, McKay's longtime friend and colleague, had written Dutton himself in support of McKay's book. On February 12, 1941, Macrae wrote Eastman to request his involvement in McKay's work:

MY DEAR MAX EASTMAN:

I had your welcome letter of January 13 in reference to our mutual friend, Claude McKay, and his proposed novel. Partly owing to your good advice, after several important talks with Claude McKay we entered into a contract with him for the writing of this novel. The plan adopted is to provide a certain amount per week for a limited period to Claude McKay. It was the feeling of Claude McKay that he probably could write the novel within the time specified in our contract.

My literary advisers were of the opinion that the outline which Mr. McKay submitted to us was too melodramatic, and that the novel written on these lines would not satisfy the artistic taste and refinement of Claude McKay. Also, it was the feeling of my literary adviser that we would not care to publish a novel so melodramatic as Claude McKay's synopsis pictured it.

As and when Claude McKay provides you with installments of his novel, I will be everlastingly obliged to you if you will assist him with your common sense advice and, added to that, the good taste which is part of your work. I do believe that Claude McKay will write a good novel, and I am taking the liberty of asking you, as far as you can, to give to Claude McKay of your wisdom and your critical sense of what a novel should be.[81]

As we will see, Eastman did give advice to McKay about his manuscript over the next few months.

McKay discussed the work in progress in many of the letters he wrote while in Maine. In a letter to a seaman, a cook on the Royal Mail Lines based in South Africa, McKay concluded a long screed about the "fraudulent international Popular Front that was promoted by the Communists" and the "ruthless and unscrupulous" Soviet regime with the news that he was "far away up here in Maine writing a new book."[82] He likewise mentioned the novel to labor organizer A. Philip Randolph, who wrote a letter to McKay in April praising the accomplishment of *Harlem: Negro Metropolis* and went on to say, "I am glad to know that you are now engaged in the writing of a new book, for not only have you a facile style of high excellence, but your ideas on the Negro liberation movement flash out like a diamond from the sands and cut deeply into the consciousness of Negro and white America."[83] McKay's agent Carlisle Smyth wrote in May that he was "very glad to know that you are in stride again. I am sure the country is by far the best place to work."[84] By the end of May, he was telling friends he was almost done. An acquaintance in Philadelphia wrote back: "I am glad that you have so little to do to finish your book. I am sure that it will be good";[85] and another from Brooklyn offered encouragement: "I am very glad to hear of your completion of your new work, I'm sure it['s] a killer, etc."[86] Simon Williamson, an old friend from McKay's days with the Federal Writers' Project and the Negro Writers' Guild, wrote toward the end of June 1941: "I am glad the work is shaping up nicely, and wish I could see it before it is published."[87] A month earlier, McKay had asked Williamson to supply him with urgently needed "items" and "facts" for his novel. "I should be happy if you could inform me whether the Spanish Civil War broke in June or July of 1936," McKay explained. "I want to dovetail the Fascist conquest of Ethiopia into it, but I need to be certain about the facts."[88] Incidentally, since he wrote the novel in Maine, *Amiable with Big Teeth* has the unlikely distinction of being the only novel McKay ever wrote on American soil—*Home to Harlem*, *Banjo*, and *Banana Bottom* were all written on the other side of the Atlantic.

It is in McKay's extensive correspondence with his longtime friend Max Eastman that there is not only this sort of intriguing circumstantial evidence—that McKay had started writing a new work of fiction that had something to do with Ethiopia and the Popular Front—but also explicit discussion of the manuscript in progress that proves beyond any doubt that it was *Amiable with Big Teeth*. On March 29, 1941, McKay wrote to Eastman:

Dear Max: I took your advice (half-way) and spent a month, not two, pottering with the plot, characters and aim of the novel. And it has worked out a little differently from the first draft I showed you. The main thing is that it has some politics in it and we had thought it expedient to keep politics out. But after building up the Lij into a really sympathetic character (albeit weak) and consulting notes and newspaper stories of the period (early 1936) in which the tale begins, I discovered that it was impossible to keep politics out, for the Aid to Ethiopia was the jumping-off of the Popular Front movement in the United States. Of course, I am keeping the political stuff in its proper place, so that it may not be a handicap to the straight tale.

I began the actual writing on the 15th and it is going pretty good and I shall send the duplicate sheets to you as soon as I have from 40 to 50 pages. I believe that it'll take as much as that to give you the lay of the tale. I have a new agent in New York and she is also keen to see the tale as it unfolds.

I am working quickly for the time is short and I am not fooling with this chance. I like the climate up here. It has been cold with a lot of snow on the ground (which is now melting and slushy) but the air is dry and keen and I feel a thousand times better than I did in New York. I have a nice large sunny room and a roaring wood fire which is regular and more dependable than the best I was getting in my place in New York. If you should be moving, please let me know as I hope to send the stuff in a couple of weeks.[89]

Soon after, McKay did send the first chunk of the manuscript as promised, for Eastman wrote back toward the end of April with praise:

Claude, I'm perfectly delighted with your book. So is [Eastman's wife] Eliena as far as she has gone. I was waiting for her to finish, but I don't want to wait any longer.

Of course I endorse absolutely your impulse to bring in the Stalinists, and make the canvas as big and significant as it can be. Put in all Harlem and all you know and think about it.

I am vividly interested in your characters, and that's the main thing.

I've written in a little suggestion here and there. I have a difficulty, just as in Tolstoy, keeping track at the beginning of which is which. You might help me a little there by repeating in some way who they are the second time you mention them. But then I'm rather dumb as a novel reader, my interest wandering from persons to ideas so easily.

The only general suggestion I have is: Don't write it <u>too</u> fast. Don't work when your [*sic*] tired. Your style is fine on the whole, but occasionally it sags a little imaginatively. I want to encounter <u>more</u> brilliant visions like "a reddish person and so covered with freckles that he looked like a cinnamon sandwich." Or: "like children with tinted candies, each one hiding its candy in its fist and insisting it had the prettiest tint."

Claude you can make those up by the basketful, when you put your mind to it in idle energy. Your poetry was full of them. Sprinkle them more thickly in your prose. You would, if you were writing a little poetry on the side, as we both always ought to be. It keeps the color in your prose. I think this is enormously important, and it is one of the things I am most certain you <u>can</u> do, if you put your mind—or rather your imagination—to it.

There wasn't enough of this in your Harlem book either, but I attributed that to haste. <u>Don't be hurried</u>. I'll get additional funds out of Dutton if it keeps up like this. That's the only big and important thing I have to say. I'm excited and happy about the book.

Tell me when you write how long your money will last at the rate you are using it. I'm going to keep in touch with Macrae. I'm sure I can get you the time you need to finish such a book. Maybe it's the great (Afro) American novel after all these years.

Put everything in it, yourself and everything else.

> Love to you and admiration,
> Max[90]

This heartfelt letter is significant because it explicitly names the publisher (Dutton) and its president (Macrae), and because it gives a clear indication that McKay was working under some kind of contractual deadline to finish the book. Most important, Eastman includes quotations from the manuscript McKay had sent him to read. And indeed, both quotations, with their vivid and unusual metaphors, are found in the typescript of *Amiable with Big Teeth*: "a reddish person and so covered with freckles, he looked like a cinnamon sandwich" is a description of Seraphine Peixota's absent biological father (p. 24), while the second passage ("like children with tinted candies, each one hiding its candy in its fist and insisting it had the prettiest tint") is a phrase used to describe Seraphine and her friends (p. 37). In other words, given the peculiar wording of these precise quotations, there can be no doubt that *Amiable with Big Teeth* was the manuscript in progress McKay sent Eastman to read.

Shortly after he received the above letter, McKay wrote to Eastman to say that he might not have enough money to stay in Maine past the end of April. Eastman wrote back again immediately, stressing that he would be happy to ask Dutton for more money to support McKay, if necessary: "I am interested in your story, heart and soul, and will do everything in my power to get you money enough to finish it. Please let me know what I have to do."[91] At the end of May, Eastman returned the first fifty pages of the typescript to McKay: "I enclose the manuscript you sent me with a few random comments in the margin. I am in town until the first of next week, and am in touch with Dutton, trying to get an appointment with old John Macrae."[92]

At the beginning of June, a letter from Simon Williamson suggests that he had heard that both Eastman and Dutton had praised the novel. He wrote to McKay: "I am glad that your publisher and the critic liked your manuscript. I believe that it will be a success since it comes at an opportune time of social change, development and disillusion of the Negro."[93] But

McKay needed more time. Eastman wrote on June 3 that he was trying to intercede with Dutton in order to convince the publisher to give McKay two more months of support. There is a handwritten, undated note in McKay's papers in which Eastman informs him that even though the deadline for completion had passed, Dutton had agreed to pay the additional $150 due upon submission as an additional advance, so that McKay could keep working.[94] The publisher wrote at the same time to McKay to confirm this arrangement.[95] And as late as June 24, 1941, Macrae told McKay that he was "very happy to learn from our mutual friend Max Eastman and from you the splendid progress you have made with your new novel."[96]

By the end of July, McKay had returned to New York. He wrote to another friend, the writer and photographer Carl Van Vechten, letting him know that he was "rushing through an important job, which I want to get off my hands + feel free."[97] A week later, it was done; he wrote Eastman on July 28 to tell him that he had finished and turned in the novel:

DEAR MAX

I succeeded in getting an old loft on this noisy busy thoroughfare for only $15 a month, no bath, no hot water etc, but it is a big barnlike room and I am glad to have it and hope I can make a little money to pay for it. Instead of working on the duplicate, I decided it was wisest after talking to President Macrae, to pitch in on the original of the manuscript. And so I did and finished and turned it in last Friday. It runs to a little over 300 pages. I should have liked to have more time to polish it up and get in some brighter phrases after resting and refreshing my mind a little, but as I lacked the necessary means I did the next best thing and finished the job to the best of my ability. I might decide to give the dedication to Eliena and you, if it comes through the test all right. I am writing with my fingers crossed.[98]

As we now know, crossing his fingers wasn't enough; the book was irrevocably rejected by Dutton's editorial department. Without offering specifics, Dutton president Macrae told McKay that the novel had turned out "so bad and so poor that I cannot offer you any hope of its being revised in a satisfactory way to meet what I believe a novel by you must be."[99] In a rather bittersweet twist of fate, the day following his manuscript's submission to Dutton on July 24, 1941—and thus before receiving news of the crushing rejection—McKay sat down for a series of beautiful portraits by Van Vechten, the last he would ever take of McKay. Viewed with the knowledge that McKay had just submitted his novel, these portraits now take on a new, affective dimension: the photographs capture a mature, smiling McKay, bearing what may be the look of a man who has the satisfaction of having just completed a monumental endeavor.

Macrae's rejection notice, along with two letters McKay composed in the wake of Dutton's decision, provides important clues regarding the novel's ultimate fate.[100] Macrae's one-page letter, dated August 7, 1941, explicitly referred to the novel as "God's Black Sheep," and informed McKay that the manuscript—the only extant copy since (as these documents make clear) McKay never had time to complete the duplicate—was being shipped back to his address at 33 West 125th Street. Openly disappointed with the way the novel turned out, Macrae decried the fact that McKay "failed to take advantage of Mr. Max Eastman's valuable and competent aid" as their original agreement had stipulated. In brutal language, without explaining the reasoning behind the verdict that the novel was "so bad and so poor," Macrae advised McKay to abandon it altogether.[101]

McKay had actually learned of the unfavorable outcome two days before receiving Macrae's letter, when his anxiety had led him to telephone the Dutton offices. Describing himself as "chagrined and depressed" by the publisher's decision,[102] McKay wrote Eastman to express how "very very disappointed" he was "after working so hard on a novel of ideas about Aframericans." At the same time, he confessed that the news nevertheless came as "a relief from the high strain under which I've been existing. There were days when I felt as if I was keeling over and only mental awareness kept my feet on the ground. I hope I shall never have to write under such circumstances again."[103] Still, McKay hoped the novel could somehow be salvaged: "I am eager to hear exactly what is wrong. Perhaps it can be revised."[104] If the book turned out to be flawed, he told his friend, it was due to the fact that he "was working under high pressure to finish the work within a fixed time."

Replying directly to John Macrae on August 8, 1941, a remarkably subdued and distraught McKay tried to explain that the lack of time and his distance from Eastman—McKay was in Maine and Eastman in Florida during most of the period when McKay was writing—impeded his ability to receive Eastman's assistance prior to final submission. "I rushed the story through to an end," he explained, "because I was writing under pressure and considered it a bounden obligation as much as possible to live up to the terms of my contract."[105] It was this "race with time" that had prevented him from sending Eastman the finished manuscript in order to get his feedback, not any "inharmony" between them.[106] When Eastman's initial reaction to the first fifty pages was "extremely favorable," McKay took it as a "signal for me to go straight ahead with the rest of the story according to my plan."[107] He again asked Macrae for more information regarding the reasons for the rejection, and attempted to elaborate his own aspirations for the novel as he saw it:

> Now, I have no idea what, in the opinion of your readers, is the worse [sic] thing about the manuscript, whether it is the actual writing, the conception or subject matter of the story or all combined that makes it bad. In conceiving the story I had the idea of breaking with my former performance in fiction. And I attempted to do a contemporary historical tale of local conflict with an ethical basis. The idea is implicit in the first 50 pages. Of course, I introduced humorous scenes to enliven it for the pot [sic] is rather somber.[108]

Without knowing "whether the objection was to structural form or subject matter,"[109] as he complained to Eastman, the frustrated McKay was left to speculate. He knew that Dutton had expressed concern that his original outline for the novel seemed overly melodramatic, but he did not think the finished book was susceptible to such a charge. As McKay told Eastman, in his own estimation the "only two items which may be considered sensational is the marriage of Seraphine to a white comrade after she has been seduced by him and the final chapter when Maxim Tasan, the agent of the Comintern is killed when he is hurled from a Harlem roof."[110]

We do not know whether Macrae ever responded to McKay's letter, but the publisher's decision was final. For all intents and purposes, the August 8 letter from McKay to Macrae appears to be the end of the Dutton archival trail. There is no further correspondence regarding the project in the publisher's files, and the next exchange between McKay and Eastman conserved in their papers does not occur until the following summer.

Macrae's August 7 rejection letter does include one detail that may help explain why the novel was prevented from being published elsewhere. In the course of his brusque dismissal, Macrae rather spitefully reminded McKay that their contract included a clause specifying that should he ever "sell the manuscript to another publisher or receive any monies from any source whatsoever in connection with the publication of the manuscript,"[111] McKay would have to return the $475 advance he had received from Dutton. For the destitute McKay, this must have seemed an impossible obstacle to surmount.

McKay never wrote about his apparently brief interaction with Samuel Roth, the publisher in whose papers the typescript was eventually found in 2009, and it goes unmentioned in the voluminous scholarship on McKay's work. The earliest evidence we have of the encounter between the two dates from September 11, 1941—in other words, roughly a month after the Dutton deal collapsed. It is a signed copy of Roth's book of poems, *Europe: A Book for America* (first published in 1919), which Roth gave to McKay and inscribed: "For Claude McKay with the unqualified admiration of Samuel Roth."[112] We do not know how they met, although they were both left-leaning intellectuals with many acquaintances in common in the modernist literary and political worlds of the interwar period (such as Max Eastman, Louise Bryant, Frank Harris, Maxwell Bodenheim, and Harry Roskolenko).

Two months after "God's Black Sheep" was rejected by Dutton, McKay entered discussions with Roth concerning the ghostwriting of a book to be called "Descent into Harlem" (see "A Note on the Text").[113] But there is no indication that McKay ever began to work on the project. It seems likely that during those negotiations, McKay gave Roth the typescript of his latest novel to read, and the two may well have discussed the possibility of perhaps publishing "God's Black Sheep" under a different title to avoid having to pay back the Dutton advance. Since Roth himself was rather cash poor at the time—indeed, one of Roth's checks to McKay for the "Descent into Harlem" project bounced[114]—the fear of having to pay Dutton close to $500 in order to release the novel may have ultimately deterred Roth from taking the risk. Evidently McKay never retrieved the typescript, and neither he nor Roth seems to have spoken or written about it publicly again.

When McKay wrote to Max Eastman again in July 1942, a full year had passed since their last correspondence. He even noted the long delay and said by way of explanation that he had been "dangerously ill."[115] Wayne Cooper notes that in late 1941, McKay's health "finally collapsed," due to a persistent flu as well as high blood pressure, heart disease, and many years of poor nutrition. Indeed, McKay would never fully recover from these ailments. In early 1942, McKay was penniless, ill, and discouraged, writing to Ruth Raphael: "I have not done much work of any value since I wrote my last book. In fact I became so broke that I took a menial job to keep myself going."[116] Sometime that winter, another of McKay's friends, the writer Ellen Tarry, found him "alone and seriously ill in a Harlem rooming house" and helped him receive medical attention through Friendship House, the Catholic social agency.[117] In an undated, handwritten letter, McKay expressed his gratitude to Simon Williamson for helping him to pay his rent and eventually helping him move: "you had attended to me through my worst illness," McKay writes.[118] His illness was so debilitating that he left all his belongings behind; as he explains to his former landlord: "because of my illness, [I have] been forced to move to my present address. In fact my condition has been of such a nature until it was impossible for me to get out of the house and get the remainder of my things and return your keys."[119]

It may seem surprising to us now, thinking of McKay as a major twentieth-century author, but it is entirely possible that McKay—given his impecunious and peripatetic existence as a self-professed "vagabond poet" for much of his life—lost track of *Amiable with Big Teeth*, as he had lost or misplaced other book contracts and manuscripts he had written but been unable to publish over the years. When Catherine Latimer wrote to McKay in early 1941 asking if he would be willing to contribute manuscripts to the Schomburg collection at the New York Public Library, he replied that "many of the original ones are lost and others scattered here and there. . . . I have not been careless about them, but one loses manuscripts in packing and moving, sometimes one makes the mistake of throwing out valuable items with trash."[120] In a 1947 letter to his agent Carl Cowl, McKay explained why he no longer had any of his book contracts:

> I lost the Harcourt, Brace contract years ago. I left it in my trunk when I went abroad and never got back the trunk from Nancy Markhoff. And I have none of my other contracts. I put them in storage when I was in New York. And when Dorothy Day sent the books to me here all the contracts (even the one with Dutton's) had disappeared and some other valuable items.[121]

If *Amiable with Big Teeth* had consumed McKay's undivided attention in the spring of 1941, perhaps it fell by the wayside the following winter as he struggled to regain his health and turned to other projects. Although McKay kept writing through the 1940s, his correspondence does not evidence any inclination to return to previous prose projects that had remained unfinished or unpublished, such as "Romance in Marseilles" (written around 1930), "Harlem Glory" (written around 1936–37), and *Amiable with Big Teeth*. It is perhaps worth recalling, too, that this is the same writer who in 1927 burned the manuscript of his very first try at fiction, "Color Scheme."[122] As is the case with many artists, McKay seems to have always kept his eye on the next project, rather than brooding over the ones that did not come to fruition, for whatever reason.

When Ivie Jackman wrote to McKay in the fall of 1943, asking him to contribute material for what would become the Countee Cullen/Harold Jackman Memorial Collection at

Atlanta University, McKay replied that aside from a number of letters from James Weldon Johnson related to the Negro Writers' Guild, "the only other thing I have here is a novel which I was to work over some day and this is the only copy."[123] He doesn't say whether the manuscript in question is the single copy of *Amiable with Big Teeth* or one of his other unpublished works. But to the best of our knowledge, the archives provide no further reference to *Amiable with Big Teeth* or "God's Black Sheep" until the typescript resurfaces in the Samuel Roth Papers in 2009.

JEAN-CHRISTOPHE CLOUTIER AND
BRENT HAYES EDWARDS

Suggestions for Further Reading

WORKS BY CLAUDE McKAY

Banana Bottom (1933). New York: Harcourt Brace Jovanovich, Inc., 1974.

Banjo (1929). New York: Harcourt Brace & Company, 1957.

Complete Poems. Edited by William Maxwell. Urbana: University of Illinois, 2004.

Gingertown. New York: Harper & Brothers, 1932.

Harlem Glory: A Fragment of Aframerican Life. Edited by Carl Cowl. Chicago: Charles H. Kerr, 1990.

Harlem: Negro Metropolis (1940). New York: Harcourt Brace Jovanovich, Inc., 1968.

Home to Harlem (1928). Boston: Northeastern University Press, 1987.

A Long Way from Home (1937). New York: Harcourt Brace & Company, 1970.

My Green Hills of Jamaica and Five Jamaican Short Stories. Edited by Mervyn Morris. Kingston: Heinemann, 1979.

The Passion of Claude McKay: Selected Poetry and Prose, 1912–1948. Edited by Wayne F. Cooper. New York: Schocken Books, 1973.

SECONDARY CRITICISM

Asante, S. K. B. *Pan-African Protest: West Africa and the Italo-Ethiopian Crisis, 1934–1941.* London: Longman, 1977.

Cloutier, Jean-Christophe. "*Amiable with Big Teeth*: The Case of Claude McKay's Last Novel." *Modernism/modernity* 20, no. 3 (September 2013): 557–76.

Cooper, Wayne F. *Claude McKay, Rebel Sojourner in the Harlem Renaissance: A Biography*. Baton Rouge: Louisiana State University Press, 1987.

Edwards, Brent Hayes. *The Practice of Diaspora: Literature, Translation, and the Rise of Black Internationalism*. Cambridge: Harvard University Press, 2003.

Fronczak, Joseph. "Local People's Global Politics: A Transnational History of the Hands Off Ethiopia Movement of 1935." *Diplomatic History* 39, no. 2 (2015): 245.

Gertzman, Jay. *Samuel Roth: Infamous Modernist*. Gainesville: University Press of Florida, 2013.

Harris, Joseph. *African-American Reactions to the War in Ethiopia, 1936–1941*. Baton Rouge: Louisiana State University Press, 1994.

Hirsch, Jerrold. *Portrait of America: A Cultural History of the Federal Writers' Project*. Chapel Hill: University of North Carolina Press, 2003.

Huggins, Nathan Irvin. *Harlem Renaissance*. New York: Oxford University Press, 1971.

Irmscher, Christoph. *Max Eastman: A Life*. New Haven: Yale University Press, 2017.

Jackson, Lawrence P. *The Indignant Generation: A Narrative History of African American Writers and Critics, 1934–1960*. Princeton: Princeton University Press, 2011.

James, Winston. *A Fierce Hatred of Injustice: Claude McKay's Jamaica and His Poetry of Rebellion*. London: Verso, 2000.

———. *Holding Aloft the Banner of Ethiopia: Caribbean Radicalism in Early Twentieth-Century America*. London: Verso, 1999.

Kelley, Robin D. G. "'This Ain't Ethiopia, but It'll Do': African Americans and the Spanish Civil War." In *Race Rebels: Culture, Politics, and the Black Working Class*, 123–58. New York: Free Press, 1994.

Lewis, David Levering. *When Harlem Was in Vogue*. New York: Alfred A. Knopf, 1981.

Makalani, Minkah. *In the Cause of Freedom: Radical Black Internationalism from Harlem to London, 1917–1939*. Chapel Hill: University of North Carolina Press, 2011.

Maxwell, William J. *New Negro, Old Left: African-American Writing and Communism Between the Wars*. New York: Columbia University Press, 1999.

Plummer, Brenda Gayle. *Rising Wind: Black Americans and U.S. Foreign Affairs, 1935–1960.* Chapel Hill: University of North Carolina Press, 1996.

Robinson, Cedric J. "The African Diaspora and the Italo-Ethiopian Crisis." *Race & Class* 27, no. 2 (1985): 51–65.

Scott, William R. "Malaku E. Bayen: Ethiopian Emissary to Black America, 1936–1941." *Ethiopia Observer* 15, no. 2 (1972): 132–37.

———. *The Sons of Sheba's Race: African-Americans and the Italo-Ethiopian War, 1935–1941.* Bloomington: Indiana University Press, 1993.

Tillery, Tyrone. *Claude McKay: A Black Poet's Struggle for Identity.* Amherst: University of Massachusetts Press, 1992.

Von Eschen, Penny M. *Race Against Empire: Black Americans and Anti-Colonialism, 1937–1957.* Ithaca: Cornell University Press, 1997.

A Note on the Text

This is the first publication of the typescript of Claude McKay's *Amiable with Big Teeth: A Novel of the Love Affair Between the Communists and the Poor Black Sheep of Harlem*, which was found in 2009 by Jean-Christophe Cloutier as he was processing the Samuel Roth Papers in the Rare Book and Manuscript Library at Columbia University. This typescript (MS 1643, Box 29, Folders 7–8) appears to be the only extant copy of *Amiable with Big Teeth*. The manuscript was first submitted to E. P. Dutton & Co., Inc., for publication under the title "God's Black Sheep."

There are two sets of handwritten edits in the 314-page typescript. One set of edits, which runs through the entire duration of the novel, appears to be McKay's own, given the striking similarity of the handwriting with McKay's revisions in the typescripts of two of his other unpublished novels, "Romance in Marseilles" (composed c. 1930) and "Harlem Glory" (composed c. 1936–37), both held in the McKay Collection (Sc MG 19) in the Manuscripts, Archives, and Rare Books Division at the Schomburg Center for Research in Black Culture of the New York Public Library. The second set of handwritten edits, which only runs through the first fifty-six pages of the novel, and then again on the final few pages of the typescript, appears to have been made by Samuel Roth, given their similarity to his writing elsewhere in the Roth Papers.

Unless otherwise indicated in the Explanatory Notes, this edition follows all of the handwritten revisions by McKay, but not those by Roth. Other minor misspellings and typographical errors have been silently emended, and the book has been lightly edited for felicity and consistency (in particular, some punctuation has been edited for the sake of clarity; and a few words that are spelled variously in the typescript—which uses both "School-teacher" and "schoolteacher," for example—have been standardized). Otherwise this edition maintains the original formatting in McKay's typescript, except that all words that were underlined in the typescript (most often to indicate emphasis in spoken dialogue) have been rendered in italics.

In the Roth Papers, the McKay manuscript is one of dozens of manuscripts by other authors that Roth kept in uniform black binders. Though written in the same typeface, the label on the binder cover gives a slightly different variation of the novel's subtitle: "A Novel Concerning the Love Affair Between the Communists and the Black Sheep of Harlem." This edition retains the subtitle as given on the title page of the typescript itself inside the black binder. Although the novel was originally submitted under the title "God's Black Sheep," the extant typescript was retitled *Amiable with Big Teeth*. It is unknown when the title change was made or who initiated it—McKay may have hoped to give the novel a new chance with a new title for a new publisher, or Roth may have asked for a title change, or the two men may have come up with the title together in an effort to avoid having to pay back the advance McKay had received from Dutton.

Also originally inserted in the black binder with the *Amiable with Big Teeth* typescript was a one-page "Publisher's Note," presumably written by Roth. This note was composed in a different typeface from the novel itself, the leading characters page, and the table of contents page (although it appears to be identical to the typeface used on the binder label and the title page). The "Publisher's Note" is at times factually incorrect: for example, it dates the Italo-Ethiopian War as having taken place in "the Twenties" (whereas in fact the conflict started in October 1935 and ended in May 1936) and states that McKay wrote the novel "just before his death" (whereas in fact he composed it in the spring and summer of 1941). It is thus likely that Roth drafted the "Publisher's Note" at some point after McKay's death in 1948, perhaps in the hope of releasing the book posthumously in order to capitalize on the fame of the writer the "Note" describes as "Harlem's most distinguished novelist."

The binder in the Roth Papers also contained a three-page typewritten document entitled "Proem." It is written in grammatically flawed English and narrated in the first person. (The "Proem" opens: "At the end of my junior year I quit the High School. I did because I was excited to radical change. It offered a chance for voyages, to see strange places and different people.") It is also narrated in the voice of a self-described "young white man" who, after traveling the world, returns to New York City in 1929. In other words, there is no connection between this document and the narrative of *Amiable with Big Teeth* aside from the fact that Roth retained them in the same binder. By all evidence, this "Proem" appears to be an initial draft of "Descent into Harlem," the book Roth hired McKay to ghostwrite for an Italian-American named Dante Cacici in the early fall of 1941, but which McKay does not seem to have ever undertaken or completed. Because the "Proem" is a fragmentary artifact from another book project and not an integral part of *Amiable with Big Teeth* (which, as explained in the Introduction, McKay had written months before Roth hired him to work on "Descent into Harlem"), it has not been included in this edition. Both the "Publisher's Note" and the "Proem" are kept with the original typescript of the novel in Box 29 of the Samuel Roth Papers.

The Ethiop Gods have Ethiop lips,
Bronze cheeks and woolly hair;
The Grecian Gods are like the Greeks,
As keen-eyed, cold, and fair.

—Walter Bagehot[1]

AMIABLE

   WITH BIG TEETH

A novel of the Love Affair

between the Communists and

the Poor Black Sheep of Harlem

BY

Claude McKay

author of
HOME TO HARLEM

The Leading Characters

Lij Tekla Alamaya	An Envoy from Ethiopia
Pablo Peixota	Chairman of the Hands to Ethiopia
Maxim Tasan	Mysterious Person Identified with the White Friends of Ethiopia
Newton Castle	Secretary of the Hands to Ethiopia and Friend of Maxim Tasan
Dorsey Flagg	Executive Member of the Hands to Ethiopia
Kezia Peixota	Wife of Pablo
Seraphine Peixota	Daughter of Kezia
Gloria Kendall	Employee of the White Friends of Ethiopia
Rev. Zebulon Trawl	Executive Member of the Hands to Ethiopia
Professor Koazhy	Leader of the Senegambians

I

". . . ETHIOPIA SHALL SOON STRETCH OUT HER HANDS TO GOD."

—Psalms 68:31[1]

From 110th to 140th Street, Seventh Avenue on this pleasant Sunday afternoon was a grandly tumultuous parade ground. The animated crowds pushed over the jammed sidewalks into the street. Every stoop was pre-empted by eager groups of youngsters struggling to hold their places and warding off newcomers. Above, the tri-color green-yellow-red of Ethiopia blazoned from many windows. Streamers were thrown at the marchers and confetti fluttered in the air like colored moths. With bands and banners and pompous feet the procession undulated along the avenue. There were Elks and Masons and other fraternal orders, political and religious organizations, social clubs and study clubs—the Ethiopian Students Class, the African Historical Society, the Senegambian Scouts,[2] Ladies' Auxiliaries, children's groups. At intervals resounding claps rewarded some section which attracted special attention by a piece of meretricious music or movement. Near the corner where the procession went down a side street to the church, a huge banner floated over the avenue, bearing the motto:

WELCOME TO THE PRINCE OF ETHIOPIA: ENVOY OF HIS IMPE-
RIAL MAJESTY.

As the tail of the march trailed by, the official cars followed
at a slow pace. There were three of them, each carrying the
Ethiopian flag and the Stars and Stripes. In the first two cars
there were the notables of Harlem; in the third the Ethiopian
envoy, a slight olive-colored youth with large calf's eyes. The
people applauded, clapping, whistling and shouting "God Save
Ethiopia!"

But as the cars rolled down to the church, from far down the
avenue came the echo of a mighty roar. The noise became tumultuous as it surged up the street. "Hey! Hey! Hey! Rey! Rey!
Rey!" It was borne along by a bigger crowd escorting an open
automobile in which stood a full-sized ebon-hued man, bedecked in a uniform so rare, so gorgeous, it made the people
prance and shout with joy. "R-e-e-e-e-e-e-e-e-e-y!" The
shouting rose to its highest point like the furious sounding of a
thousand bagpipes, like a paddock full of horses wildly neigh-
ing, like the exuberant flourish of a parade of kettledrums.

The lone personage wore a mailed shirt extravagantly covered with golden gleaming arabesques and a wonderfully high
shako, white and surmounted by a variegated cluster of ostrich
plumes. With his right hand held at salute he smiled triumphantly, almost roguishly. Responding to the thunderous salvos of acclaim, the throng that could not be accommodated in
the huge church surged up from the side street to meet the new
multitude of the avenue. Thrilled by the tumultuous spectacle,
suddenly the saluting dignitary unsheathed his sword and
brandished it at heaven. The mass roared in a frenzy while
slowly the car threaded through, turning down the side street
to the church.

The people wondered. Who was the richly bedecked appari-
tion? The ignorant said it was the prince envoy. But others
more informed said the envoy had already passed and entered

the church with the notables. It was the military aide of the envoy, someone suggested, and the gossip rustled like a wind-blown leaf from mouth to mouth.

Inside the immense church the vast audience was startled by the tremendous uproar. The choir had sung the Ethiopian an-them, and stirred by the tumult, which penetrated and filled the church, the audience was restless. Up on the platform sat the dignitaries with the young envoy in the midst of them. They were whispering to one another about the cause of the height-ened prolonged cheering, when suddenly they were amazed by the dramatic entrance of the man in uniform. The audience turned and saw him like a medieval knight framed in the portal and it rose with one accord and cheered. The envoy in formal clothes distinguished only by a red slash aslant his breast had not elicited anything approaching this warm welcome extended to the military personage.

The chairman of the meeting thought at once that the unin-vited notable could not be left unnoticed there among the au-dience. Besides, he stood there smiling, saluting as if waiting for official recognition. So after hurriedly whispering with a colleague, the chairman dispatched the chief usher to bring the soldier to the platform. Applause pursued him as he marched elegantly, deliberately down the aisle and ascended the plat-form. There he saluted and bowed to the audience, shook hands with the chairman and took the introduction to the en-voy with a deferential bow.

"Professor Koazhy!" The envoy repeated the name in a low tone, his wide eyes in wonder surveying the uniform. So he was not really a military man, but had thus adorned himself in honor of the occasion, the envoy thought. But he had pleased the crowds, and had been rewarded with an ovation greater than was given to him, the official representative of Ethiopia. Perhaps he too should have worn a uniform, as Pablo Peixota, the chairman, had suggested. But he did not like uniforms and rarely wore one, unless he was attending a state function, and nothing he might have worn could compare with the resplendent splendor of Professor Koazhy's accoutrement. But why did Professor Koazhy choose to wear this barbaric fantastic costume, which was not symbolic of the new spirit of Ethiopia? And how puzzling that that uniform had made such a powerful appeal to the senses of the crowd. For these people were not anything like the tribal Ethiopians, the envoy thought; they were more like European crowds. From the quaint and fanciful accounts he had read, from things he had heard, he had imagined a very different kind of people. These Aframericans—

Meanwhile, Chairman Pablo Peixota was calling the great meeting to order. He spoke through a megaphone. Briefly he said that the purpose of the meeting was firstly to give aid to Ethiopia and secondly to welcome the representative of the Emperor. He said Ethiopia was a Holy Land to all Aframericans,[3] that afternoon's glorious demonstration was a proof of their interest. Ethiopia was the ancient lamp of Africa, which should not be extinguished. The Aframerican people had pledged themselves to help keep that lamp burning. They were collecting the funds and sending medical aid. The Emperor of Ethiopia[4] had condescended to send a representative as a token of his goodwill and to give encouragement and inspiration to the efforts of the Aframericans. "Let us show to him the things that we can do and will do. Let us begin in a big way this afternoon."

The chairman spoke efficiently but not brilliantly. He was precise, as if he were reading from a manuscript. Next he called upon the minister of the church, the Reverend Zebulon Trawl, to say a prayer for Ethiopia. The minister was of about the same complexion as the envoy, but more heavily built. He prayed rhythmically for Ethiopia, the Emperor and his family, his advisers, his generals and the armies, the confounding of their enemies, the restoration of peace to the land. And lastly he prayed for Aframericans, dropping down to a colloquial and dithyrambic note: "Get busy and do your stuff, brothers and sisters. Begin today, start right now, put your hands in your pockets and not for nothing, bring it up, bring it out, get under your pillow, open the jars in your cupboards, open up the old family Bible where you have some bills pressed down like faded flowers, pennies and nickels and dimes, bring them in for the defense of Ethiopia. The Emperor has honored us here in America, sending to us his personal personable representative." He turned to the envoy. "Never before have our people been honored in such a grand manner. Let us show ourselves worthy of that honor. Mohammed he went to the mountain, and Ethiopia has come to us, to you and to me, to each one of us. Oh, my brothers and sisters, Ethiopia shall stretch forth her hands to God."

Many voices responded: "God, God! Amen, Amen!"

The chairman said he would ask each speaker to be brief, as the long parade had delayed the beginning of the meeting. There were seven speakers besides the envoy: another outstanding preacher, a prominent doctor, a high official of a popular fraternal order, a leader of the Back-to-Africa movement,⁵ a university professor, a woman representing the Colored Women's Clubs and a representative of the White Friends of Ethiopia.

At last the young envoy, Lij Tekla Alamaya, was announced. He stepped nimbly forward, bowing to the chairman and the other speakers, and was greeted with prolonged cheering. He thanked the people for the warm welcome they had extended to him, as a representative of the Emperor and the people of Ethiopia. He stressed the gratitude of the Ethiopians for Aframerican sympathy and help. He told of the valor of the armies in the field, but that they were fighting a modern war without modern arms. They needed artillery and machine guns, warplanes and armored trucks, uniforms and shoes, medical supplies and doctors and nurses.

He described Ethiopia as a land-locked nation unable to communicate with the outside world, except across the territory of hostile or inhospitable nations. But nevertheless the people were courageous and brave as ever, jealous of their great traditions and guarding their ancient faith, the same Christian faith of Aframericans, which had inspired them to rise up and demonstrate to defend Ethiopia as they had today. "I am nothing but the humble servant of my Emperor who has sent me to you in the name of his people. I have come to give you all the information you require about Ethiopia, the Emperor and the Imperial Family and the Imperial Army. Things that are strange and incomprehensible to you, I shall endeavor to make clear. We thank you from our hearts for all the help that you have extended to us. Oh, we need all the help that you have pledged and much more, for the enemy is strong and cunning. My Emperor sent me to you as his humble servant and now I am also your humble servant."

Lij Alamaya won a fine ovation. The sympathy of the audience was touched by his slight appealing figure and his rather quaint English which sounded as if he had learned most of it in school in a foreign country. But as the applause died down there were shouts of "Professor Koazhy! Professor Koazhy!" "Let's hear Professor Koazhy." The entire audience voiced the demand and waited expectantly.

The chairman could not do less than present the gentleman in his uniformed splendor. And the roar of applause that exploded when he stood up was visibly disconcerting to the notables on the platform. It was greater than they all had received, including the envoy, and it was not funny.

Proudly stepping forward amidst the wild plaudits of the audience, and posing erectly—elated to be so signally honored, although he had not been one of the notables invited to participate—he was a perfect picture of triumph. Who else could have conceived and executed his inimitable performance?

Professor Koazhy clicked his heels, saluted, paid his respect to Lij Alamaya and the chairman and spoke in a deep kind of preacher's voice. "Some of you here know who I am," he declared, "but I know that the majority are applauding this uniform. That is as it should be. For I did not wear this uniform for merely a gaudy show. I put it on for a purpose—a special purpose. This is the uniform of an Ethiopian warrior. I went through all the trouble and expense of procuring it so that you should have a dramatic idea of why you are gathered here. In this uniform I want you not to see me, but the great warriors of Ethiopia. A long line of them who have fought and died so that their nation should live.

"Oh, my friends, this is a grand event. And it is a wonderful opportunity for me. Here in your midst in flesh and blood you have an Ethiopian—a Prince of Africa. I pray you, I implore you to realize the significance of it. I have given many years to the study and teaching of African history. The newspapers and the professors mocked me. Yet I am a college man and as good a professor as any of them. It was because I didn't study and teach African history the way they do it in the classrooms. I gave it to those who were hungry for it, the people who came and sat right down at my feet to get it. They said I was funny in the head, that I had an obsession, because I said that African history was as noble and great as European history. To them African history was just an unimportant chip off of European history.

"But I tell you, my friends, excited and exalted now about Ethiopia, if you knew African history, you would be better equipped to help Ethiopia. How many of you know anything about the real Ethiopia? I tell you, you are ignorant and not only you but the world is ignorant. I have just heard these learned speakers inform you that the kings of Ethiopia are descended from Solomon. I am sorry to correct them, but that is not true, my friends. The dynasty of Ethiopia is older than Solomon; it is older than the Bible.

"I must humbly apologise to our envoy and prince, but even the Ethiopians themselves today do not know their great history. They imagine that their Emperor is the Lion of Judah because he was descended from the Queen of Sheba. But that is history turned upside down. The Emperor of Ethiopia is the Lion of Judah because many centuries ago the Empire of Ethiopia extended to Egypt across Judea into Persia and India. You must know the truth and Professor Koazhy is here to teach you.

"You complain and whine about the white man's attitude towards you. I will forgive the white man for all the wrong he has done the black. I will forgive him because the white man has done one good and great thing. The white man has given the black man knowledge, and that is the greatest gift that one man can give another. Take that knowledge and learn from it. Learn about the past as it relates to you and use it to do something about the present. What you should know about yourself is the white man's gift to you. They wrote the truth but they cannot open your blind eyes to see it or make your minds understand. Herodotus, Volney, Champollion, Moret, Budge, Littmann, Frobenius, and a hundred more.[6]

"What you all should know is also what the Ethiopians should know about themselves. Then they will fight better and you will help more." Professor Koazhy unsheathed the sword and held it up and said: "A sword in the hands of an ignorant man is a dangerous weapon that may destroy him. Knowledge is available. Get it. Learn, learn, and learn more."

Professor Koazhy ended with a prancing flourish of his body and the crowd wildly clacked its approval. He was a major showman, yet with all his vanity and bizarreness, there was no hint of the spirit of clowning in him. After that strenuous procrastinating parade, and the taxing ceremony of the introduction of the envoy to the people, Professor Koazhy still held them under his spell. They were reluctant to leave the building.

Again holding up his sword as a signal he cried: "Wait! If you like what I have said, if it means anything to you, I want you to prove it. If I have enlightened you any about Ethiopia, then I want you to give more to the Cause of Ethiopia. At least I want one person in this audience to bring twenty-five dollars and come and shake hands with me." One man who was about to leave pushed his way back in and went to the platform, handing twenty-five dollars over. He was followed by two others. Professor Koazhy stood them together and said: "Now if there are three persons who can give twenty-five dollars there must be one in this crowd who can give fifty." A middle-aged woman, a schoolteacher, held up a cheque-book and came forward to write a cheque for fifty dollars. She received a signal ovation. The excitement was contagious and the audience was drawn close together like a big family gathering with sugared comments and murmurs of approval. The atmosphere of the church was eager and sensuous like an African bazaar.

Chairman Peixota jumped up and declared: "Since woman is the inspiration of man, I will pair with the lady by offering my cheque for a hundred dollars." Bowing he shook hands with the schoolteacher and as the audience appropriately acknowledged this pretty play of gallantry, Professor Koazhy flourished his sword and cried: "And now all of us together again. Come along with the little pieces of money, dollars and quarters and dimes. Little things make big things. Individually we are a poor people but collectively we're richer than we imagine. Come on, a little more sacrifice, one more effort to help a valiant nation. You gave before you heard the envoy. Now show your appreciation again by giving after you have heard him."

Many in the audience were standing; they were motioned to sit down. The ushers went down the aisles with the plates. The people responded generously with the little pieces of money. And the Koazhy appeal brought in twice as much money as was previously collected. He was cordially thanked by Chairman Peixota.

Professor Koazhy's extravagant injection of himself into the ceremony of welcoming the envoy and focusing the greatest attention upon himself was at first extremely irritating to Chairman Peixota and the rest of the Hands to Ethiopia committee. But the wonderful enthusiasm the man had stirred up, coupled with the incidental raising of an unexpected large sum of money, had mitigated the harsh feeling against him. Pablo Peixota was above all a business man and the main purpose of the committee was to raise funds for the aid of Ethiopia. Koazhy was exalted by his triumphant intrusion. Greater than he had expected it to be when he planned the coup, for he had even eclipsed the envoy. He chuckled over his success as he drove home to divest himself of his uniform: "Why, they have no imagination at all, no real insight into the mind of their own people. Putting on a show like that without a first-rate actor. Why, if I had the management of it I would have hauled in five times as much money."

Professor Koazhy was one of the most curious of the local illuminati. He was a notorious authority on native African history. He was a graduate of a Southern institute and had taken post-graduate work at a famous New England institution. For some years he was a teacher in the Deep South. From that he switched to the Baptist ministry. Becoming a little too involved in the profaner side of life, he retired from the pulpit, returned to the North, and during the first World War earned high wages working at the mechanic's trade which he had acquired at the Southern institute. Since then he had resided in New York, living a largely intellectual life, chiefly devoted to African studies, ancient and modern. He had an encyclopedic knowledge of African fetishism and prided himself on being a pagan. And he was the historical mentor of a group calling itself the Senegambians. His Christian name was Matthew—Matthew Preston—but he had changed it to Koazhy after his absorption in African fetishism. Koazhy was his version of Quashie, which he pronounced "Kwà-zée." He insisted that African names often sounded ridiculous to Aframerican ears because they were pronounced badly and written wrongly. And so he had turned Quashie into Koazhy and prefaced it with "Professor."

THE PEIXOTA HOME

Lij Tekla Alamaya of Ethiopia did not share the chagrin of the Harlem Reception Committee over Professor Koazhy's outshining him and taking the major portion of the acclaim that would have been fitting for the King of Kings himself. His mind was more occupied in an endeavor to appraise the grand spectacle. Professor Koazhy, despite his primitive joy in extravagantly exhibiting himself, seemed to Lij Alamaya to be a serious and extraordinarily well-informed man. He had made apparently authoritative and profound statements about Ethiopia of which, he, the Lij himself, was ignorant. The Lij was not much of a student of history, not even Ethiopian history. And now he felt that it was incumbent upon him to open his mind to study more. The religious exuberance, the fermenting emotional élan of the Aframericans in their manifestation for Ethiopia, was strange and perplexing to him. Yet it was sincere, Lij Alamaya believed. He had felt its warmth like the heat of the African sun, so different from the pale and tepid European expressions of goodwill and sympathy for his people. He craved and prayed for a real understanding of these Aframericans, so that his mission might be crowned with success.

Lij Alamaya resided in a downtown hotel. But he was a special guest in Harlem, where his headquarters was established in the residence of Pablo Peixota, chairman of the Hands to Ethiopia, in 138th Street. He was treated as a royal guest. The entire first floor of the Peixota residence was placed at the envoy's disposal and served the purpose of reception room and office. The arms of Ethiopia, with the symbol of the lion carrying a cross, was affixed to the street door of the house, a green canopy extended from the entrance to the curb and under its full length was unrolled a red carpet. Peixota insisted upon according his guest all the respect and dignity of an imperial envoy. He wanted the envoy's visit and contemplated tour to pass off without drawing the ridicule of the powerful white world. And for that reason he had at first regretted the irruption of Professor Koazhy and his fantastic exhibition, even though his resentment was softened by the extra avalanche of dollars.

Lij Alamaya had arrived prepared for simplicity and the democratic way of doing things. He had experienced enough of the routine of ceremony abroad, and here in America, he felt, there was a chance of escape; he would be taking a holiday away from it. And he had thought that of all Americans, the Aframericans would be less interested in the formalities of titles and courts. Evidently he was not conversant with the pomp and splendor of titles and uniforms that glittered in Harlem in the heyday of the Pan-African movement.[1]

That same evening Chairman Peixota had invited some of his colleagues to dinner in order that they should become more closely acquainted with Lij Alamaya and plan immediate work for the organization. Peixota possessed the executive ability of a steam drill. And he was planning a campaign to raise funds for the organization. Alamaya's schedule was planned for him to meet a number of important persons in the vestry of the church. But the prolongation of the ceremony had caused Peixota to cancel this arrangement in order that he should rest before dinner.

The dinner was served in the large basement dining room. Those present were the Rev. Zebulon Trawl and Mrs. Trawl;

the Hands to Ethiopia secretary, schoolteacher Newton Castle; Elks Official and Chief Scout William Headley; Second
Scout Professor Dorsey Flagg of one of the Aframerican universities; Dr. Phineas Bell of Harlem Hospital and Mrs. Bell; Libby
Brace, a nurse of Lincoln Hospital; and Mrs. Leah Arzell of the
Colored Women's Clubs, tentative head of the Women's Division
of the Hands to Ethiopia.[2] In addition there were the members of
the household, the hostess, Kezia Peixota, and her daughter,
Seraphine.

Kezia Peixota was an efficient housekeeper. Not nearly as
enthusiastic as her doughty husband over the defense of Ethiopia and the issues involved, she was nevertheless his reliable
helper where the household was concerned. She was a haughty-
looking woman and very conscious of the fact that she was the
wife of one of the wealthiest men in Harlem.

The guests were assembled in Lij Alamaya's reception room,
where they had drinks: whiskey and soda and imported sherry.
The amazing mass meeting was naturally the chief thing talked
about. "I think that that Professor Koazhy is a bad actor and
something should be done about him," said Mrs. Leah Arzell.

"I would say he is an excellent actor," said Peixota. "His stunt
brought us a lot of money. At first I was disgusted when he popped
in like a man from Mars bringing all that bedlam with him. But
he dominated that mighty crowd and that's a big achievement."

Leaning against the grand piano and tossing down a double
drink of straight whiskey, Professor Dorsey Flagg said: "The
trouble with a man like that is that he wants to be a modern
scholar as well as an African medicine-man and he gets all
tangled up in a crazy jumble of information. I can't see where
he is helping our people with such antics. He's just a burlesque
of an unconvincing pedant."

Lij Alamaya said quietly that he thought Professor Koazhy
was amazingly convincing.

"You don't *mean* that, do you?" Mrs. Castle injected her affectedly husky voice. "Today's demonstration was a big build-up for you and Koazhy spoiled the effect of it with his jungle burlesque. He looked so much like one of those hideous African masks in which some white people profess to see a new art."

"If you care to have my opinion," said William Headley, "I think Professor Koazhy's part was anything but a burlesque. And he couldn't take away any worthwhile thing from the stature of Prince Alamaya, even if some of the crowd thought he was the Prince. I think he was a mighty big help to your meeting. Gee! I wish I could get him to join the Elks."

"I think you are right and I agree with you entirely," said Alamaya. "I prefer Professor Koazhy's performance with his sword and uniform to that of Mussolini and Hitler in Africa."

"I object to all uniforms," said Newton Castle.

"All the world loves uniforms and won't do without them," said Alamaya. "Perhaps the best uniform for this age is the obsolete theatrical kind that was chosen by Professor Koazhy—"

"Oh, I thought that was the same kind of uniform the Ethiopian warriors are wearing today," Seraphine said brightly.

"Oh no, that's the ceremonial uniform of the old tribal kings," said Alamaya. "It isn't worn now. The Emperor has been working for years to modernize the army and the country."

"And has he been successful, Prince?" said Headley.

"I wish you would not call me a prince—"

"But you *are* one, aren't you?" said Seraphine.

"I am not a member of the Imperial Family."

"But you are a Lij," said Peixota, "and I was informed that the Ethiopian Lij is the equivalent of the European prince."[3]

"I am a Lij and if a title is necessary, I prefer the African to the European."

"It shall be as you desire," said Peixota.

"I was wondering whether Professor Koazhy's name would not be a good addition to the Hands to Ethiopia committee," said Alamaya.

Speaking at the same time, Mr. and Mrs. Castle said "Impossible!" "Oh no!"

"Personally *persona non grata*," said Professor Dorsey Flagg, pouring a big drink of rye.

Newton Castle said: "Koazhy is a one-man show. He will frighten away the better elements. And right now we need them more than the mob. Up till now we haven't been able to pull in any of the big Aframericans—those who front for the people and can get a hearing in Washington. In an organization like this we need such people, because we'll have to depend a lot on diplomacy."

"And so it's better to leave Koazhy out of this particular picture," said Mrs. Castle.

All the guests were grouped around Alamaya except Dorsey Flagg, who was helping himself to another rye when Mrs. Arzell cried: "Shame on you, Dorsey Flagg, you're acting like a person in a barroom. Look!" she said crossing over to the piano. "He has finished the bottle."

"Sallright," said Flagg, "Peixota got plenty. Peixota, I'll take Scotch as a chaser."

"If you care to mix your drinks, I'll get some," said Peixota. "Seraphine, will you get a bottle of Scotch?" he said.

But the maid came in and announced that dinner was ready and they all descended to the dining room. Mrs. Peixota indicated the place where each guest should sit. She had made careful preparations for the dinner. She had done the marketing herself, selected a huge red snapper which had been baked, and also leg of lamb for the roast. In the place of the regular maid she had a butler in to serve.

The serious conversation was continued during the dinner. There had been a considerable difference over the question of admitting white persons to the newly formed committee. A majority of the professional persons thought that there should be a white representative and favored a member of the White Friends of Ethiopia. But led by the Elks' Exalted Ruler, William Headley, who formerly was the outstanding agitator of the Garvey Pan-African movement,[4] the masses of the people had vociferously opposed the inclusion of a white. It was also their pressure that had brought about the election of a type of man like Pablo Peixota as chairman.

"I still insist that it was a mistake to exclude whites from the committee," said Newton Castle. "That is purely black chauvinism and isolationism, and no people can stand alone today."

"The common people feel that Ethiopia was betrayed by the white nations," said Peixota. "And you've got to respect their feelings. It is unfair to say their stand is chauvinism. Ethiopia is fighting alone and I'm sure you'll get a lot more out of an all-colored organization. You've got to sell it to them: one little black nation, single-handed, almost unarmed, fighting against a mighty white nation."

"But Ethiopia is not alone," said Castle. "What about the sanctions? All the countries in the League of Nations are joined in sanctions against Italy."[5]

"The sanctions are like passing a lot of resolutions and not acting on them," said Alamaya. "Italy is importing all the essential things she needs. The League of Nations is like those curious creatures that I hear exist in Haiti—the zombies. Dead nations which act as if they were living without knowing they are dead."

"But Soviet Russia is not in that class," said Castle. "She led the fight to defend Ethiopia in the League of Nations, she insisted on sanctions—"

"Russia is selling more war goods to Italy than any nation," said Dorsey Flagg. "Deeds speak better than words, Mr. Castle, and the deeds of Soviet Russia make a mockery of her words."

Newton Castle flared: "I'll challenge any sodden foul-mouthed Trotskyite[6] who tries to slander Soviet Russia to prove the charges. I have the facts—"

"Gentlemen," said Peixota, "our aim is to help Ethiopia. That is the mandate of today's meeting. And we must work in unity and harmony to achieve anything. We must not be confused and divided by the issues of the white world. I don't know what is a Trotskyite; I don't know anything about Russia except that it is a Communist country and I am not a Communist nor is Ethiopia."

"Mr. Castle, won't you *eat*?" said Mrs. Peixota. "I won't be flattered if my guests neglect my food and imagine my dining room is a committee room. Won't you have some more snapper?" She spoke in a slightly playful manner, but her face was stern.

"If Castle is looking for a real scrap, we'll have to ship him to Ethiopia," said Flagg.

"Now I hope we'll all get along like a good team without any resignations or sabotage," said Headley. "But we are fortunate to have Lij Alamaya here, so that when there is any trouble he can arbitrate."

"Lij Alamaya is a representative of the Emperor and a symbol of our united strength," said Peixota. "He must stand above everything."

"That's perfectly lovely," said Seraphine, "and I'll stand up with him above everybody." She was sitting right opposite Alamaya and beamed broadly at him.

Everybody laughed and Seraphine said: "Well, I did make you all happy." And extracting a cigarette from her case, she lit it and smoked, although they were in the middle of the dinner.

Mrs. Peixota said, not disapprovingly: "Shame on you, Sirrie, always saying and doing what you please without any regard to the time and place."

"Are the Ethiopian girls like that, Lij Alamaya?" said Mrs.

Castle, who had the privilege of sitting on his right. Alamaya smiled and replied: "Our women are very modern in some things."

The conversation now turned on Ethiopian customs, women, dress, food, and nothing serious about the work of the committee was discussed during the rest of the meal.

3

THE PEIXOTA FAMILY

The Peixota family was one of the most remarkably interesting in the Aframerican community. Pablo Peixota was a wealthy man. He owned other private houses besides the one he lived in and three large tenement buildings. Also he was the owner of one of the best bars in Harlem. And he had interests in other enterprises that were not generally known to the public.

He was thought to be a Brazilian. But it was his father who was. His father had emigrated to Central America and, after prospecting in various countries, settled down in Honduras. Pablo was born there and came to the United States when he was a youth. He had built himself up to his present substantial position by the unorthodox method of starting in as an operator of the notorious numbers game.[1] This was long before the world became acquainted with the Aframerican racket. But by the time it was overtaken by national notoriety, Peixota had poured his huge profits into the channel of real estate.

He married Kezia Hooker twenty years ago, long before he bought his first piece of real estate. It was her second marriage. She was a Durham girl and vastly admired for her beauty, which was more sensuously South European than Aframerican in its appeal. At the age of eighteen she had eloped from a Southern college with one of her ardent admirers. They came to New York and were married. But the passionate romance could not hold its own against the difficulty of the young couple's living in Harlem and finding work in New York. They both regretted leaving school for love. They quarreled, each blaming the other for the false step. And the young husband went about his business.

Kezia could not go home to Durham. Her schoolteacher mother informed her that she could not help her now. But she did come to New York when Seraphine was born. The first two years Kezia received some help from her mother, but it was a desperately hard life. Then she was fortunate to find a place where she could work as a maid and keep the child. Seraphine was five years old when Kezia met Pablo Peixota at a Democratic club. A district captain had advised her to join, as there was a chance of her getting a better job or some help through the club.

Peixota obtained a place for Kezia as stenographer and typist in an employment agency. He did not fail to remark her beauty. And he showed his interest by promising to find her a better job and extending an invitation to dinner and the theatre. Of course, he told Kezia his business. But she was not even surprised. Five years had taught her a lot. During which she was plagued by unhappy memories of college days, of the time that whenever she entered a room she was the center of attraction and a string of young men sought the privilege of taking her to the theatre or the dance.

She had paid dear for her lesson in that school of vanity and harked back to it with hatred. Now her interest was in tangible things only. She had learned that charm and beauty could be worthless unless a woman was placed in a position to show them off.

Kezia Hooker and Pablo Peixota were married during the second year of the first World War. They agreed to give their name to Seraphine. It was the time of the beginning of the expansion of the Aframerican community and of the blacks' migration from the South to the Northern centers of industry. And also it was the beginning of the new growth of the numbers game into an enormous clandestine lottery. Having started with the racket from the cradle, Peixota was in a handsome position to exploit its growth. Cautiously he launched out and bought his first piece of property—a private house in 133rd Street. In the basement he transacted the business of numbers while the family lived on the first floor and the rest was let.

Peixota was a Mason. And also he was persuaded to join the new order of Colored Elks.[2] As he transferred the profits of his illegitimate business into respectable holdings, his influence correspondingly increased in the community. He became a power in local politics and the captains of the district always sought his advice. The white district leader consulted him about the distribution of patronage. In its early days he was Honorable Treasurer and Industrial Advisor to the Pan-African organization.[3] He was a member of an African Methodist Church and his name appeared as a patron of affairs to promote funds for churches.

Eschewing fashionable activities, Mrs. Peixota was an excellent foil to her husband. She gave gifts to the Colored Orphanage and the Co-operative Residence for Young Unmarried Colored Mothers and her name appeared as a sponsor on programmes of benefit affairs for like institutions. She was a member of the Aldermanic Committee of Christmas Cheer for Needy Colored Families. She had devoted herself to the education of Seraphine. Peixota had suggested that the girl should be sent to a colored college after her graduation from high school. But Mrs. Peixota persuaded him that an academic education in New York might be of greater value to Seraphine. And so the girl was sent to Hunter College.

Seraphine did not possess the beautiful regular features of her mother. But she was an arresting type with an extraordinary personality. Her father was a reddish person and so covered with freckles, he looked like a cinnamon sandwich. He had been nicknamed "Red" at college. Seraphine's skin was so fair that her appearance was suggestive of an albino. She had inherited her father's hair, which was a coarse dark-dull red. Her eyes were strange, the right one slightly bluish and the other of a chameleonlike yellowish tint. She was slender but taller than her mother.

In training Seraphine her mother had put a great deal of emphasis upon her making a competent hostess. She pushed her into the company of older people and to converse with them. Above all Mrs. Peixota impressed upon Seraphine's mind the value of being always in the company of persons who were outstanding in some line and bolstered by an economic asset, a business or a decent job. And so even when she was in high school, Seraphine was always seen at affairs with people older than herself. She was often escorted to parties and dances by doctors or lawyers or other persons of prominence. She never gave much thought to the youngsters of her own age and so was not popular among the younger set. They often referred to her as black Peixota's white daughter.

But the Peixota family was a power in the community, although they did not really belong to any of the various cliques, such as the fashionable upper-deck city employers who gave weekend parties in rotation, or the theatrical set, or the professional. Their status was something like that of the family of a successful preacher. Peixota was one of the few men of wealth who was active in promoting the affairs of charitable organizations. In spite of his background he was noted for his honesty, his fervent racial interest and his practical approach to racial problems. And so he was always solicited to assist in organizational work for the welfare of the group. It was not merely because he was honest that the chairmanship or treasurership of an organization was given to him, but also because he was generous in helping an organization when its funds were low.

He inspired great confidence among the ordinary people. It

was even said that he still had a hidden hand in the numbers game—that one of his old servitors who was now established as a "banker" was actually fronting for him. The manager of Peixota's bar and grill was also a former trusted lieutenant in his numbers business. Perhaps nowhere else in America but in such a community could the former promoter of a gambling game arrive at such a position of power and respect.

4

PROFESSOR KOAZHY IS FEATURED

The tides of Italy's war in Ethiopia had swept up out of Africa and across the Atlantic to beat against the shores of America and strangely to agitate the unheroic existence of Aframericans. Suddenly the people were stirring with action and churches and lodges and clubs and the streets were filled and eloquent with protesting crowds. The burden of the protests was "Help Ethiopia!" The Aframerican newspapers headlined the news of the conflict. The Garveyites[1] advocated the raising of an army. More practical members of the intelligentsia planned to send medical assistance with doctors and trained nurses.

But there was little or no coordination of the various efforts. Funds were solicited everywhere. The people generously were responding. But some of the agencies most assiduous in collecting funds had a doubtful standing in their communities and no contact with an Ethiopian government or its representatives. There was evidence of the development of another nation-wide racketeering movement on the credulity of the Aframerican masses.

Acting upon the suggestion of an eminent medical doctor who had visited Ethiopia at the time of the Emperor's coronation in 1930,[2] some prominent Aframericans organized a responsible group in an effort to coordinate the movement to help Ethiopia. They made contact with the scanty few Ethiopian legations and consulates in Europe and tried to obtain official recognition of their action. With the coming of Ethiopian representative Lij Tekla Alamaya, their work was stamped with official approval. The most flagrantly dubious organizations to aid Ethiopia apparently ceased their activities. And with advertisements, broadsides and news articles the people were warned of fake organizations.

It was a little bewildering to many that the vague religious sentiment for Ethiopia existing among Aframericans should so suddenly be transformed into positive organized action and that that country should appear on the horizon as an embarrassing new Canaan. But the events of two decades must have been slowly working on the minds of the people. The first World War and the ill-starred theatrical Pan-African movement had enormously increased the interest in African lands. And Ethiopia specifically swung into the international spotlight when it was admitted to the League of Nations in 1923, after its abolition of slavery. In 1930 the barbaric splendor of Haile Selassie's coronation was world excitement. Also it attracted a number of Aframericans to emigrate to Ethiopia. Thus the biblical legendary Ethiopia and earliest Christian state was revealed as a reality with a new significance in the minds of Aframericans.

Long after the other guests had left, Peixota and Alamaya continued to discuss campaign plans and the Lij was persuaded to remain overnight so that the discussion could be resumed early the following day. Alamaya was preparing to shave the following morning when Seraphine rapped on the door and entered his bedroom with an armful of newspapers. "Look here!" she said, spreading the papers on the couch. "Koazhy has stolen the place you should have had. They were right and you were wrong about him, the dog-faced fool." Koazhy had provided rich material for the photographers. Standing in his car, saluting the multitude, erect on the platform, brandishing his sword, he was lavishly displayed. There was not a single photograph of Lij Tekla Alamaya. The news item, "Negroes Organize to Aid Ethiopia," was written around Professor Koazhy and his gorgeous uniform.

Alamaya smiled and said: "They have spread him like an army with banners."

"And ignored you," said Seraphine. "That's a terribly bad start for your mission."

"It won't matter much among the colored people and my mission is for them."

"But it will. The colored newspapers reprint everything the white ones publish about us. And the colored people eat it up."

"Well, let Professor Koazhy take the news. Ethiopia is bad news and sad news now. The papers need a little diversion."

"And perhaps you too, Tekla. I prefer your first name and I want you to call me Seraphine or Sirrie for short. I am invited to a party tonight and promised to bring you along. Won't you come?"

"Would like to, but I'm invited to one that some of the downtown Friends of Ethiopia are giving. I wish *you* would go with me."

"Oh, I'd love to. It may be nicer downtown. The Towers, that is my club, they can wait. But they want to be the first club to entertain you in Harlem. I like that lovely wine color in your pajamas. Were they made in Addis Ababa?"

"No, they are your father's."

"Ha-ha! I must hurry, goodbye."

"Not waiting for breakfast?"

"Had breakfast. You see, I'm working in Father's office, part-time. And I must open up promptly at nine. Now he's so busy with your job, I must help take care of his."

The Executive Committee of the Hands to Ethiopia, meeting at Peixota's house, had agreed that Alamaya was the most suitable person to act as go-between in connection with their work and that of the White Friends of Ethiopia. It was conceded that the overwhelming sentiment of the people for an all-colored organization should be respected. The one most irreconcilable to this idea was the brown bantamlike schoolteacher Newton Castle. He had been very persuasive arguing that if Aframericans set a precedent by excluding whites who desire to join their organizations, it will give the whites the justification for maintaining barriers against Aframericans and keeping them out of their private clubs and public places. Peixota retorted that since most of the whites and the best of them preferred not to have the Aframericans in their groups, there was a big possibility that that small minority that was so eager to penetrate into Aframerican affairs was doing so from selfish motives and was perhaps undesirable. He cited the numbers game and that the whites who bored in to partnership with the Aframericans came from the lowest vilest sediment of society, so that even the Aframerican racketeers were ashamed of association with them.

The more cultured members of the committee laughed at Peixota's bluntness, thinking of his former connection with the plebeian racket. But Peixota quoted the popular phrase: "It's not what you do, it's the way how you do it."

"Ours are a weak people," he said, "and like all weak things they are vulnerable. They've got to build themselves up like building a house, brick upon brick. They have been building slowly; we have colored churches, colored fraternal orders, clubs, newspapers, and other enterprises. It's a long slow building, halting, without real direction, just an instinctive necessity. And now the social tea-hounds who appear to know everything but what life is all about, they tell us that we should admit any white person who wants to join in every colored organization, otherwise we are chauvinists, segregationists and isolationists. Your fathers and mothers didn't learn to organize their benevolent and protective societies from drinking cocktails with bohemian white folks. They learned it cleaning the white man's W.C. and over the washtub in the kitchen. And they learned their lesson hard enough to use it to give you an education. Yes, *you* who are using that education now to destroy the things which your parents worked so hard to build."

Newton Castle looked uncomfortable. Peixota was so obviously referring to him. He felt that he ought to reply. He never liked to give up in an argument. He said: "You are mistaken if you imagine the whites who want to join with you are gangsters or liquor heads."

"Then who are they and what are their motives?" asked Headley, of the Colored Elks.

"They are persons who believe in the solidarity of all races and want to prove their sincerity," said Castle.

"Well, let them prove it by working from their side and we will be working from ours," said Headley. "It won't be helping the situation, bringing white people into a colored organization and disrupting it."

So Newton Castle was overridden, but he was sulky and said the people's sentiment cannot always be trusted; the mob must be led by intelligence.

Peixota spent the afternoon giving Alamaya a full report of the Hands to Ethiopia activity. In the treasury there was only $5,096. Much of the monies collected by unauthorized bodies could not be accounted for. But the new organization was protected by the federal law prohibiting unauthorized public soliciting of funds. Peixota said he had plans to organize a national Help Ethiopia drive for $100,000. Under the active leadership of Alamaya, the money could be easily raised, he thought. And he was now convinced that Alamaya should wear an Ethiopian uniform or a decoration that would distinguish him from others on a platform.

"You see how the papers have made a grand hero of Professor Koazhy; they want entertainment."

"But for a serious cause as this," said Alamaya, "one would expect something different."

"Lij Alamaya, in this country our group is identified with entertainment. It is an old tradition. And even in the most tragic things, whether it is love or death, the whites are looking at the funny side of colored life. And our own people, too."

"I didn't bring a uniform but I can get one. I had different ideas, thinking that I was coming to a democratic country and that if I were simple in the democratic way, my appeal would be more effective."

"That's what most foreigners think, but they are dead wrong."

Peixota continued to outline the plans for raising funds. Units of the organization were rapidly getting organized in all the large cities. Organizers had been sent to Boston, Philadelphia, Pittsburgh, Chicago and Detroit. And Alamaya should start out on a tour while the enthusiasm was high. But Peixota warned against pitfalls. He explained the issue of race and color, the complications, the perplexities, the illogicalness, unreasonableness and bitterness of it. Alamaya should avoid becoming involved. The Aframericans were a sensitive lot and the intellectuals confused and jumpy. One mistake might turn the entire group against Alamaya and the cause of Ethiopia.

Peixota proposed that Dorsey Flagg (who unlike Koazhy was a professor in a recognized Aframerican college) should accompany Alamaya on the tour. He thought he was the best man available, for he was on a sabbatical leave from his college, engaged in a study of the comparative intelligence of urban and rural colored families. The itinerary was under discussion, when the maid announced that Newton Castle had called. Peixota told her to show him in.

Castle entered with his briefcase. He was coming straight from school. It didn't appear as if he were making just a casual call, yet he did not immediately talk. Peixota asked if there were any new developments.

"I want to suggest that we take Dorsey Flagg off the committee," said Castle.

"But the man is already elected. We don't want to start anything like that," said Peixota.

"He shouldn't be on the committee, for he's a Trotskyite Fascist," said Castle. "He's an anti-Soviet mad dog and Nazi sympathizer. A man like that should never serve with a Help Ethiopia group."

"Mr. Flagg a Fascist! Impossible," said Alamaya.

"But he is," said Castle. "He is anti-Soviet and every enemy of the Soviet is a friend of Mussolini and Hitler."

"Goddamit! I won't listen to that," said Peixota. "What's Russia got to do with *us* and Ethiopia? I won't entertain your proposition. Get that straight. We're fighting Fascist Italy in Ethiopia and Dorsey Flagg is one of us. We don't want any Soviets in our organization."

"We won't get anyplace without the Soviets, I'll tell you," said Castle. "They are the only ones who understand colored people's problems and take us seriously like other human beings. You saw what the bourgeois papers had about our grand meeting last night, but I guess you didn't see this."

Castle took the Sovietist *Labor Herald* from his briefcase and opened it out on the table. A full page was devoted to the monster demonstration. At the top left there was a photograph of the Emperor of Ethiopia, to the right one of Lij Tekla Alamaya, in the center the people were pictured massed before the church, and at the bottom the speakers were shown grouped on the platform. There was no photograph of Professor Koazhy and no mention of his speech. The accompanying article was dignified and sympathetic, with a forthright denunciation of Fascist Italy's war against Ethiopia and an indictment of the governments of Great Britain and France in abetting Italy. The article concluded with the statement that Soviet Russia is the only nation interested in the fate of and fighting for the rights of small nations and minorities and colonial peoples.

Standing shoulder to shoulder Alamaya and Peixota read the

article. It was the first time that Peixota had read the *Labor Herald*. He was impressed by the tone of the article and the fine display of pictures. Still he was not convinced that Dorsey Flagg should be ousted from the committee. He said that so soon after organizing a united group, they should not allow themselves to be divided by the Fascists and Communists. He could not see what colored people had to gain from either.

Said Newton Castle: "Now you see what it means to be in right with the Communists. What Capitalist newspaper would have played up our demonstration like that?"

"The *Labor Herald* has a very small circulation," said Peixota.

"The circulation doesn't matter. It's getting into print that counts. The *Labor Herald* is the defender of the working class and oppressed minorities."

"There is one thing that I am determined about," Peixota banged the table with his fist. "I'll fight against any white group, Fascists or Communists or the next one which wants to divide my people and disrupt our organization and sabotage our work. S'help me God!"

5

THE EMPEROR'S LETTER

Seraphine telephoned Alamaya to say that she would meet him at his hotel and go from there to the party. Alamaya thought it would be more gallant for him to go and fetch her. But she laughed at his objection and explained that she had a previous engagement to keep, after which she would go directly to the Hotel Santa Cruz.

That other engagement was only an unexpected call upon Bunchetta Facey, whom Seraphine regarded as her rival, not so much in affairs of the affections but chiefly in social affairs. Both girls belonged to the exclusive Tower Club. Seraphine was popular in the club because she was rich Peixota's daughter. But Bunchetta worked to influence the members of the club from the angle of intellectual prestige. Bunchetta was graduated from the elite colored group in Washington, where her mother resided, and her father was a member of an old Philadelphia family of caterers.

Bunchetta was a social worker in New York. She was older than Seraphine and her tastes entirely different. She read the latest books, she liked modern painting and always visited the galleries, she adored listening to symphonic music and classical singing and her conversation was carefully pitched to an intellectual key. She was a member of an interracial group and when she had a gathering of friends, there were always white persons among them. Her portrait had been painted by a painter in

Greenwich Village, where she was told that her complexion was Balinese, although her shape was full-rounded like a Southern watermelon. She was much liked by the painter and his wife and often visited them. And she held the interest of the Towers with accounts of the unusual persons she met there. Not as arrestingly different and attractive as Seraphine, she nevertheless exerted herself to be charming.

Seraphine was the last person that Bunchetta was expecting to see then, when she burst in in her trailing turquoise blue dress and a short white fur coat. The ensemble was a gift from her father and it was purchased at the first Harlem Fashion Show. This show had been organized by six of the leading matrons (including Mrs. Peixota) and downtown modistes had sent up dresses and models.

"Oh, where you going all dolled up like a princess?" cried Bunchetta.

"Perhaps I could be a princess, if I wanted to. Princes are not so hard to get, but who cares about such things nowadays?" Seraphine shrugged and stepped around.

Bunchetta told her to sit but she stood and looked admirable standing. "You must be going to a swell affair, my dear. Who's throwing it?"

Seraphine preferred to be mysterious: "Nothing going on in Harlem on a Monday night." She sat.

"Then you're going downtown, are you?"

"Is there something going on downtown?" Bunchetta had so many contacts downtown that Seraphine was in doubt whether she knew about the party. Bunchetta was always so snobbish about downtown parties, she enjoyed the sensation of having one on Seraphine which she knew nothing about. Bunchetta always went to Greenwich Village but tonight she was going to Park Avenue.

But Bunchetta gave no inkling whether she knew about the

party or not. And said: "I'll guess you're going to the theatre, or a dinner party."

"Too late for any theatre," said Seraphine. "May I telephone?"

They teased each other like children with tinted candies, each one hiding its candy in its fist and insisting it had the prettiest tint. Seraphine telephoned her father's chauffeur to come and get her at the famous 409 Edgecombe Avenue,[1] where Bunchetta was resident. The uniformed doorman neglected his post and followed Seraphine to the car to open the door for her. He stared at the Ethiopian device painted on the side and gave a nod to the chauffeur, which conveyed something like the grip of the two persons belonging to the same secret order.

The party was taking place not in Park Avenue, but off it in the Sixties, close enough to be called a Park Avenue party. The hostess was Mrs. Lela Witern. She was the young and generous-minded wife of an aged philanthropist. He had recently had a severe paralytic stroke and could speak only with great difficulty, slowly and almost inaudibly. But his mind was still actively interested in people and causes. And when Mrs. Witern gave affairs she had a practice of having her husband in the room until most of the guests were assembled. Then she introduced each one to her husband with a few words about each accomplishment or interest. It was a rather wearing and sometimes embarrassing process, as Mr. Witern also made strenuous efforts to say something sympathetic or pleasing. After making the introductions Mrs. Witern excused herself and led her husband back slowly and affectionately to his bedroom. They were married in 1933 and had had three years of wedded life. Before his second marriage Mr. Witern's philanthropic interests were conservative and devoted primarily to schools and organized charity. But young Mrs. Witern had influenced him to consider modern artistic people and things and social activities of a more radical nature.

It was not particularly a White Friends of Ethiopia party in the sense that Sunday's meeting was a Hands to Ethiopia demonstration. Mrs. Witern was not one of the "Friends" but only a sympathizer. The idea of the party was suggested to her by another sympathizer named Maxim Tasan.

Alamaya was fidgety. He knew nothing about the ways of New York parties but thought he should get to Mrs. Witern's between nine and ten. But at ten o'clock Seraphine telephoned again and he enquired if it was not late. "Oh no," she said. "You're not the guest of honor and it's better to be a little late. New York specializes in late parties. But I won't be long. See you!" She was then on her way to Bunchetta's. It was after eleven when she got to the Santa Cruz. And then she had to fool around and examine his rooms and spill a few pretty phrases.

It was nearly twelve o'clock when they arrived at the party. The place was crowded. Newton Castle was near the door as if waiting for the prince's coming and hurried him over to Mrs. Witern. "You were not very early, Lij Alamaya, and so my husband had to retire without the privilege of meeting you."

Alamaya apologised and said he had heard that most New York parties began at midnight.

"That depends on the set you belong to," Mrs. Witern said, laughing. It was a bohemian gathering and many persons had come with friends that Mrs. Witern did not even know. Some sat around in groups while many were on their feet enjoying drinks and tidbits at the buffet. Mrs. Witern introduced Alamaya to some important persons: the college professor A. Banner Makepeace, who was the only member present of the White Friends of Ethiopia committee; Mrs. Willoughby, who was specially interested in the Young China Society; and her Chinese friend Mr. Ming. There was also another professor, Joseph Bancleft, who was honorary president of the World Democratic League. He essayed a few words to Alamaya about the crisis of world democracy, but it was impossible to make serious conversation in that atmosphere with so many persons pressing around them to shake hands with Lij Alamaya of Ethiopia now that they knew he was there. So Dr. Bancleft said that he would telephone Alamaya and make an appointment for dinner with Professor Makepeace, who also was a member of the World Democratic League.

"Why, there is Bunchy," cried Seraphine. "That cat, she trumped my ace!" And she left Alamaya, surprised at her remark, to go over near the buffet where Bunchetta was drinking with Delta Castle and a group among whom were some of the first refugees from Nazi Germany. Bunchetta giggled as she saw Seraphine coming towards her.

Newton Castle steered Alamaya to the other side of the large room where, near a smaller buffet with drinks and food, there stood Maxim Tasan, whom Castle specially wanted Alamaya to meet. With Tasan was a brown girl, Gloria Kendall, and an Englishman named Aubrey Pickett. "This isn't a bad corner you picked out for yourselves," said Castle. He made the introductions, but he had not met Aubrey Pickett, and Tasan introduced him.

"I see, already you are keeping C.P.T.," said Pickett to Alamaya. "Well, it wouldn't be strange for an African."

Pickett had taken a single cruise de luxe of Africa, making one stop at Zanzibar and another at Dakar. And perhaps from enchantment, perhaps from disillusion, he liked to imagine that he was an authority on African things. Alamaya asked what was C.P.T. "C.P.T.? Why, you have acted as if you were acquainted with it, Lij Alamaya, after keeping us all waiting for hours for your appearance. Won't you explain for me what C.P.T. is, Miss Kendall?"

But neither Gloria Kendall nor Newton Castle knew. "Really? Fancy living in Harlem and not knowing what C.P.T. is." And with an amused expression as if he were imparting some special knowledge of Aframerican similarity to Africa: "C.P.T. is Colored People's Time, of course, because as they say, 'Colored people are always late.'"

Alamaya was surprised and nettled by the stress Pickett put on "colored." He had always thought of himself as an Ethiopian, an African, but he had not been long enough in America to think in terms of being "colored." Coldly and deliberately he said: "Perhaps *colored* people are never early, because they can afford to be late. They have nothing in the world to hurry about. But you English have everything. Yet you were late in Asia in 1931, you were late in Africa in 1935 and perhaps you will soon be late in Europe and in Britain itself."

Tasan's eyes turned sharply on Alamaya as if they were searching for the key to his character, then a look of approval came into his face and he nodded his head as if he wanted to say: "Fine, fine."

"I am afraid you are anti-English, Lij Alamaya," said Pickett.

"On the contrary, I am not. I am only pro-Ethiopian. Fascist Italy is the enemy of Ethiopia. Do you expect me to praise Britain and France for prohibiting the sale and transportation of arms to enable us to fight our enemy?"

"There are larger considerations," said Pickett. "I think all decent Englishmen sympathise with Ethiopia, but Britain cannot be policeman for the world."

"But even if it's against Great Britain's will, her vast empire puts her in the position of policeman of the world," said Tasan.

Aubrey Pickett regretted his little banter and its development into a serious argument. He had no inclination to discuss politics in such a place, for he felt that it was not in good taste. He was saved from his predicament by Seraphine and Bunchetta joining them, with German refugees, a Dr. Schmidt, a Professor Jacob Fischer, their wives and a young artist named Willy Rittner. The refugees wanted to meet Alamaya and were introduced.

Said Seraphine: "We were talking about you, Tekla, and Ethiopia and everything. Professor Fischer is an anthropologist and he says the Ethiopians are not really an African people in the sense that Aframericans are, that they are a Semitic people like the Arabs."

"Ethiopians don't think so. We call ourselves a black African nation," Alamaya replied coldly in a tone indicating he did not want to pursue the subject.

"And I insisted I could pass for a typical Ethiopian girl, couldn't I, Lij Alamaya?" Bunchetta asked in a gurgling treaclish accent.

"No, you couldn't, Bunchy," said Seraphine. "You want to be everything, you are passing as a Balinese in the Village—"

"I am not," said Bunchetta, "but the artists think I resemble one."

"That's all the same, what difference does it make? You tell us, Tekla, what a typical Ethiopian girl is like."

"Oh, there are various types, just like in Harlem," said Alamaya, "but Miss Kendall could be a typical Ethiopian girl."

Gloria Kendall, who had had so little to say and remained almost unnoticed, was now the center of attention. The compliment was unexpected and she smiled modestly. Her face was attractive, round and sweet-like, and the same color of a nice cup of rich warm cocoa. Seraphine had merely nodded to Gloria when they were introduced and was not even interested to know who the girl was. The compliment was quite as unexpected to her and she blurted: "Dammit! Well, it's neither you nor me, Bunchy."

The general laughter was a welcome antidote. Mrs. Witern and Professor Makepeace approached. Mrs. Witern was of the same height as Seraphine, but thinner and her complexion was ruddy. She signaled to the attendant at the buffet to fill up the half-empty glasses. "You must call him when you need something or just get it if he isn't around," she said. Professor Makepeace took a swallow of the sherry he had in his hand.

"We're getting along all right," said Maxim Tasan.

"You do have a comfortable corner," said Mrs. Witern. "I didn't expect such a crowd, but I think it's a nice party."

"Splendid!" Professor Makepeace agreed. "Lij Alamaya, haven't you an Ethiopian souvenir, any little trifle to show us?" Alamaya said he had nothing on him. "But," he added, "I have only the Emperor's letter of commendation." All were eager to see it. And Professor Makepeace said that nothing could be more interesting. Alamaya handed him the envelope. The letter was written on a square of thick white paper. Attached to it by a red ribbon was a plain gold circlet about the size of a fifty-cent piece. The circlet was curiously rounded. The letter stated that Lij Tekla Alamaya was the personal representative of the Emperor of Ethiopia and recommended him to the good graces of all officials of embassies and consulates and the friends of Ethiopia abroad. Alamaya translated it. Many persons collected around to see it and the letter was passed from hand to hand.

Seraphine of all the persons in the party was the most remarkable to the Germans. She was so fair, despite her Papuan physiognomy, so Nordic something. And so they contrived to keep her constantly in their company and put many questions to her about Harlem: *Must be a vastly interesting place. Were there many more persons like her—white of complexion, of course? Did they feel differently from the rest of New York?* She was very flattered by their attentions, considering herself a greater social success than Delta Castle and Bunchetta Facey. In her high spirits, she drank excessively, even to the extent of mixing whiskey with gin.

Maxim Tasan and Newton Castle had moved with Alamaya away from the others in what appeared to be a cabal. Seraphine and the Germans with the Englishman went from the spacious reception room, passing down the long corridor to the dining room. There were drinks there too and eatables. Mrs. Witern was prodigal in her arrangements to please her guests.

The young artist, Willy Rittner, said he would like the plea-sure of painting Seraphine. She said that her picture had already been beautifully enlarged in colors by an art firm downtown, but that was when she was in high school and she would like another. The artist thanked Seraphine and handed her a large glass of Scotch and a little soda.

"Tell us how the Harlem people live," said Mrs. Fischer. "It is so strange to a stranger. Thousands of you up there and liv-ing downtown one never would realize it. You see a few por-ters in the railway station or a maid when you go out to dinner, but otherwise a colored person is as rare as a red Indian."

"You won't feel that way when you visit Harlem," said Seraphine.

Mrs. Schmidt drew closer to her on the couch. "But isn't there popular resentment against such prejudice? Cut off from the fuller life of the city? You have heard of what is happening to the Jews in Germany. Now when an educated cultured col-ored person, just as well-bred as any white person—like you—"

"Oh, I don't know about that," said Seraphine. "This is a funny country and some colored persons get along. For exam-ple Mother is a member of the Board of Colored Charities. And last May she was invited by the Matrons of the Temple to luncheon. That's an old club and the members wanted to know about charitable work among colored people. And Mother said that after the luncheon one of the ladies told her it was the first time a colored person was ever entertained there and not a Jew had ever got in there."

"Oh there!" cried Mrs. Fischer, her glass of liquor having fallen from her hand and broken on the floor.

"That affair of the Matrons having your mother to luncheon was soon after the Harlem Riots," said a downtowner.[2]

"Yes, two months after, I believe," said Seraphine. "As I say, there are breaks and compensations and sometimes I wonder what the darkies are always fussing about. Mother and I go wherever we want in New York. We have dined at the Waldorf and I've danced at the Jardin du Ciel of the Plaza Alhambra³ and visited the Seminole Cabaret, which is the most exclusive in New York. But it costs a lot of money to go to such ritzy places. And how many Harlemites have money? Ha-ha!"

Seraphine threw herself back on the couch in a giggling fit. She was addicted to laughing spells when inebriated. Artist Willy Rittner hissed: "The silly hussy." And there was dead silence. The Germans could not understand this girl who was so closely associated with the envoy of Ethiopia, a country struggling against Fascism. She seemed to know nothing; giddy, empty-headed.

Mrs. Fischer walked out of the room followed by her husband. Pair by pair and one by one the others left. And Seraphine was alone. She looked up and saw that she was alone. And she lay back and giggled again until her body was limber. At last she pulled herself together and said: "Gee, I wonder if I made a damn fool out of myself again." And she laughed at what she said. She kicked her feet out and got up, swayed a little. She straightened up and started down the corridor. She felt dizzy again and leaned against the panel of a door. She heard voices inside and was startled by her own name, "Peixota." She listened. It was Alamaya speaking:

"Peixota won't stand for the ousting of Dorsey Flagg. He likes him. Flagg is one of the few college men—perhaps the only one—who respects Peixota. We are trying to avoid any more dissension. If Mr. Castle starts trouble with Mr. Flagg and forces him out, Peixota will resign."

"Then let him resign, we can get plenty more to take his place. We don't want any Trotskyite on that committee."

"But the colored people want Mr. Flagg, they elected him. What do they know about your Trotskyite-Stalinite controversy? What do they care? It is my poor suffering country they are thinking about; they want to help Ethiopia."

"Lij Alamaya," said Maxim Tasan, "your country is a part of the world. You're a very young man, but you are a diplomat. Tonight when you reminded that bright Englishman about the English acting late in Asia and Africa, you said a profound thing. But you are not profound when you think that the Stalinite-Trotskyite issue has nothing to do with colored people. This issue involves all the peoples of the world. Trotsky is one of the cleverest men on earth and he is one of the most powerful and dangerous agents of Fascism. We have imperative orders to fight against Trotskyism and its agents and sympathizers everywhere—to show them no mercy, fight them with every weapon, fair or foul. Soviet Russia is the only great nation that is fighting Fascism today. In all the other countries the Fascists are permitted to organize their forces, except in Soviet Russia. Ethiopia is a victim of Fascist aggression. We couldn't give you our support, if you were working with Fascists."

Seraphine passed along into the big room. What she heard had a sobering effect on her. Although she was wholly lacking in political intelligence, her curiosity was aroused. Who was this Maxim Tasan and why was he mixed up with Lij Alamaya and the Hands to Ethiopia committee?

The radio was on and a few couples were shuffling around, without much animation. There was much more space, for many of the guests had left. Those who remained were of two kinds, persons who enjoy making conversation and reluctantly break away from a convivial gathering and those who will stay until the last drink is drunk. The Germans were gone except the artist Willy Rittner, who was sitting in conversation with Bunchetta. A muscular man with the swing of a boxer was walking about the room, accompanied by a fragile kind of mollipilose youth, who was earnestly talking. The man was an esteemed writer of action tales, not the popular Westerns, but tales of social significance, of brutal and bloody incidents involving the cultured classes in the struggle for existence. The youth was praising the master in accents of adoration. Sometimes the writer glared at him, but said nothing. His glass was empty and he went to the buffet (still dogged by the young man), found a bottle that was not empty, poured a large drink and swallowed it at one gulp. Suddenly he turned round and, with a terrific swing, hit the poor young admirer in the mouth. The lad fell with a thud. A girl screamed and a crowd collected around him. He was lifted to his feet. His teeth were loose and the blood dripped from his mouth upon his shirt.

The writer had walked leisurely away. "Come to the bathroom and clean yourself up," Mrs. Witern said to the young man. She gave him a handkerchief and he held it to his mouth.

Another man remarked: "At first I thought it was one of the proletarians who had gone off his nut, but it was a highbrow."

"Yes, and I was congratulating myself that it was such a nice party," said Mrs. Witern.

Alamaya appeared and Seraphine captured his arm and said it was time for them to go. But before he left Alamaya discovered that the Emperor's letter was missing. Instinctively he had thought of it and found the thick envelope empty in his pocket. Mrs. Witern was very upset by this new incident. She and her guests looked everywhere under chairs and cushions, but there was no letter. She could only promise to make a thorough search the following day. But everyone there felt that someone had impishly appropriated the most precious souvenir of the evening.

On their way home Seraphine tried to offer some consolation: "Is it awfully serious, Tekla? Can't you get another one?"

"Such documents should never be lost. When a man loses a letter like that, he disqualifies himself—"

"Then you should have left it at home, you shouldn't have shown it around."

"Yes, you're right. Let's not talk about it."

"Poor Tekla!" Seraphine drew closer and leaned against him.

He was thinking about the party. Would he be invited to any more like it? A crowd of people coming together to drink and amuse themselves as best they could. And a few phrases spoken about Ethiopia, his country—ten million people fighting with medieval weapons against a nation of over sixty million, with colonials, with modern war machines, planes and tanks and gas. How long could they stand it, his people? In Menelik's days it was different—the rifle and the spear were mighty weapons.[4] But Haile Selassie was not Menelik. He had tried to modernize Ethiopia, but the time was too short . . . The Italians were killing off his people, overrunning his country . . . And he was drinking cocktails at a party in New York. But people must amuse themselves to keep from going insane. Even under the terror, the soldiers at the front and the civilians behind the lines, both getting bombed and gassed just the same, they had their relaxation: cards, jokes, laughter, music, wine, women . . .

"I like you a lot, Tekla," said Seraphine. "Do you like me?"

"Yes, I do."

"Then show it," she said, pouting her mouth to his. They kissed. He caressed her hand.

"That is better than worrying," she said. "Is that Gloria Kendall really very much like an Ethiopian girl?"

"H'm, yes."

"And you like her?"

"I haven't even thought of her again."

"And who's that Maxim Tasan who brought her to the party, your friend?"

"He is the big man of the White Friends of Ethiopia. What he says goes."

"Did you know him abroad?"

"No, I met him here in New York at the 'Friends' office."

"Is he a foreigner? He seems to have a strange accent."

"I don't know. All Americans are foreigners and strange to me."

"We are not strange to you. Father and Mother like you like their own son. And when Father likes anybody he stands up for him."

She thought of the brief altercation she had overheard between Alamaya and Maxim Tasan, but she did not mention it. She felt happy that Alamaya had spoken in favor of her father.

THE BRANDING OF A
BLACK FASCIST

Mrs. Peixota hovered over her husband in the office and brushed an imaginary fleck of something from his shoulder and remarked: "Sirrie said she had a perfectly lovely time with Lij Alamaya at the party. He seems to be a nice sort, charming manners."

"He's a diplomat," said Peixota. "But he *is* a nice person, the people will like him."

"Sirrie's head is completely turned. I've told her to beware of heartache."

"What do you mean?"

"Oh, don't be so stony and slow to understand when you don't want to. I can't help it if they happen to like each other."

"Nonsense, Seraphine couldn't be that silly. Alamaya is here just on a brief mission."

"Yes, but he is a bachelor and eligible and Sirrie is of age. Besides, he is a prince! If they were married Sirrie would be a princess."

"He doesn't want to be called a prince and maybe he is right. Titles are cheap nowadays. The Emperor and Alamaya and the Rasses may all soon be exes. Mussolini is moving fast. What would Seraphine do with an empty title?"

"She wouldn't be the first American girl to marry an ex-something."

"Would be better if Seraphine thought about getting herself an American husband."

"Chut! Surprised at you, Pab. You're not American-born, either. And do you believe I made a mistake when I married you?" She tapped his shoulder playfully and he rustled some papers on the desk, suppressing a laugh.

"I'd advise you, Kezia, to discourage Seraphine as tactfully as you can. You know how mean and vile our people can talk about one another. Lij Alamaya is our special guest. If anything should go wrong with his mission, they would blame it on our family."

"I don't care about colored folks' spiteful gossip. You don't want her to marry a no-count anymore than I do and I trained her to aim high. Our black young men are wriggling and slippery like eels. Duster Boley got married to a white girl last week."

"Did he? It might ruin his father." Duster was a dentist, not established in practice yet. His father was a successful medical doctor and skillful Tammany politician.[1] "I guess it's another of those radical entanglements," added Peixota.

"I don't know what kind of a tangle it is—interracial I should think. Anyway, Alamaya and Seraphine belong to the same race, and if they are interested in each other, I won't put any obstacle in their way."

The bell rang. Mrs. Peixota went to the door. It was Alamaya. She greeted him with rare cordiality and said that Mr. Peixota was in the office. She went down to the kitchen.

Alamaya told Peixota that he had come directly from the office of the White Friends of Ethiopia. His demeanor was not very prepossessing and Peixota was concerned.

"Maxim Tasan of the White Friends is opposed to Mr. Flagg accompanying me on tour," said Alamaya.

"That's none of his goddam business," said Peixota. "And I won't stand for any of his interference. We are running our show and the White Friends are running theirs. We've never attempted to tell them who they should work with and why. We decided to work along parallel lines without crossing one another. Dorsey Flagg is my friend and he is an honest man. I think he's worth a hundred Newton Castles. I won't let any Maxim Tasan tell us what colored persons we should have as officials. What does he know about colored people anyway?"

"What Newton Castle tells him," said Alamaya in a sarcastic manner.

"Do you have any objection to Dorsey Flagg?" asked Peixota.

"None at all. I rather like him."

"Then, when you start on your tour this Saturday, he will go with you."

Dorsey Flagg was not in the least agitated about the attempt to oust him from the Hands to Ethiopia committee. When Peixota told him of Newton Castle's threat and the opposition to his membership, he declared that he was not worried and that no intrigue of unscrupulous Communists could scare him to resign or prevent him serving the cause of Ethiopia. Aside from their personal friendship, Peixota desired Flagg to serve on the committee precisely because he could be influential in allying the reluctant intelligentsia to support the Hands to Ethiopia organization. Even without his actually doing anything, the name of Dorsey Flagg on the committee meant a lot. His father had been a prominent Republican office-holder, a friend of Frederick Douglass and also of Booker T. Washington; a maternal uncle was a well-known bishop of the African Methodist Church. And so besides being a college professor, Dorsey Flagg was of real importance in those Aframerican circles that cherished every item, even the dead straws of traditional value. And although he was called a rough-neck intellectual on account of his propensity often to imbibe too much and show the effects of it, he was nevertheless welcome in exclusive Aframerican circles. However, he had drawn the fire of the Communists and the powerful Popular Front because, in an article widely publicized in the colored press, he defended some students who were formerly Soviet-minded but had come out against the Soviet Dictatorship and the Communist International. And worse, he declared that Leon Trotsky was a ruthlessly honest man and one of the greatest intellects of his time, even though he did not partake of his views.

A Trotskyite group[2] asked him to address them; the meeting was widely advertised. And ever since, unexpectedly unpleasant things began happening to Dorsey Flagg. He was surprised when he spoke even at non-political meetings, to be heckled and called a Fascist. Even at purely social gatherings some gin-fizzing fuzzy-minded woman of the Bunchetta Facey type might exclaim at some statement of his: "That sounds a little like Fascism, Professor."

"I hope we don't split with the 'Friends,'" said Alamaya. "If we could only arrive at some solution. I told Mr. Tasan quite emphatically that he was damaging our cause with this Stalin-Trotsky issue. My God, I can't see what it has to do with Ethiopia."

"Lij Alamaya," said Peixota, "who is this Maxim Tasan?"

"He seems to be the most important person among the White Friends of Ethiopia, but who he is and what he is, I don't know." His manner was slightly confused, evasive.

"I would like to meet him," said Peixota.

"That can be arranged. When do you want to meet him?"

"Today, now if possible."

Alamaya picked up the telephone and called the office of the Friends of Ethiopia. "It's all right, he will meet us there at the office," he said.

If Alamaya did not know the commonplace things about Maxim Tasan, such as where he was born, nationality, married or single, he knew the essential thing, what he represented, and of that he did not inform Peixota. Tasan was a frequent visitor in the Aframerican quarter. He attended lectures, mass meetings, street meetings, church affairs and the dances at the Savoy,[3] especially those that were held under the auspices of Communists. He was a constant companion of Newton Castle. Some people thought that he was studying the community to write a series of articles or a book. There was nothing strange about his interest in the community—not to Harlemites at least. The community was one of the showplaces of New York. And other persons were as assiduous as Tasan in their interest: Hindus, Jews, Nordics and Native Americans, students, social workers, radicals, bohemians. Among dissident Communists it was said that Tasan was a key international organizer of the Popular Front.

Tasan was a small man in his late thirties or early forties. His appearance was youthful and it was not easy to guess his age. There was something about him of a furry little animal, a ferret that one might like to stroke or not, according to one's taste.

The office of the Friends of Ethiopia was on the eleventh floor of a building in Madison Avenue near Forty-Second Street. It was not elaborate like the spacious floor which Pablo Peixota had donated to Lij Alamaya and the executive work of the Hands to Ethiopia. The Friends' office consisted of two rooms containing typewriters, large and small desks, steel filing cases, a bookcase and chairs.

When Alamaya and Peixota arrived, they found Prudhomme Bishop, the president of the Equal Rights Action, in conference with Maxim Tasan. Peixota was slightly acquainted with Prudhomme Bishop, and Lij Alamaya, who had not met him before, was introduced. Peixota said that he would withdraw and wait, but Tasan said that that was unnecessary, as he and Prudhomme were also discussing the Ethiopian situation in which the latter was also interested. Tasan set two chairs for the guests.

Muscular yet quietly reserved in demeanor, Pablo Peixota

was an impressive type compared to Prudhomme Bishop, who was a dark-brown man with a bulging body and short fat hands which contrasted strangely with his small coconut-round head and excessively small feet. As he was fussy in his manner and addicted to gesticulation, he gave one the impression of being a comical figure. Yet he was the leader of a considerably influential portion of the Aframerican intelligentsia. The "ERA," the organization of which he was the thirteenth president, was founded in Boston after the sudden collapse of the Reconstruction period and the rise to power of the Ku Klux Klan. The ERA's motto was "Equality under the Law." Its programme was the Right of all the people, including Aframericans, fully to enjoy the fruits of American Civilization and to participate in the pursuit of life and happiness. For three decades it was eclipsed by the Tuskegee Idea of Special Group Development of Aframericans.[4] But it still retained its powerful hold on the imagination of the Aframericans of the North.

The orthodox Marxists with whom Maxim Tasan worked were for many years the avowed enemies of the ERA. But the profound universal social change of recent years had brought about limited sympathy between them. Prudhomme Bishop had refused to work with the Harlem Hands to Ethiopia organization, but he was an executive member of the White Friends of Ethiopia. Newton Castle was the other Aframerican member.

Clapping and wringing his hands Tasan said: "Mr. Peixota, I am glad that Mr. Bishop is here, for he might help us over our little snag." (His tone was intended to indicate that Prudhomme Bishop's being there was accidental.) "Mr. Bishop was recently appointed an executive member of the White Friends of Ethiopia. And we are working excellently in harmony together."

"But Mr. Bishop is not white," Peixota facetiously remarked.

"Now, Mr. Peixota, that's a funny thing to say, but our work is a serious affair. It isn't prudent that leaders of the people should emphasize too much the differences of race and color. Not in these times when the Fascists and Nazis are using them to feed their raging fires."

"But people were divided up by race and color from the beginning of the world," said Peixota. "I know that the Fascists are taking race and color to turn the world into a hell. But we cannot pretend that they don't exist."

"But we can set an example by demonstrating the spiritual unity of the civilized world, Mr. Peixota," said Prudhomme Bishop. "The spirit is the grandest handiwork of man and a house divided against itself shall fall. The Fascists and the Nazis will live to learn that."

"The Soviet state has abolished race and color," said Tasan, "and by that we are implacably, historically and eternally in the service of humanity opposed to the Fascists and the Nazis. The people are still ignorant and all the leaders who are opposed to Fascism must educate them. But, of course it must be done gradually. That is one reason why I supported an all-colored organization like the Hands to Ethiopia and agreed that it was necessary to have a separate White Friends of Ethiopia organization. The chauvinistic imperialists are responsible for the crisis of race. Their actions have put the colored world on the defensive against the white."

"But we cannot tolerate the destruction of our spiritual welfare," said Prudhomme Bishop. "That is why I couldn't support the Hands to Ethiopia, Mr. Peixota, although I admire your work. But I believe in the symbol of unity. Man is the Lord of creation and we are all men."

"You see, Mr. Peixota," said Maxim Tasan with a shrug, "your own influential leaders are opposed to a separate organization. But I don't see eye to eye with them, just as I can't see eye to eye with you. Mr. Bishop has just been discussing with me a new idea which I consider extremely original, if it doesn't endanger the unity of your group."

"And what is that, may I ask?" Peixota spoke coldly. He thought it was an idea that had something to do with his organization.

"It's an idea that the white people should appreciate as much as a bull moose is protected," said Prudhomme Bishop. "I am launching a campaign of national magnitude and its purpose is a predication of the security and unity of the nation. I propose to put a white person in every colored organization, great and small, as a symbol of the oneness of this wonderful nation. And I am putting into this campaign the entire administrative energy and membership loyalty of the ERA."

"Mr. President Prudhomme Bishop," said Peixota, clearly articulating each word with a little pause in between, "with your kind permission, I should like to make a suggestion."

"With pleasure, with pleasure indeed, Mr. Peixota. I have never considered my position to be such that I could not learn from experience by disciplining myself to listen to proposals from others who are not so advantageously placed as myself."

Alamaya kept his eyes fixed on the floor and Maxim Tasan stroked his face with his palm in order to conceal a faint smug smile.

"It is not much of a proposition," said Peixota. "I want to say that I imagine your campaign might be of greater national significance and symbolic effect, if you made it a campaign to put a colored person in every white institution. You might take the government first. Begin with the cabinet and then switch to the Supreme Court, the federal judiciary, and the other government departments, right down the line: Colleges and Schools, Libraries, Newspapers, Radio, Banking, Shipping, Railroads, Airplanes, Buses, Hotels, Cinemas, Theatres, Orchestras, Trade Unions. There are more I guess." Peixota counted the number on his fingers as he spoke.

"I think that's an original idea, all right, President Bishop," said Tasan. For the first time he imitated Peixota in addressing

Prudhomme Bishop as "President Bishop" and his manner was sarcastic.

"But it is not co-efficient in the practical realm of the higher manifestation of human application," said Prudhomme Bishop.

"Yet, I believe that you could make it serve the ERA or a 'New ERA,'" said Peixota. "Looking ahead I have an idea that the ERA or Equal Rights Action has served its purpose and that our people need instead a RAGLAW (Right of All Groups to Life and Work)."

"Not feasible, not feasible," said Prudhomme Bishop, rising. "My campaign will be explosive with the cannon of idealism, which is the basis of the altruistic principle of achievement."

"You are not leaving us now," said Tasan, very happy that he was.

"Yes indeed," said Prudhomme Bishop, "the duties of my office are innumerable and exacting and as laborious and overwhelming as the stars along the Milky Way. Mr. Peixota, I earnestly hope that you will change your mind and make your organization a credit to our people, by bringing in as many whites as possible to illuminate it. And Lij Alamaya"—he bowed gravely—"I am honored to make your acquaintance and I wish to extend to you an invitation to visit the offices of the ERA. We are installed in a palatial environment."

The diversion gave Peixota and Tasan a chance to take an estimate of each other. Peixota was a shrewd evaluator of persons. He had handled one special variety in the numbers game and another in his real estate business. In the former he had had the advantage of choosing men for various kinds of jobs: to canvas for players, as lookout for police movements, as dummies to take the rap for others, as reliable controllers of the game, handling temptingly large sums of money. And his judgment was mostly good. He knew for instance that a cheery, back-slapping canvasser or collector could never be good in the role of a poker-faced dummy.

It didn't take him any time to know that Maxim Tasan was the type of man who went doggedly and persistently at getting done what he wanted. And if one method failed he would find another. Quiet and undistinguished looking, Tasan was the kind of man that could make a schoolteacher like Newton Castle jump through a hoop with a whoop and stand on his head.

And Tasan too was soon satisfied that Peixota was a different Harlemite from those with whom he had become acquainted at parties and meetings. He saw in Peixota a type of conservative, intelligent businessman. He saw in him the type that could be obstinate, determined and aggressive once he was stirred to interest in a moral idea. He saw that he wouldn't be an easy man to handle.

"You wanted to talk to me about the collaboration of the Friends with the Hands to Ethiopia, Mr. Peixota," said Tasan.

"Not exactly that. I thought that after our exchange of letters and our delegates meeting with yours that all that was settled. But Lij Alamaya said you had objected to Mr. Flagg going along with him on his tour. And there was even opposition to him being a member of the committee."

"It is one of your own committee members who objects most, Mr. Peixota: the secretary of your organization."

"Yes, Newton Castle, but we can take care of his opposition. The real trouble is the White Friends supporting him. That isn't playing fair, for we had agreed to carry on the good work along parallel lines."

"Mr. Peixota, will you permit me to put a question to you?"

"You may ask any question you want and I shall be glad to answer if I can, Mr. Tasan."

"I'd like you to tell me why you and your people are interested in Ethiopia. Why you are making sacrifices to defend the country. Is it just because they are a colored people like you?"

"Not at all. The Chinese and Hindus are colored, and we don't have exactly the same sentiment for them that we have for

AMIABLE WITH BIG TEETH

Ethiopia. But Ethiopia is African and our people have their roots in Africa. It is the same sentiment that different white Americans have for Europe. They can't feel just the same way about Africa and Asia, because their roots are European. It is a natural human feeling. If a native state can maintain its existence in Africa and hold its head up among the white nations, it adds to the self-respect of the colored Americans. For Africa is the land of their ancestors, who were brought here in a state of degradation. When an African people do something that is fine and noble it also gives our people hope and courage to fight race and color prejudice here and strive to lift themselves up in a noble way. I don't know if you will understand me, but a people live by tradition and self-respect as much as they do by food and drink."

Said Tasan: "I understand perfectly, Mr. Peixota, and I agree with everything you say. I wish only that you could understand me too and believe that the white man also can be sincere in his attitude towards the colored man."

"I have never doubted that a white man can be sincere towards the colored man. Many are as individuals. But we are all subject to limitations. Our views are influenced by our training and environment. Even God when he made the world could not make it perfect, so I don't expect the white man to be perfect more than any other."

"Now I think we understand each other, Mr. Peixota. I know now that you believe that the White Friends want to help Ethiopia as much as the Hands to Ethiopia. You want to work without friction. You hate the Fascists who sprung this abominable war on Ethiopia. Why should you want to keep in your organization a man who is said to be a Fascist? Just for the sake of harmony I think you should let out Dorsey Flagg."

"Dorsey Flagg is not a Nazi-Fascist, Mr. Tasan. I know that. How can a black man in America be a Nazi-Fascist? I could never believe that about Mr. Flagg. And besides, he says the whole thing is preposterous. He says it's a Communist frame-up, Stalinites against Trotskyites and the Soviet Russia conundrum.⁵ I don't understand the thing very much, because I am not educated about Soviet Russia and foreign politics. And I don't want it to disrupt my organization."

"But, Mr. Peixota, it *is* disrupting your organization. I know that you haven't got the large professional group of colored people behind your organization. I could swing them to you if you would only compromise on this issue. With just a little pressure exerted from the right direction, Prudhomme would jump into your arms."

"Better let him stay in the white man's arms, for I can't use him," said Peixota. "He is only good for a white tool and fool."

"But he is the leader of an influential body of colored people."

"It is no credit to them that he is."

Two girls entered, a white and a colored. They had been out to luncheon. Lij Alamaya recognized the colored girl as Gloria Kendall, whom he had met at Mrs. Witern's party, and he introduced her to Pablo Peixota. She worked as a file clerk in the office and the other girl was the typist.

"So you still insist that Mr. Flagg must accompany Lij Alamaya on his tour, Mr. Peixota?"

"Unless Lij Alamaya personally objects to him."

"I am entirely at the disposal of the Hands to Ethiopia committee," said Lij Alamaya.

Peixota was irritated by Tasan and especially when he declared that he could swing the professional group of colored people to him. A white man declaring that he could deliver the colored people to a colored organization! Peixota was more angry because there was a probability that Tasan might be able to do it. He was a manipulator of men and undoubtedly possessed power or the means to wield power and delighted in it.

But he could not understand why he should want to have power over colored people. He could understand white Democrats and Republicans seeking to capture the colored vote. He had played the political game and understood. But the Democratic and Republican game was something quite different from the influence that Tasan desired to exert over colored people. Maxim Tasan wanted power over the life and thought of his people, to turn their mind to Soviet Russia as a Promised Land. Peixota was convinced that the man cared little about Ethiopia. Yet he marveled that he should be so interested in the social existence of his group of people. What could they contribute to the prestige and the future of Soviet Russia? He arrived at the conclusion that as the Soviets were in principle anti–Nazi-Fascist and Italy a Fascist state, they were merely using Ethiopia as a strategic base of propaganda. And suddenly he had a suspicion that Lij Alamaya knew more about Maxim Tasan than what he had told him. He was so strangely silent during the conversation and wore such an obviously distressed expression, as if he were worried about Tasan's taking offence. Was it conceivable that there was a possibly secret understanding between them? But immediately he scouted the idea and felt ashamed of entertaining it. No, Lij Alamaya was the Emperor's personal envoy, with authentic credentials. Yet the perverse thought persisted in pursuing him.

THE TOWER AND THE AIRPLANE

With the benevolent encouragement of Mrs. Peixota, Seraphine embarked on a gay flirtation with Lij Alamaya. Yet Seraphine had no clear idea of what she wanted from this association. Alamaya was a personage and it was a rare distinction to be his constant female companion. At least the other girls would be envious and she enjoyed arousing their envy. It was not the easiest thing for a girl of discriminating tastes always to find a distinguished male escort, not in Harlem at least, in whose limited area competition was as keen and entertaining as the ravishing beauties of the Apollo Theater[1] dancing around the leading man.

When Bunchetta teased Seraphine at Mrs. Witern's party and said, "You're a fast one—how nicely you have manicured and painted your claws for him," Seraphine replied, "I'm not thinking of hooking anybody, cat, just having a good time."

"But you like him, don't you?" said Bunchetta. "He has wonderful baby eyes."

"I like him all right, but not so much in the way you imagine."

Seraphine's mother informed her of Mr. Peixota's reaction, when she playfully hinted that there was a possibility of an attachment between her and Alamaya. "—and he said he didn't want you to marry a foreigner. Mussolini might conquer Ethiopia and then Alamaya's title wouldn't be worth anything."

"Father said something there," said Seraphine, "and who knows but Tekla may have a harem in Africa."

"Then it would be safer if you *were* married to live in America," said Mrs. Peixota. "If Mussolini licks Haile Selassie's black hide and conquers Ethiopia, Alamaya would have to stay here and find a job. And why shouldn't it be as easy for him as it is for the other titled foreigners? He's got an advantage of color like you and he can work both ways between white and black."

"But, Mother, he's not in the same class as a European prince or count, he's just an Ethiopian Lij."

"Nonsense, child, you're confused by glamour in the spotlight. Lij Alamaya is in a nobler class, if you ask me. Ethiopia is the oldest empire on the face of the earth. A Lij is a prince and if Alamaya marries you, I will make him use the title of prince."

"Oh, and I would be Princess Seraphine!"

"Yes, and his princely arms would be engraved on your furniture and stationery. *And your bed linen too.* You'd be better off married to him in America than in that barbaric African land, even though the dynasty is grander than that of King Tut of Egypt. Why, if I ever had to visit you there, I'd have to travel in a caravan, just as if I were going on a pilgrimage to Mecca or Jerusalem."

"But, Mother, the way you *talk*, though. Why, you make me dizzy. I don't know that Tekla is any more serious about me than I about him. He might prefer marriage in his own country, where he can sit all wrapped in silk and satin on a golden stool, with his docile native women groveling at his feet."

"You can prevent that happening, if you play a clever game. Even though he is an African, Alamaya is not so different from others. All the world loves American women."

Seraphine dropped to the studio chair and gave herself up to a hectic spell of giggling.

The Tower had the privilege of being the first club in the community to entertain Lij Alamaya. Seraphine had promised that the club should have that distinction, and she luxuriated in the feeling that the other members were indebted to her for the realization of their aristocratic desire.

The Tower was a women's club of twenty-one members. It was founded during the last World War. Its founder was a distinguished clergyman's daughter and an official of the Home for Colored Working Girls. She was a militant of the Votes for Women movement and a very effective speaker. Her name became famous when a group of Southern politicians declared that although they were in sympathy with the Votes for Women campaign, they could not support it, because it would mean the extension of the privilege of voting to Aframerican women. This woman was publicized as one of the many Aframerican women who were quite as qualified as other women to vote. The original founder intended the Tower to prove that its women were a tower of strength to the Aframerican group. But she was an aristocrat by conviction and limited the membership to twenty-one. It was her hope that similar groups would be formed in other cities which by example would influence Aframerican womanhood to strive for higher things.

But when the founder died, five years after starting the club, her successor directed it from an idealistic into a sophisticated channel. Elegantly placed in the form of a right angle reversed and embossed on its official stationery, the name of the club was artistically arranged to indicate its character, thus, in the upper left side:

T-alent
O-riginality
W-ealth
E-ligibility
R-efinement

These were the five attributes requisite to membership. Eligibility was the most important and next Refinement. Originality was more a matter of manners than of ideas and Talent was determined by cleverness instead of originality. Wealth was rather a potential than an actual requirement. It meant chiefly that a member was materially able to keep up with the social standards of the club. If her background and its traditions were rich—that is, if she were connected with a historically notable Aframerican family—she was considered as important as a member whose parents or husband were well-to-do. Thus a prominent member who came from Washington, D.C., was admitted because of "her wealth of beauty and traditions and associations." But there were moneyed Harlemites who could not obtain the coveted privilege of membership. There was one matron who had accumulated her fortune from two divorces and the tragic death of one husband and certain personal investments which were outside of the province of the legitimate financial market. She possessed the first three qualifications for membership and ardently desired admittance to the Tower. But she could not get a member to sponsor her candidacy. Once she persuaded a man of solid professional standing to take her as his partner to an exclusive invitation dance of the Tower and she was rejected at the door.

Among the twenty-one active members, there were city employees and social workers, doctors, wives of professional men and daughters of prominent city officials. There were a few honorary members, chiefly former members who were no longer permanent residents of New York. The president in office was Miss Lucy Lincoln Washington, who was a great-granddaughter of one of Abraham Lincoln's servitors. The secretary was Miss Bunchetta Facey.

The Tower was meeting with Lij Alamaya at the home of Seraphine. It was a hurriedly arranged affair, as Lij Alamaya was leaving on his tour on Saturday. As usual when the club entertained a male, a couple or more men were invited. Newton

Castle, whose wife Delta was a member, was asked. And he had prompted Delta to suggest that Professor A. Banner Makepeace be invited. Professor Makepeace brought Mrs. Witern along.

It was a very quiet gathering compared to Mrs. Witern's. It began early, for it was scheduled to end by twelve o'clock. Highballs were served, but drinking was moderate. There was something of the atmosphere of a small forum. Mrs. Peixota came in and met the guests, but she did not remain. It was Seraphine's club and her affair.

The tone was set by Bunchetta Facey, who said that the members were eager to hear Lij Alamaya talk informally about the general conditions in Ethiopia. Alamaya said that there were so many things to talk about that he did not know which would be the most interesting for such a select audience. And he proposed that they should ask him questions.

Only twelve of the Tower girls were present, for Bunchetta had telephoned and written to members just the evening before, when Seraphine informed her that Lij Alamaya could meet them on Thursday. They fired questions at Alamaya about the Emperor and the Empress, the Ethiopian Church, the Europeans in Ethiopia, the flamboyant Aframerican Hubert Fauntleroy Julian,[2] whom the Emperor made a colonel, the Rasses, the Queen of Sheba, the status of women, the kind of specie and the kind of food.[3] Lij Alamaya acquitted himself admirably and his answers were considered satisfactory.

Miss Lucy Lincoln Washington presided at the head of the long table and she expertly kept the meeting at the desired intellectual level. Getting fresh and unusual firsthand information about an interesting land is a rare pleasure and everybody felt that they had a good evening.

Professor Makepeace had a chance for a brief illuminating talk with Alamaya. (He was the only other male present; Newton Castle did not attend, as he was summoned to an emergency final meeting of the Hands to Ethiopia committee where the final arrangements for Alamaya's tour were discussed.) The girls considerately gave the two men an interval to converse together. Alamaya discovered that although Professor Makepeace was the chairman of the White Friends of Ethiopia committee, he was ignorant about that organization's operation and work. Maxim Tasan had more to do with the actual direction. Professor Makepeace's relationship to the World Democratic League, of which he was also chairman, was about the same. He spent most of his time lecturing to liberal and radical audiences on modern social changes and adjustments (he had retired from academic work) and he knew little about the practical direction of the organizations with which his name was connected. Once he was satisfied that they were progressive and not reactionary organizations, he informed Alamaya, he was always ready to cooperate and lend the prestige of his name to help.

It was Mrs. Witern's first visit to Harlem. She said she liked the party, it was lovely and restful, so different from the usual ones downtown. Bunchetta, laughing, said she should not take that as a sample, for it was not a party; it was an intellectual exercise.

Newton Castle came in about 11:45, when they were all preparing to leave. He explained why he was late.

"It's a nice night," said Seraphine, "too early for good friends to break away from each other."

"Have you anything to propose?" said Delta Castle.

"We might take Mrs. Witern to some spot—it's her first time in Harlem," said Seraphine.

"But where can we go?" Bunchetta asked. "It's too early for a cabaret and I'm sick of Harlem cafés."

"The Airplane is the only place that I can think of," said Newton Castle. He poured himself a highball.

Only Bunchetta of the Tower was a frequent visitor to the Airplane. Delta Castle went occasionally and Seraphine said that

she had dropped in twice. None of the other members besides
the three felt like going to the Airplane except former Washing-
tonian Iris Marlow, who was a little jealous of Seraphine's fashionable popularity. She decided that she would see the Airplane
for the first time. Lucy Lincoln Washington declined the invitation a little coldly. She was the oldest and most precisely formal
member of the Tower and disapproved of the modern fad of
slumming parties which was recently developing among the
Aframerican elite. Mrs. Witern and Professor Makepeace (who
was rejuvenating himself under the stimulus of new people's
movements) were happy to string along.

Of the variety of dens and dives that pullulated in Harlem
during the glorious intoxicating era of Prohibition,[4] the Airplane was the only one of highly stimulating interest that was
carried over into the revolution of Repeal—the only one that
maintained its allure amidst the bountiful blossoming of bars
and grills beckoning with gaily glittering neon lights and lux-
urious interiors.

The Airplane was ingeniously located on the top floor of a
tenement on Seventh Avenue. Two rooms of a three-room apartment were turned into one to make the Airplane Tea Garden
and it still held the atmosphere of an old-fashioned apartment.
Its location on the top floor was an asset. Customers had to ride
up there in a creaking old elevator. Riding in that elevator with
the regular tenants was enough to give the customers who came
from a more salubrious environment a funny feeling of going
somewhere.

The proprietor, Buster Quincy, in Prohibition time operated a
basement joint in which he dispensed synthetic gin and other
hot alcohol. Risky and energetic Buster broke the law like the
rest of them, when everybody—gangster, reformer, radical and
plain Mr. Citizen—was itching to beat the law in those wild
artificial fermenting days. But when Repeal ushered in a new
era Buster decided that he would keep the commandments. He

took a chance on changing his luck and hoisted himself from the basement to the top floor. And his luck did not desert him.

The fast-spending gentry of the general staffs of the policy game,[5] no longer affluent, were not as heretofore the best customers. And the downtowners who formerly appreciated the exotic sultry nutshells of Harlem speakeasies, now that those landmarks had disappeared, were more inclined to the neighborhood amenities of their own café society. But a few staunch regulars followed Buster in his heavenly hike and new faces appeared.

Buster installed a replica of an old-fashioned bar, but served no alcoholic beverages. Not to his best friend. If any guests asked for stimulants, he offered to go out and get it. If they offered him a drink he was effusive with thanks in declining and explaining that he never drank while he was working and he was working all the time. But many of them would leave something in the bottle (sometimes as much as a half) for Buster to drink at his leisure. And this he would resell when someone else asked for liquor and he "went out to get it."

Yes, Buster Quincy was a very shrewd fellow in the age of Repeal, for the time was ungodly tough for God's swarthy step-children. Above the bar there was a crudely executed but arresting painting of an airplane in the sky and a descending parachute jumper caught up in a tall tree. Many thought that this picture was intended to represent the exploits of the notorious Aframerican Hubert Fauntleroy Julian, who had visited Ethiopia at the time of the coronation of Emperor Haile Selassie, and by whom he was decorated and made a colonel of aviation.

But Buster said that the artist and himself had something different in mind. That when the idea occurred to him to move his place from low down to high up, he wanted to call it the Lindy Hop because it was a handsome name and he was also an amateur of the dance. But the Aframerican gossip said that

Lindbergh detested Aframericans, because they had desecrated the sublimity of his glorious hop across the Atlantic by immortalizing it in a popular dance.[6] Lindbergh was said to be so incensed that later when a colored man also discovered the poor body of his kidnapped baby, he was not given any credit for it. Buster, deciding that he did not want to contribute anything to increase Lindbergh's anger against his race, discarded the name of the Lindy Hop in favor of the Airplane.

A happy incident gave the Airplane its successful boost in the winter of 1934–35. An old beau mondish friend and former customer of Buster's arrived from abroad and brought a party of five to his place one night. Also present was a new thespian group that were planning to launch a Marxist theatre. With them was an actress, once famous, who hankered after a comeback in a new type of drama. When Buster was told who she was he asked her for her autograph. She loudly and indignantly refused, much to Buster's embarrassment.

Buster was saved from his unfortunate fix by his beau monde friend, who said that his group would be honored to donate their autographs to the Airplane, which they did. They were the Countess of X., Lord and Lady Y., the honorable daughter of a Baron, and Mr. A., an internationally famous and rich writer. That incident gave Buster the idea of procuring a large guest book in which his customers should inscribe their names. There were some exciting international signatures in that book,[7] among them: Marlborough, Ostrovsky, Bourbon-Parme, Colonna, Braganza, Glenconner, Torby, Boris, Louis-Ferdinand, Windermere, Hohenlohe, Murat, Vanderlinden, Segur, Bibesco—besides notable American names, scions of real estate houses and merchant princes and names of the high bohemian and fine arts world— such names in such a setting that might have stimulated even the exquisite surfeited appetite of a Marcel Proust.[8]

Some Aframerican visitors thought that many of the famous

signatures in the Airplane's log book were fake. Buster never wasted any time trying to prove that they were not. As a master of ceremonies of his Aquarium (he sometimes called the Airplane by that name, as he sold no liquor) he tried to please all his customers. Mr. High-up may be rubbing shoulders with Mr. Low-down at the bar, but he wouldn't attempt to introduce them, unless he was aware that the desire was mutual.

Buster had had visits from the plainclothes police, who were tipped off that there was something phony about a joint which was frequented by richly dressed downtowners going up in an elevator carrying Harlem rags. But his conduct convinced them that nothing was wrong. Friends suggested that he should embellish the place with modernistic fixtures. But he wouldn't make any changes: the best customers liked it more as it was.

Although prices were very low, the same as in any ordinary lunch counter, Buster's Harlem customers were not from the common crowd. Neither were they from the smarter set. They were mostly young men and women who were working hard to achieve something in one of the arts—writing, painting, music or the stage. Among them were a few students and journalists and some of the more easy-going professional persons.

On a Saturday night when it was crowded the place could accommodate forty people. But there were not many this night that the members of the Tower chose to show the place to their guests. There was a downtown party of two men and a woman, three young men sitting at the bar with an out-of-work cabaret entertainer, a couple of old regulars of Buster's former place and, seated by himself, reading an Aframerican magazine, there was Professor Koazhy. His coat pockets were bulging with pamphlets and papers and a small bottle of ginger ale was set before him. He adjusted his glasses attached to a black ribbon to regard the Tower party as they entered. He got up and went over to Lij Alamaya and they shook hands.

"Well, it's nice to see you here, sir," said Koazhy. "I see you're stepping out, sampling everything." He winked and nodded in the direction of the women who were divesting themselves of their wraps.

Lij Alamaya introduced Koazhy to Professor Makepeace as "Professor." Newton Castle was irritated; he did not consider Koazhy entitled to the dignity of "Professor." Also he resented Koazhy's wink and leer, when he greeted Alamaya. Besides, he disliked his politics.

"Won't you join me at my table?" said Koazhy. "I'm all alone."

Alamaya was willing, but Newton Castle interrupted him, saying, "We have a special party of ladies."

"Oh, I don't mind at all," said Koazhy. "That makes it so much pleasanter."

The women joined them now and the Tower girls were displeased by the embarrassing presence of Professor Koazhy. Bunchetta and Seraphine, Delta Castle and Iris Marlow took the introduction to him very coldly, scarcely opening their mouths and not offering their hands. But Mrs. Witern held out her hand to his and casually sat down. And so the girls sat likewise.

Buster came over and spoke to Bunchetta, who presented him to the group. They ordered ginger ale and orange drinks. From an inner pocket Koazhy extracted a pint of bonded rye and placed it on the table. "You must share with me," he said.

"Oh no, we couldn't, we just couldn't," said Newton Castle. "That is unfair—"

"Unfair to what?" said Koazhy. "There's no strike on here, unless you want to strike. Ladies and gentlemen, allow me to offer you a drink from America's bonded golden treasury."

General laughter warmed the chilly civility and Mrs. Witern said: "I like the joke on the Treasury."

Buster brought the soft drinks and glasses and Professor Koazhy poured his stuff.

"This is like speakeasy days, with a little difference," said Bunchetta.

"A big difference, if you ask me," said Newton Castle. "Wasn't it strange how all the speakeasies vanished so quickly like snowflakes in springtime?"

"They didn't altogether," said Koazhy. "The speakeasies have gone back to the old-style buffet flats of pre-Prohibition days."

"This place is extremely interesting," said Mrs. Witern. "It is like a clever trick. Riding up here in the rickety elevator and then coming through that iron gate and finding this bar. You would imagine it was an opium joint or something worse."

"It reminds me a little of a place in Paris, Le Bateau au Ciel, up on the hill in Montmartre," said Mrs. Castle. "It's not the same, but it's the same crazy idea."

"That's the thing," said Newton Castle. "This place is for the crazy crowd, the Harlem remnant of the lost generation.[9] They don't think, for they can't think—they sneer at the Popular Front and the Proletariat. They're still existing in the hectic speakeasy past and they can't realize that something is rotten with the world."

"Don't be so oratorical in a place like this, my dear man," said Professor Koazhy. "Something has always been rotten with the world ever since it was created."

"If this place is for the crazy crowd, Mr. Castle, then we are crazy too, for we are here," said Mrs. Witern.

"Newton will never believe that he's crazy until he lands in a lunatic ward with a straitjacket strapped on him," said Bunchetta, in her extra syrupy malicious accent.

"Why, Bunchy!" Delta Castle exclaimed.

Mrs. Witern tactfully changed to something else: "I was fascinated by all the questions you people put to Lij Alamaya and his illuminating answers. But there is one thing I didn't find out about and I think it is important. What is the Tower actually doing in the Hands to Ethiopia campaign?"

"Oh, we're working with the medical unit," Bunchetta spoke up quickly, as if apprehensive that somebody else might say the wrong thing. "We are raising money to help buy equipment."

"Bunchetta, you may as well be honest and tell the truth," said Newton Castle, seizing the opportunity to get back at her. "You know perfectly well that the Tower is not supporting the Hands to Ethiopia, just like all the rest of our professionals. I mean to say all of our intelligentsia."

"I never knew there was such a wide cleavage within your group, Mr. Castle," Mrs. Witern said. "I was under the impression that yours was a movement of all the people and I don't quite understand your saying that the intelligentsia is not supporting it. How is it then that Miss Peixota's father is the chairman of the Hands to Ethiopia?"

Seraphine felt a little confused and fidgeted nervously with her bag. How could she explain to Mrs. Witern that although she was ranked among the best element of the community, her father, who made it possible, could not belong.

Delta Castle ventured the explanation: "Our people cannot be judged entirely by the standards of yours, Mrs. Witern. We still have a long ways to go. Many of the parents of our professional class are working for your people as domestic servants. And even when they retire after they have educated their children to obtain decent positions when they might help their parents, they make no pretense of belonging to the intelligentsia."

Seraphine showed her annoyance at Delta Castle's explanation: "I am not sure that your explanation is the correct one. My mother came from the best people in Durham and your husband is from Chicago, where there is no society at all. And Father had as much solid property as the best of them in Harlem. If he doesn't fool with *society* it's because it seems so stupid to him."

"I wasn't thinking of your *family*, darling," said Delta. "I was speaking generally. Bunchetta understands what I'm trying to show. She's a student of sociology and a social worker."

Mrs. Witern was curious to know more about Mr. Peixota and how he made his money. But she said instead: "I believe I understand and that no offence was intended. But you should not be starting out on the wretched road of class differences and become a divided people. For the world is going a different way, a finer way. This is the people's day. This is the hour of the triumph of world democracy."

"Democracy is a luxury of modern civilization," said Professor Koazhy. "I am always drumming that into the heads of my students. People are talking loosely about democracy as if it were a social religion. But it is not! It is a system of social evolution exactly as a civilized human being is a creature of natural evolution."

"I believe that democracy is an idea," said Bunchetta, "and you might change your mind about what it is, Mr. Koazhy, if you were engaged in social work."

Like Seraphine, Iris Marlow was not interested in serious social discussions and she fondled her empty glass and said: "What about a little drink?" The bottle was empty and Newton Castle said he would go out and get some.

"Buster will get it," said Bunchetta. But Castle preferred to go himself. Soon after he was gone, Dorsey Flagg entered the Airplane and was invited over to the Tower group. He sat in Castle's chair and, noticing the glass, asked if the seat was reserved. Seraphine said that Newton Castle was sitting there but he had gone out to get something to drink. Flagg scowled and said he would sit at the bar. But they all insisted that he should join the party.

Flagg and Newton Castle had met earlier in the evening at the emergency executive meeting of the Hands to Ethiopia at which the twenty-four members were present. It had been convened to make a final decision on the debatable issue of Flagg's accompanying Lij Alamaya on his tour. Thoroughly coached by Maxim Tasan, Newton Castle had marshaled all the reasons to impress the committee that it was undesirable that Flagg should go. The most important reason was the White Friends of Ethiopia were opposed to Flagg because he was said to be sympathetic to the Fascists. Castle pointed out that Lij Alamaya needed all the publicity he could get. Some of the Friends were powerfully influential and could make it possible for Alamaya to get the right kind of publicity. But they would not use their influence in his behalf if his manager was a Fascist sympathizer. Castle said that Flagg had made a big blunder by supporting the Russian exile Leon Trotsky, who was anti-democratic and a spy and informer for the Fascists-Nazis. It would be preposterous to send a friend of Fascists to introduce to the American public the envoy of a country which was invaded by the Fascist state.

Flagg defended himself. He said he was not a Fascist nor was he a Communist. He said the Fascists, Nazis and Communists all believed in and practised a ruthless dictatorship over the peoples. He was not a friend of Leon Trotsky but as a democrat, he had defended his right to express his opinions. He had opposed the Popular Front and its drive among Aframericans, because it was promoted by the Soviet Dictatorship. He could not imagine how a nation which held down millions of people under an iron dictatorship could be the chief sponsor of a People's Front to safeguard Democracy. It was as fantastic as the idea of an incorrigible gangster and law-breaker starting a campaign for legislation to make the nation safe for legality and honesty. Flagg finished by saying that he was ready to resign from the Hands to Ethiopia committee and let some other person accompany Lij Alamaya on his tour if that were for the better interests of Ethiopia. He warned the committee against irresponsible agitators who, seeking to serve other interests, were trying to divide the Aframerican people with the highly intellectual issues of Fascism and Communism.

Dorsey Flagg was stoutly supported by Chairman Pablo

Peixota. And the majority of the committeemen were with him. They all had a deep detestation of the Communists from observation of their propaganda tactics in the Aframerican community. And they were also aroused to hatred of the Fascists because of the Italian attack on Ethiopia. They were aware that the Nazis believed that the great blond European race was the superior of all and the fittest to control the destiny of the world, that they were proscribing the Jews, as colored people were proscribed, and that Hitler said in *Mein Kampf* that black people were half apes.[10] They could not believe that any colored person in his sense could be a Fascist-Nazi. What on the face of the earth could he and his people gain by adherence to the Fascist-Nazi social philosophy? But neither could they understand why some sections of the Aframerican intelligentsia were fascinated by the idea of Communist Dictatorship. Under a dictatorship they could imagine only the ruthless rule of an unscrupulous white clique with no regard or consideration for the rights of a colored minority. Existence was difficult and hard enough under a Democracy. Yet a Democracy was circumambient and elastic, there were byways of grace and surcease. But a dictatorship was all of human life drawn relentlessly, ruthlessly together in a well-greased hangman's noose.

And so the committee voted to sustain Dorsey Flagg. Infuriated, Newton Castle had stamped out of the room. It was a disagreeable surprise to Castle, finding Flagg at the table upon his return. And if Mrs. Witern and Professor Makepeace were not there he might not have stayed. At that time Mrs. Witern and Professor Makepeace were not yet fanatic anti-Trotskyites. They were intellectually stimulated by the grand duel that was being fought between Stalin and Trotsky and as intellectuals they admired Trotsky's destructively incisive style, although they considered it a little morbid with the fury of futility. But their real exalted respect went to Stalin, the strong, silent leader who

had captured the Soviet State and was slowly but surely direct-
ing the movement of the Russian steam-roller.

Professor Koazhy's interest was excited by a knobkerry that
was hanging behind the bar.[11] And he had asked Buster's permission to look at it. Buster explained that it was a gift from
one of his titled patrons, who had brought it back among his
trophies from a hunting trip to South Africa. Carrying the
knobkerry to the table, Professor Koazhy became lyrical over
its exquisite workmanship. He passed it around for the guests
to scrutinize and wondered how many of the Aframericans
who visited the Airplane had shown any interest in the knobkerry as a work of art.

Although pooh-poohed by the intelligentsia, Koazhy in his curiously dogmatic way was also a local authority on artistic things.
There were artists among his students of history, archeology, fetishism and anthropology. He lectured to them on Art and said
they could be good artists only by serious research in African
anatomy and physiognomy and hard apprenticeship to the execution of African and Aframerican form and figure. When colored
artists painted Aframericans, he said, they turned out to be white
people dyed in dark tints. Some white artists did a better job with
Aframerican material. And once he made pointed reference to a
successful Aframerican artist who executed excellent portraits of
white persons but could do only caricatures of colored ones.

He had collected in his house a fairly interesting assortment
of African material, mats and masks and beads and carven
sticks and bowls, photographs extracted from books and newspapers and reproductions of ancient Egyptian figures. When a
critic once pointed out to him that West African crafts were as
different from those of the Congo as Hungarian music from
Irish, Koazhy replied: True, but Ireland and Hungary *were* European nevertheless, just as Egypt and the Congo were African,
and there was closer affinity between Egypt and the Congo than
between Ireland and Hungary and that was all.

Addressing Lij Alamaya, Koazhy said: "I have some Ethiopian objects, pictures and fabrics and metalware, and I'd like you to come to my house and inspect them and tell me whether they are genuine."

Alamaya accepted the invitation and Mrs. Witern, who kept pace with all the trends in modern art, asked if she could not anticipate the pleasure of a visit to Professor Koazhy's. Koazhy stood up and bowed to her and said: "I should appreciate the honor, Madam. I should like you to come some evening when I am lecturing to my class of Senegambians."

"How very interesting! Are there really Senegambians in Harlem?" said Mrs. Witern. The Tower girls giggled.

"Not in my class, although there are some native Africans in Harlem," said Koazhy. "My students appropriated the name of Senegambians for its artistic and historical quality."

"I think the whole business is futile and silly and it's a pity that this Harlem should be an incubator for a lot of crazy artificial ideas," said Newton Castle. "Aframerican students must go forward, keeping time with the radical movement, they cannot go back to the primitive forms of savage Africa."

"You are more savage in Harlem, Mr. Castle," said Koazhy, "and it seems to me you need a lot of education yourself. You should join my Senegambians and let me teach you something."

Dorsey Flagg guffawed and everybody was tickled. Although Flagg considered Koazhy a sort of pedantic eccentric, he delighted in his putting something over so neatly on Castle. He preferred a thousand Koazhys to one Newton Castle, who ate and slept hugging the radical movement and was always ready glibly to explain everything by Marxist theory. He said: "So Professor Koazhy thinks that the radical paragon, Dr. Newton Castle, with all his degrees, should sit at his feet and learn again. You said something there, Koazhy, shake hands!" He extended his long arm across the table and vigorously shook Koazhy's hand.

"It isn't a laughing matter," said Castle. "Who are the white people who are interested in so-called primitive African art? They are the rich, reactionary, anti-Soviet crowd. Here they buy and sell African *art* at fancy prices. But the savages who made them get nothing. And our own artists never get a chance. Who but the radicals and a few liberals care anything about the work of our young artists and writers? What newspaper pays any attention to them except the *Labor Herald*? It is only through the radical movement that our young artists and writers can express themselves. The powerful rich art cliques prefer the primitives of the African savages, because they don't have to recognize them as human beings as they'd have to recognize the poor artists here."

"They recognize Dixon Davis Lee," said Koazhy.

"That is merely an exception to the general rule," said Castle. "And Dixon Davis Lee is not a great artist, he's merely a clever opportunist."

"If there is one exception there will be others when they learn their stuff and how to take advantage of opportunity," said Koazhy. "And that's why I insist they must learn that stuff from the foundation."

"There is no opportunity for our artists unless they can follow the Soviet example," said Castle.

"What Soviet example?" said Flagg. "The best Soviet literature was written when Tolstoy, Dostoievsky, Turgenev, Chekhov, Gorky and the rest of them expressed themselves under the Czarist regime.[12] Also the best dramas were written and the best pictures painted. Today the Soviet writer is just a prostitute of the pen for the Communist Party. They have reverted to the practice of the Oriental writers producing panegyrics for the party and persons in power to make a living. That's what the thousands of well-paid writers and the millions of books mean in Soviet Russia. I would rather there were no colored artists and writers than for such a travesty of art and literature to exist in America."

Newton Castle jumped from his seat as if a pin had pricked him, and pointing in Flagg's face said: "You're a fool and a Fascist. You're a disgrace to humanity and a traitor to your race. You have no place in any people's movement and shouldn't be a member of the Hands to Ethiopia Committee. When we Marxists take the POWER, I hope they make me Commissar of Education and I'll clean out the stinking academic niggerati renegades like you."

Flagg said: "The Hands to Ethiopia business is settled and I want to hear no more about it from you." He rose from the table and strode towards the bar.

But Castle followed him: "You think it's settled but it isn't. We will find a way of blocking you, you degenerate anti-Soviet reprobate, you academic cad, you stiletto-up-your-sleeve Fascist."

Bantam-sized Castle was right up against the powerfully built Flagg and beating his fists against his breast. Flagg said: "You're making an ass of yourself and taking advantage of your size. Please go away or I'll give you a swift kick in your rear."

"I'm not afraid of you," cried Castle at a hysterical pitch. "The power of the party will protect and give me strength to fight you murderous Fascists." His high voice went higher and higher.

With a sudden gesture Flagg reached down and grabbed Castle by the seat of his pants and held him up in the air: "Your *power*, fool, is in my hands," he said.

"Put me down, you Fascist! Put me down!" cried Castle.

"All right, I'll put you down," said Flagg. And he dropped Castle to the floor and walked out.

"Well, here is Tekla's car," said Seraphine. "Who wants to be taken home?"

Mrs. Witern's car was waiting too. She told the Tower girls she thoroughly enjoyed the evening, reminded Professor Koazhy of his promise to have her at his house and drove off with Professor Makepeace.

Delta Castle said she preferred to walk: "Come along, Newton, a little walk might have a sobering effect on you." And her face and her voice appeared as if she would like to give him a spanking on the way. Seraphine and Alamaya drove Bunchetta Facey and Iris Marlow home on the hill. They were relieved that Delta and her husband did not take a ride with them, as they were embarrassed by Castle's creating too much of the wrong kind of excitement.

The two girls were driven to the Sugar Hill mansion.[13] Seraphine said: "Tekla, I don't feel the least bit like going home. What about a spin or something?"

Alamaya replied: "Anything you like makes me happy."

"Let's take a swing up the Parkway then," and she instructed the chauffeur to drive into the country.

"Are you sentimental, Tekla?"

"Sometimes," he said.

"I'm always sentimental," she sighed charmingly. "And you have hardly arrived before you will be gone again."

"Yes, I must go among the people in other cities and tell them about Ethiopia and get them to help."

"And Mr. Flagg is going with you. What luck. He's a big strong fellow and will look after you. Father likes him a lot. It was so silly for Newton Castle to start that nonsense at the Airplane. Since he became inoculated with the Soviet system, he's no good in society."

"He *was* very excited."

"And rude. Three years ago he was just a harmless teahound skipping with his sister from one tea party to another. Then his sister died and he got Communism, although he says he isn't a Communist. And now he's like a man who never started to drink liquor until he was old and stays intoxicated all the time."

"That's a neat way of fixing Mr. Castle," said Alamaya.

"Wouldn't life be a glorious thing, if there weren't so much wickedness in the world! People fighting and killing one another just for the love of it."

"The Europeans say we Africans are savages," said Alamaya, "and it is their destiny to civilize us. They said the tribes were always fighting among themselves and it was necessary to bring peace among us. But our tribal wars were like bright fireworks compared to the Europeans' annihilating wars. We never fought to exterminate one another. The Europeans fight to exterminate us and call it civilizing us."

"Poor Tekla! Poor unhappy Africa. But Tekla, did Father show you those revolting pictures of what the Ethiopians do to the Europeans in war? They were so hot he was ashamed to let me see them, but Mother said I was of age."

"That is Italian propaganda against us. But even if a few Ethiopian warriors conform to an ancient tribal rite and do that when their victims are dead, there are many Europeans who practice it among the living. And to us that is a greater shame."

"Yes, there is savagery and barbarity everywhere among uncivilized as well as civilized people. Tekla, supposing Mussolini wins in the war against Ethiopia, would you stay in America?"

"May God save Ethiopia," he said. "It is the last torch of national independence and native aspiration left in Africa."

"You didn't answer my question. You don't like America?"

"Oh yes I do. They are a strong new people and everyone likes newness and strength."

"And would you like to live here?"

"If I had no country to return to and the authorities permitted it, I would be glad to live here."

"And you would become an American citizen and marry—you are not married, are you?"

"No, I'm just starting my career as a diplomat."

"Do you imagine I could qualify as a diplomat's wife?"

"Perfectly!"

"You darling! Do they marry in Ethiopia the same as we do here?"

"There are four or five different ways of marrying."

"Yes, what are the marriages like?"

"Oh, we have trial marriage, religious marriage, civil marriage, transient marriage and permanent marriage. And the women have more freedom than the men."

"Oh yes! Then you're all just as modern as we are in America. I thought you followed the Oriental pattern, but I am always forgetting that Ethiopia is African."

Seraphine called to the chauffeur and asked where they were. He said they were passing through Bronxville. And she told him to turn back to the city. She switched off the light, saying: "It is cosier without it."

8

SAYING IT WITH KISSES

Schoolteacher Newton Castle came to New York from Chicago. He came with his only sister, Annabella Castle, who was older than he, and who presided over their home. Castle took the examination to enter the New York City schoolteaching system. And after thirteen months on the waiting list he was appointed to teach in a junior high school. He was a proficient pedagogue, a doctor of philosophy. He was progressive in his profession and had taken post-graduate work at Chicago, Wisconsin and Columbia, besides special summer studies in Paris, Berlin and at Cambridge, England. He might have had a superior professor's position in any of the high-standard Aframerican universities in the South. But he said he preferred to be a schoolteacher in the great metropolis, where there were social and educational privileges which he could not obtain in another place. Besides, the remuneration was high.

He was a meticulous type of person and his sister was prim and punctilious. Theirs was a perfect hand-and-glove association. They lived in one of the best Harlem houses. Every Friday afternoon a few friends were invited to tea and one evening every week they indulged in a card party. Their tastes were similar and together they visited the art galleries and attended concerts. They never missed a concert downtown, when any outstanding Aframerican artist was featured.

Annabella Castle was more strong-willed than her brother,

and although it appeared as if she were devoting her life to serve, she also managed him. Yet despite their exemplary way of life in Harlem, they never moved in the inner circle of the professional world of doctors, lawyers, musicians, teachers and other city employees. Perhaps because their emphatic propriety irked a little the exclusive members of the professional set, who considered them to be Westerners from what Carl Sandburg dubbed the "hog city."[1]

The Castles got a little deeper in, when they became close friends of Delta Buckton. For Miss Buckton was "in" in the right way and not even her straitened circumstances could keep her out. She was the grand-niece of one of the famous Jubilee Singers.[2] She retained in her possession the cameo brooch that was presented by Queen Victoria to her grand-aunt, the celebrated mocking-bird of the Jubilee Singers. And that distinction opened the best doors to her in Aframerican Philadelphia, Durham, Charleston, Baltimore and Washington, D.C.

Miss Buckton, on becoming attached to the Chicago Castles, carried them along with herself through those difficult doors. The Castles often visited Europe during the summer vacation and once they had taken Miss Buckton along, paying all her expenses. Miss Buckton's companionship influenced the Castle pattern of living, which became more elastic and informal. She substituted cocktail for tea and convinced them that gin should not be taboo, because white folk believed that it was black folk's indispensable tonic.

But suddenly in the midst of their charming change of life, the inseparable brother and sister were divided by death claiming the latter. The change that Delta Buckton was gradually bringing about in the Castles' life must have been more revolutionary than she realized, for the occasion prompted Newton Castle to stage an original unforgettable performance.

He invited his friends to a cocktail party and when they

arrived they found his sister arrayed in one of her finest dresses and laid out on a couch. Newton informed each guest that the occasion was a final tribute to his beloved sister and that they should drink, eat and be happy, for thus she would have liked it. He was an amateur piccolo player and, taking his instrument from its case, he entertained with snatches of gay operatic airs. He finished the party by playing dance tunes on the phonograph and, standing before the couch upon which lay his sister's corpse, he strenuously danced an extravagant modernistic combination jig-and-shimmy.

Broken like an egg by his sister's demise, Newton Castle might have remained in a protoplasmic state if he had not been saved by Delta Buckton offering to marry him. "Annabella would have desired it," he said, and acquiesced. And so he was enabled to come back to a semblance of his normal self again and to continue teaching.

But he was never quite the same to the ultra-sophisticated set that was coming round to acceptance of him when his sister went out of his life. His marriage to Delta patched him up a little and made him externally presentable, but he was not cured inside. For a while he was fascinated by fetishism and secretly consulted Harlem's occultists. But his delicately refined sense could not be long deceived by the manifestations and crude evocations of illiterate occultists.

A new world opened before him when he was invited to attend a meeting for Scottsboro's boys and accepted.[3] His name appeared on the programme among other prominent names. For the first time he was associated with Marxists. His state of mind was purely emotional when first he felt the proselytizing power of the Marxists. Clearly he saw the Scottsboro boys as a persecuted lot and vaguely he felt that he was being persecuted by unkind fate in the death of his irreplaceable sister.

Shrewd evaluators of personalities, the Marxists found Newton Castle malleable material, a type of intellectual that could be dominated and disciplined and who once converted would remain faithful to their cause. And Newton Castle was emotionally ripe and ready to have the Marxists take up the burden that his sister had carried.

His first year among the radicals was one of disciplined study of Marxism as interpreted by the Leninist-Stalinist school. The word "Communist" was still generally unpopular in America; besides, one might be politically and socially penalized for being a Communist. To distinguish themselves from the Socialists, Social-Democrats, Trotskyites and other innumerable fractional groups who adhered to the Marxist-Proletarian-Dialectical interpretation of History and Society, the Communists called themselves the Leninist-Stalinist Marxists.

But in the beginning of the second year of Newton Castle's apprenticeship, the Soviet Dictatorship in a worldwide maneuver launched its People's Front movement against the weak undefended ramparts of the Democratic world. Intellectuals and intelligentsia as a group always regarded with contempt by the Marxists were now courted, fawned upon and given preferential treatment over the proletarians.

And suddenly Newton Castle found himself pushed ahead as a Harlem leader. His surprise was immense, for when he first went over to the Marxists, he had thought that it would take him years to qualify as a Marxist proletarian. He had thought that he would have to show by exemplary living that he had divested himself of all snobbish accoutrements. He was an excitable speaker and splendid for the exciting ferment of the People's Front, whose movement was a universal crusade against the all-destructive hydra-headed power of Fascism and Nazism.

Castle was catapulted among the elite of those opposed to the Satanic threat to Christian Civilization: liberal politicians, philanthropists, scholars, ministers, diplomats, merchant princes and captains of industry, musicians, artists and writers—all conscripted in this vast movement of the world to combat the forces of evil.

If his speeches were more rhetorical than substantial, if he merely parroted phrases about Marxist action and people's power under the aegis of Soviet Dictatorship sweeping the death and destruction of Fascism from the world, he was nevertheless eloquent. And though he thought less of it than his white colleagues, he was a symbol of the non-civilized peoples of the world, even heathen Africa, joining hands with the civilized to save Christendom from destruction.

But in his unbridled zeal for the people's movement Newton Castle had precious little sentiment for the particular position of his own people. In fact he despised them. The great masses of his people ignorant, provincial and superstitious, they were nothing in his eyes in comparison with the illimitable spreading masses of the world. Black masses! He hated the phrase. He had only a religious conception of masses of the world all united, who were one without difference in the People's Front like the hosts of angels in heaven.

To him the Hands to Ethiopia was not interesting as one means of defending Ethiopia, but only as an organization that might be captured by the Marxists to help expand the gargantuanesque inflated maw of the Popular Front. His uncompromisingly fanatic attitude was disconcerting even to the cynical Maxim Tasan. Never had Tasan possessed so perfect an instrument for his purpose. Indeed Tasan sometimes regretted that Castle was not of another race than Aframerican, as he might have been of multiple services to him.

Castle was such a zealot of Marxism that Tasan did not even find it necessary to conceal from him his contempt for the cause of Ethiopia. It was merely a sideshow, Tasan said. When he was ordered to give his attention to Aframerica, he felt as if he were taking a vacation. He remarked to a comrade that the Aframericans were merely "chicken feed."

Maxim Tasan surveyed the new field with the help of Newton Castle and other Aframerican friends. In Harlem he was noted at all the popular places, at the Savoy dancing palace, the Renaissance, the Witoka,[4] the popular bars and restaurants. He was introduced as a guest in some of the Elks Clubs, met present and past Exalted Rulers, and paid for many rounds of drinks. He attended services at the most important churches—Methodist, Baptist, Episcopalian—and he ate at the Romanish orgiastic Banquet Board of the Harlem Deity, Father Divine.[5] He could often be spotted in a crowd listening to a street corner orator. Thus he was a familiar figure in Aframerican public places in that early period of the People's Front. And Maxim Tasan also attended secret meetings of which only the members could know.

Naturally people were inquisitive about his origin and his purpose. Some said he was a Russian and agent of Stalin, others thought he was an agent of Trotsky and still others believed he was agent-at-large of the Communist International. An anti-Communist Indian Nationalist said that he had seen Tasan in Shanghai and that he had arrived in the United States by way of the Pacific. But thoughtful Aframericans would not give credence to the general gossip. If Maxim Tasan was such an important person, they reasoned, why should he be wasting his time among the comparatively insignificant Aframerican group? However, they became doubtful of their own judgment when it leaked out in the Aframerican press that Mr. and Mrs. Newton Castle had had the privilege of meeting the Soviet ambassador and his wife at a private reception, when the ambassador arrived in New York as the dinner guest of an organization of conservative businessmen. In spite of her husband's proletarian mindedness, the fashionable streak in Delta Castle made it impossible for her to withstand the itch to let the item out.

Yet to Harlem the item was no more than a week-end surprise. For despite its general aspect of a mass of people, like a great army of crabs all crawling on the same level, there are many un-usual personalities in Harlem, like famous actors dropped into obscurity, who have rubbed shoulders with greatness. Apart from the high bohemian world, such as is represented by the list of guests at the Airplane, there was the more important domain of politics and government. There were individual Harlemites who had enjoyed handshakes with presidents of the United States and sat on the same platform with congressmen. Some had con-versed with the ex-King of Spain, the ex-King of England and the late Queen of Romania. Others preferred to boast that they had shaken the hand of the President of the Soviet Union, and had listened to Lenin and talked to Trotsky and Zinoviev[6] and even Stalin.

And so the activity of Maxim Tasan in Harlem was not so strange a thing. There were others like him in Harlem: Ger-man exiles, Spanish, Arabs, Hindu, full-caste and Indian half-caste, and Japanese, besides a horde of Union Square comrades and friends.[7]

Prompted by Maxim Tasan, Newton Castle had persuaded the Hands to Ethiopia Committee to have another mass meeting on Friday night to speed Lij Alamaya on his tour on Saturday. Castle said that many of the White Friends of Ethiopia desired to attend as a demonstration of their sincerity and solidarity with the cause of Ethiopia. The members of the Hands to Ethiopia agreed that a joint meeting with the White Friends of Ethiopia might create a favorable impression among Harlemites. Pablo Peixota pointed out that there was hardly time to promote a large meeting. It was too late to get a notice in the weekly news-papers. But Newton Castle said that he would use every means to publicize the meeting locally.

That Friday night the meeting was held in the church of the Rev. Zebulon Trawl. As Pablo Peixota had feared, there was not a great crowd, but it was a fair gathering. The back pews and the balcony were empty, but there were enough people assembled to give warmth and cheer to the meeting. One un-usual aspect was that about one-third of the audience was white.

On the platform there were Lij Alamaya, Pablo Peixota, Newton Castle, Dorsey Flagg, Mrs. Leah Arzell, Elks Exalted Ruler William Headley, Rev. Zebulon Trawl and other mem-bers of the Executive Committee of the Hands to Ethiopia. Also Professor A. Banner Makepeace and four other white men of the White Friends of Ethiopia.

The meeting started with Rev. Zebulon Trawl again pray-ing for the triumph of Ethiopia and that God bless the tour of Lij Alamaya. And too he prayed that God should bless and enlighten the white friends who were also working to help save Ethiopia. "Give strength and wisdom to the white friends to confound and defeat the white enemies of black people," he said.

Pablo Peixota followed the Rev. Zebulon Trawl. He stated they had called an emergency meeting on the eve of Lij Alama-ya's tour, which was mainly for the White Friends of Ethiopia to make manifest their goodwill to the people of Harlem; the people could see, by the large number of white persons pres-ent, the sincerity of their purpose. He introduced Professor Makepeace.

Professor Makepeace said that in joining the White Friends and working with the people of Harlem for the freedom of Ethiopia, he was merely heeding the call of his blood. An English ancestor was a pioneer agitator for the abolition of the African Slave Trade and his American grandfather was an ar-dent abolitionist. He said the Italian aggression against Ethio-pia was but one step in a worldwide plan of the dictators to remake the world according to their will. And it was necessary that the colored people should see the Italian-Ethiopian cam-paign not merely as an isolated event, not as a struggle of black against white people, but as a struggle of the ruthless and re-actionary white powers against the progressive white powers of the world. If the reactionary powers should win all colored and native peoples would be reduced to a greater slavery than the world has ever known. Professor Makepeace chose simple words and spoke objectively but eloquently and with such manifest sincerity he won the people's hearts and they vigorously cheered him.

Newton Castle was then asked to give a joint report of the parallel efforts of the Hands to Ethiopia and the White Friends of Ethiopia. And Newton Castle made it a very lengthy report. He reviewed the work of the Hands to Ethiopia group, telling of plans to send ambulance units to Ethiopia and efforts to enlist doctors and nurses, of various committees that were working along different lines to the same purpose. He named the important organizations which were participating and showed how certain elements were working among the colored masses and others among the intelligentsia. He stated that the plan of the work was his idea and he hoped when the time was ripe and opportune to combine all together in the People's Front. He switched to the White Friends and described their work in raising funds and conducting propaganda for the cause of Ethiopia. He stressed their specially superior role in exerting their influence in the diplomatic spheres. He aptly pointed out that the White Friends could reach and influence certain powerful persons and governments which the Hands to Ethiopia could not. And then he launched forth in an appeal to unite the two organizations immediately so that they could combine their efforts instead of continuing along parallel lines.

Dorsey Flagg interrupted Newton Castle, declaring that the issue of separate organizations was settled and asking Chairman Peixota to correct him. Newton Castle apologised but said that these were not times to adhere to punctilious points of order when the Fascists were making disorder and spreading terror everywhere among all the peoples of the world. And then he shot into a wild-eyed frenzy about Fascism: "Fascism is the enemy of all the world, of all the people of the world, the black people, the brown people, the white people. We, the people, all one and the same under the epidermis, the same veins, the same red blood. Against us are the anti-Soviet plotters, the imperialists, the colonial exploiters, the anti-democratic capitalists, the war-makers, the blood-letting investors, the anti-Semites, the anti-Marxists, the anti-Christ—

"Fascism is the enemy. Fascism declared war on Ethiopia and all the people of the world. The machine and the mechanized units of hell are fighting against the people. There is no race and no color, no class and no nation in this hellish fight. It is all the people in one people's front against the scourge of life. The Soviet Union calls the Democracies to war against the dictatorships and enemies of the people. The Soviet Union leads in the fight to defend Ethiopia and all the peoples of the world, regardless of race and color.

"Only under the mighty Proletarian Dictatorship is Democracy real, a vital challenge of the people's will to live and an expression of the Democratic hopes of the people of the world. Oh, let us defend the Soviet Union and thus save Ethiopia. Let us accept and exalt the leadership of Stalin, of the people, by the people and for the people of the world. Let there be no other leader before him! Let us organize our forces by the pattern of the Soviet Union with the sacred image of our great world leader Stalin in our hearts.

"The triumvirate of the Fascists, Hitler, Mussolini and Trotsky, cannot triumph against him. And we will tolerate no Fascists in our midst deceiving and misleading the people. We cannot defend Ethiopia, we cannot save Ethiopia with Fascists in our organizations. For the Fascists are the fangs of the serpent and the claws of the dragon, the tiger, the hyena and wolf destroying the free life and security of the people—

"I have been called to order. But there are those who make hypocritical pretense of order and law, while they are sewing the seeds of disorder and lawlessness. Such are the Fascists. I was called to order, but the issues of the life and death of this grand world in which we live—this wonderful world of the people, by the people and for the people—the defense of Ethiopia, the fate of Ethiopia—these issues are greater than points of order.

"The Fascists started with Ethiopia first to demonstrate their strength, because the African people are weak. My friends, let us start now and here and organize to be strong. Let us rid ourselves of Fascists in our midst. Let us send the Ethiopian envoy, Lij Alamaya, on his tour with a man who is not a traitor to the people and of his people, with a man whose heart is pure and purged of Fascist ideologies."

Sternly pointing at Dorsey Flagg, Newton Castle said: "I accuse this man of being a Trotskyite Fascist and enemy of the Soviet Union and of Ethiopia. I say that he is unfit to tour the country with Lij Alamaya. I want you people to decide here and now in open meeting by a show of hands—decide against the man, vote him out of the Hands to Ethiopia organization— We, the People, and You, the People! Demonstrate your power against the Fascists as a unit of the Popular Front. Drive this black Fascist out of your organization—"

"Stop that black fool of a white man!" shouted Professor Koazhy from the audience. He was not in uniform and had been sitting apparently unobserved in the seventh row. Now he attracted attention as he stood out in the aisle and his voice boomed impressively: "Stop him! Our people don't want that nonsense! Stop him!" Other voices joined Koazhy's: "Kick him off the platform!" "Throw him out!" "The crazy spade!" Pablo Peixota pulled at Castle's coat from behind. But Castle bounded at Dorsey Flagg and cried: "This is the man to throw out, this Fascist!"

Professor Koazhy rushed to the platform, followed by a number of young Aframerican stalwarts. Simultaneously, the whites in the audience started stamping and chanting in unison: "Throw the Fascist out! Throw the Fascist out! We want Castle! Throw the Fascist out!"

"Yes, you want Castle, because he is speaking for *your* people, not for *our* people!" Koazhy shouted back. Dorsey Flagg threw off his coat and stood out conspicuously in his white shirt. Raising his hands he shook his fists and cried: "Come on, you! Come and throw me out! Throw me out of Harlem! It's you I want and not your stooge, Castle. Come on, you Union Square soldiers!"[8]

But the Union Squarites continued chanting: "Throw the Fascist out! We want Castle!" Chairman Peixota raised his hand, crying: "Quiet please, you're breaking up the meeting, quiet!" But Newton Castle started prancing and shrilled: "Fascists! Fascists! Black Fascists!"

A young man pushed him off the platform. He fell over to the parquet and was quickly surrounded by angry people. The church was in an uproar.

Lij Alamaya stepped to the edge of the platform and held up his hand. The audience quieted down a little. Lij Alamaya spoke: "Friends all, American friends of Ethiopia, I appeal to you as the envoy of the Emperor of Ethiopia. Let us have order. Let's not fight against each other here. My people are fighting desperately against the overwhelming Fascist army in Ethiopia. The big fight is there. Let us have peace among ourselves, as workers carrying on behind the lines and serving those who are actually fighting.

"I need not say that I am anti-Fascist—all Ethiopia is anti-Fascist, for we are fighting against Fascist Italy. I came to America to enlist your support in the fight against the Fascists. I did not come here to divide you people into Fascists and Communists. I don't believe that such an issue here will help Ethiopia over there. There are no Fascists among the Ethiopians. And I don't believe that there are any Fascists among the Aframericans.

"The Ethiopians stand in need of your united help. If we are divided the Fascists who are united will win. Then let us all work together. The Executive Committee of the Hands to Ethiopia has made certain decisions. I have put myself at the disposal of that committee. I will abide by its decisions and cooperate to the best of my ability. I want my mission to the Aframericans to be a success, so that in the future you may more closely cooperate with your Ethiopian brothers. I am an envoy of the Emperor, but I am also a servant of the people. With your united help my mission will succeed, my service will be worthwhile."

Suddenly divesting himself of his coat, Lij Alamaya stepped across to where Dorsey Flagg, also coatless, stood and said: "I think Mr. Flagg is what you say—okay! I am sure he hates the Fascists like all the Ethiopians and all true friends of Ethiopia. The Hands to Ethiopia has elected Mr. Flagg to a responsible position and I have confidence in him. We will all work faithfully and unitedly together. God help Ethiopia, God bless America."

There were a few hesitant hisses among the whites, but they were immediately suppressed by the mighty applause, which broke like a thunder-clap. Despite the smallness of the audience, it was more spontaneous and prolonged than Lij Alamaya received at the previous mass meeting, when he was officially welcomed. Twice when the clamor was fading out Professor Koazhy boomed: "Hep, hep up Ethiopia! Long live Ethiopia!" And it started again, filling the church like a riotous picnic.

A voice started singing "John Brown's Body,"[9] and the crowd excitedly joined, singing and dancing, with happy heavy stamping, exultingly shouting the glory chorus. Not a vestige of formality remained and many of the people mounted the platform to greet Lij Alamaya. One woman kissed him and it was a signal for many others to emulate her. Dorsey Flagg received a share of the kissing also and he was as pleased as a pigeon. Long before the joyous demonstration had ended all the whites had disappeared.

Alamaya was bewilderingly happy that his speech had changed the furiously angry crowd into a merry mob of demonstrators. He did not imagine his speech was so good. Later he mentioned it to Peixota. Peixota told him that it was his unexpected gesture, throwing off his coat to take Flagg's hand, which had fired the enthusiasm of the people. "But I did it merely from politeness," said Alamaya, "as Mr. Flagg had no coat on." But Peixota explained that shirt-sleeve diplomacy was one of the pillars upon which rested American democracy.[10] And every American, even the most humble and ordinary, was aware of it. And so when Lij Alamaya threw off his coat to shake hands with Dorsey Flagg, the people thought that he was staging a little exhibition of Americanism for their benefit.

9

MRS. PEIXOTA CHAPERONES HER DAUGHTER

Mr. and Mrs. Pablo Peixota were at breakfast on Saturday morning when the telephone rang. The maid called from the vestibule: "It's for you, Mrs. Peixota." It was Mrs. Leah Arzell of the Colored Women's Clubs calling: "Having breakfast, Kezia? I've just finished and couldn't wait, as I wanted so much to have a little chat with you about last night's hullabaloo."

Mrs. Peixota: "It was perfectly disgraceful and those no-count white people ought to be shamed out of their skins. For Newton Castle is irresponsible. Just a phonograph which they wind up to spout what they want him to say."

Mrs. Arzell: "Yes, Newton is a pest and a pain, but what he did was nothing compared to the way the women carried on with Lij Alamaya. Don't you think?"

Mrs. Peixota: "What women, the white or the colored? What did they do?"

Mrs. Arzell: "Didn't Peixota tell you about it?"

Mrs. Peixota: "No, he only mentioned Newton starting to fight with Flagg again and the white people supporting him and breaking up the meeting. But what did the women do? Tell me."

Mrs. Arzell: "But how strange for Peixota not to tell you. Just like a man to be so indifferent about the most exciting thing."

Mrs. Peixota: "Was it the white women? They're all so

radical these days, they'll do things that colored women'd be ashamed to do."

Mrs. Arzell: "But it wasn't the white ones, Kezia. They only indulged in a little hissing, but our own sisters started kissing. Really, you're fooling—didn't Peixota tell you?"

Mrs. Peixota: "No, and I'm just itching for you to tell me everything. Kissing how? Kissing what?"

Mrs. Arzell: "The Harlem sisters started singing and shouting and shaking their feet as if they were celebrating with Father Divine¹ in his kingdom. And Kezia! They raided the platform in a body and started hugging and kissing Lij Alamaya all over the place. My dear, it was contagious and wilder than you can ever imagine. I could hardly keep my seat myself. But I had to remember that I was on the platform and that I was there representing the higher type of colored women."

Mrs. Peixota: "Oh, I'm so sorry I wasn't there. But how did Lij Alamaya take it? Wasn't he angry?"

Mrs. Arzell: "No, he was a perfect darling. Embarrassed, of course, but just as charming as his brogue and his ravishing eye. He's sure going to go places. He has all the women on his side."

Mrs. Peixota: "Well, I never—all that public smacking—"

Pablo Peixota had finished breakfast, and was about to leave the dining room, when his wife came back to the table. A few high phrases had reached his ears and given him a drift of the conversation. She reproved him for withholding from her the exciting incidents of the previous night's meeting.

"I did tell you about Newton Castle with his delegation of white comrades creating a disturbance and breaking up the meeting," he said.

"Don't be so trifling, Pablo," said Mrs. Peixota. "Everybody except the white folks knows that Newton is crazy and queer like an angel of Father Divine. You know quite well that the most exciting thing to a woman would be the women flocking to the platform to kiss Lij Alamaya."

Peixota said the women were carried away by their feeling for Ethiopia and expressed themselves that way because Lij Alamaya was a living symbol of Ethiopia.

"Symbol, Pablo! You make me laugh and you don't believe that either. You know as well as I that those women were not excited about Lij Alamaya as a symbol, but because he's just plain *it*."

Mr. Peixota tried to suppress a smile and went on upstairs.

At noon time Seraphine came from the office with more gossip about the incident. "All Harlem is wild about Tekla, Mother. I stopped at the beauty parlor to see my hairdresser and all the girls were talking about him. He made a big hit last night."

"I am sorry now we didn't go," said Mrs. Peixota, "but public meetings make me tired and I didn't imagine it would have been so exciting last night."

"They say his speech was better than the first time. But, Mother, it's too strange to be true. Imagine all those women smacking him like that. It makes me jealous."

"You ought to be and you'd better get busy before you lose him. When any man is being built up like that, the women have a way of just going nuts. I'm sorry for him, he should have brought a princess with him."

"Oh no, Mother, then I wouldn't have a chance. Shall we see him again before he starts on his tour?"

"Certainly, he's dining with us tonight with Dorsey Flagg. No other guests."

"Suppose we drive downtown and pick him up at his hotel?"

"Well, that is not such a bad idea. I have to do a little shopping and in the meantime, you could be visiting. You'd better telephone and tell him."

Later, Mrs. Peixota chaperoned her daughter downtown and went shopping, while Seraphine visited Lij Alamaya at his hotel.

Alamaya was packing his traveling bag when Seraphine entered. "Go on with your packing," she said, "and don't let me bother you." But he couldn't go on. Instead he sat down on the couch beside her. "I thought it would be nice to be with you a little while, as we won't be seeing each other for some time. Are you glad I came?"

"Very."

"Well, you might be a little more demonstrative about it," she said, turning to rub her cheek against his.

They kissed. "I thought you said you were coming with your mother when you telephoned."

"She did chaperone me downtown, but she had to go shopping." She got up and inspected his bag and some neckties and other articles on the bed. She picked out a dark-green necktie with diagonal yellow and white stripes and said: "This is lovely, but you should have a valet to pack your things and all that."

"Oh, your father had one ready for me, but I didn't need him. What's the use of a valet in a hotel? To lace my shoes and give me my hat? I still want to feel that I can use my hands. So I let him go."

"I don't think you should. That was a job for somebody, and there's a lot of agitation about the scarcity of jobs in Harlem."

"I didn't think of that. I only felt I didn't want a personal servant hanging around and no work to do—like an empty title. I couldn't feel right."

"That's fine, Tekla. You will make a good American."

"I thought you would prefer me to be a good Ethiopian. But perhaps you don't think so much of Ethiopia."

"Oh, please don't say that, Tekla. I like you and prefer you as you are—a handsome man, with all the women so mad about you. But, Tekla, how did you feel with all those women round your neck, like a satyr or a sultan in his harem?"

"Neither. I was really a little frightened at first. But I quickly thought that maybe it was an American custom and surrendered myself. I remember I had read about prominent American statesmen always kissing babies at public meetings."

"That's true, Tekla. And so you took your share of baby-kissing too. You *are* a diplomat. Well, I don't feel so terribly jealous, as it was many and not *one*. Although they say the savage Africans—forgive me, honey, I mean tribal Africans. They say one man is accustomed to many females. But you are civilized—you wouldn't keep a harem, would you, Tekla?"

"I am not a Moslem; I'm a Christian."

"Oh, you darling, forgive my ignorance. I forgot all about Ethiopia being a Christian nation."

"It was the first nation to embrace Christianity—long before Rome—and every Ethiopian is proud of the fact. You know the legend. It was the eunuch of the Queen Candace who fanatically fell in love with Jesus, and as he was a person of great authority, he succeeded in converting the Ethiopians to Christianity.[2] Before then, they were pagans, each man possessing many wives, like the other Africans and the Arabs."

"It is a lovely story and your voice was so beautiful in telling it, Tekla, but—h'm—you're not sorry that the Ethiopians were converted from the Barbarism of many wives to the civilized practice of one wife, are you?"

"Not at all. I'm a good Christian."

"That's nice. It seems silly to me that a man should want a lot of wives. How can he love all of them unless he's an abnormal sexomaniac. It would be more natural for a woman to have many husbands."

"Do you think so?"

"Well, not for myself, but for cats like Bunchetta, yes. And the majority of women are feline. But me, I want one man I can worship and who will adore me."

"You are adorable, Seraphine."

"You dear darling duck"—she embraced him—"you say such lovely sweet things as if you were raised on palm wine and wild honey. It's no wonder all the women are batty about you."

"But I don't like bawdy women."

"I didn't say 'bawdy.' That's a bad expression. I said batty women, but perhaps there isn't much difference. There was something bawdy about last night's performance, even though it happened in a church."

Alamaya laughed. "They certainly did prance around on the platform. Your people are wonderfully demonstrative."

"My people nothing. But I warn you, Tekla. No more orgies of kissing, even if you were captured by an army of black Amazons. For in spite of my education and training, I'm just another savage woman when my feelings are aroused. I don't believe in everybody sipping out of the same cup like taking Communion, for I'm no Communist one way or the other. And your mouth is not a public piece of property, even though you may be the symbol of Ethiopia."

"To receive one must be willing to give. And when a person is a symbol he must submit to things like Harlequin at a carnival,[3] things which might be worse than public kissing."

"But a symbol is also something like a fetish, is it not? Something sacred that should not be touched by everybody?"

"Yes, there is the symbol and there are symbols. They may be more important than what they seem to be. Many may touch a symbol and never reach the symbol. Or I might say many may feel the body, but few, perhaps only one, can move the heart." She was leaning on his left shoulder with her right hand hanging against his breast and he caressed it.

"Tekla," she said, "your thoughts are so perfectly beautiful, you could make even Cleopatra your slave. Promise me, you will never say these last words to another woman, will you?"

"I'll promise you anything."

"Oh, Tekla, I'm the happiest girl in Harlem and I would like to make you the happiest of men."

"You are very nice and sweet," he said.

"Please don't flatter me, Tekla, or I'll become hysterical. Bunchetta says I'm selfish and spoiled and I know I'm not a sleek purring tabby cat like her around men, but when I fall for one man I do in a big way. I want you to understand me."

"I'll try to," he said, and kissed her.

"Yes, but go on now and finish packing. Mother may call for us at any moment now. Go on, Tekla, hurry up. Oh, I wish I was your secretary or something and going on the tour with you instead of Mr. Flagg."

She picked up a magazine and started turning the pages.

"ALL WE LIKE SHEEP HAVE GONE ASTRAY"

—Isaiah 53:6[1]

That night while they were on the train traveling west, Dorsey Flagg extracted from his briefcase a copy of Saturday's issue of the *Labor Herald* and drew Lij Alamaya's attention to a little article on Harlem. It contained an oblique reference to Lij Alamaya and was headed: "Ethiopian Prince?"

Harlem is the magic quarter, which thrives lustily on sensations, even though hunger ravishes the increasing ranks of its vast army of unemployed. The masses recklessly indulge in the luxuries of numbers game, the aggrandizement of cultists, and the animistic manifestation of mystic magic makers. The brazen swing bands drown out the pitiful bleating of underfed children and the Lindy Hop exhibitionists perform from sundown to sunrise like specters merry-making at a carnival. Chauvinistic social profiteers of a people's misery raise their standards at street intersections and entertain the crowds with wisecracks about their unenviable situation, even as the ebony masters of ceremonies, those peerless princes of their profession, tickle the jaded passions of the privileged few in the hot cabarets.

The latest sensation is the hectic excitement stirred by the Fascist war against Ethiopia. Many bogus organizations have been formed with the sole purpose of milking the poor credulous colored people, who retain a strong religious feeling for Ethiopia and are keenly interested about the fate of that country. And besides bogus organizations there also are equivocal envoys who pretend to be personal representatives of Emperor Haile Selassie and lay claim to the title of "Prince."

There is evidence that some of these fakers are tools of the Fascists. The Fascists are at work in Harlem, penetrating the organizations of the colored people. These international gangsters have sent their spies among the Harlemites to discover the strength of the sentiment for Ethiopia. They secretly support the bogus Aid to Ethiopia organizations, because they are afraid of the power of the Popular Front gathering the broad masses of all peoples, regardless of race and color, under its banner to crush and annihilate the evil forces of Fascism and Nazism.

The colored people must be awakened to the danger of Fascist agents in their midst. They must be made to realize that all Fascists are not white, that there are also black Fascists of their own race and blood who must be exterminated. They must be weaned from their simple faith in "race" leaders and vicarious hankering after African "princes" tricked out with trinkets and plumes. It must be drilled into them that Soviet Russia is the only nation that is a true friend of Ethiopia and of all the colored and colonial peoples of the world.

The article was signed by a well-known pro-Soviet Harlem journalist. When Alamaya finished reading, he said: "Well, they have given me a fine bon voyage prick in my hide."

"Yes," said Flagg, "they're assassins in ambush. When they were hounded by the Czarists they developed that offensive weapon. And when they got the power they could not rid themselves of it, for it had become an ineradicable attribute of their minds, which carried it over into their new system."

The Sunday edition of the *Labor Herald* carried an elaborated full-page feature of the previous day's article regarding the Fascist penetration of Harlem. There was a photograph of Lij Alamaya with the statement that it was rumored he was not really a representative of Emperor Haile Selassie nor a Prince of Ethiopia. There was also a photograph of the turbaned Sufi Abdul Hamid in his Oriental makeup,[2] with the subtitle of "Black Hitler." And he also was designated as an anti-Semitic leader of Harlem, an active member of the pro-Japanese Pacific movement and chauvinistic Aframerican race leader and labor racketeer. Professor Koazhy too was pictured there as the philosophical mentor of the Harlem Fascists, and the Rev. Zebulon Trawl had a niche of honor as their religious leader.

On this Sunday the Rev. Zebulon Trawl had announced a special service to further publicize the Hands to Ethiopia. Without being officially denominated as such, his church, because of his active interest, had become the devotional center of the Hands to Ethiopia activities. The Rev. Zebulon Trawl was eminently fitted to rally the religious-minded Harlemites to the cause. He was one of the clerics who had led his church, exalted to action, in support of the grand upsurge of the Pan-African movement,[3] when the Back-to-Africa slogan stimulated the heartbeat of thousands of Aframericans. He was frequently criticized for permitting persons like Sufi Abdul Hamid and Professor Koazhy to proclaim their heresies from his platform. But he was rewarded in his church becoming something of a social center, where groups of different persuasions met to exchange opinion. And secular-minded visitors this Sunday were Sufi Abdul Hamid, Professor Koazhy and Pablo Peixota.

Just before the service began a group of people appeared with placards and started marching back and forth on the pavement before the church. The placards proclaimed their purpose:

DRIVE THE FASCISTS OUT
OF HARLEM

COLORED AND WHITE UNITE
TO DEFEND ETHIOPIA

JOIN THE FIGHT AGAINST FASCISM
NAZISM ANTI-SEMITISM

REV. TRAWL AIDS FASCIST AGENTS
OF HITLER AND MUSSOLINI

WE PROTEST UNFAIR TREATMENT
OF WHITE FRIENDS OF ETHIOPIA

WE PROTEST AGAINST THE FASCISTS
IN THE CHURCH OF GOD

The pickets were led by Newton Castle bearing a large American flag. It was a considerable squad of them, about three-fourths white and the others colored. They marched in silence. On the other side of the street, there were many more whites. A curious crowd soon gathered to watch the parade and it was increased by many of the late churchgoers. It was whispered in the church what was taking place outside and the people began to desert the pews for the street.

The Rev. Trawl was astonished and upon making enquiries a deacon informed him of what was afoot. He stepped down from the pulpit and strode to the front of the church. He stood at the top of the high flight of steps for a brief moment and watched the pickets, reading the signs. His shining dark features wore a

strange expression of bewilderment, and then they were sad-
dened as he seemed to perceive what the demonstration meant.

The Rev. Zebulon fell on his knees and uplifting his hands
he prayed like a wailing saxophone: "Oh, Lord, this is one
hour of trial for thy people and the testing of thy humble servant. Lord, I have labored all these years to build this church
for thy glory, so that thy faithful people may serve thee and
sing thy praises and give thanks for thy goodness.

"Lord, I have tried to build a clean church for thy worship
and otherwise make it serve my people. For thy poor black
sheep need guidance, oh Lord, pushed aside in the back ways
of the world, they need guidance to shuffle through the little
alleyways. Oh, Lord, I have tried to do my duty in thy service.

"But the wicked are setting themselves up to be the righ-
teous ones and keepers of the law. They have carried their
baseness to the very portals of thy house, seeking to desecrate
it and dishonor me. Lord, I have asked thee to guide my foot-
steps and lead me in all things. I have endeavored to walk by
thy light only, invoking thy wisdom in my planning and thy
approval of my actions. Thou seest and understandest all
things deep into the heart of thy people. Lord, if I have not
been a good shepherd to my flock, thou knowest. If I have
sinned, thou art the one to admonish and chastise me.

"Lord, the white ones have swarmed up here like hornets
and peckawoods to sting and peck at God's black sheep. What
have we done for the white people to invade us in this high
reservation to frighten and stampede thy black sheep? Lord, I
have tried to be a good Christian in the spirit and, in spite of
the flesh, in my heart. I have labored in thy service to lead my
flock to walk circumspectly in thy light.

"But, Lord, thy light is burning dim in this dark Harlem.
Harlem is the stamping ground of false prophets. The racketeers of Satan are posing as angels to deceive your black sheep
and lead them astray. The brazen black rams of the unblessed

goats are creating havoc among the vain and weak and foolish ewes and lamblings. Some profess to know the secret of your holiness and omniscience and set themselves up as priests and priestesses, mingling your sacred words of eternal life with the honeyed jungle brew of Satan. And some even set themselves up as gods before thee.

"And now, Lord, even the white ones are worse than the black jugglers of Satan. For they are trying to fool God's poor black sheep with the magic of their white fleece. They take the magic and the strength of their whiteness, which is like a fetish, to break down the confidence and hope of thy people. Lord, they are trying to turn the spirit of my people against the leadership of thy servant. Lord, I pray to thee for strength to stand up against them. Let them not desecrate this thy sanctuary. I have seen the picketing of business places, plants and factories and stores and offices and private houses by thy working folks, oh Lord. But I have never yet seen or even heard anywhere about the picketing of thy house, oh Lord. Is it because this is a place of worship for God's humble black sheep? And my Lord, these pickets are not even workers. None of them wearing overalls, they are all wearing silk stockings and nifty clothes. Hear my prayer, oh Lord, and show me the way to defeat the machinations of the strong white ones against thy poor black sheep."

Meantime Professor Koazhy, Sufi Abdul Hamid and Pablo Peixota were circulating among the large crowd, which rapidly filled the block. And they observed the contemptuous regard of the white friends of the pickets and heard some of their comments: "The oily-tongued old black hypocrite!" "We will show him what it means to dare to fight against the Soviet line of action." "The preaching son of a bastard, he ought to be gagged."

Professor Koazhy whispered to Sufi Abdul Hamid. Then he clapped his hands and boomed, "Senegambians! Senegambians!" And Sufi Abdul Hamid shouted, "Any Sufists in the crowd, step forward!" Quickly appeared a number of Professor Koazhy's students, and the bodyguards of Sufi Abdul Hamid surrounded him. "Seize that flag," Professor Koazhy commanded, "and stop that damned demonstration."

A broad-busted hefty Senegambian approached Newton Castle and with one grab he wrenched the flag from him and bore it into the church. "A splendid trophy!" cried Professor Koazhy. Other Sufists and Senegambians elbowed their way through the crowd and in among the pickets. They quietly edged each one from off the pavement into the street. They formed a solid line before the church in which they were joined by young members, who were aroused from their astonishment to a vague understanding of the shame of the disorder.

Pulling from his pocket a large red handkerchief, stamped with a white hammer and sickle, Newton Castle waved it from the iron railing across the street from the church upon which he had perched himself. "Comrades," he cried, "down with the Fascists in Harlem! Destroy the Fascist snakes in your midst! Drive them out of Harlem. Make Harlem safe for Soviet Russia, the defender of the World Proletariat and all oppressed people. Many Harlem preachers are Fascist-minded! Drive the Fascists out of the church and organize—"

A Senegambian pulled him down. He was so small and funny, like a rabbit, that no one wanted to hurt him. But his voice was as noisy and shrill as a bagpipe as he yelled: "Leave me alone! I'm an American citizen! I demand the right of free speech!" And he waved the red face cloth.

Three Senegambians seized him kicking and scratching and hustled him into the dim corridor of a tenement and down to the basement. There they gagged Newton Castle and would have tethered him. But there was no cord. Instead they divested Castle of his suit, which they carried off, leaving him shivering in his underwear. "I guess that will hold you a little while," said one Senegambian, as they mounted the basement steps.

While Newton was performing his antics on the railing, Pablo Peixota saw a man half hidden behind a barbershop sign and watching the exhibition. Peixota felt certain that the man was Maxim Tasan. He whispered to a Sufist to go after him. But before the Sufist could reach him the wily fellow had disappeared in the crowd.

The Rev. Zebulon Trawl had returned to the platform, when the Senegambian entered triumphantly with the Stars and Stripes, which he had wrested from Newton Castle and poised against the platform. But someone had turned in a riot call. The congregation was streaming back into the church, when a police patrol came furiously clanging into the block and three police cars with sirens screaming. The pickets and their friends had already disappeared. But some of the considerably diminished crowd remained, gossiping with the policemen, while an officer entered the church.

The Rev. Zebulon Trawl had started the service. Fondling the trophy he said: "Oh, Lord, I knew that my prayer would not be in vain. I knew that the Lord would come to the rescue."

11

THE EMPEROR'S STATEMENT

It fell upon the Hands to Ethiopia organization like a mighty cloudburst, when the news was published that the Emperor of Ethiopia had declared that Ethiopia was not a "Negro" state, that he was the Lion of Judah and descendant of King Solomon and that the Ethiopians did not consider themselves kin to the Aframericans. Further, the declaration stated that the Emperor had sent no special envoys to the Aframericans.

The news article bore the trademark of one of the reputable news-gathering agencies. It was conspicuously printed in the national newspapers, some giving it the front page. Under the heading "Ethiopian Emperor Repudiates Self-Styled Representative," the *Labor Herald* carried the photographs of Emperor Haile Selassie and Lij Tekla Alamaya looking at each other from opposite columns.

Prominent Aframerican weeklies retailed the news under flamboyant headlines of red, black and green. The influential conservative organs had never enthusiastically publicized the Hands to Ethiopia movement. And now their comments were biting in their criticism, not only of the Emperor's attitude, but of those Aframerican leaders who were turning the thoughts of the people to native African problems instead of concentrating upon vital Aframerican issues. Now they nursed their hurt pride and retaliated by publishing pictures of the Ethiopian types, depicting them as backward, barbarous and unprogressive, compared to the

Aframericans. Some of these pictures, evidently originating from Fascist sources, were so particularly offensive, they could not have appeared in any national newspaper. The Emperor Haile Selassie and his spokesmen were compared to the "brass-ankles" of the United States and the West Indies—those equivocal near-white types who had no roots either among the Euramericans or the Aframericans.

Lij Tekla Alamaya was trounced as a fake representative, a swindler and parasite upon gullible colored people who were enamored of tinsel and title. They published the rumors that had floated about him, saying that he had lived all of his adult life in Europe, he was not an authentic Ethiopian, that he was fair of countenance because his father was a Levantine[1] (some said a Greek) who had married an Ethiopian woman. He was depicted as a sybarite[2] in his private life, enjoying a dandy's bohemian existence in a hotel downtown and posing as a prince in Harlem with the arms of Ethiopia engraved upon his car and the door of his reception room.

The Executive Committee of the Hands to Ethiopia decided to act quickly to save their movement from complete disintegration. Pablo Peixota sent a telegram recalling Lij Alamaya from his western tour. His chief idea was to try to establish the authenticity of Alamaya by releasing to the newspapers the imperial letter, with the Emperor's signature and the Ethiopian seal, accompanied by an authoritative statement from Alamaya. In the telegram Peixota cautioned Alamaya not to make any public statement or discuss the matter before seeing him. Also, Peixota sent a telegram to Dorsey Flagg asking him to protect Alamaya and prevent him from talking to any reporters.

There was no way of proving that the Emperor's declaration was authentic by communicating with him, for the Emperor was with his troops at the front and communication between Addis Ababa and the outside world had broken down. Even the radio station could not be operated.

Pablo Peixota believed that the Emperor's declaration was fabricated to torpedo the Hands to Ethiopia. He was already quite convinced that the White Friends of Ethiopia organization was no friend of the Aframericans or the Ethiopians, but that they were the friends of Soviet Russia. He felt that the real object of the White Friends was to create sentiment among the colored people in favor of Soviet Russia.

But he was puzzled by the situation. He saw what the White Friends, using Newton Castle as their instrument, were aiming at—the control of his organization. But he could not understand why they should seek such control, why they should be expending so much energy and subterfuge to obtain their ends. For he could not see the colored group as an effective asset in furthering the policy of Soviet Russia. If it were to win the colored people over to the Communist Party, their tactics were absurd, he thought, for political converts are not made by that type of propaganda.

Peixota's mind did not go beyond the horizon of the traditional method of playing politics. Alien to it and incomprehensible was power politics as a religious ecstasy gripping and sweeping people off their feet to imagine that they could find social salvation in a pharisaism such as: "Soviet Russia is a Workers' State."

To him social feeling was an apprehension purely apart from religious emotion. When he availed himself of the channel of the church to promote the Hands to Ethiopia, it was not because he felt that Aframericans were good Christians, but because the church was a social center and perfect rallying point. In the same manner he found the church useful for Democratic rallies. But intellectually he could not combine the sentiment of religion with the aptitude for politics. His conception of politics was something like the numbers game, which had elevated him to his position of responsibility and which, although played in the home, he had managed to keep so severely separate from his respectable family life.

Thus lacking in the imaginative perceptions of social idealism and its international reverberations, Pablo Peixota was psychologically incapable of plumbing the well-spring of Newton Castle's wild antics or to grasp a hint of the vast web of thought and action of which Maxim Tasan's penetrating into Harlem was but one little spider's spin. But of one thing he was concretely aware: Maxim Tasan and his White Friends of Ethiopia desired to destroy the Aframerican Hands to Ethiopia.

Less than a week from their departure, Lij Alamaya and Dorsey Flagg returned to New York. They were met at the Grand Central Station by Pablo Peixota, accompanied by the Rev. Zebulon Trawl and driven to his home. No other committee member was present. Peixota wanted to discuss with Lij Alamaya alone the crisis caused by the Emperor's declaration and agree with him upon a definite plan of action. As the new secretary of the organization and traveling companion of Lij Alamaya, Flagg's presence was necessary. Peixota himself was not adept at making notes. Also he relied on the good counsel of the Rev. Trawl. He had already called an emergency meeting of the twenty-four members of the Executive Committee of the Hands to Ethiopia, immediately following the Emperor's alleged blast. And they endorsed his recalling Lij Alamaya to New York in an effort to resolve the crisis.

Dorsey Flagg doubted that the Ethiopian Emperor would choose such a moment deliberately to offend the Aframerican people. He was emphatic in his belief that the thing was a hoax engineered by Newton Castle and Maxim Tasan with the help of powerfully influential persons. He said bluntly: "It is a Comintern plot." Peixota did not know what "Comintern" stood for and Flagg told him that it meant the Communist International. Even then Peixota did not grasp its full meaning. Communist was similar to Socialist in his mind. He understood more when Flagg explained the difference between the Communists and the Socialists, but he did not understand in Flagg's intellectual way. He could, however, apprehend the fact of Communism as the political system of the Soviet State, but not as a doctrine any more than he could understand a doctrine of Democracy.

Lij Alamaya was partial to Dorsey Flagg's opinion. He said that Maxim Tasan was an extremely clever man, who he considered far more important than he appeared to be. He said he regretted being drawn into a conflict with him, but developments had made that inevitable. Dorsey Flagg told Alamaya not to regret anything, for the only effective way of dealing with persons like Maxim Tasan was by fighting them. But Alamaya was not as forthright and positive of attitude as Flagg. He said that sometimes it was the better policy not to be too aggressive, that an individual might do better to compromise where the larger interests of people were at stake. There was no doubt that Alamaya was genuinely sorry that he had taken a course that had turned Maxim Tasan into an enemy. And again Peixota wondered if there had been some previous secret dealing between Lij Alamaya and Maxim Tasan. But looking searchingly at Alamaya's gentle and sincere face he felt ashamed of the thought.

Peixota said that had he felt convinced about the Emperor making such a statement, he would wash his hands of the organization. But he would not believe that Haile Selassie could be so discourteous to Aframericans. Alamaya said that even if the Emperor had said anything, he believed that the newspaper item was an exaggeration. He continued to explain why Ethiopia considered itself an African and not a "Negro" state and said that "Abyssinian" was also objectionable and never used. And just as many thousands of Aframericans considered "Negro" an offensive word and even banned it in conversation and in print, so the Ethiopians preferred to be designated by their ancient original name, "Ethiopian."

The others were in agreement with Lij Alamaya. Dorsey Flagg said that Koazhy was not just a fool eccentric, when he took an African name and declared that Aframericans and Africans should abolish the word "Negro" because it did not originate among the Africans, but was of European creation. He pointed out that other peoples and countries had changed names, Ireland to Eire, Persians to Iranians. The largest circulating New York daily newspaper never used the word "Negro" but "colored" instead, and it looked better in print than "Negro," sometimes with a large and sometimes with a small "N," which was favored by the other newspapers. It was awkward to see a newspaper print, "Mrs. Ada Jones, Negro." Such a rule was not followed in printing the names of Spanish, Italian, Jewish, or Mongolian people. He, Flagg, was not partial to "colored"; he preferred "Aframerican." The Rev. Zebulon Trawl suggested that the Aframerican churches should call a national conference and decide upon a name. Dorsey Flagg questioned whether the churches were representative enough to deal with such a matter and thought the Aframerican colleges more suitable. Pablo Peixota thought both churches and colleges might work together, but he considered the first more important, as most names had a religious origin and churches played a primary part in the naming of people.

Peixota submitted his plan of releasing to the press the Emperor's letter to Lij Alamaya. He suggested that they should work upon a statement from Alamaya to go with it in which he should make a declaration of the real attitude of the Ethiopians towards the Aframericans. And he thought it would be a good idea to get together those Aframericans who had returned from Ethiopia to publish a signed statement. Dorsey Flagg and the Rev. Trawl agreed with the outline of the plan. But Lij Alamaya remained ominously silent.

"And what do you think of our plan, Lij Alamaya," said Peixota. "It depends on you."

Alamaya fidgeted uncomfortably in his chair, thrusting his hands in his pockets and removing them.

"Well," said Peixota. He too was embarrassed. Again his suspicions were aroused. Would Alamaya refuse the publication of the letter? Was he playing fair with them?

"But I have no letter!" Alamaya said in an anguished tone.

"What!" Peixota jumped from his seat. "But you do have a letter from the Emperor. I saw it myself."

"It is lost," said Alamaya with a sorry gesture of his hands.

"Good God in Heaven!" shouted the Rev. Trawl. "My good Prince, how could you lose such a precious document?"

Peixota strode back and forth: "But why didn't you tell me, Lij Alamaya?" His voice was hard, his suspicion stronger than ever that Alamaya might be playing a double role. "When did you lose the document?"

"Soon after my arrival. It was the night of the party at Mrs. Witern's and Miss Peixota was with me."

"But how did you lose it there? Was it stolen?" asked Peixota.

"I believe it was. I was asked by Professor Makepeace if I had a souvenir of Ethiopia. But I had nothing. Then I thought of the letter with the gold circlet in its leather envelope, which were both native made. And I showed it to Professor Makepeace. Others were interested to see it. Everybody wanted to talk to me. I had no thoughts of treachery in such a place. When the leather case was returned to me I slipped it into my pocket without looking at it. That was the correct thing, for I had no suspicion that anyone there would want to keep for himself such a very personal thing. Even now I don't know what to think, whether it was stolen for a political purpose or for the value of the gold."

"It might be either," said Dorsey Flagg. "There are so many down-and-outers mixed in with the wealthy comrade snobs at those leftist parties."

"This is a terrible blow, Lij Alamaya," said Peixota. "It is worse than the Emperor's statement. Now I don't know what we shall do. I wish you had been frank with me and told me when it happened."

"I couldn't," said Lij Alamaya. "A diplomat should not lose his documents."

"Bad business, bad business," said the Rev. Trawl. "Only God can save the organization now."

"It is a very unfortunate situation," said Peixota. "This week I received one thousand and seven dollars. It was collected from the poor struggling colored people, doing their part for Ethiopia. Over there the soldiers are fighting barefooted with spears and rifles against tanks and machine guns, fighting against gas without a single gas mask. And we have bungled our little bit over here. Now Lij Alamaya, it's up to you to find a way to save our organization. As you've lost your letter, my plan is worthless."

They sat in an uncomfortable silence. At last Lij Alamaya said: "I am in a tight spot and don't know what to do. I am sure the Emperor was misrepresented in that news dispatch. But it's impossible for me to communicate with the Ethiopian government."

"Couldn't you do something through one of the European legations?" Dorsey Flagg demanded.

"The Fascists have cut off all communications with Ethiopia," said Alamaya. "Perhaps we could end all this trouble by coming to some understanding with Newton Castle and Maxim Tasan and amalgamate the Hands to Ethiopia with the White Friends of Ethiopia."

"Like hell we will!" said Peixota, bouncing up again and walking to and fro. "No working together with those two incorrigible rats. Not me. I'll resign the chairmanship and let you others carry on. Before I work with them, I'd sooner see the organization in hell."

"And I'm with you, Brother Peixota," said the Rev. Zebulon

Trawl. "I'm with you every time. When those White Friends attempted to destroy my church, parading and creating a riot in front of it, I prayed to the Lord for assistance and He assisted me. And now that they want to blast our Hands to Ethiopia, I will pray to Him again. And if the Lord won't help—before I work with those kind of 'White Friends,' I'd be like Brother Peixota, I'd sooner be in hell!"

"There's nothing for me to do," said Flagg, "for I'm the real cause of all the trouble. When Lij Alamaya speaks of an understanding with Maxim Tasan—Newton Castle doesn't count—he isn't including me, because he knows that Maxim Tasan wouldn't work with me. But one thing I can do. I'll give up the secretaryship and resign from the organization in order to save it."

"No, Dorsey, you won't," said Peixota. "If you resign, I will resign and Trawl will and the entire Executive Committee. We won't let that white snake get you or run our organization. Better no organization at all than one dominated by him."

Dorsey Flagg jumped up and grabbed Peixota's hand. "Fine, Peixota. I love a real fighter. They may destroy the organization, but they can't lick us. Peixota, you may know very little about the vast network of international political plot and the tug-of-war power politics which is spreading out over the world, even to Harlem to spread confusion among our people. And perhaps you don't care, but you should. It's a bigger thing than you imagine and you should know what is really trying to destroy our organization."

"I guess they will be forcing me to get some understanding," said Peixota. "It's a pity I wasn't college educated like you to understand what is shaking the world to its foundation."

"I don't know but you're better off without it," said Flagg. "Without it you became one of the solid pillars of Harlem. But with it you might have been only another Newton Castle."

"Then God saved me from such a calamity," said Peixota.

They all laughed and the tension was lessened.

Lij Alamaya said: "Gentlemen, I cannot express all that I should like to say. But, please believe me when I say I am sorry. I am miserable because my carelessness has placed us in such a disadvantageous position. I can think of nothing except to go and see Mr. Maxim Tasan. It may be very humiliating for me, but I will go."

"You may go, but not on behalf of the Hands to Ethiopia, Lij Alamaya," said Peixota. "We will not discuss our organization with Maxim Tasan. Personally I would sooner see him dead than alive. I don't know why such a viper should live."

12

ALAMAYA MAKES HIS SUBMISSION

That evening before dinner, Pablo Peixota was sitting dejectedly at Lij Alamaya's desk thinking about the future of the Hands to Ethiopia when Seraphine entered very agitated. Her eyes were red and she continually mopped them, which was very astonishing to her father, because he rarely saw her in tears.

"Tell me, Father, is it true you have sent Tekla away, when he is in great trouble?"

"I didn't send him away, he went himself."

"Then it's true. He's gone. Father, how could you be so mean to him? A poor lonely stranger—"

"Don't be silly. I didn't send him away. He left himself to go to the hotel in which he lives downtown."

"Oh, you've made up with him then," she said in a less distressful tone.

"Made up what?"

"Mother said you had quarreled with Tekla and he was gone and you had washed your hands of him and the organization."

"Your mother should have told you that the Hands to Ethiopia is in a hole and only Alamaya could have pulled it out, if he had not carelessly lost the Emperor's letter."

"It wasn't his fault, Father. It was just carelessness. I believe somebody played him a trick. I was with him at the party, you remember?"

"What do you mean, somebody played him a trick? Do you know something about the letter? Do you have any idea what happened to it?"

"I mean some person tricked Tekla and stole his letter as a souvenir. Maybe it was some woman who fell for him, for everybody likes him. But it isn't his fault, Father. He's a prince and he had to be courtly and grand when they asked him to show a souvenir."

"Better he had shown them his tongue," said Peixota. "He couldn't have lost that. But he stupidly lost the Emperor's letter. And never told me, that's the worst of it. I made myself responsible for him, doing everything to put him over in a big way. Yet he kept back such an important thing from me. It's sly, like cheating."

"Please, Father! He told *me* about it. But there was nothing to be done and we agreed to forget it. I think perhaps that man named Tasan had something to do with it. That night he kind of monopolized Tekla in a familiar way and I even overheard him talking about you."

"You did? What did he say?"

"He and Tekla were in a little room by themselves and didn't know I was outside. And that Tasan was all hot about Stalin-white and Trotsky-red or -black or what is it? And he said that Mr. Flagg was a Trotskyite and shouldn't be on the Committee of the Hands to Ethiopia. And Tekla said, 'Mr. Peixota won't stand for the ousting of Dorsey Flagg.' I remember clearly, Father, Tekla stood up stoutly for you. And I felt so proud I fell in love with him right away, for I love you so much."

"So Maxim Tasan was plotting and trying to corrupt Alamaya from the very start!"

"Yes, Father, and if I had known it was so important I would have told you everything. But you'll forgive Tekla for my sake. I love him, Father. He's so charming and with grand ways, just like you, Father. It's the first time I've felt a big feeling of love."

"My dear Seraphine, how can you fall in love with Alamaya? I am not sending him away, for I haven't the power. I wouldn't want to do anything to hurt you. But he is here only on a special mission; he may be recalled tomorrow. It will be better for you to put him out of your mind altogether."

"But I love him, Father. If you wash your hands of him, you must wash your hands of me too. If you send him away, I will go with him."

"But I'm not sending Alamaya away, Seraphine. This is just too trifling when there are so many heavy things on my mind."

"Trifling, Father! Do you believe my love for Tekla is trifling?"

"Seraphine, won't you go and talk to your mother? She may be—"

"But I did talk to Mother and she told me you said you were washing your hands of Tekla and we both would be separated."

"I said nothing about that." Peixota put on his overcoat and said: "Tell your mother I have gone out and not to wait for me for dinner."

At that time Maxim Tasan and Newton Castle were leaving Lij Alamaya's hotel. They had invited Alamaya to join them in a few rounds of drinks. But Alamaya had refused. He would have been drinking to their triumph over him. The poor young Ethiopian was terribly softened up. And when they left he locked the door, threw himself facedown on the couch and cried.

Newton and Maxim entered a bar on Broadway, where both together could be served without creating an incident. They chose a table that was set a little apart where they could talk with enough freedom. Newton appeared more nervously emphatic in his manner since Sunday when the Senegambians left him in his underwear and Delta had to hurry down to bring him another suit. Before his wife arrived the superintendent had removed the gag from his mouth and the experience had apparently made him more loquacious. He felt as if he had earned his medal as a hero of the cause. He talked unceasingly, agitating his hands.

"Now that we have Alamaya on our side and he's going to work with the White Friends, we must see that he doesn't keep up his contact with Peixota and Dorsey Flagg and their gang."

"Yes, but we mustn't push him too hard at first," said Tasan. "He's a sensitive kid and may turn mulish and kick us to hell away from him, without giving a damn."

"You're right. He's got an independent streak," said Newton. "I'll never forget Friday night when he suddenly threw off his coat and gripped Dorsey Flagg's hand. It was a good act."

"Sure he's independent enough, or he wouldn't have been interested in the Soviet idea. If we ever corral him and break him down in body and spirit, he'll be a riot."

"And now as far as Newton Castle is concerned the Hands to Ethiopia can go and crawl through the sewers of New York," said Castle.

"Is that intended to be profanity or obscenity, Professor?" Tasan laughed like dry leaves shaking in a little breeze.

"Both. That gangster Peixota, he thinks he is a big bug and I'd like to swat him with a Soviet brick bat."

"Now, that's wholesome revolutionary opinion," said Tasan, "but it isn't when you want to dump the Hands to Ethiopia in the New York sewer system. It's a people's organization and we need the people. The leaders may go stink in the sewers as far as we are concerned, but we need the people. And that's why we must go slow with Alamaya. He can help us there."

"He might help us more in Ethiopia."

"What do we care about Ethiopia, that savage-feudal state? The Emperor is a tyrant worse than Ivan the Terrible. Mussolini will soon clean up for him. Alamaya can help us with the colored people here who think of Ethiopia as a sort of Canaan."

"Canaan is right," said Castle. "There is a Zionist streak in the hearts of the colored people. It isn't really a Back-to-Africa Promised Land that they yearn after like the Jews' desire for Palestine, although they did support the Back-to-Africa movement. It is more of a spiritual hankering after a Land of Beulah.[1] And that explains the amazing interest of the masses in Ethiopia. It's the ancient Ethiopia-shall-stretch-forth-her-hand-to-God of the Bible that is stirring them up. My God, just imagine wasting all that splendid mass feeling on the jungle Empire of Ethiopia when it could be put to work for enlightened Soviet Russia."

"But it could be very interesting as a social study—from an anthropological or a psychological angle," said Tasan, "especially as there is such a large admixture of persons of European blood in your group."

"Yes, and some of those are the most chauvinistically *African* in their ideas," said Castle. "I don't think I ever did tell you about Mrs. Arzell, one of the tops in the Colored Women's Clubs. She was presiding at a meeting sponsored by one of the Apex lodges— the Apex is the women's division of the Elks. And she said that since an Ethiopian prince had arrived as an envoy to the Aframericans, the colored women should demand the sending of an Ethiopian princess to represent the Ethiopian women."

"A Princess of Ethiopia! That's not a bad idea," said Tasan, and he vigorously scratched his flanks and laughed. "We might find them a princess as a diversion. She may go over better than the prince."

"Are you serious?" asked Castle.

"Sure I am. We Marxists can do anything. We have exterminated kings and princes to gain our ends and we have resurrected and honored them when it suited our purpose. The prince cuts a pretty sorry figure now. I think we should have a Princess of Ethiopia. I'll see what can be done about it."

Castle said: "I think it's better to forget the fantasies and think about settling our score with the four Harlem horsemen of the Trotskyite Apocalypse."

"Who are the four?" said Tasan.

"Pablo Peixota, Dorsey Flagg, 'Professor' Koazhy and Sufi Abdul Hamid. And dangerous as Flagg is, I believe Peixota to be still more dangerous, for he's a wealthy man, nigger-rich."

"What was that last word?" Tasan asked.

"It's a Harlemism," said Castle. "I'll explain. We have some wealthy persons in our group who look like millionaires to the average type of colored people. But in the white world our wealthy ones would be just comfortably fixed persons with a tolerable income. So we of the elite call ours nigger-rich."

"That's interesting," said Tasan. "So this Peixota person is nigger-rich. Shouldn't be so hard to handle. Couldn't we plant something on him? Make him out to be a pervert or pimp or anti-Semite?" Again he scratched himself with the vigor of a dog full of fleas.

"He's a respectable married man, more solidly so than you and I," said Castle. "And the anti-Semite tag wouldn't work any more than the Fascist label is working on Dorsey Flagg. The Harlem folk may hate a mean Jewish landlord or an Italian bar-keeper. But you can't get them steamed up over such issues as anti-Semitism and Fascism. My people are not like white people. I'm ashamed of them, they're so goddam unintellectual."

"Then can't we expose the bastard as a pervert or degenerate? We've smeared a lot of undesirables with that and railroaded them into oblivion."

"There's a skeleton in every closet in Harlem. Look here, Maxim, you may be an expert in getting hold of people and pushing organization. But what works like magic with one group may not with another. A skeleton in a colored closet may be like a fetish or a mascot, when in a white closet it may haunt you to death and destruction."

"Harlem is a freakish spot, anyway," said Tasan.

"It is full of freaks," said Castle. "Take Professor Koazhy and his glittering Ethiopian uniform and his West African name. And Sufi Abdul Hamid, who posed as a Guinea fetisher and mind reader. And Pablo Peixota was a policy king[2]: now he's a big realtor and a pillar in Trawl's church. Just think of it—a man who made his money skinning his people."

"But you're too goddam moral to be a Marxist, Castle," said Tasan. "The whites do a lot of skinning of your people and their people, too. Life is one big skin game. What's the difference between a policy game and a stock exchange game, except that under bourgeois law, one is illegal and the other is legal?[3] Comrade Stalin was marked for the leadership of the Bolsheviks and the World Proletariat when he robbed a bourgeois bank. His physical courage and daring set him high above Trotsky and his apocalyptic logic."

"You're right," said Castle humbly, "I was too intellectual in my attitude."

"Of course you were. The Soviet State is proletarian, at least in theory. And although we're building up a broad Popular Front movement with the Democratic governments and intelligentsia and the bourgeoisie, we are still anti-bourgeois, at least in theory. There is a place in our movement for men like Peixota and Sufi Abdul Hamid. We fight them because they are such fools, unable to see that by every rule of the game and from their place in society they belong with us and not against us."

"But you wouldn't want a charlatan metaphysic-mystic like Sufi Abdul Hamid in the movement?"

"Why not, if he would submit to discipline? He is no worse a charlatan and mystic than the monk Father Gapon,[4] who led the Russian workers to demonstrate before the Czar's palace and drew the fire of the soldiers."

"He'll never work with us like Father Divine,"[5] said Castle. "But I hate the idea of our working with Father Divine for I despise his guts. When I listen to him spouting that religious rigmarole and his followers calling him 'God,' I feel not only ashamed of my people, but of the whole world of peoples."

"Every jackass with his tail up imagines he can bray better than his brother," Tasan said cryptically. "The Imperial Family of Russia and all the nobles and ladies of the court were not ashamed of Monk Rasputin;[6] they worshipped him instead. So you and I need not be ashamed of the human race because of Father Divine. He's easy to handle, for he stays in his field. Our programme is, 'All aboard to build the Popular Front.'"

"Well, perhaps now that we have Alamaya safely aboard in a specially reserved compartment, I shouldn't worry so much about Peixota and the Hands to Ethiopia," said Castle.

"You leave it to me and I'll handle them. Peixota may be rich, but Harlem is a poorhouse. I can get a promoter to organize a benefit affair at the Savoy, which will net us more in one night than the Hands to Ethiopia could raise in a year. I can get movie stars and socialites not only to sponsor it but to appear."

"I know all of that is possible," said Castle. "But can we get the Hands to Ethiopia organization to climb aboard? That is the problem."

"You leave that problem to me, I say, Comrade Castle. Ever since we decided to stake the International movement on financial pressure in a big way instead of using moral suasion as formerly, we have bought up not only individuals and organizations, but even governments. And you want to tell me that a little organization of colored people, most of them on relief, is a problem!"

"The rich are corrupt from having too much power," said Castle, "and as the more they have the more they want, it is sometimes easier to buy the rich than to buy the poor."

"I suppose you still believe in bourgeois propaganda about the virtues of the poor," said Tasan.

"Not at all, but the majority of the poor are so dumb, it is

difficult to bargain with them and fix a price. They either un-
derrate or overrate their own value."

Tasan said that he was hungry. They had accounted for
many glasses of Scotch and soda. He beckoned the waiter and
paid the bill and they left.

THE MERRY-GO-ROUND

In his conference with Maxim Tasan and Newton Castle, Lij Alamaya had consented to continue the work of his mission to the Aframericans entirely under the direction of the White Friends of Ethiopia. The alternative, as it seemed to him, was the wrecking of his mission and the disillusioned Aframericans turning in hate against Ethiopia. The situation was bad enough, his new approach might save it from getting worse.

He realized that he had blundered badly in his initial steps, that there could be no rapprochement between the ideology which motivated the activity of the White Friends and the sentiment which moved the black Hands in their endeavor to help Ethiopia. He saw clearly that the cleavage between the two groups was as enormous as the social chasm which separated the life of the colored from the white people. He would have preferred to work intimately with the Hands. For he had a sincere admiration for the Aframericans. Now that he had become acquainted with them, his attitude had considerably changed from what it had been when the idea of the mission was conceived in Europe. There, the Aframericans he had met in the various capitals were few and mostly entertainers in cabaret and theatre, and occasional students who lived lavishly and convivially as one might expect from their inimitable prodigal gestures on the stage.

Alamaya and the rest of the Ethiopians had imagined the

Aframericans to be a wealthy group, insouciantly living and capable of raising large funds to assist his homeland in its unequal struggle. But upon his arrival in America he discovered that conditions were actually different, that the Aframericans in their social relationship to other American groups were comparatively like the Ethiopians in theirs to the European nations. Like Ethiopia there were a few outstanding and privileged personalities among a large mass of pitifully baffled creatures of circumstance and poverty, except that the privileged Ethiopians did enjoy the privileges of spatial living, while all the Aframericans were crowded together in the same ant-hill. Alamaya's earlier attitude of cavalier curiosity in the Aframericans had changed to active sympathy.

He appreciated their extraordinary efforts to extend to him a royal welcome and treat him like a prince. And although Newton Castle had taken the precaution to inform him at the outset that Peixota had acquired his wealth by gangster activities, Alamaya nevertheless highly respected the man and his family. The quality of Peixota's character was such that Alamaya felt that if the man had had a less limited sphere to develop his special ability he might have been a big financier—were he born an Ethiopian he might have been a Ras.[1] Even though it was excessively deferential, the attitude of Peixota and his friends towards him was tolerable compared to the blithe arrogance of Maxim Tasan. The Aframericans were instinctively aware of his different cultural background. They tried to understand him and enlist his cooperation on the basis of their understanding. They were flexible, suggesting things he might do instead of insisting what he should do. But Maxim Tasan was blind to social backgrounds and nuances. In his orthodox Marxist missionary mind, differences of culture were unimportant and individuals counted only as instruments that might serve to teach all the peoples of the world to pronounce the shibboleths of the same social and political doctrine, even though its substance was meaningless to them.

Peixota was prepared when Alamaya informed him of his final decision to collaborate with the Friends. He had anticipated it by calling a meeting of the twenty-four members of the Executive Committee of the Hands to discuss the issue. In spite of the demoralization that the Emperor's alleged statement had created in the ranks of the organization, the committee, through the initiative of Peixota and Dorsey Flagg and the Rev. Trawl, had worked hard to hold it together. Statements were published in some of the colored weeklies which doubted the authenticity of the Emperor's utterances. Special columnists were inspired to write articles in defense of the proud Ethiopian nation and Aframericans were cautioned against blandly accepting without question all statements which appeared in the "white" press concerning their African brothers. Also those Aframericans who had visited Ethiopia and were favorable to the Imperial regime were invited to address mass meetings and give details of their experiences.

To men like Peixota and Flagg and Trawl, the Hands to Ethiopia was more than a mere vehicle for rendering material help to Ethiopia. They saw in it also an instrument for helping the Aframericans here, to give them the dignity of human beings with a background that bridged the enormous pit of slavery, something that could shake them in their skins to feel that they were no less men because they were different from other men, something that could make them feel that the physical aspect of man was not less noble because it was diversified.

Peixota and the Rev. Trawl did not come by their opinions through vague theorizing. Peixota had used his dime tips as an elevator runner to launch his illegal lottery and make it a success. And the Rev. Trawl had started his church in a cold-water railroad flat and carried it forward to the acquisition of a splendid edifice. They belonged to the old school of self-made men, but they were modern in the ideas of their group striving as a unit to overcome some of its disadvantages. Dorsey Flagg did not have their experience of practical struggle, but his sharp mind could see clearly through the inadequacy of the old theoretical panaceas, such as a group of people demanding equal rights without possessing the economic assets or the organized political machinery to press their demands.

And so they were united in their opposition to Marxist mercenaries like Maxim Tasan and the modern school of neo-liberals who advocated that Aframericans should surrender the right to think and act as a group to their "white friends." It was emphasized that these "white friends" could be trusted more than others by the forlorn blacks simply because they were converts to the regime of Soviet Russia, which they believed to be the paradise for all oppressed people of all races, the Promised Land of the Millennium, where the lion and the lamb would lie down together in the same den and the wolf and the sheep would frolic side by side in the green pasture.

And so in order not to destroy the faith and dampen the hopes of their people, Peixota, Flagg and Trawl had influenced the executive members of the Hands against publicly withdrawing all support from Alamaya. It was agreed that an organizational front should be maintained, but that the Friends of Ethiopia should not be permitted to absorb or dominate the Hands to Ethiopia. The office in Harlem was still nominally held at Alamaya's disposal. By patronizing Lij Alamaya the Friends could rescue him from utter disgrace. Dorsey Flagg felt certain and was able to convince Peixota that Maxim Tasan had a sinister hand in that supposed interview with the Emperor, in which he offended the Aframericans. He thought that Alamaya's approval of him to go on the tour and the ousting of Newton Castle as Executive Secretary of the Hands were the real anonymous authors of the Emperor's statement. Flagg even suggested that the Emperor's letter might be in Tasan's hands. Peixota was incredulous. Dorsey Flagg enlightened him. He told how the Russian Marxists, shielding themselves behind the Popular Front and now the White Friends of Ethiopia, had used every weapon they could find to injure him, by charging that he was a Trotskyite Fascist and Nazi sympathizer. They had employed something of the technique they did to build up Sufi Abdul Hamid into an anti-Semite. But their methods were less crude and spectacular, for he had not yet been arrested and hauled into court. But they had petitioned the president of his college to oust him as a Fascist. They had secretly approached members of the faculty with the proposition that they should isolate him, arguing that being a Fascist, he must be hostile to Ethiopia and that as a Trotsky sympathizer he also was an anti-Semite.

"Then is Trotsky supposed to be an anti-Semite too?" Peixota demanded.

"Sure," said Flagg, "not supposed to be, but actually is. The Soviet had conferred upon him the title of: Mad Dog Fascist Foe of the Proletariat and Hitler Spy and Anti-Semite."

Peixota grimaced as he often did instead of smiling: "If Hitler can make a Jew an anti-Semite he is much greater than I thought he was."

What Dorsey Flagg related to him sounded incredible, fantastic. But he reasoned that the times were fantastic in a way that was beyond his imagination. Principles had become meaningless in the universal social ferment, yet leaders of the people still talked as if principles were the same principles. It was no longer merely unscrupulous politicians who were changing principles quicker than a chameleon its color. But everybody was doing it: great liberal and radical leaders of the people who formerly appeared as gods crowned with halos of honesty. And even nations. Not some little unstable military Central American[2] or

Balkan nation, but great nations whose constitutions were founded upon high principles. Yet no one seemed willing to tell the people the truth in a great way. And so they were left in confusion to run after any popular panacea and shouting the slogan of the hour, whether it was the Soviet "Dictatorship of the Proletariat" or "People's Front" or the Democratic "Make the World Safe for Democracy" or the Nazi-Fascist "Workers of the World, Unite against Jewish Capitalism."

It was infernally fantastic, Peixota thought. Even his illegal business had had to be based on sound principles to make him successful. He had built up his reputation by always paying the winner of a lucky hit, always paying his agents every cent of their commission, besides their bonuses. And thus he had come to be known as Honest Peixota in Harlem.[3]

The Sufists, assisted by sympathetic groups, had organized a monster anti-Italian demonstration. Elks Lodges, clubs, students' associations, churches, professional and political groups were participating. Leading preachers, politicians and professional men were among the sponsors, including the Hands to Ethiopia and the White Friends of Ethiopia.

It was a fortnight since the Emperor's statement had fallen like a heavy frost upon the heads of the Aframericans. But their naturally warmth-generating blood soon melted the chill. If the Emperor of Ethiopia did not need them to serve, they needed Ethiopia to serve their interests here. And so they were again zestfully carrying on with the work they had begun.

Newton Castle was not merely shocked when he read the broadsides which were distributed in Harlem, but he was grieved that the name of the White Friends of Ethiopia had appeared as one of the sponsors. He gathered a bunch of the offensive things and hurried to the office of the Friends downtown.

Maxim Tasan and Lij Alamaya were there. Castle frisked about like a squirrel in his agitation. Why had the Friends permitted the use of its name to sponsor an anti-Italian demonstration?

he demanded. Why had they not insisted that it be anti-Fascist? The Aframericans should not be encouraged to manifest animus against the Italian people, for it was the Fascists who were warring against Ethiopians and not the Italian people. But the Sufi broadside was using the Fascist war to attack the Italians in Harlem and incite the Aframericans to boycott Italian businesses.

Maxim Tasan admitted that it was a serious error, but he did not know who had given permission. He turned to Lij Alamaya. Alamaya knew nothing about it. He summoned Gloria Kendall from the adjoining room. Miss Kendall explained: the Sufi organization had telephoned when she was alone in the office, asking the Friends to be one of the sponsors of the demonstration. She telephoned Professor Banner Makepeace and he gave the necessary permission. She said, however, that the Sufi official had distinctly stated that it was an anti-Fascist demonstration. She had made a note of it in shorthand, which she had preserved.

It was Tuesday. The demonstration was set for Saturday. There was time to get a notice in the Harlem weeklies and to print new leaflets. Tasan asked Lij Alamaya if he would make contact with the Sufists and suggest the changes. Alamaya declined. He said it would be more correct if Pablo Peixota as chairman of the Hands were asked to do it. Besides, the Ethiopians themselves did not make any nice difference between the Italians and the Fascists; they were both the same thing to them.

Newton Castle excitedly cried: "But there is a big difference, Lij—"

Tasan arrested him: "That's all right, Newt. Don't forget that Lij Alamaya is not a Marxist."

Now that Lij Alamaya had made his submission, Tasan was carefully considerate of attitude towards him. Even as Pablo Peixota had ideas about the Hands to Ethiopia, so did Maxim Tasan. Tasan also did not desire the disintegration of the Hands. He hoped to get control and bring it into the Popular

Front and he was planning to use Alamaya to realize that hope. He knew that although Alamaya's was a sensitive nature, he was not a mere weakling. So he handled him cleverly. Furthermore, the situation was more favorable to Alamaya since he had gone over to the Friends. The *Labor Herald* was puffing up his stature and had said that although scandalous rumors had been printed about his status, there was no question but that Alamaya was a true representative of the real interests of the Ethiopian people. Tasan knew that if he should break away from the Friends again, it would be less easy to besmirch him. And so he treated Alamaya with deference, not with the honest dignity of Pablo Peixota, but with subtle hypocrisy. For example, when Tasan would sometimes address him as "Prince" Alamaya, Alamaya would correct him and say that it was not "Prince," it was "Lij," and he preferred plain "Mister." Thereupon Tasan would apologize and tell Alamaya that he was a regular democrat.

Tasan was of the opinion that it might work to better advantage if Professor Makepeace talked to Peixota. He telephoned Professor Makepeace and instructed him what to say. Professor Makepeace got connected with Pablo Peixota and, introducing himself, said that he was speaking on behalf of the White Friends of Ethiopia. He pleaded with Peixota to exert his influence upon the Sufists to postpone their demonstration to the following week and to print new leaflets in which "Fascists" should be substituted for "Italians." Professor Makepeace particularly stressed the readiness of the Friends to pay all the expenses of the change.

Peixota told the professor that he was sorry he was unable to accede to his request, but he could not agree with his point of view, because he could not differentiate, like him, between the Italians and the Fascists. The Italian nation was Fascist and making war against Ethiopia. It made little difference if a few Italians preferred to call themselves non-Fascists or Communists. He asked Professor Makepeace if he were aware that the Italian-American communities had organized their own mass meetings even in Harlem to raise funds which were donated to the Fascist war chest to prosecute the war against Ethiopia. And they, the Italians, had drawn no line between the Ethiopian people and the Ethiopian Empire. He could see no reason why Aframericans should be generous in sentiment to a people who were fighting their Ethiopian brothers without mercy.

Professor Makepeace said that he knew all the facts of the situation, but it was the policy of the Friends of Ethiopia and other liberal organizations to which he belonged always to make a distinction between the government of a country and its people. He added that Maxim Tasan had specially requested him to talk to Peixota, as he considered the moment opportune to bring the Hands and the Friends into closer collaboration.

As if a wasp had whizzed out of the receiver and stung him in the ear, the mention of Tasan's name infuriated Peixota. He said: "If Mr. Tasan is there I'd like to talk to him." Professor Makepeace replied: "I'll put you in touch with him immediately." He felt relieved in ending the awkward conversation. In his heart he felt that Peixota was right, but he had pledged himself intellectually to uphold Marxist principles.

When the telephone rang again Peixota's finger twitched as he grasped it in eagerness to talk to Tasan. Said he: "Mr. Tasan, Professor Makepeace was just talking to me about you. He said you wanted to stop the Sufi demonstration. But I think it would be better for you to keep your blood-hound's nose out of Harlem and take your filthy leprous hands off our organization. You've done every damnable thing possible to hurt our cause. You caught Lij Alamaya in a trap. You can work your will on him, you abominable bashibazouk.[4] But we others will be a match for you, you understand? I know your type. You don't mean my people any good; you don't mean any people any good. Human life to you is like playing a game of cards which you aim to win by hook or crook. What do you care about working people of any race and their miserable lot? How can you care when you're only a cold-blooded international sloganizer, a phrase-touting racketeer? What can you do for humanity when you're no more human than a viper? What can humanity expect of a despicable whoreson, a proletarian prostitute like you, yes, you—"

He stopped, having used up all available words, but he still held the receiver.

"Thank you, Mr. Peixota," Tasan spoke calmly, "you are very eloquent."

Peixota turned from the telephone in disgust. His anger was suddenly gone and he thought: "I should have faced him man-to-man and said it. That would have been more effective. But perhaps I would have made a big ass of myself." Had Peixota been able to see Tasan's face, livid with hate, he would not have thought that what he said was not quite effective.

Peixota had not been very enthusiastic about the Sufists' demonstration, when he permitted the use of the name of the Hands to Ethiopia as one of the supporting organizations. As a would-be labor leader and Harlem agitator he considered Sufi Abdul Hamid, in his attractive Oriental costume, more picturesque than practical and much too volatile of character to hew steadily and unswervingly along the hard line of labor organization of an overwhelmingly unskilled body of workers who were the victims of discrimination by white employers and workers. Also as a property owner and employer, Peixota saw the problems of his people more from the anthropological than a labor angle.

But the conversation with Tasan had resulted in quickening his sympathy for the Sufists. He visited their headquarters personally to give Sufi Abdul Hamid the assurance of his support. The Sufi informed him that he had been approached directly and indirectly by persons who desired him to use the word "Fascist" instead of "Italian" in the demonstration, but he had refused. He added that even if he were willing to make the change, all of his followers were against it. For "Fascist" to them was like an unfamiliar word that one had to look up in the dictionary and even then not quite grasping its clear meaning. But "Italian" was as real and obvious as spaghetti and tomato sauce and as full of meaning for Aframericans as it was fraught with danger for the Ethiopians.

That Saturday afternoon the parade was held according to schedule. It was a grand mass demonstration of marching and music. The people flocked together, a mighty host with bands and banners and flags. There were religious and lay groups from churches and clubs, political and professional leagues and associations and plain people's organizations of the sons and daughters of the Southern states and the Caribbean islands. Organized into sections, each headed by a band of music, they assembled at the upper end of Seventh Avenue. Arresting signs proclaimed the object of the demonstration:

ITALIANS EXTERMINATING
ETHIOPIANS IN AFRICA

ITALIANS DEBAUCHING
AFRAMERICANS IN HARLEM

ITALIANS DECLARE AFRICANS ARE
SAVAGES UNFIT TO LIVE

ITALIANS SAY THERE SHALL BE NO
ACTIVE AFRICAN STATE

ITALIANS SPRAY ETHIOPIANS WITH
POISON GAS

ITALIANS BOMBING ETHIOPIAN
WOMEN AND CHILDREN

AFRO-AMERICANS—HELP YOUR
ETHIOPIAN BROTHERS

PEOPLE OF HARLEM—DON'T
PATRONIZE ITALIAN BUSINESS

The parade went down Seventh Avenue to 135th Street, crossed to Lenox Avenue and continued to 125th Street, turned to reach Seventh Avenue again, streaming on to 110th Street, thence east to Lenox Avenue and headed north. It was followed by a cavalcade of cars decorated with flags of the United States and Ethiopia. Seated in a big Buick, the heavy-muscled Sufi Abdul Hamid resembled a black Buddha in his turban and baroque Oriental costume, but he was out-dazzled by Professor Koazhy, who sat beside him in his glittering uniform of an Ethiopian Ras with his shako of many-colored plumes. The parade stopped above 125th Street, where the speakers' stand was erected.

The speakers' stand was opposite the notorious Merry-Go-Round bar and grill, which was Italian-owned. As the Sufi and Professor Koazhy mounted the stand, four Sufists unfolded a large banner before it, which was lettered:

ITALIANS EXTERMINATING
ETHIOPIANS IN AFRICA

ITALIANS DEBAUCHING
AFRAMERICANS IN HARLEM

Suddenly unfolded there directly in front of the café, the huge banner was a surprise even to the demonstrators, having upon them the effect which the Sufi intended. Murmurs of approval arose from the crowd: "Exactly right!" "A fine idea!" "It just hit the nail on the head!"

The Sufi's job as a community and labor leader combined the role of the sidewalk agitator and muck-raker, whose obsession was the morals of Harlem. It was a subject upon which he was always pounding. It teamed perfectly with his labor leader activity. Aframericans had no fixed and worthwhile place in the good ship, Labor; they were flotsam dumped to please any captain's whim, or workers' caprice, therefore Harlem morals were low. And in his bitter harangues, standing on a step-ladder on the avenue, the Sufi usually picked the Merry-Go-Round as an example to prove that Harlem morals were low.

The Merry-Go-Round was the largest and bawdiest bar in Lenox Avenue. It had the commodious aspect of a barn-big everybody's drinking-joint on Forty-Second or Fourteenth Street. Its liquor bar was a gigantic horseshoe centrally fixed, with tables ranged on either side. There was an enormous room in the rear, which was filled with customers every night. Ordinarily it employed six bartenders besides waiters, and on Saturdays, Sundays, and holidays the number was doubled. There was no orchestra, only two elaborate music boxes, one in front and one in the rear. It was the haunt of the gutterbugs of Harlem and the place par excellence where its elite went slumming. And like flies attracted by sweet scum, its customers came from all parts of New York. Polite-speaking Harlemites nicknamed the place the Marys-Go-Round, but the gutterbugs called it the Fairy-Go-Round.

The Sufi had campaigned against the establishment for months, planting his step-ladder on the opposite side and demanding that it be closed by the City Fathers. "The white folks say we are degenerate and dirty and diseased," he shouted, "but this Merry-Go-Round proves that they are pushing us down to be what we are. They wouldn't permit any Afro-Americans to run an open cesspool like this."

The Sufi was probably right. A group calling itself the Jitter-bugs had started in the hub of Harlem a place similar to the Merry-Go-Round. But one night the doughty one and only Aframerican police officer led his men in, armed with hatchets, and hacked it to pieces. He declared that no such den of abomination would be run by Aframericans as long as he had any power in the community! But evidently his power was not great enough to stop the Merry-Go-Round.

Sufists and Senegambians had frequently precipitated quarrels and fights in the Merry-Go-Round. For sometimes when the Sufi was agitating the crowds from the step-ladder some of them would enter the bar and attempt to induce customers, especially persons with whom they were acquainted, to leave. The management was compelled largely to increase its staff of able-bodied Aframerican bouncers to handle the intruders.

The great crowd was not aware of the intention of the erratic and unpredictable Sufi Abdul Hamid to make the mighty demonstration for Ethiopia serve as an instrument of agitation against the Merry-Go-Round. Professor Koazhy spoke first and chiefly emphasized the ideas of the speech he made at the mass meeting of welcome to Lij Alamaya. His uniform was still thrillingly exciting to the crowd and he was rewarded with warm salvos of applause. Other speakers followed with vivid details of the horrors of the war in Ethiopia. A doctor who had lived in Ethiopia gave a pathetic idea of the wounded soldiers and civilians, because there was a dearth of physicians and nurses and no adequate hospital service.

The altercation with Maxim Tasan had intensified Pablo Peixota's interest in the demonstration and he and Dorsey Flagg had walked down to the pavement parliament. The Sufi had just started his attack against the Merry-Go-Round when they got there. Peixota was delighted with the man's pithy phrases and sarcasm and the adroit manner in which he took advantage of the Ethiopian conflict to press his drive against the Merry-Go-Round. He had never visited the bar and had not even heard of it, so far was he removed from the bohemian life of Harlem. Now he decided to go in and see what it was like. Dorsey Flagg, of course, had indulged a Black-and-White occasionally at the Merry-Go-Round when he was out slumming with a regular gang of intellectual good fellows, among whom was Newton Castle. But he seldom went there now, as most of them had become collectively serious adherents of the People's Front and had black-listed him as a Fascist.

So while the Sufi was pounding away at the Merry-Go-Round the two men elbowed a way through the crowd, crossed the street and entered the bar. They stood on one side of the horseshoe and ordered Scotch. Being Saturday afternoon, there were a considerable number of customers. Some of them, chiefly young men, went outside awhile to listen to the Sufi and, titillated by his sharp jabs at the establishment, they came back giggling and singing: "Oh, Mary goes round and round."

Peixota looked around at the place and naively asked Dorsey Flagg why so many lads had charcoaled and elongated their eyebrows and rouged their cheeks like the girls and spoke from the tip of the tongue a kind of unintelligible jargon. Flagg explained that they were chorus boys of the lower type from the cabarets and music halls.

"I don't like it," said Peixota. "It is very insipid. It is as bad as Sufi describes it, or is he plastering?"

"To tell the truth, it's bad enough, sometimes worse," said Flagg.

They went back into the rear. The music box was playing and, although dancing was not permitted, a group of chorus boys with arms linked were shaking their legs together, while some girls sitting were rhythmically clapping and prompting them to continue. The tables were nearly all occupied and there was general hilarity, a hectic reckless wave of intoxication sweeping all together.

In one corner a group of nine persons—six girls, two youths, and an older man—were imbibing many rounds of double "shorties" (a Harlem special) of rye.⁵ One of the girls was white. She was svelte with regular features, not very pretty, but she had beautiful orange-burnished bobbed hair. It was difficult to tell to what white group she was a member. She was limber from inebriation and tossed excitable amorous phrases at the Italian waiter each time that he attended to their table.

At last, when he came and set down another round of drinks, she jumped up and embraced him and cried: "Tony, for all the passes I'm making at you, you'll hardly look at me. I guess you imagine I am white, but I'm a real nigger with all that nigger stuff, just like my darker sisters have." She clung to the waiter, kissing, and the ribald older man of the party cried: "Look out, Carrot, don't choke him with your tongue."

"Don't worry about me," said the waiter. "I'm used to it."

Peixota and Flagg were going out by the side entrance and the same man called to Flagg: "Lo, Dorsey, come and have a shot with us."

The girl he called Carrot looked round and waved: "Dorsey, you bum, come right on over here."

Flagg shouted, "No!" And he went out with Peixota.

"Who is she? They know you," said Peixota.

Flagg mentioned her name and said she was an important city employee.

"I met her father in Philadelphia," said Peixota. "Her family is among the tops. But, good God, can't she drink without making a slut of herself in public?"

"If she keeps it up, she'll lose her job," said Flagg. "Some of her own drinking pals will write in to her department. I know them for what they are: skunks and rats."

"She must be sex crazy to put on such an exhibition in such a place," said Peixota. "It's a rotten dive, raw and slimy like the afterbirth of a cow."

Peixota's first reaction to the place was not unfavorable. It had appeared to him like a big carousing depot for disoriented young people, of which it was regrettable there were so many in Harlem. And he was inclined to conjecture that the Sufi perhaps had a special grudge against the owners and was overstepping his license as a popular agitator to hurt their business. He was opposed to bigotry and would combat it in a Sufi Abdul Hamid as much as in a Maxim Tasan. He could not apprehend what disgusted the Sufi about the establishment, for his eyes were not keen nor his ears sensitive to detect the secret signs and suggestive erotomania of the underworld.

But the spectacle of the Titian-haired[6] member of one of the best Aframerican families and a swinish white waiter was upsetting to his innate feeling of respectability. It hurt his dignity and that pride in his group which he fostered and held sacred against all the humiliating circumstances of living that continued to undermine it. In a flash he had understood the fundamental cause of the Sufi's agitation.

"Are there many more places like this in Harlem?" Peixota said to Flagg.

"Not any large licensed establishments," said Flagg, "but there are lots of reefer joints or tea-shops and the hooch dives where they sell rot-gut for a nickel a glass. They're worse because the fools who drink that stuff are getting poisoned and going insane at the same time. I don't approve of Sufi making a racial issue out of his agitation against this joint. They have them downtown too. The underworld must also have its relaxation."

"But you can't compare downtown with Harlem, Dorsey. Downtown the whites run such places for *whites*. Up here the whites run them for *colored* and we can't get away from the racial angle. The Sufi says it is an orgy of debauchery and it is. And then the white people declare we are degenerate and bestial. In science books and schoolbooks they try to prove we are inferior. The Nazis and Fascists say we are half apes. And these same white, these Fascists are exploiting our vices for profit! I agree with Sufi. If we don't wake up the whites will destroy us in the same manner that the Europeans and Japanese encourage the Chinese to have their opium and make laws to prevent the sale in their own countries."

Outside in the keen March weather the Sufi was mightily booming against the Merry-Go-Round. One of his scouts had espied Peixota and Flagg and informed the Sufi of their presence. He invited both to the stand and presented them to the crowd. Peixota spoke for three minutes in congratulation of the demonstrators and in praise of the Sufi and invited all to work together for the salvation of Ethiopia. Dorsey Flagg spoke just as briefly in the same vein.

There was a little commotion in the midst of the crowd as a white man struggled to approach the stand. "Let him through, let him come!" commanded the Sufi. The white man pushed his way through and after exchanging words with the Sufi, he was permitted to mount the stand. Murmurs of disapproval arose among the crowd: "Throw him off!" "We don't want any white man up there!"

But the Sufi held up his hand and silenced them. "Listen, friends! This is a member of the White Friends of Ethiopia. This is a democratic country, where we all believe in freedom of speech. I want you to hear him."

The man was an Italian of average height and appeared to be an ordinary workingman. Said he: "My friends, I wanta you see yourself one Italian no wanta war against Etiopia and there are a lotta more like me. Mussolini and Fascisti notta real Italy. Mussolini hema big bandit kidnappa our King. But our King no wanta Etiopian Empire anda Pope no hate Etiopian people, for alla people white and colored in the church.

"We Italians alla good Americans and we believa in liberty for oda people. Me no likea Fascists. Fascisti badder for my country, but America my country now. Fascisti killa Italia for Fascisti hate the working class. I'd geeva my life a-fighting with you all for Etiopia. I joina da Friends of Etiopia to helpa fight against Fascisti and if all of us a working people stick togedder no Fascisti can leek us. Only Party Communista fighta with Fascisti. Only Soviet Russia help alla people fighting with Fascisti, alla working people. Join the Party Communista for Soviet Russia—"

The crowd booed and yelled: "Take it away!" "We don't want that crap!" "To hell with Soviet Russia and give us Ethiopia!" "Down with Italy!" "Boycott all Italians!" At the northern edge of the demonstration a voice shouted: "Help! Help! Murder!" There was a general stampede toward the spot. Many were asking what was wrong; some said a white man was hit, others that a white man was killed. The police patrol had been considerably increased for the occasion. Police hurried to the corner when the cry of "Murder!" came. Others ordered the people to disperse, driving them like cattle and poking them with their sticks. The people were sullen. Some of them damned the police. One fellow would not move on quickly and argued with a policeman about his rights as a citizen. He was prodded hard in his backside. He turned and grabbed the policeman's stick. The policeman felled him to the pavement with the butt of his gun. The Sufi tried to convince the police that the people would disperse and go home quietly, if they were not badgered. He was arrested for creating a disturbance and obstructing a policeman in pursuit of his duty. But it developed late that the cry of "Murder!" was a grim joke. No person, white or colored, had been molested.

PEIXOTA'S HUMILIATION

Pablo Peixota and Dorsey Flagg had left the scene of the demonstration immediately after speaking, before the disorder occurred. The Sufi, despite his bizarrerie, was a stimulating tonic to the Harlem kraal, they both agreed. So long as they were not wholly unconscionable fakers, men like Sufi Abdul Hamid and Professor Koazhy were performing a real service to their people, filling that lacuna in their lives which the privileged world had studiedly neglected.

Peixota went home to dinner. He had another engagement for the later part of the evening. The Good Old Pals of which he was a member were having a pig knuckles feed and card game. He had promised and wanted to attend. The Good Old Pals was Peixota's pet club. It was founded long before he became a wealthy man by a group of young men, elevator runners and others, who were close associates. Now they were really "old" pals. Most of them were married and had children and only two of fifteen members were still operating an elevator. But every three months they got together in a midnight stag party to play cards until dawn.

The secretary and leading spirit of the club was at one time one of Peixota's most trusted lieutenants in the policy game.[1] Now he was the owner of a restaurant. Another lieutenant of Peixota's who was a member was the proprietor of a flourishing little cigar and candy store, and it was said that he still held a small kingship in the policy. Another member was the proprietor of a bar and grill. One of the Good Old Pals had plodded through many years to become a lawyer and he was the only professional member.

For a decade, starting in during the hey-day of the Prohibition era, when money started coming easy to Peixota, he had provided the liquor for the get-together. As the wealthiest man of the Old Pals Peixota made this contribution with a generous gesture, always sending plenty and a variety of good liquor. It was such acts—remembrance of old friends and treating them just as in the past—which caused many Harlemites to be so loyal and ever ready to defend him.

The Good Old Pals were meeting at the home of their secretary. He lived in a private house, renting some of the rooms. His wife and daughter had carefully prepared the basement rooms for the event. They cooked the pig knuckles and left them simmering on the stove. They set the dishes and plates on the buffet, with dill pickles, horseradish, olives and bread. They set out a package of paper napkins. And when everything was perfect, mother and daughter went off to a midnight show, leaving the Good Old Pals to enjoy themselves as if they were a secret fraternity.

Twelve of the Old Pals were already there when Peixota arrived. His coming perceptibly changed the spirit of the atmosphere. Because although the others had started to play cards and had had something to drink, their mood was like actors doing minor roles as a preliminary to the appearance of the principal. Although Peixota was just one other member, the others all looked to him without subserviency as the natural leader.

They all stood together and drank a toast to the Good Old Pals and sang, "We All Are Jolly Good Fellows." Then they started their games. There was no gambling. They were friendly games played for prizes, chiefly boxes of cigars. At intervals each pal helped himself to a feed of pig knuckles and poured his own drink.

As the blanket slipped a little from the friendly body of night, the joviality of the pals increased its volume. About the hour when the scarcely visible hand of dawn was lifting, the house was raided by a colored and white squad of plainclothes sleuths. They were armed with hatchets, intent upon chopping up the roulette wheel which they imagined to be there. But they found only a small group of respectable persons mildly amusing themselves. Disappointed, the sleuths insolently charged them with gambling, bundled all into a patrol wagon and took them to the police station.

On Monday morning the city newspapers reported the raid of a Harlem gambling club, magnifying it into a big affair. There were details of the flourishing of the numbers game in Harlem in spite of efforts by the authorities to break up the syndicates, and Pablo Peixota was specially mentioned as one of the men arrested and a leading promoter of the numbers game. There was no reference to his respectable interests.

The *Labor Herald* put the story on the front page with a photograph of Peixota, who was called a gangster and racketeer and the most vicious exploiter speculating upon the vices of the unfortunate people of Harlem. On Monday all the accused were released under bond. When the case was brought to trial their lawyers easily demolished the charge of the police with irrefutable proof that the Good Old Pals were a respectable fraternal group and that the secretary's house was not a gambling rendezvous, but a family residence. The magistrate rebuked the police and dismissed the case. There was a Fusion mayor[2] in office who was sincerely opposed to the indiscriminate and aggravating high-handedness of police activity in Harlem.

But there was no report of the outcome of the trial in the city newspapers. The Aframerican weeklies copied the reports of the arrest from the dailies under big headlines and published photographs of Peixota. Inconspicuously printed at the end of the accounts it was stated that the case was dismissed.

That Monday evening Alamaya called to see Peixota. He had quickly perceived that the unfavorable publicity given the man's arrest was an underhanded attack on the Hands to Ethiopia. And it had followed so soon his own miserable experience, he felt that the same persons who had smeared his own reputation had perhaps indirectly engineered the raid. He felt personally involved in all the trouble. He wanted to tell Peixota how he felt, he had such a high regard for him. He was unhappy knowing that there was nothing he could do to help.

Alamaya found Peixota calm as always, with plans already formulated. "Don't agitate yourself about it," he said to Alamaya. "It's just a dirty frame-up. But I have to resign as chairman of the Hands. It would hurt the organization if I didn't resign. It is more than seven years since I washed my hands free of the numbers game. And those people who wrote that filthy slander about me know it. They know I am not a professional gambler. Their one aim is to destroy the organization."

"But if you resign, that *will* destroy the organization," said Alamaya, "and that is what they desire."

"I don't think it will if we can find a courageous fighter to head it," said Peixota, "and I'll work just as hard behind the scenes. But as a front man my usefulness is at an end."

"My God! What a pity," said Alamaya. "The war news from Ethiopia gets worse and worse. Our soldiers have only spears and battle-axes and old-fashioned rifles to fight against Italian machine guns and tanks and airplanes. And my effort to do something here is futile. I am helpless."

"Don't give up in despair, my son," said Peixota. "Life is a grim struggle all the time. Your experience here will be useful in the future. You discovered that your European Friends were 'Greeks bearing gifts.' And it is the same with our Friends. Friendship between individuals must be based upon common self-respect. It is the same with nations as with individuals. Each side must possess the wherewithal either materially or spiritually to maintain its self-respect. We have very little beside the spirit to sustain us to exist and work with hope for the future. I have fought against the influence of the Friends in our organization, because I saw very clearly that they did not want us to retain a spirit of our own, they wanted either to control or break our spirit."

"I am afraid that my mission is a failure," said Alamaya.

"It may appear to be in the eyes of those who expect immediate results. But sometimes what looks like a failure may be only a necessary setback in a grand cycle of events which foreshadows a new dispensation," said Peixota.

"You're optimistic," said Alamaya.

"On the contrary, I'm not. No Aframerican can be overoptimistic, but I am a man. I must have faith to live. Those who feel so sure, because they have the power to possess the world today, they may have the wrong kind of faith. You have more cause than I to be optimistic. You have a little corner of Africa, and Africa is a land of vast resources still undeveloped. Your Empire may be destroyed by the Italians. But your people may live and if they guard their native spirit intact, they may yet become the Light of a new Africa."

"God help my people," said Alamaya, putting his hand to his face in a gesture as of prayer.

"God help us all," said Peixota. "Now, I believe that you're here not merely to talk, but to know what I plan to do. I think the best man to take over the chairmanship is Dorsey Flagg. Even though the White Friends hate him, he has no questionable past which they can use against the organization. Then, I don't think my house should continue to be your headquarters, even as a front. It would only be a handicap to you in your present position. Better for the present that you cut off all contact with me. Later on perhaps we may be able to collaborate closely again. This time of ferment and high tension can't continue forever. It must burn itself out and people will have a chance at least to think before they act."

"Then you don't want me to come here anymore," said Alamaya, "and you and your family are the only real friends I have in New York. You have been so good to me."

"It is not that I don't want you to come," said Peixota. "I like you personally, but I think it is better for the Cause if you stay away for a while. After all the Cause of Ethiopia comes first. Circumstances may change and conditions become more favorable and then—"

The door opened and Seraphine looked in and said: "Hi, Tekla, I didn't know you were here. Busy?"

Tekla nodded and forced a smile.

"Awright, see you afterwards."

Seraphine closed the door and Peixota said: "How are you getting along with the Friends?"

"Tasan is the Friends and the Friends is Tasan," said Alamaya. "I drop in at the office occasionally. He has been acting exceptionally decently. He's considering a new plan of campaign with the cooperation of Mr. Bishop."

"Prudhomme Bishop, that wishy-washy humbug!" Peixota spoke with emphatic contempt. "You'll find plenty of optimism there. He's as wholesome as pasteurized milk and his superlatives are grander than Hollywood's. Well, whatever happens, I wish you better luck, Lij Alamaya. Personally I think you're a nice young man, too clean to touch that stinker Tasan. It's a pity we're such a weak and vulnerable people."

Alamaya said: "Mr. Peixota, I want to thank you for all your kindness. I shall never forget it. I tried my best and if I have failed—I have tried to be frank with you and yet—but perhaps someday you will understand."

"I understand the difficulty of your position very well, Lij Alamaya," said Peixota, "and don't forget I am still your friend.

Let's take a drink, a straight drink." He opened a cabinet and took out a bottle of whiskey. He filled two glasses and said: "To the freedom and future of Ethiopia!"

Seraphine was hurt because Lij Alamaya left the house without seeing her. Peixota said that he had been summoned by telephone to an important rendezvous. But that did not satisfy her. Her mother's attitude was disquieting. Mrs. Peixota was fretfully reiterating that the publicity her husband's arrest had received would affect their relations with Alamaya. She wasn't worried about his position in the Hands to Ethiopia and Seraphine felt about the situation exactly like her mother.

She telephoned Lij Alamaya the following day, but he betrayed no eagerness to see her; his manner was evasive. Vexed but undaunted, she surprised him at his hotel the following evening. In a wretched mood Alamaya was unable to hide his embarrassment.

"What is it, Tekla?" cried Seraphine. "Aren't you glad to see me or are you tired of me already?"

"I am not tired of you and you should not say that."

"Then why do you act in such an *un-American* way? Why don't you kiss me?" She hugged and kissed him, but there was no warmth in him. "I don't believe you like me anymore. Do you?" she asked.

"It isn't anything personal, Seraphine, but things aren't going right. I'm in trouble and your father too. You saw what the papers had about him."

"Yes, but what has that to do with *us*? I am not responsible for my father's affairs. And he isn't guilty of anything except that he keeps low company. Mother often told him he's too big a man in Harlem to associate with trash."

"Your father is a real man, Seraphine, and I like and respect him very much. I'd prefer to visit his house and associate with—with his family more than any other in New York. But he doesn't want me to and I believe he's right."

"Why?"

"How can I explain? You know I'm here on a mission for Ethiopia. Your father thinks it is better for my mission if I keep away. I'm not a free person. I have made mistakes and I must pay the cost of those mistakes."

"But you don't have to pay for Father's mistakes," said Seraphine, "nor have I. If you won't come to the house, then I can visit you downtown. I'm sick of Harlem anyway."

"I made a promise to your father and I'll keep it, Seraphine. I won't cheat, for I have too much respect for him."

"You mean you don't want to see me then. You don't like me?"

"Don't say I don't like you, *please*. But do try to understand. I cannot help myself. I'm not a free agent."

Seraphine buried her face in the cushion of the couch and sobbed. Alamaya sat beside her and put his arm across her shoulder. "Please don't, don't be upset," he said. "I'm not worth it." But her sobbing increased, her body violently shaking almost as it strangely did when she was inebriated and giggling.

Alamaya caressed her hair and murmured: "Don't do that, please. Please, forgive me." At last she calmed down and, holding a handkerchief to her face, she went to the bathroom. She dipped her face in cold water and vigorously rubbed it and applied powder and rouge.

When she came out she said: "Goodbye, Tekla."

"I'll accompany you to your car," he said.

"I came down on the subway, but I don't want you to come with me, goodbye."

"Au revoir, Seraphine."

SERAPHINE LEAVES HOME

Seraphine did not wake up as usual the next morning to go to her father's office. The maid served her breakfast in her room, but she only drank orange juice. Her mother went up to her bedroom. Seraphine said she was miserable in her mind and in her body and would not be able to breathe in the atmosphere of her father's office. Mrs. Peixota informed her husband that Seraphine was indisposed.

Peixota opened the office himself. He had neglected it since he became so immersed with the work of the Hands to Ethiopia. Now he plunged into it again, giving his attention to details of things which had accumulated. In his largest tenement building most of his tenants had joined the recently formed Mutual Association of Harlem Tenants and had presented demands for a reduction in rent. He was arranging with his lawyers to discuss the situation. There was a strike of tenants in many other apartment buildings owned by white people. For many reasons, but specially because he was connected with the Hands to Ethiopia, Peixota did not want his tenants to go on strike. He expressed his willingness to meet the officials of the tenants' group in conference.

Seraphine kept to her room all day. And in the evening, when Peixota came home from the office, he went to see her, taking a bouquet of violets, which he thought of when he was passing the florist's.

"I've brought you some violets, Seraphine," he said, putting them in a vase on her dressing table. "People asked for you at the office."

"I don't want any flowers and I'm never going back to that office," she said. "If you want to be nice, you should be nice to Tekla."

"Now what is wrong with you?" said Peixota. "I haven't been unkind to Alamaya or anyone."

"Yes, you have too. You've stopped him from coming here and seeing me. But nobody can stop me from doing what I want. I'm not going to stay here cooped up in Harlem."

"If Alamaya cannot have his office here anymore, there are reasons for it. The young man is here on a mission, which is more important than his having an office here. And I wish you would try to understand and not make a simpleton of yourself."

Seraphine jumped up from her couch-bed, drawing her blue and orange satin kimono around her: "I'm not a simpleton and I won't be called a simpleton. You imagine you're the only wise person in Harlem and everybody else a fool. But I am not and I won't stay here for you to insult me."

"What is happening now?" Peixota said sharply. "Are you going crazy?"

"I'm not crazy either and I won't be talked to that way. You can't treat me like Lij Alamaya. I think you're hard and mean and cruel and smug with it. I won't stand for it, I won't. Indeed not. You're a wicked man, o-o-oh!"

Mrs. Peixota came in: "What's all this noise about? What's wrong with you, Sirrie?"

"Father says I'm a simpleton and a fool because I like Alamaya and I won't be treated like a child. I'm a woman, I know my own mind. I won't stay in this house and be insulted—"

"Shut up!" said Mrs. Peixota. "If you were a woman you wouldn't be acting like a child."

"I'll show you I'm a woman, yes I will. I'll leave this house and to hell with it."

"Why, Seraphine, you don't know what you're saying," cried Mrs. Peixota. "Pablo, go out and leave us alone."

"And take your damned flowers, I don't want them!" cried Seraphine, smashing the vase on the floor.

Her mother slammed shut the door: "Are you going insane, Seraphine, speaking that way to your father?"

"He's not any father of mine."

"If you say that again, I'll spank you for the first time in my life, you miserable ungrateful wretch. What other father do you know but Pablo, who raised and educated you to become what you are today?"

"I'm not a miserable wretch and you can't spank me either," said Seraphine. "Understand that I won't be treated like a little child. I won't stay under this roof, not if I've got to go to hell!"

"There!" cried Mrs. Peixota, sharply slapping Seraphine's face. "Go to hell if you want to—the devil may teach you good sense."

"O-h-h!" Seraphine cried, pressing her palm against her cheek. "That ends it!" She rushed to the closet and started to take out her clothes, tossing them on the couch.

"You may go as quick as your feet will carry you, if you have no respect for your father and me," said Mrs. Peixota. "Perhaps it's my fault. I must blame myself for bringing you up too indulgently." She left the room, banging the door behind her.

That night Seraphine stayed with Bunchetta Facey at her apartment on Edgecombe Avenue. The girls talked the greater part of the night. Bunchetta was more excited about Seraphine Peixota's actually leaving her parents' house than the cause of it. For some years Bunchetta had maintained an apartment of her own, finding existence more elastic living away from her parents. But Seraphine had always appeared to her set as the type of girl that could exist forever under the parental roof, because she enjoyed such unlimited freedom there.

"I hope I can find a really good job," said Seraphine. "Then I wouldn't have to worry about anything."

"It won't be difficult for you to find a place," said Bunchetta. "I wouldn't mind taking an apartment with you in the Village or some place downtown. I'm fed up with living in Harlem and feeling that it's the only place I can live in New York."

"That's just how I feel myself," said Seraphine. "Mother and Father are content, but I won't be content with Harlem. All of us crowded together in the same pen. I love plenty of space and change of scenes. I want to feel free to live my life like any American girl."

"Certainly and why not?" said Bunchetta. "I like a modernistic life and Harlem is not modernistic. Our downtown friends think it is because Harlem is abnormally hectic and jitterbuggering on the surface. But I tell them that Harlem is no more modernistic than Chinatown."

Seraphine's eyes seemed stranger than usual; while the yellowish one was glowing like a cat's, the bluish appeared half-asleep between the lashes. She said: "I've never mixed much with the downtowners like you, Bunchy, I guess because Mother always discouraged it. We've gone to a lot of places downtown, but never made friends. Mother always said that white folks' opinion of colored was either patronizing or sneering, but never genuine."

"I've discovered that to be true enough," said Bunchetta, "and that is the chief reason why I like to keep up with my contacts downtown. I try to correct wrong impressions of colored people among whites. Information is like daily bread to people. We eat and we talk and read. The white people control all the best means of information and so colored people cannot pretend to ignore them like—well, like the Peixotas."

The remark made Seraphine smile: "I wish I could get interested in those interracial contacts like you, Bunchy. But I can't see that they mean so much in the life of colored people. Interracial contacts are not really normal social contacts. Some charitable whites meet colored social workers with maybe a singer or a doctor from the group. They drink tea together or if it is a bohemian crowd they drink liquor. Everybody is very polite. But it's like going to church and sitting beside a stranger and both of you listening to the sermon and singing hymns together. But colored people don't live that way really, nor white people either."

"But that's one way of social contact, all the same," said Bunchetta.

"It's the worse way," said Seraphine. "It is oily with hypocrisy. I prefer Mother's way. She's got to meet the downtowners too because of her connexion with colored charitable organizations. But it's business with her, to prod some politician to act or get the city to do something. She doesn't pretend it's social like you all. There can't be any really normal social enjoyment and contact between people who have something and people who have nothing."

"Then you wouldn't entertain the idea of living downtown," said Bunchetta.

"Sure I would. But it's because I want space to move around with freedom like other people and enjoy life; it's not because my heart is breaking to shake a white person's left hand. I'd like to sit and eat in any restaurant on Broadway with a dark man, if I enjoy his company. I'd like to see him treated as an American, so that I could be proud of him. In spite of his money Father has never had the privilege to enjoy it and walk like a man with Mother along the American way of life. Otherwise he would be different and not so ingrown and hard like rock that resists even dynamite. He wouldn't be so buried in racial movements."

"The enjoyment of life is worth fighting for and a man must be hard as a rock either in his body or his mind to fight," said Bunchetta. "If you had specialized like me in economics and sociology instead of music and interior decoration, you would understand that man was not born to enjoyment of life—he has to fight to get enjoyment out of life. I'll tell you, Sirrie, you're missing plenty by not associating more with white people who are thinking about social problems. They're fighting like Mr. Peixota, but from a different angle. Take Lij Alamaya, for example. He is wrapped up in the fight for Ethiopia, just like Mr. Peixota, but he lives downtown, where he has important contacts. The average white person wouldn't think he was Ethiopian, he's so fair-skinned."

"That's just it," said Seraphine. "The light ones have some freedom of movement by themselves, but with the dark ones together we are all doomed to discrimination. I don't know if I wasn't crazy about Tekla because he was fair and we could circulate together anyplace without creating curiosity. Once I said to him that it was nice that we two could 'pass' together. He didn't understand, so I explained to him what 'passing' was and he was very angry. He said he was not 'passing,' he was proud to be an Ethiopian. I told him that he couldn't live in the Santa Cruz if he were a dark Ethiopian. He said he didn't care where he lived and he thought 'passing' was cheapening to the person who was 'passing' if he had any pride in being himself. He couldn't understand the American point of view."

"He's perspicacious," said Bunchetta. "The human point of view is more important than the American point of view. It is the American point of view, the German point of view, the British point of view and all the different nations' point of view that make a mess of the world. Now we have the Popular Front to which all peoples with the right human point of view can belong."

Seraphine yawned. "I wish I wasn't so plumb dumb about politics and social problems. But you may be right, Bunchy, when you say I should associate more with social-problem people. Maybe I'll learn something for my benefit."

———

The opportunity of a new orientation for Seraphine was right at hand. Bunchetta telephoned at noon the next day (from the lower Harlem office of Social Service) to inform Mrs. Witern that Seraphine had quit her parents' house and was staying with her. She did not omit to mention that Seraphine was looking for a job. Mrs. Witern communicated the interesting report to Professor Makepeace. And long before Harlem's rubbernecks had reached out to sample the choice morsel, Maxim Tasan had heard that Peixota's daughter had left home.

That evening Bunchetta informed Seraphine that Mrs. Witern had invited them to dinner on Friday. Seraphine had not followed up her contact with Mrs. Witern since their visit to the Airplane. Twice she had received invitations to visit her, once through Bunchetta and another time by a direct note, but she had found some excuse for not going. But now she grasped eagerly at the chance. Anything was welcome which offered some relief from thinking too much about Lij Alamaya and the consequences of her leaving home.

It was a small dinner party at Mrs. Witern's. She never had many people to dinner, because of the state of her husband's health. Besides Bunchetta and Seraphine, there was Mrs. Abigail Hobison, who was accompanied by Mr. Hall Ming, a young Chinese, and Mr. Montague Claxon. It was a plain dinner, hot broth in cups, a platter full of appetizers (olives, celery, pickles, shrimp, miniature frankfurters), mashed potatoes, boiled carrots and grilled filet of beef.

No kind of liquor was served before or during the dinner. Mr. Witern was once a connoisseur of wines and liquors but he could no longer take any alcoholic drinks because of his physical condition. Out of consideration for him, Mrs. Witern never had any with meals. As his right side was entirely paralysed,

Mr. Witern ate with his left hand only. The butler had his meat cut into small pieces before it was placed before him.

Mr. Witern, to the right of his wife, was eager like a child interested in new surroundings. It was the first time he had dined with a Chinese or an Aframerican and he was pleased with the invitation. He adored his wife and her intellectual outlook, so elastic and varied. Her approach was so different, so superior to the cold philanthropic routine to which he was formerly accustomed, such as sitting in his office and discussing the possibility of an endowment with an emissary from an educational or charitable institution. His wife's attitude was the ideal human way. And he appreciated her more because withal her activities, she was so exquisitely considerate in her attentions to him.

The conversation about the worldwide social ferment and the Popular Front was like a substitute for rare wine to the taste of Mr. Witern. For many years he had supported the intransigent position that Mr. Secretary Hughes[1] took against the recognition of Soviet Russia in the society of states. But his paralytic body was miraculously thrilled when Soviet Russia at last accepted the democratic formulas of the comity of nations and with a grand gesture of goodwill promoted the universal movement of the Popular Front. But Mr. Witern's enthusiasm was dampened by the knowledge that at the time the Russian nation made this conciliatory move the great Nazi nation had ostentatiously withdrawn from the society of Democratic nations.

Mrs. Abigail Hobison was seated opposite Mrs. Witern at the other end of the table, with Seraphine to her right. Like Seraphine she was tall, but remarkably stately with her white hair sitting like a crown upon her head. She was a widow and the scioness of an abolitionist family which became rich through wise investments in the dynamic industrial expansion that developed from the Civil War. She was the promoter and benefactor of the *Interlink*.

The *Interlink* was something of a correspondence school of information, a human-interest school. Its chief object was the dissemination of valuable and authentic information concerning the way of life and the thought of different groups of people. This information was condensed and sent to members and other persons in the form of a monthly newsletter called the *Interlink*. The *Interlink* had member correspondents in Argentina, Brazil, Chile and other South American countries, Panama and the Caribbean Islands, Mexico, Canada, Alaska, Australia, the Netherland Indies, China, Korea, Japan, the Philippines, India, Iran, Egypt, South Africa, North Africa and West Africa, Spain, France, Italy, Austria, Turkey, Greece, Czecho-Slovakia, Finland, Scandinavia, Great Britain. It had no correspondents in Germany.

Its original name was the *Interracial Forum*, but after the Nuremberg decrees[2] were promulgated, setting the Nordic race apart from and above all other races, the name was changed to *Interlink*. Mrs. Hobison believed that the word "race" had become like a danger signal, threatening the existence of Civilization, and that decided her to drop "Interracial." Her newsletter was circulated among important people: bankers, industrialists, scions of great fortunes, brokers, heads of corporations, merchants, ministers of religion, editors, publishers, educators, social workers, governors, congressmen and other politicians. It was slanted to combat prejudice of all kinds and chiefly race prejudice, class prejudice and caste prejudice. It advocated the free promotion of literature, art and science, and also the aristocratic conception of society.

After the launching of the Popular Front movement, Soviet Russia was listed among the countries in which the *Interlink* had correspondents, but no reports from that land were ever published. But sometimes excerpts were reprinted from Soviet newspapers and magazines.

The social highlight of the *Interlink* was the once-a-month luncheon at which an informal discussion was initiated by an invited guest who had accomplished an achievement in any field of civilized endeavor. Mrs. Hobison was not like Mrs. Witern, bohemian-inclined and proletarian-minded. She lived an aristocratic life, but she believed in the aristocracy of service. She was extensively and intelligently informed about the affairs of the world and her keen mind was as alert as a bird's to the rustle of a leaf. She held that more than any the wealthy classes should be political-minded and aware of the social conditions of life on a world scale. She was contemptuous of people of consequence whose outlook was narrow and contended that misinformation was the chief cause of international confusion and misunderstanding. And so she had founded the *Interlink* as her contribution to the greater understanding and knowledge of human beings.

Mr. Montague Claxon was the director of the *Interlink*. The office was on lower Madison Avenue. It employed a considerable staff whose main work was to read and translate and clip excerpts from newspapers and magazines. Among them were a Chinese, a Mexican, a Hindu, a Brazilian, a Tunisian and a German exile. Claxon was a former newspaper correspondent who had lived in China in the late 1920s and had traveled in Japan, the Philippines and South America. He shared Mrs. Hobison's ideas and was an efficient executive.

When Maxim Tasan learned of Seraphine Peixota's predicament and that she was looking for a job, he immediately thought of her finding a place in the *Interlink*. Tasan had previously asked Montague Claxon why there was not an Aframerican on his staff. Claxon replied that he had not thought of it.

"But you should," said Tasan. "The Aframericans are like a small foreign nation within the United States. As foreign as the Chinese in China and Eskimos in Alaska. Did you ever think of that? Some thoughts in their newspapers need translating into American as much as an article from Iceland or Arabia."

"What you say is very illuminating," said Claxon. "The Aframericans have become so matter-of-course among us that few white persons realize they are practically strangers among us."

"They are your most problematic minority," said Tasan, "and the readers of the *Interlink* should know it."

"I'll tell Mrs. Hobison exactly what you say," said Claxon. "Of course, I could take on an Aframerican employee without telling her, for I have complete control over the staffing. But she'll be excited over your idea and surprised that we never thought of it. She's a true-blue descendant of abolitionists."

And Tasan said: "There are some people who are so encrusted in the aristocratic shell of a great tradition that they are apt to forget the true spirit of it." When Tasan was introduced to Abigail Hobison he had immediately formed an unfavorable opinion. He distrusted her lofty ideas about intellectual and cultural achievement and her bourgeois egoism in bracketing the class struggle with class prejudice and race prejudice. However, as a loyal soldier of the Soviet, he was fulsome in praise of the *Interlink*, hoping thus to win another recruit for the Popular Front.

In this case, as in many others, Tasan was successful. He was a close friend of Montague Claxon and was often at the offices of the *Interlink*, the entire staff of which were enthusiastic adherents to the Popular Front against war and Nazi-Fascism.

Tasan's view concerning the Aframericans was a novel and a pleasing surprise to Mrs. Hobison. It had never once flashed into her mind that they too were a subject people like Zulus and Indians and Malays. She had always seen them from the angle of a domestic problem. But quickly her prehensile mind was illuminated to see, like Tasan, that Aframericans were a colony of subject people within the nation. Perhaps the only reason why she and the others had not seen the thing before was because of the lack of perspective. The human eye is at its best when it is long-sighted and accustomed to look at horizons and beyond; the proximity of the Aframericans placed them in a disadvantageous light.

Mrs. Hobison was eager to have an Aframerican representative on the staff of the *Interlink*. But Seraphine was a little disappointing to her, when they met. Mrs. Hobison had anticipated an Aframerican as distinctly representative of the type as the Chinese and Hindu members of the staff were of theirs. But Seraphine was so astonishingly typically Euramerican! However, she was doubly interesting as a type and as a symbol, thought Mrs. Hobison; she would be excellent to illustrate the absurdity of the new Nordic theories of race.

Mrs. Hobison got Mrs. Witern's attention across the table and said: "We are using a very interesting item in next month's *Interlink*, a splendid letter that Mr. Ming has received about living conditions in Manchukuo. From a member of the Comintern, was it?"

"The Kuomintang, the Chinese National Party," said Mr. Ming.

"Oh, thank you," said Mrs. Hobison. "Sometimes I become confused about the names of the innumerable radical movements. But the Comintern is mentioned in the letter, am I right?"

"Yes," said Mr. Ming, "the Comintern is cooperating with the Left wing of the Kuomintang in an effort to bring the entire party and all of China into the Popular Front."

"Please excuse me for being so stupidly ignorant," said Seraphine, "but what *is* the Comintern?"

"It is the Communist International, my dear," said Mrs. Witern. "That is all the Communist parties in the world that are sections of the Russian Communist Party."

"Excuse me, please," said Mr. Ming, "but that is not technically correct. The Russian Communist Party is also a section of the Comintern. The Comintern or Communist International consists of all the Communist parties of the world that are recognised by the Executive Committee of the Comintern, which has its headquarters in Moscow. And the Executive Committee is composed of delegates from the various international parties."

"Thank you," said Seraphine, "although I still find it kind of complicated."

"You'll soon get on to it," said Mrs. Hobison, then speaking generally. "Now that Soviet Russia is collaborating with the democratic nations in mutual collective security, it is important that we should know the precise meaning of all those abbreviated words and algebraic letters which the Bolsheviks have loosed upon the poor world. I must confess that they appear to me sometimes like a pernicious epidemic."

"We are getting quite as bad ourselves in imitation of the Russians," said Claxon, "with our innumerable CCC and NLRB and FHA and AAA and TVA and NYA and FBI,[3] and I'd like to know why."

Everybody laughed and Mrs. Hobison said: "I suppose we'll have to learn them as we did our ABCs. This vast multiplying of abbreviations may have greater significance than we imagine. In Russia they sprung up after the Revolution. Who knows but that with us they may be the signs and portents of social revolution."

"There are more real signs and portents in what is taking place in Africa now," said Mr. Witern. "Mussolini has started the conflagration in Africa, but no one knows how far it may spread."

"Yes, the war in Ethiopia is an extremely dangerous adventure," agreed Montague Claxon. "I am publishing an interview with Lij Alamaya in the next issue of the *Interlink*—"

"Oh, I invited him to dinner too," said Mrs. Witern, "but he had a previous engagement."

Seraphine and Bunchetta winked at each other.

"I met him with Mr. Tasan at the office of the *Interlink*," said Mrs. Hobison. "A charming young person and very seriously concerned about the fate of his country. The Fascist attack upon Ethiopia is outrageous."

"And extremely dangerous," Montague Claxon repeated, "because it is motivated by the idea of the possibility of new imperial conquests and there can be no new imperial conquests without starting another world war. Mussolini might have gained more by employing methods of economic pressure with peaceful penetration. The Fascists shout insults at the British for opposing their action in Ethiopia. They charge that the British Empire was created by ruthless imperial conquests. They refuse to realize that such conquests were accomplished in another age before the industrial revolution was consummated. Today any highly industrialized nation can exploit a backward country by peaceful penetration. The United States set an example to the great powers, when it withdrew its naval and military forces from Haiti and signed an agreement with the Filipinos eventually to withdraw from the Philippines."[4]

"The withdrawal from Haiti was a masterstroke," said Bunchetta Facey. "We Aframericans were almost as jubilant as the Haitians. Because it filled us with hope that even as this country could excel in diplomacy and treat Haiti justly as a member of the family of nations, so likewise it might someday seriously apply itself to solve the problem of our people as citizens and members of the family of humanity."

Said Mrs. Hobison: "That was beautifully said, Miss Facey, and I wish that I had spoken it. If you develop the idea into a short article, we may feature it in the *Interlink*. Don't you think, Mr. Claxon?"

"It would be splendid," said Mr. Claxon, "if she will write it just as she said it."

"I'll do my best," said Bunchetta, "although my writing machinery has gone quite rusty." She was one of the promising talents of the Harlem literati, when they enjoyed a vogue in the 1920s. She had ideas about writing a sociological novel of Aframerican life and was encouraged by other writing people, but the job was never begun.

"I may be talking too much like a one hundred percent American," said Claxon, who had the appearance of a refined and shrewd type of Yankee salesman, "but I can't imagine any social problem too big for this nation to tackle and solve if it sets its mind to it. We are in the most enviable position of any nation and we can be the teacher of the world. We have the greatest natural resources and the finest industrial and technical equipment. We hold no colonies against their will and we're a young and vigorous and idealistic people."

The butler cleared the table of the dishes and served a fruit cup.

"Russia is the only nation that may be compared with us," said Mrs. Witern. "She hasn't reached our industrial standard, but she has the natural resources and no colonies. I believe that the hope and the future of the world lie in the United States and Russia working together. We can export our industrial technique to Russia and the people will understand our ideals, for they are being transformed with a fresh challenging outlook on social problems."

"And now that the Soviet had declared itself forthrightly for the democratic idea of world organization," said Montague Claxon, "both nations can work faithfully together for the ideal of Collective Security."[5]

"The Popular Front is the evangel of Collective Security," said Mrs. Witern, "and we must honor the genius of the Soviets for its invention. It has injected new life into the moribund League of Nations. Only Russia and America working closely together can defeat the abominable Nazi power and its barbaric pagan and ante-Christian conception of race and nation."

"You should include the British Empire," said Claxon, "for only Collective Security can save the British Empire from eventual collapse."

"The colonies of the Empire are a mill-stone around the neck of the British," said Mrs. Witern. "The British Empire is the greatest political anachronism of the industrial age. It is like a vast unending forest full of dry brittle brushwood in the path of the Nazi fire."

"Russia . . . Russia . . ." said Mr. Witern, speaking slowly with painful difficulty and shaking like a leaf. "Czarist Russia was an abomination, corrupting the body of the civilized nations. But Communist Russia was a menace to Civilization. But now that the Soviets have entered the League of Nations to work side by side with the democratic powers, perhaps our civilization will get a new lease of life. I believe in the Popular Front and Collective Security . . . anything that can save the world from Fascist vengeance, because I believe in humanity."

Mrs. Witern beamed and leaned over to stroke her husband's hand. But the effort to speak was so taxing, his head dropped as if he were falling asleep. Mrs. Witern rose and motioned the guests to the sitting room. Then tenderly she helped Mr. Witern to his feet and led him from the room.

By the time she returned to her guests the butler had already served them wine and other liquors, and warmed up by the spirits they animatedly continued the discussion.

A PRINCESS OF ETHIOPIA

The Hands to Ethiopia was reorganized with Dorsey Flagg elected chairman and secretary and the Rev. Zebulon Trawl treasurer. Newton Castle was unable to rally a group to support him. He was definitely shelved. But in Harlem and among the various branches throughout the country, the high enthusiasm which had perceptibly subsided could not be revived. And the war news from Ethiopia did not contribute to inspire confidence and bolster morale.

In spite of strenuous efforts by the newspapers to make the news favorable, the man-in-the-street in Harlem was aware that the Fascists were striking with moral thrusts at the last of the native empires of Africa. The big Aframerican weeklies excelled in clever devices to brace the courage and enthusiasm of their readers. Improving upon photographs of brave Ethiopian soldiers, they doctored them so that readers could not detect the unshod feet under the trim uniforms. The mild-looking Emperor Haile Selassie was pictured in his most martial pomp and shown at the front operating an anti-airplane gun. But Aframericans knew that there were few such guns in Ethiopia and that equestrian Ethiop officers with swords and battle-axes astride noble mules could not match their equipment against gas, airplanes and tanks.

Most undermining to Aframerican morale was the sudden return to the States of the jaunty and irrepressibly adventurous

Aframerican Colonel Hubert Fauntleroy Julian, a onetime favorite of Emperor Haile Selassie. Colonel Julian made statements which conveyed the impression that the Ethiopians were
already licked and blamed Haile Selassie for not coming to
terms with Mussolini. He was damned as a defeatist and Fascist spy and so enraged the militant-minded Aframericans that
they even suggested employing the exclusive Nordic exercise of
lynching against him. But his views were widely publicized
and inwardly the Aframericans were dismayed, for they knew
that the picaresque Colonel Hubert Fauntleroy Julian was not
the type that would desert a good ship, if it were not in danger
of sinking.

However, an unanticipated occurrence uplifted the flagging
spirits of the Aframericans. It was the exciting news of the
arrival of a Princess of Ethiopia. Her picture adorned the met-
ropolitan publications, an arresting marvel of jet radiance
whose lovely features were heightened by a gorgeously filigreed
gown and antique jewels ornamenting her neck and arms. The
Aframerican weeklies whipped up the item with banner headlines of primary colors.

The Princess Benebe Zarihana was heralded as a messenger
of hope and faith from Ethiopia. She also was an amateur pantomimist who had graciously condescended to give a few special performances for the benefit of Ethiopia. Princess Benebe
Zarihana was identified as a direct descendant of Falasha
(Black Jewish) Queen Judith, who ascended the throne of Ethiopia in the year 937 and reigned for forty years. She had arrived under the sponsorship of the Friends of Ethiopia. Unlike
the coming of Lij Alamaya, Harlem had no part in the glory of
welcoming the princess. Her sponsors may have agreed that
that was the best way of avoiding misunderstanding and exciting the jealousy of rival groups.

Most of the upper strata of Harlemites were partial to the
way in which the visit of the Princess Benebe was handled. The

fiasco of Lij Alamaya's spectacular debut in Harlem was fresh and irritating to their thoughts. They considered it more appropriate to the dignity of Ethiopia as a nation that the princess should be launched from downtown. Downtown was the seat of wealth and power. Harlem had little to offer besides excitement. Harlemites who desired to see her could go downtown as they usually did to see any celebrated Aframerican star resplendent in an Aryan setting.

Lela Witern, Abigail Hobison and Professor Banner Makepeace were chief among the sponsors of Princess Benebe. Her first appearance at the City Casino was a successful affair socially and financially. Lij Alamaya was her interpreter, as Princess Benebe did not speak English. Arrayed in striking rich costumes, the princess executed the following striking series of tableaux of the women of Ethiopia:

> A queen of Ethiopia in coronation robes
> Ethiopian woman in a bazaar
> Ethiopian woman in negligee
> Ethiopian noblewoman in her boudoir
> Ethiopian woman after the visit of the hairdresser
> Ethiopian woman in bridal costume
> Ethiopian bride reclining in her tent
> Ethiopian equestrienne
> Ethiopian woman arrayed for the battlefront
> Ethiopian mother and child

At the end of the pantomime Princess Benebe sang a plaintive Ethiopian song. Her voice was not great, but it was pleasingly rarely modulated and effective. It might have made its mark in a small concert room.

The distinguished audience threw off its dignity in generous applause of the Falasha Princess of Ethiopia. By its attitude one could gauge the degree of sympathy for the beleaguered

Ethiopian nation. There were present important personages in social, professional and political life. Their presence there was as much of a protest against ruthless aggression as it was an appreciation of an unusual talent among an obscure African people. Princess Benebe was just as fortunate in the impression she registered among the representatives of the Fourth Estate. The reviews of her tableaux were favorable, but it was particularly her personality that fetched the critics. The emphasis was on her poise and aplomb, her gait and charm and composite magnetism. One enthusiast marveled at the nobility inherent in her consummate African dignity, the indefinable artistry manifested in every shade of her movement. Another declared that she combined the classic grandeur of Duse with the wild wonder of the original appearance of Josephine Baker.[1]

But none of the notices equaled the *Labor Herald*'s in spread and length and abundance of phrases. The column and a half of the mellow and authoritative *Era* and *Forum* appeared parsimonious against the full-page modernistic extravaganza of the *Labor Herald*. The deftly arranged poses of Princess Benebe in her gilded costumes and golden slippers and jeweled tiara whipped the eye to dance with delight. And the purple blocks of baroque passages that heralded the artistry of the Imperial pantomimist appeared as if designed to whet the appetite of blasé sophisticates rather than for the instruction of proletarian readers. The *Labor Herald* did not neglect to mention Lij Alamaya's little contribution to the success of the performance. It carried his small photograph in an inset and commended him as an excellent interpreter.

Of goodly height, lissome and beautifully proportioned, despite the extravagant costumes which rarefied her performance, Princess Benebe Zarihana herself was entitled to all the praises. Her sponsors arranged for her to give special subscription performances for persons of means. Efforts were made to induce her to turn professional; one impresario made a juicy offer. But it was considered incompatible with the dignity of the Imperial House of Ethiopia that a princess should become a professional actress. Even in the extreme crisis of Ethiopia, Princess Benebe could not become a professional artiste without Imperial permission.

With the debut of Princess Benebe, the Friends of Ethiopia had held the limelight as the chief agency of aid for Ethiopia. Prudhomme Bishop, the president of the Equal Rights Action, was marshalling the elite and professional groups of Aframericans to support the Friends. Little was published about the progress of the Hands. And actually the work of the Hands was at a standstill. Dorsey Flagg was excellent as an animator on the platform, but he did not possess Peixota's organizing ability. And the defection of Lij Alamaya to the Friends was like the pulling of the main pole out of a tent.

Seraphine was employed on the staff of the *Interlink*. With Bunchetta's help she listed the important Aframerican publications to which the Society should subscribe. Her chief duties were the clipping of important pieces and pasting in the Aframerican scrapbook. Also from the Aframerican Division of the Harlem Library she obtained the names of Aframerican publications in the Caribbean area and of native publications in Africa. Seraphine liked the work and the atmosphere of it. But she had plenty to learn about modern social and international ideas and she applied herself assiduously. She learned rapidly and soon she was able to converse tolerably with her co-workers about the important topics of the times, such as the New Deal, war in Ethiopia, Nazism, Fascism and Communism and the Popular Front.

She and Bunchetta moved downtown. Not actually in Greenwich Village, they found a comfortable place on Second Avenue, below Fourteenth Street. Maxim Tasan was a frequent visitor to the *Interlink* offices to see his friend Montague Claxon. He was interested in the Aframerican newspapers and often glanced through them. He became better acquainted with Seraphine, ingratiatingly chatted with her about the work, appreciated her efforts, and she considered him a nice person.

It was a surprise to Seraphine when Tasan asked her if she would like to work in the office of the Friends of Ethiopia, to fill the place that was formerly held by Gloria Kendall. Seraphine said she liked her work with the *Interlink* and besides, Montague Claxon was exceptionally nice to her. But Tasan assured her that he had already talked about the proposal to Claxon and the salary would be forty dollars weekly, twice the amount that Seraphine received for part-time work with the *Interlink*. It was good pay and Seraphine agreed to make the change, especially as Claxon was agreeable to it. At her suggestion, Claxon employed one of the Tower girls, Iris Marlow, in her place.

Seraphine zestfully devoted herself to the new job. She still nursed some resentment against Lij Alamaya, but it was cooled by the elation she felt when he was humbled to take a secondary role in the triumph of the majestic and inaccessible Princess Benebe. Once when he visited the office of the Friends, unaware that Seraphine was there, it was he who was embarrassed. And she tried to make him feel at ease, talking about trivialities as if there had never existed a sentimental attachment between them.

Tasan never mentioned Pablo Peixota nor tried to get Seraphine to talk about her parents and her attitude towards them. He was perfectly satisfied in having Peixota's daughter working with the Friends of Ethiopia and safe in the bosom of the Popular Front. He would have listened eagerly had Seraphine wanted to tell him anything. But she had not even considered the idea of his being interested. She had never attached any social significance to the difference between the Friends of Ethiopia and the Hands to Ethiopia and when the latter was indirectly the cause of her misunderstanding with Alamaya, she was disgusted with it. Now that she was working for the Friends she was convinced that it was the superior article.

One Friday evening Tasan invited Seraphine and Bunchetta to dinner. He also had as his guest a Frenchman named Jean Danou. The Frenchman was an ardent Popular Frontist. He was an adherent of the Socialist (International) Center group in France. Up until 1933 he was militantly anti-Soviet. But like thousands of other Left Republican and Socialist Frenchmen, his social ideas underwent a profound change after the 1934 riots when Royalists and Right Republicans gave battle to the Leftists in the streets of Paris. Since then he had swung clear over to the support of the Soviets with intense Gallic ardor and Latin realism, armed with the conviction that only the Soviets in alliance with the remaining Democratic countries could stop the march of Nazism and Reaction.

Jean Danou was the son of an industrialist who was an extreme Rightist. He visited Russia in 1934 and had arrived in America by way of Japan and China. America was a puzzling phenomenon to Jean Danou. In spite of the Great Depression and mass unemployment that he had read about, the inhabitants, unlike Europeans, did not appear to be profoundly agitated by the social catastrophe. The social tension in France had been destructive to governments and political parties, while refugees were pouring across the border from Germany. The lights of Montmartre and Montparnasse were dim in La Ville Lumière, while the Broadway façade of New York was as scintillant as ever.

Maxim Tasan and his guests had dinner in a Broadway bright spot. Tasan had arranged to see a Soviet film showing in Forty-Second Street. It was specially for the benefit of Danou, who had not seen the film when it was first released in Europe, because until 1935 France had maintained a ban against Soviet motion pictures. The picture was entitled *A Song of Lenin*.[2] It portrayed Lenin more as a social crusader with emphasis on his love of children than as a lion-hearted revolutionist. It was saccharine sentimental and soaked in sanctimonious music.

In the middle of it Seraphine exclaimed: "Why, it's just like the gospel story for kids." She spoke loudly enough and drew reproving sh-h-h-h's from members of the rapt audience. The Frenchman whispered: "It is very good propaganda for the Popular Front."

When they left the theatre, Maxim Tasan said that it was an educational picture and it had been one of the most successful Soviet films among the backward peoples in the distant provinces of Russia.

Jean Danou said: "We should make a film like that in France about the life of Jean Jaurès.[3] He was a great good man. If he had not been assassinated at the outbreak of the war in 1914, the history of France might have been different today. He was our greatest leader and statesman."

"Yes, Jaurès was a big man," Tasan agreed, "but I've often wondered if he would have been big enough to support the Bolsheviks."

"I believe he would have been big enough to understand and support Lenin and prevent the split in the Socialist Party," said Jean Danou.

"The night is still young and inviting," said Bunchetta, "and what shall we do with it?"

"I imagine Danou would like to visit Harlem," said Tasan. "You haven't been there yet, have you?"

"That's precisely what I want to do," said Danou.

The party proceeded to Harlem and went directly to the famous Lindy Hop Rendezvous. It was a mammoth hall enlivened by twinkling bands of eurythmic adepts who demonstrated the Lindy Hop in its exhilarating variations to the clashing artillery of two orchestras, a black and a white, which galloped over the course like two racehorses in hot competition for a grand prize.

Those who could not make the extravagantly fantastic paces

enjoyed from the sidelines the performance of the more proficient, who essayed to follow the promptings of the galaxy of
professionals. During the interlude of a waltz Tasan danced
with Seraphine and Jean Danou with Bunchetta. And when a
one-step followed the waltz, they changed partners.

From the Lindy Hop Rendezvous they went to a cabaret
which specialized in elaborate floor shows. Jean Danou was not
particularly impressed. "I don't like the evolution of the cabaret
into a kind of variety show," he said. "I prefer the theatre for
that. It was introduced in Paris after the war by the Americans
and the Russian émigrés. But the best cabarets are still the small
intimate ones in which one good performer excels."

"The Russians who could afford it were always ostentatious
and prodigal in their amusement," said Tasan. "When they
fled from Moscow and Petrograd they carried the style to Berlin and Paris, Istanbul and Shanghai. You pampered too many
émigrés in France; they should have been sent back to Russia."

"The Nazis have sent us their émigrés, besides swamping us
with refugees. Now we are almost demoralized with émigrés
and pitiful refugees on our hands who are more of a hindrance
to the operating of the Popular Front. New York is lucky with
business and amusement going on as usual. While those Lindy
Hoppers were performing with such wonderful agility and élan,
sans souci, I was thinking of the week when the Camelots du
Roy spread havoc[4] in Montmartre and Montparnasse, breaking
up the amusement places and insulting the performers and the
guests, especially foreigners."

"And did they insult the Aframericans too?" said Bunchetta.

"Everybody," said Danou. "They didn't show any discrimination."

"Civilization is in a sweet mess," said Bunchetta, "like a big
jar of assorted sweet pickles."

She suggested their going to her favorite place, the Airplane, where they could relax as if it were a house party. "I don't care much for cabarets. A bar is better."

There was one other party at the Airplane when they arrived there. It consisted of Dorsey Flagg and two members of the Executive Committee of the Hands to Ethiopia, Elks Exalted Ruler William Headley and the taciturn Dr. Phineas Bell, who was active in working out the details of the ambulance unit. Dorsey Flagg had imbibed copiously and was still at it, but his hefty coeur-de-lion body was capable of absorbing an enormous amount of alcohol without deleterious effects. He was talking when Maxim Tasan and his guests entered and he did not respond to the casual greetings of Bunchetta and Seraphine. Apparently he intentionally ignored them.

"Ethiopia was sold from the source of the Nile down the river," he was saying. "And the world knows it. Europe has no use for a native nation in Africa. They can pull wool over black folks' eyes, but they can't fool me."

"I can't see any sense in taking sanctions against Italy and not allowing arms to be shipped to Ethiopia," said Dr. Bell.

"Why, Italy has enough war materials and supplies to lick ten Ethiopias," said Dorsey Flagg. "Besides, the sanctions aren't real. Soviet Russia, the goddam viper, is sending Italy all the oil and other supplies she needs."

"But I thought it was Soviet Russia that started the Popular Front to fight the Fascists and the Nazis, isn't it?" said Headley.

"The Popular Front!" Flagg sneered. "Take it from me, Soviet Russia started the Popular Front in the interest of Soviet Russia. The Popular Front is an instrument designed by the crafty Stalin and his fellow conspirators to confuse the nations and take Democracy on a grand ride of destruction. I have opposed it and will continue to oppose it. But who wants to listen to the voice of a black man in America unless it is trained to sing spirituals or blues?"

Tasan grunted and looked fixedly and grimly at Jean Danou. Impulsively Danou got up and went over to Dorsey Flagg's table and said: "Pardon me, my friend, but what you're saying is very important. I'm a stranger, a Frenchman and I'm an ardent supporter of the Popular Front. Perhaps if you had recently lived in Europe like me, if you had seen the Fascists and Nazis organizing and marching in the heart of Democracy, if you had seen their bullets whiz by to drop your comrades dead, and frightened refugees, men and women and children, fleeing from their vengeance, you might have thought differently about the Popular Front. I am not a Communist. I am a Socialist, but we Socialists were convinced that we could stop the Nazis only with Soviet Russia."

Flagg was astonished when the Frenchman accosted him. The unwelcome sight of Maxim Tasan had stimulated him in his attack on the Popular Front, but he was a little touched by the emotional intensity of Jean Danou and inclined to listen. "You have great faith," said Flagg, "but I also am convinced that Stalin and the Communists will never be loyal allies of the Socialists and Democracy. The only decent Communists who might have kept their pledged word with Socialists and Democracy have been assassinated or otherwise liquidated by the Stalinists. You talk about the Hitler purges and the desperate condition of the refugees. I know they are frightful beyond description. But the Stalin purges and system are just as bad. Besides, it was the Soviet Dictatorship that destroyed German Social Democracy, when it ordered the German Communists to war against the Social Democrats and open the road to conquest for the Nazi Dictatorship."

"That is the Trotskyite point of view, comrade," said the Frenchman. "I too used to think that Trotsky was right in his attacks upon Stalin as an unscrupulous and diabolical dictator. But I am convinced now that Trotsky is wrong. He is too purely intellectual, too much of a theorist. Trotsky is not a practical statesman."

Flagg excitedly thumped the table. "I am not a Trotskyite. Trotsky is a Communist. I am not a Communist. Trotsky believes in the Dictatorship of the Proletariat, even though it is crucifying him. I don't believe in any dictatorship. But Trotsky is a great intellect and I believe he should have the right to speak to the world. Jerusalem had its Jeremiahs and Troy its Cassandras. But the Stalinites are making use of the Popular Front to silence and persecute all those who are opposed to them. They make tools of the near-sighted liberals to do their dirty work. They have revived the Inquisition; they have a blacklist of organizations and individuals: teachers, ministers, labor leaders, ordinary workers, doctors, publishers, editors, artists and writers—all those whom they cannot dominate or influence. My dear Sir, the Popular Front is a fraud and the prostitute of Stalin. God save the world from the Popular Front."

The Frenchman said: "You are emotional, but—"

"Pardon me, but I am not," said Flagg. "I have to use my head against the Stalinite hyena."

"I regret, my friend," said the Frenchman. "Once upon a time we French Socialists felt just like you about the Communists. But now there is no middle way. It is a clear-cut issue of choosing between the Fascists and Nazis on one side and the Communists on the other. A few years ago we used to sneer at the Fascists purging the Italians with castor oil; today they stand with the Nazis ready to purge the world with bayonets. We cannot oppose guns and bayonets with razor-edged, lightning-flash words like Trotsky—"

"But why Trotsky, always Trotsky!" shouted Flagg.

"Because he is the spearhead of the opposition to Stalin," said the Frenchman. "But you should understand the Popular Front is not merely a movement. It is a world organization with nations backing it. The French government has a defensive treaty with Soviet Russia. The French Socialist Party is allied with the French Communist Party in the Popular Front. Spain, Czecho-Slovakia, and China are in it. But we need Britain and the United States—especially the United States. We need all the people and the people are coming fast. You are lost if you are not in the Popular Front."

"I think France is lost if she stays in the Popular Front," said Dorsey Flagg. "What is a pact with Stalin worth? It is worth no more than the lives of the Old Bolshevists who made a sacred pact among themselves to overthrow the Czarists. Any government or people who put their trust in Stalin will be betrayed."

"I hope you are wrong," said the Frenchman, "but I admire your courage. Won't you shake my hand? They call me Jean Danou." He gave his hand and Flagg grasped it, saying: "And I am Dorsey Flagg." He introduced his companions.

When Jean Danou returned to his table, Buster, the boss of the Airplane, had served ginger ale, which was flavored by Tasan with the liquor he had previously purchased at Bunchetta's suggestion.

Tasan said in an undertone: "You shouldn't have shaken hands with that Trotskyite scoundrel."

"He pleases me somehow in spite of that," replied the Frenchman. "He is brave, with a mind of his own. Most of those of his race I have met from our African colonies are bright parrots echoing undigested ideas."

"The Aframericans do not have a native colonial mentality," said Tasan. "They are very American, more than some of the white groups, and their intelligence just as high on the average and higher in many individual cases, according to my observation. Their weakness is their not having consolidated any economic assets as a group. And because of that they have no political power that is worth a damn. But you should beware of taking them for exotics, the way you French regard your colonials. That kind of romanticism is only a miserable democratic bitch."

"Every intelligent Frenchman knows that true romanticism was the herald of modern individualism," said Danou. "But individualism is in a state of agony today. And that is why that colored man is so very interesting. His is the real rugged individualism. A rare thing to find in any person today. I am convinced that he is neither a Trotskyite nor a Stalinite."

"And that makes him even more dangerous," said Tasan. "He stands alone and may succeed in commanding a following. No influential man must be allowed to stand alone. For these are times when people must be converted or compelled to mass thinking so that the engineers of the new world order can obtain the maximum of mass action. As you said, the era of individual thought is ending. The modern age of mass production and social revolution also demands mass thinking. We have correlated both in Russia and are developing it far and wide in the Comintern. We have a secret admiration for the Nazi bastards, because they stole our blueprints to develop a wonderfully successful totalitarian organization."

"I hope we can overtake and beat them with the Popular Front," said Danou.

"We can do it, but only if the Comintern can control and eradicate the disease of international democracy," said Tasan.

For a moment Danou was a little more thoughtful. Then he said: "Democracy *is* diseased, it's true. But it can be cured, if the Socialists become the dominant partner in the Comintern. We are closer to the middle classes, who are the backbone of the Popular Front."

Tasan hunched his shoulders and laughed with his tongue between his teeth, hissing like a snake.

Sitting together between their escorts, Seraphine and Bunchetta conducted a whispering conversation between them, chiefly gossiping about Harlem and the Tower group. Sometimes Bunchetta cocked her ears to catch an important statement from the men talking. But Seraphine drank a lot, which unfitted her to fix her mind on serious topics, so she relaxed into her regular ways and claimed most of Bunchetta's attention.

Dorsey Flagg had heard that Seraphine had moved from her parents' house and was living with Bunchetta downtown. When he was leaving with his friends Seraphine waved at him and said in a tipsy tone: "Don't go yet, Dorsey, come and sit with us." Flagg gave her a sharp unfriendly "no" and went to the bar to square his account with Buster.

Seraphine giggled and leaning on Tasan she put up her hands around his neck, agitating her shoulders and amorously rubbing her back against him. She giggled all the time and as Flagg was going out she cried at him: "Don't be so high-hat and nasty, Dorsey, because you can't have everything your own way. You and Father make a nice pair and I hope you two will save Ethiopia. G'bye, Dorsey dear, I'm in the Popular Front now."

Flagg turned back and bending over he whispered in her ear. Seraphine instantly straightened up: "You pig!" she shouted, and, as Flagg lumbered out, "Pig! Black pig!"

A PRE-NUPTIAL NIGHT

In the afternoon of the following Monday, Seraphine went to Harlem to get some personal belongings which were left behind when she departed from her parents' house. Her mother went to the door when she rang, coldly responded to her greeting and let her in. Seraphine said she had come to get her things and went up to her room, carrying a suitcase.

While she was packing her things, Mrs. Peixota entered the room. She had resolved at first not to say anything to her daughter, when she opened the door. But Seraphine's coming had started a fire of tumultuous feeling which she could not put down. Seraphine's impulsive action had struck like a gravedigger's shovel into an old coffin and pitched her mother back into the Gethsemane[1] of her maidenhood, overwhelming her with agony. And wrestling with the heavy thoughts of unhappy memories more sharply remembered than ever, Mrs. Peixota felt that she must speak to her daughter.

"So you've completely made up your mind, I guess," she said. "You're making a final move."

"Yes, Mother, I've made up my mind to go for good."

"You may go for good and find bad and live to regret it. There is still time for you to beg your father's pardon and stay under this roof."

"But why should I ask Father's pardon, Mother? I have not done him any wrong—I don't think. And if he has done me any wrong I forgive him. I've moved because it is best for me. Downtown I have more freedom."

"Freedom!" Mrs. Peixota cried contemptuously. "You had too much freedom here and that's the real trouble. Your father and I gave you a ninety-nine-year lease of freedom and the means to enjoy it more than any other girl in Harlem. But it was my mistake to encourage you too much to fool with Lij Alamaya—"

"Lij Alamaya, Mother! I have more important things to worry about. I moved because I want more room to live in. Harlem is suffocating. But downtown I can breathe. Down there life has more meaning."

"Nonsense! Life may be full of meaning anywhere, if you have eyes to see and a heart to feel and a mind to understand. But you have been spoiled by comfortable living with so much misery around you in Harlem. And you're blinded by the bright lights of Broadway."

"That's so old-fashioned and funny, Mother. The lights of Harlem are just as bright. I am not living on Broadway of the bright lights. I am living way down on Second Avenue, which isn't as nice a street as Harlem's Strivers' Row. But it's different and that means a lot. I'm not playing downtown, I'm working."

"I know. With the White Friends of Ethiopia. You know how your father detests them. But I'd guess you went to work for them to spite him."

"I didn't, Mother. Why should I worry my young life with Father's hates and prejudices?"

"They are prejudices that were forced upon your people by the whites that you adore. You will come to understand that much."

"I have no people. Why should I be limited to any special group of people? I believe in the Popular Front."

"So that's it!" said Mrs. Peixota. "You're crazy like all the rest about the latest fad. And you may be the most 'popular front' downtown for all I know. And that may be the freedom you like so much. But let me tell you this, if you get mixed up in that Communist comradeship with a lot of free-loving and easy-riding white men, you're no daughter of mine, you understand?"

"Mother!" Seraphine whined.

"I mean what I say. I have heard enough about your free and easy carrying on with white men. And let me tell you: no decent colored girl can afford to be careless with a white man. For she isn't protected by the law or by public opinion. Our black mothers paid the price in servitude and concubinage so that we could learn and acquire a little self-respect. You chits imagine you're modern and can teach your elders. White men are modern and ready to make a 'popular front' of you all right, but they won't marry you. They'll use you—"

"Mother, please!"

"I'll say what I want to say even if the truth hurts. I'm warning you about white men and if you're crazy about them, it is better for you to pass white than remain a disgrace to the colored race." Mrs. Peixota flung out of the room and the bang of the door startled Seraphine like the shooting of a gun.

Upset by the encounter with her mother, Seraphine did not go to work that afternoon. At five o'clock, before leaving the office, Maxim Tasan telephoned Seraphine at her apartment. She informed him that she had not worked because she was upset and worried after a visit to Harlem. She was not sure she could continue on the job. Tasan was concerned. Perhaps Peixota was trying to influence Seraphine to quit. He said he would go to see her that evening. But remembering that Bunchetta and Seraphine stayed together and that Seraphine might be handicapped in talking he telephoned again and invited her to dinner at his apartment.

Tasan lived in the Seventies, off Central Park West. Previously he inhabited an apartment in one of the palaces of Central Park

West. But there were complaints from the tenants, because of the various assortment of visitors of all types. And he had moved to avoid complications. His new place, situated in a private house renovated and made over into apartments, was exactly suited to his needs. He had an entire floor of four rooms, which assured him enough freedom and privacy.

When Seraphine got there Tasan was preparing cocktails. Another visitor was cooking the dinner. Tasan introduced him as his friend, Augustus Nordling. He was a hulking big young fellow with a shock of hair that stood up flaming like a cluster of dandelions. Perhaps it was because of this that he was called Dandy. He was excessively ruddy, as if the blood had burst his veins and flooded over the dam of the epidermis. He was bubbling urbanity and greeted Seraphine as if he had known her all her life.

All three drank a cocktail each. And Dandy, saying the dinner was nearly ready, went into the kitchen, while Tasan proceeded to set the table. Meanwhile he appeased Seraphine's curiosity about Dandy. He had a job with the *Labor Herald*, and was often a visitor at Tasan's place. He was an excellent cook and on rare occasions when Tasan ate in his apartment, Dandy volunteered to cook the meal.

The dinner was solid fare, an enormous juicy steak with fried potatoes, peas and creamed onions, lettuce and tomatoes. From a cabinet Tasan took two bottles of imported French wine, a Sauternes and a Pommard, and placed them on the table. Seraphine said she preferred Sauternes. Tasan pulled the cork from both bottles. "Let us drink a toast to la belle France," he said, "who leads all the nations in the Popular Front. Long live the alliance between the French Republic and the Soviet Republic—the greatest achievement in Soviet diplomacy since Lenin died."[2]

"Do you imagine that that was a greater victory for the Soviets than obtaining United States recognition?" said Dandy.

"Many of the comrades believe that that is the biggest feat of Soviet diplomacy in ten years."

"You Americans are too provincial, Dandy," said Tasan, "and American Communists have the same faults as the rest of their countrymen. They imagine that everything American is the biggest and the best, because their thinking is dominated by skyscrapers and tractors and steel spans. The America that recognized Soviet Russia in 1934 is an entirely different nation from the America that did not recognize her in 1924, when Lenin died."

"And Europe in 1934 is a vastly different place from Europe in 1924," said Nordling. "In 1924 Germany was a Social-Democratic vassal state. In 1934 it became the Nazi terror of Europe. I appreciate your political insight, but I can't see that it is provincial or chauvinistic to recognize the fact that for ten years since the World War, Europe was economically dependent upon America."

"That is true, but it wasn't practical economics and the result was financial collapse and social chaos. To be of constructive value economic dominance must be accompanied by superior cultural influence. But culturally America is dependent on Europe and even industrially, if you take a long view of the international setup. America is big and brawny, but Europe has the best brains. And France's is the subtlest and supplest. That is why the Soviet alliance with France is more important than the biggest deal it could make with America. It is the big beginning of a grand new era in Europe."

Nordling was profoundly impressed. "And the world," he said. "I agree with you that Europe dominates the mind of the world. It will be wonderful, if the Soviet does not encounter a setback, if France doesn't double-cross her."

"France cannot even if she wanted to. We've got the cock moulting in the chicken coop," Tasan chuckled. "If France double-crosses Soviet Russia, she'll be cutting her own throat and ending her national existence. The advent of Nazism was God's gesture in favor of Soviet Russia. We've got the number of bourgeois democracy and the key to its future. As for the Socialists, for fifteen years they've been calling us bloody assassins and refusing to shake our hands. Now we'll make them eat out of our bloody hands."

"But Jean Danou thinks the alliance will help the Socialists," said Dandy. "Make them the dominant partner in the Popular Front and give them control of France."

"Jean Danou is an idealist sentimentalist and hopelessly confused," said Tasan. "A sentimental Frenchman is something awful, like a dose of sugared castor oil. It is easier to take the platitudes of an Englishman, because he is a sentimental realist. The Socialists will either be wiped out in next month's elections in France or have a temporary minority success. But they won't be in a position to do anything Socialistic without the power of the Communists. The Popular Front is a Soviet ship and the officers and crew are all Soviet. The passengers are the bourgeois elite, but we've got the Socialists jailed in the hold."

Seraphine had kept up interest in the drift of the conversation, not altogether understandingly, but considering it a social necessity to function at the table otherwise than as a mere wine-bibber, she said: "Tell me, Maxim, how will Aframericans figure in the Popular Front? What place will they get? My father says that the Popular Front will help them about as much as the League of Nations helped Ethiopia."

Tasan looked indulgently at Seraphine as a distinguished dinner guest might turn a complimentary eye upon the decorative monogram of his serviette. "Mr. Peixota is a cynic," he said. "The League of Nations is the instrument of imperialist nations. Only Soviet Russia tried to make it serve the needs of the people. But alone Soviet Russia could not change an imperialistic instrument into a people's weapon. Ethiopia has served the world, for it will be the grave of the League of Nations and the Popular Front will triumph. The Popular Front will give Aframericans their second emancipation and end all prejudice and discrimination."

"Bravo!" said Dandy. "We'll have to intensify the drive to convert the Aframericans, even against their will. During the Civil War thousands of them sided with their oppressors."

"Let's drink to the Aframerican minority and its conquest by the Popular Front," said Tasan.

They stood up and drank and Tasan started singing unmelodiously:

> All hail the power of the Popular Front,
> Which all the people of the world unite,
> Armed with Democracy we march to hunt
> And slay the dragon, Fascist-Trotskyite.

"Let's dance it too and be happy," said Tasan. And he and Seraphine and Dandy held hands and danced into the sitting room. It had the appearance of a spacious study, with many pieces of small and low bookcases set between little tables, chairs, and other furniture, against the wall. They were stacked with books in many languages: Russian, English, German, French, and there were a few in Italian and Spanish. The majority of the books were new and mainly about politics, sociology and travel. Magazines and newspapers were set on end tables and leather cushions and a lot of them were piled up unkemptly on a chest in a corner.

"Let's mix the drinks and make a punch," said Tasan. "It's easier than cocktails and more fun."

Dandy fetched a bowl from the kitchen and they dumped the rest of the cocktail in it, adding lemon juice and orange juice and more whiskey and wine. Seraphine made herself comfortable on the broad couch-bed.

"Have you seen Newton Castle recently?" said Tasan. "He didn't keep an appointment with me last Saturday."

Seraphine said she hadn't seen Newton, but that Mrs. Castle had visited their new apartment the first week she and Bunchetta moved downtown.

"He's having trouble with her, I believe," said Tasan, "ever since he led the pickets against the Rev. Trawl's church. She thought his action was too extreme and that his position as a teacher will be in danger if he keeps it up. Newton is very worried and we might have to find him another woman." Tasan laughed and scratched his thigh.

"Delta was always a pretty good sport," said Seraphine. "But the last time I saw her she did say that Newton was getting on her nerves. Life is a messy business anyhow and Harlem is a big mess."

"But you're out of Harlem now," said Tasan. "You're out of the mess."

"I wish I was, but actually I'm not," said Seraphine. "I'm a Harlemite, even if I am living downtown."

From a cabinet which contained a set of modernistic old-fashioned tumblers, Tasan took two and filled them with punch. He handed Seraphine one and sat down beside her.

"Where is Dandy?" she suddenly asked.

"He went out," said Tasan. "I suppose he had a date."

"But he didn't even tell us he was going!"

"That's nothing. He's informal like all of us, but you'll see him again. Now we can talk more freely about yourself."

"Yes, that's really why I am here," said Seraphine. "But it's a nice evening and it's a shame that it should be spoiled with my troubles."

"Nothing that you say could make an evening unpleasant," said Tasan. "Besides, I am really concerned about your troubles, when they interfere with your work. I was more worried than you perhaps, when you said that you might have to quit the job."

"Were you? That's real nice of you," said Seraphine. "I wish my mother was a teeny bit as sympathetic and understanding as you are. But she's as hard as nails and annoying as a horsefly all because of that old man Peixota and his crazy ideas about Ethiopia."

"What did she have to say?"

"I guess Dorsey Flagg must have told them about my being with you at the Airplane. You remember when Dorsey whispered in my ear and I called him a pig and you wanted to know why and I wouldn't tell you? Well, Mother said the same thing to me except that her language was not so filthy—she didn't make an obscene rhyming pun on the Popular Front like him, the pig!"

Tasan was excitedly curious: "But what did he say exactly?"

"Oh, I won't repeat it. It isn't funny and yet it is in a way. Life is full of nastiness. But what Mother said hurt me more. She put a curse on me. She said if I go with a white man, she will disown me, I will be no more daughter of hers, o-o-oh!" Tears sprang to Seraphine's eyes and she hid them with her handkerchief.

"Don't be upset by that," Tasan spoke soothingly. "Why should *you* be colored? You're colored because you *imagine* you are. But you are whiter than I—as white as Dandy Nordling. Maybe I've got a lot more colored blood than you, and I am white. I am not certain what I am, except that I'm an internationalist. There are millions of white-colored people who imagine they are pure white, whatever that absurdity is. Southern Spain and Southern Italy, the Balkans, the Caucasus, Turkey and the rest of the Near East have been absorbing the gulf stream of colored blood for hundreds of years. South America too and also these United States with their childish ideation—their damnable ludicrous reiteration of white! White! WHITE! Idiotic braggarts! Acting as if they know their corpuscles are tainted and are trying to hide the fact."

"But American culture and science is based on that," said Seraphine. "This thing you call 'ideation of white.' Americans are cradled in it. It is the basis of their moral code, out of which they have created laws like those of the Medes and Persians."

"The United States have no culture and no science beside engineering," said Tasan contemptuously. "Americans are merely the wandering tribes of Europe, who accidentally discovered a kingdom of marvelous natural resources. They possessed the skill to exploit these natural resources to build the biggest industrial system in the world. But the achievement dwarfed them intellectually. We Europeans have a sense of the cultural unity of Europe. We think of ourselves as Europeans. There are Europeans who are almost as swarthy as Africans. We could not think of 'race' and 'white' in the provincial American way."

"But how can that be with so many European nations asserting their independence and always fighting one another? I can't see any unity in that," said Seraphine.

"But in spite of the conflict, they are all European nations," said Tasan. "Under the ancient Roman Empire, a citizen of the Empire was a Roman whether he was born in Africa or Asia. And the Holy Roman Empire was based upon the unity of Europe and the oneness of humanity. And though Europe retrogressed and was split up by national rivalries, the basic cultural unity remains. We have no ideological 'race or color' conflicts such as create an infernal cleavage in the cultural unity of the United States."

"But I don't understand," said Seraphine. "Europe has the Nazis and the Jewish problem; America has the Ku Klux Klan and the Aframericans, but the Ku Klux Klan is not the government."

"The Jewish problem is not a race problem," said Tasan. "It is a problem of religion and rooted in primitive mysticism. The Nazis have copied the methods of the Ku Klux Klan and the ideas of pseudo-scientists—Hitler specially exalted the false

American conception of race in his *Mein Kampf*. He got ideas from a mad Englishman named Chamberlain and Frenchman called Gobineau.[3] We are fighting the Nazis with the Popular Front. And they will be defeated. If the democratic nations refuse to follow the leadership of Soviet Russia, then the Nazis may conquer Europe, but they cannot win out with their wild racial theories. Europe will finally tame them. Europe will never accept the Nazi ideas of race, for Soviet Russia is the biggest and greatest European nation and it is half Asiatic."

"Your ideas sound very fine," said Seraphine. "But in reality there are black people and white, yellow people and brown. And they *are* divided into races. God willed it to be so, whatever He may be."

"Don't be such a fatalist," said Tasan. "God made you white and you imagine you are black. Did you ever hear of Pushkin?"[4]

"Yes," said Seraphine. "Aframericans claim him as a great colored genius."

"Pushkin was a Russian," said Tasan. "And he was the father of Russian literature. His grandfather was black, an Ethiopian slave. Czar Peter the Great made him his personal attendant. The Czar was a mighty Russian and a great European. He valued men for what they were worth and not by the texture of their skin or the quality of their birth. He discovered big potentialities in his Ethiopian and made him an officer. And he married him to a Russian noblewoman. Today the descendants of Pushkin are scattered over Europe; they marry into the best European families; they are proud of their paternity, which is generally known. But they are Russians, not Russafricans."

"In America, they would have been Aframerican like me," said Seraphine.

"Yes, and that is why I insist that European values are sounder, in spite of the eruption of the diabolical Nazis."

"And you imagine I could be like the descendants of Pushkin?"

"Yes, you should not hog-tie your life. You should dare to

do and do, get every ounce of living you can out of the scale of life. Be venturesome and pioneering out of the blackness of Harlem. Look at me. I have gone around and across the world, kicking bourgeois prejudice in its fat face."

"But you are a *man*," Seraphine cried. "I'm a woman and colored—while your parents are alive, it isn't easy to cut yourself loose. I thought I could be as free among white as among colored. Mother was always broad-minded and encouraged me to flirt with colored men. But she called me a whore for acting the same way with white. And Father was worse—he threatened to stick the cops on me if I went around in the company of white men. And Father has political power. He could fix it and have me arrested and disgraced, even if nothing came of the charges. Just like his case."

Pablo Peixota had not seen or spoken to Seraphine since she walked out of his house. Yet deliberately she concocted this lie about him. Regarding him in her resentment as the principal cause of her troubles, her misunderstanding with Lij Alamaya and her quarrel with her mother, she endeavored to represent him as the embodiment of evil.

"The damned scoundrel," said Tasan. "I always felt that in his blind hatred and distrust of all whites he was capable of the vilest act. He ought to be lynched. I tell you, Seraphine, you ought to marry a white man."

"You think so? But I hate the idea of 'passing.'"

"Passing hell. You should never imagine that you are 'passing.' How much more can I explain that to you? Only imbeciles play at the game of 'passing.' Just be yourself, sure of yourself and proud of being what you are. Any so-called white would be glad to marry you—any goddam son of a Nordic would go down on his knees to you."

"Oh, do you really mean that?" said Seraphine, leaning heavily and warmly against Tasan.

He adjusted himself to accommodate her. "Sure I do, and I

would even include myself if I were handsome and a Nordic. But I guess I'm only good for propaganda."

"You're as fine as the handsomest," said Seraphine, "and you're even finer because you have a real heart."

Tasan fondled Seraphine's face. "In my work there is little time for sentimentality," he said, "but you are not like other women. You're a jewel. I knew it the first time I set eyes on you."

Tasan seemed to be undergoing a miraculous transfiguration by the magic of the moment and he appeared like a tropical chameleon tautened from head to tail and strangely gradually changing the color of his skin.

Seraphine whispered: "You're a darling."

They remained silent for some time, Tasan brooding-like over the relaxed figure of Seraphine. Suddenly she started up and cried: "Oh, it's late, I've got to go home."

"You haven't *got to go home*," said Tasan. "We have just finished arguing about daring to be yourself and living venturesomely. Let us relax now and forget about problems, you and I. We both need the tonic of relaxation. Let's drink some more and forget." Seraphine replied with only a long sigh.

Tasan went to the electric ice box to get fresh cubes of ice for the bowl. And then he poured an assortment of liquor in it.

SERAPHINE DISCOVERS
THE LETTER

In Maxim Tasan's apartment the following day at high noon Seraphine stirred and sighed and opened her eyes to gaze wonderingly at a flaming head resting on the cushion against hers. Two strange eyes, pale-purplish like April violets, looked archly at her and she gasped: "Dandy!"

"Sokay," said Augustus Nordling.

"But where is Maxim?"

"Gone to Chicago, I guess to see Princess Benebe."

"And how did you get here beside me?"

"Oh, I've been here all the time. You don't like it, you hate me?"

"Why should I hate you? But it's all so strange—I'm afraid—I feel kind of lost."

"You don't need to feel that way. We'll be married right away."

"Married?" Seraphine started and sat up.

"Why, sure! Don't you want to? I thought I shouldn't compromise you and I didn't intend to. Unless you have any objection to me."

Seraphine made no answer.

"Have you any objection?" Dandy reached up and grasped her shoulder and she eased back against the cushions.

"But Maxim—"

"So you prefer Tasan, you like him better," said Dandy.

"I didn't say that."

"It's me then. I'm so happy, darling." He kissed her on the forehead.

"Oh, I feel as giddy as a chicken with its head cut off," said Seraphine. "I wonder where my head is gone?" She clapped her palm upon her forehead.

Dandy smiled and said: "I'm sorry, let me get you some aspirin. And I'll make you a cup of strong coffee. I'm sorry, but I never guessed you were so innocent."

And while Dandy was preparing the coffee, reacting from the effects of a prodigal night, Seraphine's head was swimming in an agitated sea of confused thinking: I guess it is better to marry him and get it over. It'll fool Mother and Father and prove that a white man *will* marry a colored girl. And I won't have to "pass." Yet I thought it was Maxim, but it turned out to be Dandy. Maybe I'll like him better, though I couldn't say it right away. He's so blond and big—yet nice and handy at everything. Maxim is so like a little monkey and I don't like the color of his skin—it's so dead. Yet he has brains—big brains—but brains isn't everything. Mrs. Seraphine Nordling! Nicer than Alamaya or Peixota, both of them so foreign-sounding and un-American. Always having to tell people how to pronounce Peixota. Mrs. Nordling—I'll be the same Seraphine in Harlem and downtown—no cause to cover up my origin. But won't Alamaya be flabbergasted, though! Damned Ethiopian nincompoop—just a regular sissy—always belly-aching about "my country"—like a sniveling kid with the whooping cough. I'm glad I'm American—where it's easy as a snap to get a man and a license—sweet lady of liberty. . . . Gee, but won't Bunchetta be jealous! She's been a ballyhooing Balinese downtown for ever so long and never did get anywhere with it and pretending to be so over-intellectual. I'll tell her it was an elopement—love at first sight.

Dandy brought the coffee. "Remember when we get the

license, you're white," he said. "I don't care a whoop about it, but we're not going to let them get away with murder and draw any color line."

"All right," said Seraphine, "I leave all the details to you."

"There's another little item. I want you to sign this card."

"What is it for?"

"Your membership in the Communist Party. I'm a disciplined member and it's preferable that I should marry a person who is a comrade." He had the pen ready.

"All right," and Seraphine wrote her name.

They obtained the license and were married that same afternoon. Dandy had influential friends and a magistrate was found to waive the time limit and perform the ceremony. When it was over, Seraphine asked: "And where are we going to live?"

"In Tasan's apartment of course, until we furnish our own," said Dandy. "I guess Tasan will make us a wedding present of one. He's a regular fairy god-father. We'll take a week off."

"But I'll have to stay in the office, as he isn't here," said Seraphine.

"I'll telegraph Tasan in Chicago. The office will feel better after closing a week in honor of our honeymoon."

Mrs. Lela Witern entertained the newly-weds at dinner in a reserved room of a large downtown catering establishment. The invitees were Director of the *Interlink*, Montague Claxon, and his fiancée, Iris Marlow, who had replaced Seraphine at the *Interlink*; Bunchetta Facey; Newton Castle, unaccompanied by his wife Delta; and Professor Banner Makepeace. Mrs. Witern was a perfect hostess for the occasion. She made a little speech. She said that the occasion was exceptionally unusual and that the marriage of Seraphine and Augustus Nordling was not simply a private affair, but that it should be regarded as one aspect of the movement of humanity against the inhuman Nazi theories of race. Mrs. Witern said that she had never been merely a blindly sentimental advocate of mixed marriages. Because she was aware that mixed marriages, like morganatic and international ones, even if they were conceived in heaven, had to go through the test of hell on earth. For such couples cannot create an isolated island for themselves: they must often live their lives in an unsympathetic or hostile environment. In her opinion mixed couples were the martyrs of the social system of today and the pioneers of the social system of tomorrow. They were courageous couples who dared to challenge the social taboos, much braver than the great majority who lived according to the established patterns. But she did not believe in martyrdom: it was too vicarious. The world has grown hypocritical and mean under the symbol of man upon the cross. And so, said Mrs. Witern, she hoped that Seraphine and Augustus would make their marriage not a martyrdom but a challenge to the world.

Seraphine made little changes here and there, which transformed the mussy bachelor's haven of Maxim Tasan into a place more suitable even for a brief honeymoon. While she was rearranging the nuptial couch, she discovered a tiny leather case which had worked its way down between the cushions. It was stamped with the initials "M.T." and contained three keys. Two Seraphine immediately recognized as the keys to the apartment and the building respectively; the other probably belonged to a suitcase or cabinet.

Seraphine was always curious about Tasan, his work, his connections, his real origin. She was aware that his activity with the Friends of Ethiopia was only one small phase of the work in the Popular Front. But to her mind the Popular Front was vague, like a vast multitude of people assembled without leadership to gaze at a comet. She had no idea of it as an international organization with active agents scattered throughout the world. She knew that Tasan had real influence among influential people and that he disposed of considerable funds, but as his business was not something tangible like Pablo Peixota's he remained to her a man of mystery.

The idea impinged on her mind that the key in her hand might be sesame to a secret. She tried it in one of the locked drawers of the dining room buffet and in a box in the unused alcove-like room, which contained a couple of suitcases and discarded shoes and clothes and a pile of books. It didn't work. Then she tried the chest in the corner parallel to the studio couch. It fitted. She pushed off the pile of magazines and pamphlets and opened it. In the top drawer there were a lot of canceled cheques, many letters and various business papers fastened together with clips.

Seraphine glanced hastily at some of the letters and examined the cheques and business papers. She lifted the drawer and the first thing she saw underneath was a large thick envelope marked "Ethiopia." Seraphine pounced on it. She pried up the fastener and drew out a set of photographs held together by a rubber band. There were half a dozen photographs of Princess Benebe in different costumes and poses and four of Gloria Kendall, the young woman to whose job Seraphine succeeded at the office of the Friends of Ethiopia. The resemblance between Gloria Kendall and Princess Benebe was obvious; the elaborate costume of the latter could not conceal the close facial resemblance. Gloria Kendall and Princess Benebe Zarihana were the same person. Am I crazy? thought Seraphine. Princess Benebe is a *fraud*?

But the evidence was right there. Looking at the back of one of the photographs, Seraphine read: "This costume is Persian—unsuitable." The handwriting was Alamaya's and on one of Gloria Kendall's in ordinary clothes there was written: "I like you more as Gloria than Princess Benebe." A sensation of jealousy jabbed Seraphine. But the astonishing discovery did not contribute to her comprehension of the mystery. Why such an elaborate trick? Why should Alamaya, who was an authentic Ethiopian and patriot, become an accomplice to such a fantastic imposture? And what was Tasan's game? How could he, with all his lofty ideas and noble utterances, lend himself to such a cheap deception? Of Gloria Kendall masquerading as an Ethiopian princess, Seraphine was merely contemptuous. Harlem was infested with many such as she, Seraphine thought: individuals who indulged the vicarious pretence of being African princes and princesses, sheiks and sharifs of Araby, Balinese and Javanese, Red Indian and East Indian, Angels and Gods—anything but plain Aframerican. But the role of Lij Alamaya and Maxim Tasan was inexplicable. She shook the envelope and a smaller one fell out. It was sealed but she opened it and found the Emperor's letter which Alamaya had lost at the Witern party. So it was Maxim Tasan who had stolen the letter. Seraphine was convinced now that Alamaya was the victim of a vile frame-up.

Into her bosom she thrust the Emperor's letter and the two photographs with Lij Alamaya's penciled comments. She locked the chest and heaped the magazines and newspapers upon it. She put the leather case with the keys on the mantel. And she wondered what she should do next. She felt a warm sympathy for Alamaya and a desire to help him. And she felt ashamed of herself for her failure to understand him. Perhaps her father was right. If she could only bring herself to go and see him. But it was impossible now that she was Mrs. Augustus Nordling.

Perhaps her mother would soften and see the situation with a woman's understanding. She would telephone her mother. She sat down to the telephone and fingered the number. She got the response. "Mother, it's me, Seraphine. I want to come up and see you. It is very important."

"Well, have you changed your mind?" said Mrs. Peixota.

"I want to tell you I'm married, I want to see you."

"Who did you marry?"

"It's a nice person—he's white and—"

"You can keep him to yourself. I don't ever want to see you or him." Mrs. Peixota clamped down the receiver.

Seraphine put her hands upon her bosom, feeling the envelope: What shall I do? she thought. I wonder if I was right or wrong to marry him. Can I tell him? Lord no! Maxim Tasan is like a god to him. But I *must* talk to somebody. I can't carry this thing alone in my bosom.

"I'll hide it!" she said aloud.

She dashed out and hurried to her apartment on Second Avenue and locked the letter and photographs in her trunk. When she returned to Tasan's apartment, her husband was just arriving there. "Tasan telegraphed asking if his keys are anywhere about," he said.

"I saw them on the mantel, where he left them I guess," she said.

"Seen this?" said Dandy as they entered the apartment. It was the early edition of an evening paper, with the banner headline: "Italians Converging on Addis Ababa: Emperor Flees Ethiopian Capital."[1]

Seraphine had been too excited about her find to pay any attention to the newsstands.

"What a strange little coincidence," she said, thinking about the Emperor's letter.

"What?" asked Dandy.

"I mean it's so sudden, the Emperor's flight, so unexpected. Well, that's the end of the Ethiopian Empire. I guess all the little mock fights between the Aid to Ethiopia organizations will stop, now that the real big fight is ended over there."

"The Fascists may conquer Ethiopia, but they cannot win in the end," said Dandy. "The Popular Front will finally defeat them."

Seraphine giggled, slightly hysterically: "All the same, I'm out of a job."

"It'll be easy to find another for you, even though there is an army of unemployed. You'll see," said Dandy.

"What will become of Lij Alamaya and Princess Benebe Zarihana?" said Seraphine.

"I wonder," said Dandy. "They must be speeding back here from Chicago."

"H'm." Seraphine had been pondering over the idea of a trip to Chicago. "I don't want to live here any longer," she said. "Can't we move to your place?"

"It's just a lousy room on Fourteenth Street," said Dandy. "You couldn't live in it."

"I could clean it up."

"I'll show it to you, but we can't live there. Why can't we stay here until we find a nice place?"

"I don't want to, and I don't want Maxim Tasan to furnish a place for us. I believe it'll be better if we are independent."

"Anything to please you," said Dandy. "I haven't any money right now, but I'll have enough in a couple of weeks. If you're determined to leave here, couldn't we stay in your Second Avenue apartment for a couple of weeks?"

"I don't like the idea of moving in on Bunchetta with a husband—it'll be kind of crowded. And you're *white*. You see, colored persons have a fixed idea about white people, which is difficult for a type like you to understand. If you were a Southern white man, you'd understand. They expect you to keep up a *white* standard of living. If we moved in on Bunchetta, it would soon be known in Harlem. And they'd be gossiping about Peixota's daughter marrying a no-count white man who couldn't even furnish an apartment for her to live in. I don't want Mother and Father to hear that kind of thing. I'd prefer to stay in your place, even if it is just a cubby-hole, until we can furnish an apartment. If you only knew my people—you see— oh, I'm so unhappy!"

"Oh, please don't say that, Seraphine," said Dandy. "I see

your point perfectly. I was a fool, just a stupid bohemian bum. But I'll do better for your sake. I'll hunt up a place right away, don't worry. I know where I can borrow money. Gee, Seraphine, you're a pure diamond."

He took her in his arms and she dissolved limber like a branch in the breeze against his blond bigness.

19

PRINCESS BENEBE AND GLORIA KENDALL

On Friday Seraphine went back to work. She was inexorably pushed to go, so that she should be occupied with something else besides love. She could not make herself contented, could not suppress a psychic revolt against purely physical sensations, which were adulterated by the dismal feeling that she might have made a false step.

And also she was tormented by an increasing resentment against Maxim Tasan and the fraud he had perpetrated. The burden of the crisis was too heavy for a person of Seraphine's disposition to carry alone. In the excitement of first finding the revealing documents, she had decided against this course when she reflected that it could do irreparable harm to many people and especially Lij Alamaya, whom she no longer hated but pitied. She did not even imagine then how difficult it would have been for her to get any such item published.

At eleven thirty the telephone rang. Seraphine took up the receiver and said, "Friends of Ethiopia."

"Is Tasan there, Seraphine?" It was Lij Alamaya's voice.

"No," she said. "Did he return from Chicago?"

"We came back together yesterday."

"Then you've seen the news about Ethiopia?"

"Yes, we got it before it was published in the newspapers. That's why we came back."

"I want to see you very much," said Seraphine. "Where are you staying?"

"In the same room at the Hotel Santa Cruz. What is it?"

"I can't tell you over the telephone. I'll come over right after I get through with my work this afternoon."

After lunch she went to the Second Avenue apartment and took out of her trunk the envelope with the Emperor's letter and the photographs and put it in her handbag. She returned to the office to work on the indexing of some lists of names and addresses. But when she placed her bag on the desk, she imagined that it might develop wings and fly out of the room. She imagined that somebody might come in and pounce upon it. She imagined the funniest things and, feeling that the bag was not safe unless she was holding it in her hand, she could not work. Nervous and scared she seized the bag, holding it tightly, as if it were an eel trying to wriggle out of her grasp, and rushed out of the office.

Seraphine thought she would not wait but instead go straight to see Alamaya. But he, not expecting her until the afternoon, had left his hotel. Disappointed and strangely agitated, although she did not desire to see Tasan before talking to Alamaya, her genie pushed her to go back to the bridal apartment. When she arrived she found Alamaya there with Tasan and Gloria Kendall.

Tasan was speaking: "You have nothing to worry about, Alamaya, for the Movement will take care of you. Ethiopia is conquered, but the Comintern is unconquerable. Fascism will collapse with the triumph of the Popular Front and Ethiopia will be restored as a Soviet nation. You must stay here and carry on propaganda through the Popular Front."

"I will do nothing of the kind," said Alamaya. "At last I am *free*. I have no country and no Emperor. No country to suffer from my mistakes and no Emperor to disgrace. For myself I am not afraid. I am through. I am FREE!"

"You are not through and you are not free," said Tasan. "You're a member of the Comintern and subject to its discipline."

"I am through with the bloody Comintern," said Alamaya. "It was the biggest mistake of my life when I joined the Party in Paris. But there was hardly any other alternative. I was sincere. We were all frightened by the sudden challenge of the Fascists—all of us who believed in the brotherhood of humanity. And I thought I was doing a progressive thing when I joined up. I felt that the future of our country depended on what we younger Ethiopians did. I believed that we should lead the older men who were conservative; that we should tie up with progressive forces. I thought the Comintern was progressive, but I thought wrongly."

"The Comintern cannot be blamed for the mistakes of the democracies," said Tasan. "Ethiopia was betrayed and sold by England and France and the League of Nations."

"And Soviet Russia too," said Alamaya. "In spite of the sanctions, Russia continued to sell Italy the oil for the airplanes and tanks, and the food for her army to defeat Ethiopia. The Soviet government—"

"The Soviets had a trade treaty with Italy!" cried Tasan. "They had to respect the terms of the treaty."

"Hell," said Alamaya. "One of the things that Communism taught me was that no Communist regarded a treaty with a bourgeois as binding. Do you as a Communist consider a treaty with Fascists as more binding? Any treaty can be denounced in a crisis. When the members of the League of Nations took sanctions against Italy they broke treaties. But your league of Communist parties of the Comintern is just a drove of contemptible pigs eating slops out of the Soviet trough. It stinks."

Tasan showed red at his ears. The training for his career had accustomed him to maintain an exterior of Oriental imperturbability even when his heart was raging, and his poker face, aided by the general pallor of his skin, was a perfect foil. But Alamaya's outburst, his sudden refractoriness, had caught him off guard. Besides, despite his professions his real attitude towards Africans and Aframericans was still influenced by childish fairy-tale pictures of them as primitives. Alamaya's sharp penetrating appraisal of the Comintern and Soviet Russia was totally unexpected.

"Who are you to criticize the Comintern?" said Tasan. "What do you know or understand about treaties and diplomatic action among civilized peoples? Ethiopia is only a land of howling black savages, over-sexed cannibals with many wives gorging themselves with raw meat. Africa is the black plague of Europe. It can't rule itself or exploit its resources. European nations are lured there to quarrel with each other and fight like wolves and die in its jungles. You ought to be glad and grateful if the Comintern takes a *human* interest in Ethiopia."

Said Alamaya: "If I must make a choice, I would prefer the European wolves as real wolves to the Comintern wolves hidden in fleece. We African savages are used to fighting wild animals in the open; but we're not accustomed to fighting them in disguise. I have learned my lesson the hard way and you and the Comintern can go to hell where you belong."

"Understand this," said Tasan, "you can't fight the Comintern. It will crush you like a worm."

"I don't care," said Alamaya. "I have made a mess of my mission. I failed Ethiopia and I failed the Aframericans who wanted to help Ethiopia—"

"What help could Aframericans give to Ethiopia?" said Tasan. "They're all venal beggars and sycophants, always stretching out their black hands and praying to the white gods. Aframericans with their airs and antics imitating white people are a big joke, and so is Ethiopia."

"I guess it's because you imagine we're a joke that you had to put the Princess Benebe over on us," said Seraphine.

"Who told *you* about that?" said Gloria Kendall, jumping out of her chair.

Ignoring Gloria, Seraphine continued: "Aframericans are a joke indeed, just a toy for your amusement."

Tasan wondered how much Seraphine knew and what was the source of her information. He said: "Mrs. Nordling, you're a new couple and shouldn't be involved in this thing. Lij Alamaya was welcomed in Harlem as a prince and the people wanted a princess. They have the kingdom of heaven with angels and a god in Harlem—why not princes and princesses? The Communist Party was hot stuff in Harlem, when it made a pact with god."

"The colored people are not a joke," said Seraphine. "And if Alamaya cannot expose you, I will."

"Who would believe you and what newspaper will publish it? Do you think the newspapers want to show themselves up? I've got the influence to block every move you make. Besides, Alamaya was a party to it. When you expose Princess Benebe you also expose Lij Alamaya and make all Harlem ridiculous."

"I am fed up with everything and don't care what you all do," said Gloria. "I agreed to masquerade as a princess, because I was told it was for the good of the movement. I did it as a part of my duty. I believed that Lij Alamaya and the Hands to Ethiopia were wrong to oppose the Friends and the Popular Front. I believed that they were leading Aframericans down the wrong road. They told me it was my job as Princess Benebe to hold Lij Alamaya to the party line. But I soon discovered that Lij Alamaya was a real person, a patriot who loved his people. And I was nothing but a tool . . ."

"Then you abandoned the party line so you could land the Ethiopian sucker with your own hook and line," said Tasan with a simian leer.

"You be damned, you slimy skunk. Why shouldn't I abandon your party line when you use it to hang Ethiopia and hamstring Aframericans—"

"It is the Ku Klux Klan stringing up your people and not the Comintern," shouted Tasan. "The whole goddam colored race should be grateful to Soviet Russia and the Comintern. Look what we did for them in the Scottsboro case.[1] We summoned the United States before the bar of the world to be judged and condemned for degrading and outlawing its colored minority. Yet their treacherous ungrateful Uncle Tom boot-licking leaders try to poison the minds of the people and turn them against the Communists. I wish I had the power to turn loose a band of Cossacks among them to teach them a lesson."

"The Cossacks are far away," said Alamaya, "but the Ku Klux Klan is right here. I wouldn't be surprised if you made a deal with them to ginger up their persecution of Aframericans, just as you supplied the Fascists with materials to conquer Ethiopia. Blackmail and gangsterism are Communist tactics just as they are the Fascists'."

Tasan grimaced. "You will find that out in Ethiopia."

"Here, Alamaya," said Seraphine, "the Emperor's letter I discovered right here in Maxim's apartment."

"You fiend!" cried Alamaya. "You—" He bounded forward and clipped Tasan with a stinging punch to his brow. Tasan thudded on the floor like a sack of sand thrown from a truck.

"I'm getting out of this hyena's lair," said Alamaya.

"And I'm going with you," said Gloria.

"I'm coming too," said Seraphine.

But as they reached the sidewalk they met Dandy Nordling, bare-headed and beaming like a Sunkist orange with good humor. He gathered Seraphine in his arms and said: "Darling, I have found the coziest thing you can imagine. Right in the heart of the Village in Eighth Street. Come on, I'll show it to you right away. We'll soon invite you all to a little house-warming," he said to Alamaya and Gloria. And holding Seraphine's hand, he led her off.

20

ART AND RACE

In one of the assembly rooms of the Parthenon Hall the *Inter-link* was sponsoring a meeting in appreciation of the work of the Aframerican artist Dixon Davis Lee. Mr. Lee was a graphic artist with a powerful punch. For many years he had wrestled with charcoal and brush. But only recently he was hailed as a genius and welcomed into the ranks of the serious artists.

Mr. Lee had earned his first money as an artist drawing likenesses of customers in Aframerican cafés. He was a mere youth when he started making drawings of the habitués of a cabaret in Atlanta, Georgia. He had no training, but he possessed talent. And he pushed it with a mighty will, for he was ambitious. He studied drawings in the newspapers and appealing types in all the popular magazines he could get his hands on. In those early efforts, his drawings of Aframericans appeared as if the models were white.

When he came to New York he got his chance to study at night at a commercial art school and to see a better quality and variety of drawings in newspapers and finer pictures in magazines. He never attended any of the pure art schools or made contacts with students of pure art.

In Harlem he made a little more money and wider contacts, making drawings of convives in café and cabaret. He attracted the attention of visitors from downtown. There was potential power in his work and his seriousness in his subject set him apart from the ordinary café artist. Besides, he himself, broad-shouldered, chocolate-hued, was an interesting type.

Dixon Davis Lee got his first New York start when he made a drawing of the editor of *Broadway Balcony* in a Harlem nightspot. Editor Pat Conman invited the artist to bring some of his stuff down to his office. Lee was lifted off his feet and riding the air like a singing lark. He thought he had already reached the heights. But when he went to the *Balcony*'s office Pat Conman brought him back down to earth. Conman looked through Lee's portfolio and told him that he had a powerful punch in his line, but that he was like a man possessing a superb tool who didn't know how to use it, because he was not trained in his craft. Conman pointed out to Lee the fact that his best work was his Aframerican types but that the features of all of them were like anemic whites. He exhorted Lee to make his people real.

"Make your Aframericans brutal and bloody and big with life—'bawdacious' as they say in Harlem," he said. "Do caricatures of the better-known Broadway sepians, so that the public can guess who they are without their names being mentioned. And I'll give you a break in my weekly."

Pat Conman gave Dixon Davis Lee a stack of the *Broadway Balcony* and told him to study the type of illustrations. The *Broadway Balcony* was a little gadfly weekly which specialized in brief items full of malice and innuendos about stage people and the more or less prominent personalities of Broadway and café society. It was started during the earlier part of the regime of President Hoover[1] and quickly attained considerable local popularity. Its illustrations were not of a high standard, but they were funny and peptic.

Lee heeded Pat Conman's suggestions and applied them to his work and soon he was turning out some startling Aframerican types. Working for the *Broadway Balcony* brought Lee into contact with other artists and sophisticated persons, which extended his artistic horizon. His Aframerican contributions featured the Southern black in the cotton field and in the chain gang and in his cabin; as porter, handyman, roustabout and entertainer. Lee overcame the unconscious habit of making his Aframerican features appear like "stereotype whites," but he could not make them look human. Upon the powerful energetic bodies he invariably placed gorilla-like heads, with incredibly vacant, vicious and depraved faces. They produced a strange sensation of the grotesque photographic trick of a person's posing his head and becoming a part of another strange body. Sometimes in his drawings Lee created a white figure as a foil to his black, in which he reverted to his originally unsophisticated manner: the white faces were always rose-pink sweet, like the girl on the magazine cover.

Pat Conman persuaded Lee to coin a name from his initials and sign his drawings "Dèdé Lee" instead of "Dixon Davis Lee." He said that that was more artistic and suitable to the spirit of his *Broadway Balcony.* Lee's work soon established itself as the most distinctively artistic contribution in the *Balcony.* His drawings were remarked and appreciated in the more exclusive art circles. He was fortunate in obtaining an assignment to draw for a newspaper.

After a three-year spell of successful notoriety, the *Balcony* began losing circulation. Life had changed a lot along Broadway and many balconies were empty. The *Balcony* faded rapidly and suddenly died in 1933. Editor Pat Conman turned with disgust from the scandals of Broadway, which were scarcely shocking in that bleak wolfish year, and became seriously interested in the social developments of the nation. In 1935 he became an assistant in the editorial department of the Sunday supplement of the *Labor Herald.* He was soon active in the organizing of artists and writers. Also he was a zealous worker in the ranks of the Popular Front.

Pat Conman had not lost contact with Dèdé Lee. He still

found time for relaxation in the amusements of Harlem. But his reactions were not the same. He wrote pieces about dark fingers weaving the anguish of a race into the swing notes of the piano and the social protest inherent in the Aframerican pattern of tap dancing. And to the Sunday supplement of the *Labor Herald* he contributed an illustrated two-page appreciation of the work of Dèdé Lee and its profound social significance.

Up until that time Dèdé Lee had never been troubled by ideas of the social implications of his art. If he had it might have handicapped the cunning of his hand and spoiled his success. Like every normal Aframerican, he resented the discrimination to which he was subjected as one of the untouchables of the nation. But his art had materially provided him with the means of escaping from some of the harsher realities of discrimination. He was married to a pretty Aframerican girl who liked fashionable clothes and parties and they associated with the smartest pleasure-seeking set in Harlem. No one of that set ever thought there was any social meaning in the drawings of Aframerican types which Dèdé Lee contributed to the white newspaper. He made a good living out of his work, which enabled him to live up to their standard, and that was enough.

Dèdé Lee's art had enlightened him more from the angle of social experience than of social significance. Many of those who delighted in it had no notion that he was an Aframerican. On one occasion he was invited by the exclusive Ante-Bellum Club of New York to visit the club. The distinctive mark of this club was that its members were descendants of Southerners who were slave owners and gentlemen, but none of whom were slave traders. Dèdé Lee accepted the invitation, which specifically stated that the afternoon would also celebrate a revival of the custom of the drinking of mint julep. But when he arrived at the club and announced that he was Dèdé Lee, the custodian was so confused that in his agitation he stepped on the artist's toes. He asked him to wait in an anteroom, forgetting the usual courtesy of relieving a visitor of his top-coat and hat. He took Lee's card and hurried into the club room. He returned with a responsible member. This personage made an attempt of an apology to Lee, explaining there was a mistake about the date, the secretary was not there, but he would communicate with him. Lee did not receive any explanatory communication. He did not expect any. He knew the cause of the mistake. The members of the Ante-Bellum Club had imagined that artist Dèdé Lee, who so perfectly rendered the popular Southern point of view in his art, was white.

Dèdé Lee was not unappreciative of the effort of his original benefactor, Pat Conman, in ranking him in the company of artists whose work possessed significant social substance. It meant much to him to be rated among the real artists instead of remaining just a popular caricaturist. And also it meant perhaps even more to Mrs. Lee to get acquainted with the advance guard of socially serious artists. There were some big names, some aristocratic names among them. Magnus Chetwind was one of those names that were big in the popular as much as the exclusive sense. He was a popular lecturer in esthetics and had successfully sold the public his ideas of making the people art-conscious. He had established the People's Art Gallery, which was a signal success. He was in constant demand as an art populariser on the radio. He was a rare combination: an art dealer and art critic whose opinion on art was generally accepted as authoritative.

It was Pat Conman who snapped the interest of Magnus Chetwind in Dèdé Lee and convinced him that Lee's masterly portrayal of degenerate Aframerican types was an uplifting achievement, a manifestation of minority courage in the face of the challenge of Fascism and a generous contribution to the programme of the Popular Front. And Chetwind performed such a superb job in launching Dèdé Lee as one of the imaginatively possessed that the latter was almost afraid of the golgothic picture of himself that was built up to establish social seriousness in his drawings.

Magnus Chetwind's crusade for popular art with a social purpose was dynamic with urgency. Listening to him over the radio, one received the impression of unselfish lion-hearted courage and quixotism. But a close-up view of him made one think more of an admirably mounted fox in a museum.

It was a very impressive gathering of people who were assembled for the *Interlink*'s reception in honor of the realist social-impressionist Dèdé Lee. Liberal and radical people of importance who were alert to all the social and artistic trends of modernism, connoisseurs of art, educators, critics, writers and artists and artistes. There was a bright crowd of Interlinks, with Mrs. Abigail Hobison easily dominant, wearing a dress that was a rare modern edition of old-fashioned imported lace.

Harlem was worthily represented by its professional and intellectual groups, with the familiar faces of Newton Castle, Dorsey Flagg, Prudhomme Bishop, Bunchetta Facey and Iris Marlow. Delta Castle was noticeably absent, especially since a downtowner, Miss Lublu Lubov, had such a monopoly on Newton's attentions. The anti–Popular Front Dorsey Flagg was invited by a mistake; the girl who forwarded the invitation to the chairman of the Hands to Ethiopia had confused that organization with the Friends of Ethiopia. Maxim Tasan was there and also Seraphine and Dandy Nordling.

Moving around in groups the visitors scrutinized examples of Dèdé Lee's drawings on the walls, with appropriate exclamations over their punch and power. Abigail Hobison announced that Magnus Chetwind would give a short talk and the seats were quickly occupied. Those who could not find seats remained standing.

Chetwind stood in front of a desk. The occasion was unique, he said. And he proceeded to explain why: "Great artists are the rarest flowers of any Civilization. Their works are like the stars that shine down through the darkness of night. Like the stars in the sky, the galleries of the world are bright with shining works of art. But we have not enough great artists. Our modern artists are neglected, while the world is worshipping at the shrines of dead masters. But dead men need no cheer and comfort, no warmth and food. It is enough that the works of the dead masters illuminate the path of the progress of Civilization like signposts pointing the pilgrim to this way or that. Instead of blindly worshipping the dead masters we should learn from the sad penurious lives of many of them that we should honor and help our modern artists while they are *alive*.

"In the works exhibited here this afternoon, we discover the soul of an Aframerican artist of consummate skill and portentous social implication. They are a miracle of achievement— an achievement which is more amazing when we remind ourselves that great art is a rarity and a luxury—the perfected fruit of the carefully cultivated soil of Civilization—the fine vintage of our ripened years of culture. A nice distinction between young artists and old artists is an absurdity, when all spring from the same soil. For a warm advanced spring may precipitate the buds and a late summer retard the golden harvest of the corn. It is the growth of the soil of our common culture, which nurtures alike the young artist and the old, that is important.

"But in the case of this supreme artist, Mr. Dixon Davis Lee, we are confronted with an astonishing phenomenon of enormous significance. For this artist is not a product of the cultivated soil of our common culture. He is a product of the neglected God-forsaken Aframerican soil. He has sprung vigorously out of the midst of our abominably brutalized native minority. Out of this abandoned miasmic boggy soil, screened from our penetration by a thick growth of poisonous weeds and thorns, which we imagine to be peopled with pestiferous insects and horrendous reptiles, there has issued a miracle of artistic flowering.

"These drawings are a challenging expression of the highest art. They are not for puny souls, but they are edifying to strong vigorous minds. They are violent, bestial and monstrous, but they express the hidden qualities, the unknown soul of a people. We know very little about the Aframerican soul. The Aframericans are a humiliated and crushed minority in our midst. Here for the first time their soul is revealed to us by an artist of their own who possesses the mighty strength and violence of a Samson. His art is not like the beautiful flower of the cultivated soil of our common culture. It is a strange wild flower. But it is great art. I want you to appreciate it for itself and for its social significance. I want you to take its message like missionaries and spread it far and wide throughout the nation, for it is a part of our national heritage. I thank you."

Mr. Magnus Chetwind was awarded a hearty round of applause. Mrs. Abigail Hobison rose and said that Mr. Prudhomme Bishop, the president of the ERA (Equal Rights Action), desired to say something as the representative of the Aframericans.

Prudhomme Bishop stepped to the desk, adjusted his glasses, posed his mahogany hand on the lapel of his neat gray coat and said: "On behalf of the Aframericans I wish to give thanks to Mrs. Hobison and Mr. Chetwind for their glorious gesture in arranging this reception and exhibition to focus the attention of the elite upon the serious social significance in the work of Dèdé Lee." (His voice sounded like the tone of the well-worn sole of an old shoe.)

And Prudhomme Bishop launched forth: "Art is the glory of success and a tribute to the visibility of intelligence and the germs of culture in the crucible of common understanding. It is the yardstick to measure the test of achievement and the honey that sweetens the precious nectar of the beautiful life, when we partake of the melodious wine of the sacrament of human fellowship. For the wine of life is in the comprehension of the bright star of the golden chain, which binds all of humanity in one link.

"Mr. Lee has marvelously distinguished himself in the artistic designation of Aframerican types to the glory of the educational processes of all Americans. Art is the comprehension of God and humanity is its handiwork. Let God be glorified and humanity worship him among the masterpieces of the beautiful and true.

"The Aframerican people are ennobled here in this temple of art, where there are no barriers or disqualifications arising from the God-created differences of race and color. Out of the common culture of our American heritage we have raised our musicians and singers and dancers, our poets and novelists, to attain the benevolent standard of your comprehension. But this is the first time we have approached you with the burnt offering of a perfected artist, an expert in the execution of the general character of a race. Ladies and gentlemen of the high places, we thank you."

As if they considered his speech more entertaining, the audience accorded Prudhomme Bishop an applause more prolonged than was given Magnus Chetwind. While Bishop was talking Dorsey Flagg was engaged in whispering to the fastidious consort of one of the outstanding Harlem doctors who had accompanied him. He walked over to Abigail Hobison and, handing her his card, exchanged a few words with her. Mrs. Hobison stood up and announced that the chairman of the Hands to Ethiopia would speak briefly. This occasioned sharp whispering among some of the visitors who were supporters of the rival Friends of Ethiopia. Newton Castle hurried from his post against a window to consult with Maxim Tasan.

But Dorsey Flagg was already speaking. He announced himself as chairman of the Hands to Ethiopia and stated that he was also a professor of history. He said he had not expected to speak, but he was glad of the opportunity and as it was a liberal group he would speak frankly, but with no intention of offending anyone. Then he started:

"It was certain remarks of Mr. Chetwind that made me wish to speak. Mr. Chetwind is a noble humanitarian who is interested in artists as artists regardless of race and color. He and Mrs. Abigail Hobison should be honored for their helpful interest in the art of Mr. Dèdé Lee. But important things have been said here and elsewhere about Mr. Lee's work as a representative of the racial group to which he belongs. Now these are times when minority problems, which are always grave, have become acute. These problems are not merely concerned with the social and political status of a minority, but also with their special artistic and literary contributions. In National Socialist Germany, democratic art and literature is proscribed. They have burned books and pictures and destroyed statues and other monuments.

"The rise to power of National Socialism has focused the mind of the world on the words 'minority' and 'race.' Some pseudo-scientists would like to abolish the word 'race,' because the Nazis have put an evil interpretation upon it. To do that we would have to abolish the phrase 'human race' or 'human species.' Whatever we may call it, a group of people that has specific biological or social traits in common must be distinguished by a name. I suppose that more than any other region in the world, the United States is a nation of many minorities and each one is distinguished by a name. I would say the United States is a nation of people of different races, and I would describe Japan as a nation of people of one race. I think the minority groups should be very watchful and cautious in their approach to the issue of racism. We cannot deny that racial differences exist and at the same time make demands of minority rights on the basis of race. And this applies specially to the Aframerican group to which I belong. At the same time we will not accept the Nazi definition of race and its idea of the innate superiority of one racial type over the other.

"Mr. Chetwind made some serious and pointed references about the Aframerican group. It is the largest minority and the greatest problem to the American nation. We are so far and away behind the other minorities that I suspect that when our gallant American writers and speakers indict the Nazis for their harsh treatment of minorities, they forget the existence of the Aframerican minority. Against the threat of Nazism, all minority groups in this country are taking stock of themselves, clearing away encumbering rubbish in their group life, challenging defamers wherever they appear, in the press, in the theatre, in literature and art and at political and even religious meetings. Public men have been censured for adverse statements, newspapers and magazines criticized, theatres boycotted, books withdrawn from circulation, songs suppressed and exhibitions of pictures prohibited. I should have said all minority groups except the Aframerican. More than any group we are daily held up to ridicule in the press, in the motion picture, and in popular magazine and newspaper pictures or drawings and in the theatre. In Congress we are frequently referred to with contempt and in words that are a disgrace to the national seat of government.

"And now in these drawings exhibited here it appears to me that Aframericans are held up to national opprobrium by a member of their own group. I salute Mr. Dixon Davis Lee as a powerful original artist. I hope he makes money—plenty of money—for artists need money to exist and many Aframerican artists and writers are always hungry. But I cannot agree with Mr. Chetwind that these graphic delineations of certain Aframerican types represent the soul of my people. What soul? It is not the soul of myself or any of the Aframericans here in this gallery. It is not the soul of our brothers and sisters who work for you white folk as porters, errand boys, elevator operators, waiters, cooks and chauffeurs.

"Mr. Chetwind declares, and I agree with him, that these drawings are violent, bestial and monstrous. They represent the extreme of depravity, imbecility and criminality. I cannot say they are immoral, for to be moral or immoral one must be human. But these Aframerican types are all inhuman. Look at them again and see as I see: colored persons snarling like hounds, posed like baboons in the chain gang, working like zombies in the cotton field, crazy with unreasonable anger. Their sexual attitudes are also shown and I was about to say that they were like wild animals in their sexual life. But the sexual life of animals, though savage and wild, is beautiful. The sexual attitudes of the types depicted here are like that of enraged centaurs or monkeys in the zoo.

"It puzzles me that many of these pieces are relieved by a white foil and, as you all can see, the features of Mr. Lee's white people are beautiful, composed and dignified. And then I observe, but I am not sure if you see them as I do—but I observe that Mr. Lee's blacks have no human features at all. In place of features I find an ugly leer or sneer, a crooked grimace or insane lust.

"You noble spirits and high-minded critics who denounce Fascismo-Nazism and its racial doctrine as inhuman, you expect my people to accept this distorted exhibition of their race as human. We will not accept it. If we do, then Hitler is right when he says in *Mein Kampf* that Negroes are half apes. And the South would be certainly correct in its attitude, for such types as these should be quarantined.

"If such types of pictures or drawings are not good for other persecuted minorities, then they are not good either for the under-privileged Aframerican minority. I suspect that you white people see in these savage delineations what you expect the

Aframericans to be because of your vile treatment of them. You experience a vicarious thrill from the artist's version of the abysmal depravity of others. But we are not like that and we will not be like that. We refuse to accept this exhibition as the interpretation of the Aframerican soul. It is if anything an assault upon the sanctuary of our soul. Praise the work of Mr. Lee for its power, its originality and artistry. But do not try to convince us that of such is the black man's soul. We need Raphaels to picture the mothers of the race with their children, Millets to show us black workers in the field and Gauguins[2] to paint the exquisite beauty of brown flesh."

Only the Harlemites cheered Dorsey Flagg, except Newton Castle, who was wholly for Magnus Chetwind's point of view. Even Seraphine was enthusiastic, even though she was still a little resentful of Flagg. But there was some hissing, which was initiated by Newton Castle, and perhaps this caused Abigail Hobison to clap her hands vigorously, in which she was joined by a few more of the whites.

Magnus Chetwind endeavored to get Dèdé Lee to speak in defense of himself. But he declined, saying that he had spoken with pencil and paint and that was enough. Thereupon Chetwind held up his hand, signifying that he had something more to say. He said that he had tried to have Dèdé Lee say a word, but he had refused. He conceded that Dorsey Flagg's objection to some of his remarks might be valid, as he was not on the inside of the Aframerican group to be intimate with the movement of its mind and the stirrings of its soul. But he believed Flagg's criticism of Dèdé Lee as an artist was unjustifiable, for an artist's feeling about the soul of his group is not like the layman's. The artist plumbs more profoundly to the depths, untouched by the ordinary individual. Fortunately Dèdé Lee was born an artist and was self-taught. He was never influenced by the Italian and French masters whom Mr. Flagg reveres, but still he is warmly partial to the works of such masters as Goya, Rembrandt, Frans Hals, and Hogarth, John Sloan and Georg Grosz.[3]

Again Magnus Chetwind was rewarded with heavy-handed plaudits from the downtown sophisticates who, more than the fashionable Harlemites, were aware of the significance of what he was talking about.

"AS BEAUTIFUL AS A JEWEL"

Maxim Tasan thought that after the pedanticisms of the *Interlink*'s reception for Dèdé Lee, it would be a nice diversion for a select group of the guests to go to his apartment and take art and life a little easier. Tasan especially wanted Dèdé Lee to go along and, as he was not well acquainted with him, he asked Pat Conman to suggest it. Lee was favorably disposed and Tasan and Conman quickly circulated the idea among certain of the guests.

Of the Harlem guests only four, who were recommended by Newton Castle, were invited. Tasan was fascinated by the arrestingly chic copper-complexioned Harlem matron who had accompanied Dorsey Flagg. And he sicked Newton Castle on to persuade her to desert Flagg and join his group. But as a leader of Harlem's matrons, the doctor's wife was a precisely meticulous person regarding her engagements. And she refused to go to Tasan's party without her escort. Besides, she did not approve the idea of such an improvised party. She preferred one to which she could be formally invited, as she was to the exhibition. Of course, Dorsey Flagg could not be invited.

On their way to Harlem, the matron laughingly informed Dorsey Flagg of what had been afoot. And Flagg explained to her that they (the Tasan-Castle clique) were adept at employing such dirty tricks to irritate the persons whom they disliked and could not influence.

Abigail Hobison and Professor Banner Makepeace and other such sedate persons were not asked. But Mrs. Witern went along with Magnus Chetwind and Montague Claxon of the *Interlink*. The crowd arrived at Tasan's place in cars and taxicabs. After the intellectual necessity of the enjoyment of art, everybody was ready to appreciate a highball or a cocktail.

Dandy Nordling was a kind of self-appointed majordomo. He selected the liquor and mixed the drinks and a couple of girls volunteered to help him. Enormously good-natured and eagerly friendly, he circulated around to see that everyone had something to drink and he brought in trays of crackers and caviar, cheese and olives, for those who also wanted a bite. Dandy's generous activity gave Tasan the chance to act as a guest, which he preferred, instead of a host. He installed himself in a corner to chat with Dèdé Lee and Mrs. Witern.

But Seraphine Nordling was not in the happiest of humors. As she watched her Nordic husband paying assiduous attention to the needs of all alike, including herself, she was acutely aware of his boyish flexibility. She saw him big and blond and plastic in serving others, happy to be the disciplined member of a party, leaping at the call of so many Tasans, but almost useless to plan and act for himself. She had discovered that he was merely a kind of errand boy in the circulation department of the *Labor Herald*, ebullient and ready always to speed to any destination, proud of the honor of being called "comrade," happy to be merely a footman of the great cause.

Seraphine had quit the Friends of Ethiopia and Montague Claxon had taken her back at the *Interlink* on a full-time assignment. Her husband was so indifferent about a decent paying job and a place to live in, she was faced with the realization that she might have to become the responsible partner. Yet she would not entertain the idea of giving him up. For he was *white*. If she did, it would be proof that her parents were right. And Harlem would have a glorious gossip holiday. It gave her a little consolation that if Dandy was impractical, he was at least presentable, but nevertheless her heart was heavy.

Meanwhile Tasan kept his eye on Newton Castle and Lublu Lubov. As Delta Castle had wavered, fearful that her social prestige was endangered by Newton's Popular Front antics, Tasan had discovered the buxom Lublu to divert Newton and assist in holding him steadfast. The relationship between Castle and his wife was in a precarious state. He had become a byword in Harlem's elite circles because of his habit of using every occasion to sloganize: "Defend Soviet Russia and achieve the second emancipation of the Aframerican race." Like a zealous missionary, he was a frequent visitor to poolrooms, barbershops and bars, in which he distributed free five- and ten-cent pamphlets on various aspects of the Comintern and the Aframerican. His public school briefcase was always bulging with propaganda material. And it was rumored in Harlem that in his classroom he injected something of the history of Soviet Russia into every subject. To more effectively proletarianise himself, he started to wear soiled collars and old down-at-the-heel shoes when he made the rounds of the poolrooms and barbershops. Desperate Delta gathered up all his old shoes and old clothes and asked the superintendent to give them to the junk man.

As the crisis between Castle and his wife increased, he found more relaxation among his downtown friends. However, he always dressed neatly when he went downtown. He and Lublu Lubov often went joy-riding in his car, sometimes with other friends. Lublu was a W.P.A. teacher[1] and lived with an aunt in an old house in the Chelsea district. Castle was the first Aframerican that the aunt got to know intimately. She admired him, especially because of his social-political affiliations.

Tasan was pleased with himself for arranging to bring his guests from the gallery to his apartment. They all showed their appreciation, some saying that the evening's treat was the tonic to the afternoon session. He was an expert fixer of little as well as big things. His arrangement of the little affair of Newton Castle and Miss Lublu Lubov to checkmate the rebellious Mrs. Castle was perfecting itself as planned.

When all the guests had departed, except Lublu and Newton, Tasan exhibited a couple of bottles of fine Caucasian wine which, he said, he had received as a present from a friend attached to one of the Russian missions visiting America. Tasan fetched clean glasses, extracted the cork and the three sipped the delicious strange wine as if it were reserved for special communion.

"Ah, Soviet Russia, Soviet Russia." Tasan smacked his lips. "Blessed land of perpetual promise and proletarian opportunity. Dear Fatherland of Lenin and Stalin. How I long to touch thy soil and breathe thine air again."

"Amen," responded Newton Castle.

They emptied the bottle and Tasan offered to take Lublu and Newton to dinner. But flushed by the excellent liquor and wine and the exquisitely stimulating freshness of the spring night, Lublu insisted that she had no appetite; what she wanted was a nice spin in the car.

"You should eat," said Tasan. "All the others went home to dinner. And remember you have a weak heart."

Lublu shrugged. "What do I care?" And pirouetting on her toes like an overweight ballet dancer, she sang, "Tra la la, tra la la, la la." She popped a large olive into her mouth, saying, "That's enough for my dinner. Come on, Newton, take me for a ride."

"Be good, children," said Tasan. "I am going to eat."

"We'll be as good as the angels in Harlem," said Newton.

With Lublu sitting beside him Newton Castle drove over to Broadway and on the West Side Driveway. With no pedestrians to watch and no traffic lights to heed, the car spun along as smoothly as the unraveling of a silken thread. Lublu snuggled against Newton and declared she was enchanted.

"New York could be made as beautiful as a jewel," she said. "When they finish the East Side Driveway the city will be like a great big unending escalator with broad silver bands. This city could be beautiful, eh, Newton?"

"It will be, when we change the system," said Castle.

"When we change the system and the world too. Then instead of 'All the World Aboard the Popular Front,' our slogan will be, 'The Beautiful Life for All.' Then the purpose of governments will be to make life beautiful for all. No more fostering of prejudice and hate between people. All the world will be one united humanity."

Castle eased away a little from Lublu. He was more than ever a victim of nerves as his estrangement from Delta increased. The firm strands that had held him physically balanced to a person stronger than himself and kept him performing a perpetual St. Vitus dance[2] were loosening one by one. And the psychological elation which he experienced from being a member of the Communist Party and a partisan of the Popular Front did not wholly compensate for that special loss. Yet being an esteemed member of a mass organization was the more powerful influence, for he was always more of a mental than a physical case. He was haunted by a sensation of a person suspended afraid in the void between heaven and hell, yet deriving a certain gratification from the sensation. His association with Lublu did make him feel that his destiny was more closely linked up with the Movement, but not exactly in the way Tasan expected. Lublu was no substitute for the Aframerican Delta, whose sharp consciousness of holding a superior place within the barriers of Harlem society was tempered with bitterness. To Newton Castle Lublu was a sprite of the Movement whose body was tattooed with slogans of inspiration.

They drove along the Hudson Parkway. Lublu's voice kept running along like a brook babbling about life and beauty. At last Newton decided to return by way of Harlem. As the car zoomed along the speedway, Lublu suddenly uttered a sharp cry and, clutching her breast, she slumped down. Newton stopped the car and gripped her around the waist, asking, "Are you ill?"

She replied with a nod and a long sigh. He adjusted the cushion and she listed back as if life were going out of her. He held her wrist and said: "Is it very bad?" She gave only another and weaker sigh.

He remembered she had told him of previous attacks. He thought it was the best thing to drive straight to the Harlem Hospital. He was alarmed and kept touching her, endeavoring to get her to speak as he drove along, but Lublu did not reply. He turned into Seventh Avenue and, waiting for the light, he desperately tried to rouse her. But she gave no sign of life.

Panic gripped him. She can't be dead, he thought. What could kill her? A few glasses of liquor? It wasn't poisoned. I drank it myself and more than she. Good God! What a mess I've got myself into.

He drove into Lenox Avenue towards the hospital. But he stopped before he reached the hospital and parked against the curb. I can't go in there, he thought. Lublu is not sick, she is *dead*. And she is WHITE. I'll be arrested. They will jail me. And how will I ever get out of it? She is WHITE! Once when he was an errand boy he had surprised a white woman in the nude and had never quite recovered from the shattering effects of that encounter.

He propped up Lublu as if she were sleeping and stepped out of the car. He walked quickly away. Midway down the block he ran into a strapping black fellow with whom he had become slightly acquainted one afternoon, when he was distributing proletarian pamphlets. The young man was usually employed in a downtown theatre, but he was not working, as the theatre was not running that season.

"Hello there," said Newton, and then, as if immediately enlightened about his problem, "will you do me a favor?"

"Sure, if I can," said the porter.

Newton went back with the porter to the car and asked him if he would watch it until he returned. "See that girl in there? She is dead drunk," he said, "and I don't like to leave her alone, as she is white. Some of our bad boys might want to act funny. I'm just going down the block to get the rest of the crowd who are at a party." He gave the porter fifty cents.

"Why thank you, mister," said the porter. "This is no favor you're asking. You're paying me."

"Oh, that's nothing," said Newton. "When I come back with the others, they'll give you a dollar or two. White folks like to get drunk and spend money like lords when they come to Harlem to amuse themselves."

And Newton Castle hurried off. Oh, what shall I do, he thought, as he was seized with the feeling of a person who had swallowed an enormous purge, which was beginning to aggravate his colon. Tasan, Tasan! I will telephone Tasan. It was his fault, forcing his white slave of the movement on me against my desire. Lord, but I dare not telephone, for the whole police department might be listening in and the fire department besides. Fire, Lord, fire! Fire, I'm a going to burn! Flesh and body burning and it's never going to save my soul! Lord of the jungle of my dreams! Lord of the slave plantation, have mercy upon me! Why did I do it? Why did I stray? If I could only drive her home to her aunt! But she may have the posse there waiting for me with the rope and faggot.

Thus pursued by the wild terror of his imagination, Newton Castle wandered in a confused circle through the streets of Harlem. Meanwhile the porter was waiting and waiting, faithfully watching the car. Lenox Avenue was not brightly animated. People passed by and none paid any special attention to the car. The subway admitted and discharged its scanty after-midnight passengers, who quickly vanished into the side streets.

But the man said he was just going down the block, thought

the porter, and it's a hellavo long time. Why, it's two o'clock. And all the time the gal has never moved, not even a wink. She's some drunk. Lemme see. He opened the door of the car and shook her. "Seems lak to me she's more dead than drunk," he said. He reached over and touched her face. "She's daid," he said.

But the porter felt not the slightest sensation of fear. He had been asked to watch on a car in which a helplessly drunk young woman was sitting. He discovered that the woman was dead. She was *white*, but that circumstance did not make him afraid any more than if she were black. He could easily prove his innocence. The car had its license plate. The worst the police could do would be to take him into custody, pending enquiries. So the porter calmly reasoned and he decided to drive the girl to the nearby Harlem Hospital.

But at that moment Maxim Tasan came along and, recognizing the car and Lublu apparently asleep in the front seat, he asked the porter if he knew where the driver was. The porter informed him of what had occurred and said he believed that the young woman was not drunk but dead, adding that he did not know the name of the owner of the car. Tasan was startled by the probability of Lublu's death, but his composure was perfect. He examined Lublu, aware that she was subject to swooning spells. He realized that the porter had apparently guessed correctly.

"No, she's just dead sick," said Tasan. "She's a friend of mine and the owner of the car too. He was looking for me when he asked you to watch. It's all right now, I'll take charge of this." He gave the porter a dollar and he said, "Thank you, Colonel," saluted and walked off.

Tasan climbed into the driver's seat and started the car. As he curved the corner he saw one of the cleverest reporters of the most sensational of New York's newspapers approaching the scene. He was nicknamed "the Bloodhound." "I beat him to it," said Tasan. "I'm always here, there and everywhere, just at the right time."

He was not expert at driving and so he drove slowly, thinking of the unusual exit of his strange passenger and the blundering jeopardising action of Newton Castle. Thought Tasan, "The despicable coward, the yellow cur, ridden by the nightmare of fear, scared of a white shadow, screwy and jerky and jumpy like a rabbit. Trying to get an ignorant black working man in a mess of trouble. What an utter fool! Who would ever believe that such a man was mixed up in an obvious bohemian mess? Educated chut! Of what use his education when he carries his brain in the seat of his pants? Repulsive yellow louse."

Thus thought Tasan as he drove to the house of a doctor who lived in his neighborhood. The doctor was a comrade and friend. He was annoyed to be wakened at that late hour when he was snuggled in the lap of sleep. But his vexation vanished at the sight of Tasan. For he knew that there was a princely fee in anything Tasan wanted to be done. He invited Tasan to enter, but Tasan informed him that he had an urgent case just outside in the car. The doctor wrapped himself in a heavy robe and went out. He confirmed the fact that Lublu had been dead about four hours, from heart failure.

Tasan explained the circumstances under which she had died, filling in with his theory of what happened during the joy-ride, and informed the doctor that Lublu had had such attacks before. He enlisted the doctor's aid to liquidate the matter and keep Newton Castle's name out of it. They placed Lublu's body on the backseat. Then Tasan telephoned Lublu's aunt, informing her that the girl had had one of her frequent attacks, which was perhaps fatal, and he was bringing her home. The doctor got dressed and rode with Tasan to Lublu's apartment. The aunt, who was prepared for the worst, received them. They said what they could to console her. She was a "fellow traveler" along the party line and held Tasan in high estimation. He reassured her and promised to return at daybreak to arrange and defray all the costs of the funeral.

"Well, that's settled," Tasan said to the doctor as they drove away. "And I wish I was near a high cliff with that African jackass in this car; I'd send him hurtling over."

Meanwhile Newton Castle had wandered like a somnambulist through the streets of Harlem and finally arrived at home. Without removing his clothes or his shoes he threw himself facedown on the couch in the sitting room, lying motionless like a person in a heavy trance.

Towards dawn Delta called to him from the bedroom: she had heard him enter. "Newton, Newton! What have you brought into the apartment? It stinks as if it was flooded with all the sewers of Harlem."

Newton Castle gave no reply. Delta slipped into her kimono and went into the living room. She grasped Newton's kinks and vigorously shook him: "Newton, I am suffocating. What have you done to the place?"

He stirred without changing position and groaned: "She's DEAD!"

"Who's dead?" cried Delta. "What d'you mean, dead?!"

"She's DEAD, I say. I killed her!" He groaned again.

"Are you crazy?" Delta said. "Who did you kill? Who is dead?"

Again Newton Castle groaned: "Dead! Dead! DEAD!"

"I don't care who is dead," Delta cried hysterically, "but I won't stand this deadly stench and you like a helpless baby without its diaper. You're full of filth and more offensive than a skunk. You come on into the bathroom and clean yourself."

Delta prodded him up and into the bathroom, ripped off his clothes and pushed him in the tub. She turned the cold water on and he quickly added the hot himself. While she was scrubbing him, the telephone rang. It was Tasan calling.

"What is it?" snapped Delta. Tasan said he wanted Newton on the telephone.

"You can't get him," she said. "He's acting like a crazy man and won't see or talk to anybody. Said he killed somebody."

"Tell him that he didn't kill anybody," said Tasan. "The doctor pronounced the person dead from heart failure and his car is safe in my hands."

Delta delivered the message. Newton Castle leaped from the tub and, dashing naked into the sitting room, started singing, "I am free! I am free!" and dancing exactly as he had danced on the day when he invited his friends to convive at the death party for his sister.

"When you've finished your Salome number," said Delta, "you can throw out all the Russian rubbish that nearly landed you in jail and then I'll disinfect the house." She began by calling the elevator runner to take away Newton's filthy clothes. "You can burn them," she said.

ALAMAYA LANDS A REAL JOB

"Now that I'm no longer Princess Benebe Zarihana and a party member," said Gloria Kendall, "but only a member of the millions of unemployed, I guess I'll have to go on the block." She was conversing with Lij Alamaya in her one-room apartment in the Edgecombe Avenue section of Sugar Hill.

"What do you mean by 'go on the block'?" said Alamaya. "I thought that that was associated with some form of white slavery."

"I never could understand the nice distinction that was made," said Gloria, "unless it was a white euphemism to ignore the black side of the game, but what I meant was nothing more or less than the good old-time slavery of the block, which exists today in the Bronx Slave Market, almost as it does in Ethiopia."

"I wonder if I understand you rightly," said Alamaya. "Slavery in the Bronx, New York, in the most highly civilized city in the world? One of the main charges the Italians made against Ethiopia was that the Emperor had abolished slavery by decree only, but that it still existed in reality. And now you're trying to tell me that the same situation exists here. Do I look like a joke?"

"I will take you to see it with your own eyes," said Gloria. "There are over half a dozen blocks in the Bronx where starving colored women sit and wait for white women to come and buy them to work at ten cents an hour. Ten hours of lugging and scrubbing down on their knees to make one dollar. We call it the Bronx Slave Market, for the black women line up there and wait for the white mistresses just as the slaves down South waited for the masters to come and buy them. There are coolies in Asia and peons in Mexico, share-croppers in the South and slaves in the Bronx."

"The slaves don't starve in Ethiopia," said Alamaya, "for only wealthy people have slaves. But I've always thought that in the modern civilization, it is something of a luxury that a few people *should* starve. You know the Moslems starve themselves from dawn to twilight during the month of Ramadan and that is a luxury of faith. Luxury is like a warm bunch of beautiful orchids in cold New York which only the rich can afford."

"Tekla, I'm talking about bread and you're thinking about orchids. You're a born prince alright, but you might feel differently if you had to face starvation, or you might not. Life is so full of contradictions. When I was investigating the Bronx Slave Market for the Comintern, I had to look up some of these employers who were paying the black slaves ten cents an hour. And I discovered a lot of comrades among them: persons who live in two- and three-roomed apartments and can't afford a regular servant. So they hire one by the hour to clean up. Most of these comrades are well-paid workers. But they must pay party dues, buy tickets for party affairs, contribute to so many and plus more party drives from this and that cause and keep up with radical café society. When I rebuked them for hiring the black slaves at ten cents an hour, they were angry and said that they hired servant labor in the cheapest market according to the law of supply and demand. And it was the fault of the black slaves of the Bronx not to organize!"

"I'd like to go with you to see the slave blocks of the Bronx," said Alamaya, "but even though the comrades boycott you,

you won't need to go there to sell your labor. Tasan gave you a pretty name and you have a nice voice. He can't file an injunction against your using the name Princess Benebe with your voice. You can put them to work yourself and make them produce for you."

"I never thought of that," said Gloria.

"Ah, but you should," said Alamaya. "All your people should think more about doing things on their own initiative. Otherwise the Tasans among the whites will seek to hamstring your initiative and control your thinking. If Tasan used his imagination to create a Princess Benebe Zarihana out of Gloria Kendall, why not try to use your own to profit from Tasan's hoax? Go and see the impresario who wanted so badly to get you in the regular theatre. Tell him you are free to turn professional now that there's no Emperor of Ethiopia to object."

"But, Tekla," said Gloria, "you're full of bright ideas like any American salesman! How did you get that way?"

"One learns fast in America," he said.

"Yes, but not all the bright ideas turn out brilliantly. For instance, I may not be worth a bright new dime to the impresario now that Ethiopia is conquered by the Fascists. Haven't you noticed how quickly and easily the newspapers have changed their tone? They say the Fascists may modernize Ethiopia. And what the newspapers say today reflects the attitude of the democratic nations tomorrow: 'Ethiopia is an embarrassing subject. Let's try to forget it.'"

"To put it plainly," said Alamaya, "you mean that while Ethiopia was still fighting the Fascists, it was a good racket and easy to fabricate princes and princesses and excite people to contribute to help Ethiopia."

"That's just it," said Gloria. "All the fakers, whether they are individuals or organizations, must fold up now. Then the genuine people may have their break. You, for example, Tekla, you're worried about me, but what about yourself?"

"Me? Oh, I was thinking I could become the manager of Princess Benebe," said Alamaya. "As an Ethiopian princess you would be as genuine an article as myself as a Lij. 'Ethiopian' is a generic word and you are entitled to be called 'Ethiopian' exactly as you are called 'colored' or 'Aframerican.' And as for being a princess, well, you're lovelier than any of the princesses of Ethiopia."

Gloria crossed over to Alamaya and, sitting on the broad arm of his chair, she cuddled against him. Her face was warm against his and he kissed her.

"I love you, Gloria," he said.

"And what about Seraphine?"

"She's married in the Comintern church, but we are free, FREE!"

"To be each other's slave?" said Gloria.

"Why not?" said Alamaya. "Better to be the individual slave of love that is human than to be the mindless slave of a movement."

Gloria and Alamaya agreed that she should essay the perpetuation of the role of Princess Benebe as a professional performer. But when Alamaya, as her representative, tried to promote her, he discovered that Gloria was more correct in her estimation of the situation. Where Maxim Tasan with his large experience and influential contacts was expertly successful in selling a fraudulent alloy, Alamaya was a failure in separating the pure metal from the dross and trying to sell the genuine article.

The impresario who previously was so eager to flash the spotlights on Gloria parading in her gorgeous costumes was now haughtily indifferent. He rudely informed Alamaya that Ethiopia defeated was nothing but an unimportant and worthless "back number" and that princes and princesses of Ethiopia were less important to the public than Harlem porters and scrubwomen. Alamaya was told that the only Ethiopia now that might prove a profitable attraction as entertainer was the

Emperor Haile Selassie himself. And he was offered a splendid commission as an agent if he could use his influence to persuade Haile Selassie to leave Palestine for the United States. The impresario was confident that the Emperor could make up for the fortune he had lost to Italy, if he would consent to appear in a dervish dance on the American stage.

Alamaya was exceedingly angry. The high-powered salesman of modern amusement had humiliated him even more than Tasan had ever done. Apparently he took a clown's delight in getting over a cheap joke at the expense of the defeated Ethiopian nation. However, Alamaya tried to conceal his anger under a mask of dignity. He had invited the affront, he reflected, in his naïve attempt to enlist the professional help of this man, who, a friend of Tasan, was also his counterpart in the world of entertainment.

"I'm sorry," said Alamaya quietly, "but I'm afraid that the Emperor of Ethiopians could not be persuaded to perform a dervish dance for the American stage, even though there's a fortune in it. He may prefer to remain a poor exile in Jerusalem."

The impresario rubbed his enormously fat fingers together and champed his fine cigar, which appeared in his mouth like a fetish of smug self-satisfaction. "Don't stand so pat on your Ethiopian dignity, my good fellow," he said. "We have had the Queen of Romania,[1] the granddaughter of Queen Victoria herself doing her stuff on the vast American stage. Your Emperor has a chance to make his now, while Ethiopia is still half alive. Colored people are all natural-born actors. Better for Haile Selassie to become a dancing dervish making good money in America than to stay in Jerusalem, where he may eventually be reduced to the status of a street Arab hanging around the Mosque of Omar."[2]

"I suppose I should show my appreciation of your counteroffer and thank you," said Alamaya. He picked up his hat and walked out.

_____

As the excitement leading up to the execution of a man ends with a public sigh of respite when the deed is done, so a wet blanket of silence had descended heavily upon the defeat of Ethiopia. Like a fall of late hoar upon the verdant earth quickly dissipated by the rising sun, Ethiopia had suddenly evaporated from the headlines and disappeared from the front page and the sidewalk forums of conversation.

Going to Harlem alone, Lij Alamaya had a feeling of an unknown, unnoticed visitor in a strange indifferent country. In that territory which conveys such a warm impression of insouciant general intimacy of everybody knowing one another, Alamaya explored the blocks in bright daylight and nobody recognized him. The grand acclamation that was accorded him upon his first visit to Harlem appeared now as unreal as the extravagantly glittering armor of Professor Koazhy. Ethiopia is as remote and strange now as the Einstein Theory[3] to these people, thought Alamaya. When they were stirred up about it, it was like a sudden collective flare-up, like one of our tribes running amok.

One morning Alamaya was making preparations to leave his hotel, when Pablo Peixota called on him. Alamaya was surprised and expressed his gratification for the visit of his former colleague and friend.

"I can see that you are surprised," said Peixota, "but I hope you will not be displeased. As you would not come to see me, I made it my business to come to you."

"I wanted to come to see you," said Alamaya. "I made more than one attempt, but I literally fell by the wayside—I could not go through with it. I was ashamed, because I was a failure."

"The shame is on our side," said Peixota. "And if your mission is a failure, it is because we failed you. I think you acted your part with distinction. It was a difficult job. You were the representative of the government of a nation of people, accredited to a

people with vague nationalistic group yearnings but with no actual experience of what it means to be a nation. Between the
white wire-pullers who understood the significance of the movement and their colored stooges who could not understand, you
were like a man dancing on a tightrope and I think your performance was excellent."

"You are very generous, Mr. Peixota," said Alamaya, "but I
know that my performance was indifferent. I might have done
better. You believed in me, you had faith in the cause of Ethiopia, but I was never entirely frank with you."

"That's nothing and we may do better forgetting it," said
Peixota. "You were a diplomat and must have had diplomatic
secrets. I know enough of the game from my experience with
the diplomats and fixers of what they call the underworld."

"But I was not as genuine a diplomat as I pretended to be,"
said Alamaya. "I may just as well be frank with you. I did not
tell you the whole truth about the Emperor's letter."

"Oh, I know all about the letter," said Peixota. "I heard that
you found it on that dirty rascal Tasan. We ought to find a way
to make him pay for it. I think I can help you get a good lawyer
to sue him and get your share of the Comintern dollars."

"I wish I could," said Alamaya, "but I'm not in a position as
favorable to prosecute Tasan as he is to persecute me. I must
confess I did not tell you all the truth about myself. I joined the
Communists when I was in France."

"I am not really surprised to hear that," said Peixota. "I always thought that there was some secret you did not want to
reveal, but in spite of that I was convinced that you were fun-
damentally sincere and honest and patriotic."

"I joined when the idea of the Popular Front was sweeping up
the world," said Alamaya. "It appeared then as if the world
were divided between the Liberal Left (including the Communists) and the Conservative Right with the Fascists. Every
decent-minded man sided with the Left if he believed in the

traditional ideas of freedom and liberty and self-determination and tolerance for minority groups and small nations. And it was exactly that time when the world was fermenting with the new idea, that the Fascists chose to launch their war in Ethiopia."

"I understand perfectly," said Peixota. "If I was young like you, I might have been tempted to take the same stand. The young impressionable mind believes in miracles. It believes that if the rod of Democracy is transformed into a serpent, it can swallow the Communist snake and become the same good old rod again. Like Aaron's rod, eh?[4] You don't need to explain anymore. I understand everything, except why Tasan should have so much power over you."

"Because I haven't explained everything," said Alamaya. "The Emperor's letter was not genuine."

"Not genuine!" Peixota cried. "Impossible! That seemed to me the most authentic thing of all."

"It was authentic, but it was not genuine," said Alamaya. "I'll tell you all about it. The letter was written about twelve years ago, when the government of Ethiopia had made arrangements to send a mission to the Aframericans. Some prominent Africans, Haitians, Cubans, Aframericans and others who were identified with the Pan-African movement of that period had interested the Ethiopians in the idea of sending a mission. But the plan was abandoned just before it was put into execution, because powerful states of the League of Nations disapproved of it. The letter in my possession belonged to one of the originally designated members of the postponed mission. It was alright as an exhibition, when so few people can read the official Amharic language of Ethiopia, but it couldn't stand close scrutiny, and Maxim Tasan knew that."

"Then you were not a representative of Ethiopia?" asked Peixota.

"Yes, I was—I am," said Alamaya. "But I am more representative of the secret organization of the progressive Youth of

Ethiopia than of the official moribund Ethiopia. I am a patriot. I believe in the future of my country and of my people. And that is why I would not follow the lead of the Comintern, when my eyes were opened to see that it was no good for my country or my people or Aframericans."

"That is all I want to hear," said Peixota. "My confidence in you is not shaken. Indeed it is greater, for you have had your baptism of fire and you are stronger. I came here to find out if I could be of any help in your future plans. I don't know just what your plans may be, but I know that you must need help now that Ethiopia is defeated and deserted as much as you did when Ethiopia was fighting with thousands cheering from the sidelines. Perhaps your need is greater now."

Alamaya informed Peixota that he had not formulated any plans. He had broken decisively with the Friends of Ethiopia. He considered himself an ordinary refugee and would start looking for a job.

"You are not any ordinary refugee," said Peixota. "You're an important refugee. And I am here to offer my help. There's a place in my office for you, the place that Seraphine had. I will give you a better salary and you will learn something about one phase of the American housing system. Someday you may need the experience, if Ethiopia should ever regain her independence."

"Do you mean that you are giving me a responsible place in your office, even though I have no experience?" said Alamaya. "How will I find words to express my gratitude for your help—for your confidence in me?"

"It is enough appreciation when you accept my offer," said Peixota. "The white people are taking care of all their important refugees and even the unimportant ones. Yet they have so many big talents among themselves, they could afford to neglect a lot without losing anything. But we Aframericans—we have so few in comparison—nothing compared to the whites.

Yet we neglect the few persons of talent in our midst. If it were not for the whites recognizing and giving them a helping hand, we would have nothing at all to show."

"Mr. Peixota, I shall work like a fellah[5] and live like an ascetic to show my appreciation of your kindness," said Alamaya. "You say I should not thank you, but I must—"

"Don't thank me, I beg you," said Peixota. "If you must show your feelings that way, you should thank the young woman who came to see me yesterday. If I were young like you with such a girl who believed in me, to stand up with me, I would be the happiest man in the world."

"Gloria Kendall!" said Alamaya. "She went to see you about me?"

"Indeed she did," said Peixota. "And a wonderful advocate you have in her. She told me everything, except about the technical details of the Emperor's letter. And so I was prepared for your revelations."

"She's a lovely lovable girl," said Alamaya, "with a splendid head on her shoulders."

"And her wonderful heart in your hands," said Peixota. "Be careful how you handle it, Alamaya. Hearts like hers are the reservoirs of the pure lifeblood of the manhood of our group."

"She will always be enshrined in *my* heart as Princess Benebe," said Alamaya. "Maxim Tasan planned the role for her as a cheap masquerade to ridicule Ethiopia and Aframericans. But she fooled him. She made a beautiful part of it and she inspired me to have hope and confidence in myself."

"Neither Ethiopia nor Aframericans can be ridiculed," said Peixota. "The Aframerican comedy is the big tragedy of American Civilization. And I firmly believe that Ethiopia—the oldest Christian nation—must rise again, if Christianity continues to be the religion of modern Civilization."

"I predict that Ethiopia will be the jinx of the League of Nations," said Alamaya. "I am a mystic, for Ethiopia is half

African and half Asiatic. It will jinx the world. I remember early last year when the crisis became acute and Ethiopia was finding it extremely difficult to get her case before the League of Nations. The Czecho-Slovak minister was the president of the League Council. And when the Ethiopian envoy to Paris kept right on worrying him like a gadfly, one day the Czecho-Slovak minister said, resentfully, that Europe was too busy with important problems to attend to the affairs of backward Africa. The Ethiopian envoy said to the Czecho-Slovak minister: 'Africa is Europe's backyard and if an epidemic starts there and Europe ignores it, it will spread to the front yard.'"

"The Ethiopian envoy said exactly the right thing," said Peixota. "It excites me to think how closely the problem of Ethiopia and Europe parallels the Aframericans in America. When we organize and protest many liberal whites warn us that we are better off than Jews in Germany. That's the attitude of the big guns of the Popular Front. Well-meaning whites are weighing Aframerican minority problems by a European standard. They quite forget that our group position has never approached the high estate of the Jews in Germany. Short of exile or extermination, what the Nazis are attempting in Germany is to reduce the Jews socially and politically to the level of colored people in America. I often wonder if the Nazis have made a secret comprehensive study of the laws and customs covering the status of the Aframerican minority."

"Africans and Aframericans everywhere," said Alamaya, "we have the stupendous task of demonstrating always before the white world to prove that humanity is not a special privilege and that we also are part of the human race. The fate of Ethiopia has proved that such ideals as Collective Security and Popular Front will work only if organized on the basis of practical and mutual self-interest."

"Precisely," said Peixota. "I have held consistently to that point of view. Our Tammany Hall[6] is a Popular Front of the

kind you describe. Every group composing it has its own interests and the strength of its vote to promote them. Irish, Italians, Jews and the rest of us. It certainly isn't God's love among
them holding them together in Tammany Hall. It's just good
old-fashioned horse trading, but it works. And at last we
Aframericans are breaking in, since we're beginning to learn
how to organize in a practical way. But we've hardly begun
before the Communists and their friends start maneuvering to
capture our organizations. What for? Not for *our* interest but
for *their* interest. To control us for *their* purpose. When we
resist them they try to put us on the spot, saying we believe in
segregation. They use their superior white position to promote
a lie against our vital interests and whitewash it to make it
appear like truth. The Maxim Tasans of today are the carpet-
baggers of yesterday. They mean us no good. They use our
Newton Castles and Prudhomme Bishops against us."

"And with apparent success," said Alamaya.

"Because such men have no principles of life and no feeling of
fundamental human fellowship," said Peixota. "To grow to an
understanding and appreciation of universal human fellowship,
you must first be nourished and reared with the feeling of fellowship within your own group. A man with a sense of the obligation of family life will appreciate family life in general. And
a nation built upon the principle of self-respect will appreciate
such principles in other nations."

"The Maxim Tasans do not believe in the principles of human
fellowship and national self-respect," said Alamaya. "They regard
such things as bourgeois virtues."

"How a principle of human relationship may be bourgeois
or proletarian, or Aryan, Mongolian or African any more than
the sexual act can be, only Communists and Fascists can tell,"
said Peixota. "I am going now. But I almost forgot to tell you
that your former rooms at my house are still at your disposal."

"Thank you, Mr. Peixota. I wish to ask you if the report

about my friend Dorsey Flagg is true," said Alamaya. "Gloria said she heard he was fired by his college."

"Yes," said Peixota. "He was notified that his services ended with his sabbatical because of his political activities. But Newton Castle still holds his job, although everybody knows that he's too extremely neurotic to continue to teach. But that's the way it goes. It's the better men who always get it in the neck. They got Koazhy too."

"Professor Koazhy!" said Alamaya.

"Yes, indeed," said Peixota. "He had been living in a little old private house for twenty years, reserving one floor for himself and renting the rest. And we were all under the lasting impression that he owned it. So it created quite a stir last week when his furniture and a huge pile of books were dumped on the sidewalk. His landlord refused to renew his lease. The landlord said he had received a report that Koazhy was a Fascist and anti-Semite and was teaching Fascist doctrines to his Senegambian students. It was a terrible blow to the old professor. He had lived such a long time in the house and had piled up such a lot of books there that he regarded it as his permanent home and university. And he had it cheap, couldn't get anything like it now. And he's become so obsessed and mystical with African magic and glory that he has lost the skill of taking care of himself in a practical way."

"Then how is he making out? What's become of his big stack of books?" said Alamaya.

"I found a dummy to find him a temporary place to stay at," said Peixota. "I have to do it secretly, for there are many more like him needing help in Harlem. It's better for my health that I should live up to my reputation as a strict landlord instead of acquiring notoriety as a good samaritan."

"Perhaps Friend Tasan had a hand in these new developments," said Alamaya. "He is devilishly impish. I heard him say that Aframerican life passed through a bottleneck that was easy to control and he could make it hot like hell for any Aframerican who had the effrontery to fight the Comintern and the Popular Front."

"He may turn on the heat all right, but it will only warm us up to keep on fighting," said Peixota. "And now I must go," he said, taking his hat.

THE LEOPARDS DANCE

There were seven weeks of calm like a truce. And the Aframerican community was sobered like a high-spirited person convalescing from the frenzy of an emotional collapse. Suddenly the Spanish Civil War[1] belched its flames and roared, shaking like Samson the pillars of Civilization. The heat of its passion spread and seared and divided the Latin-American colony of Harlem and its sparks flared over the horizon of the Aframerican community. And soon it too was touched by the ardent agitation of the Spanish-Americans and the powerful, organized efforts to help the cause of the Spanish Republic.

The White Friends of Ethiopia was rechristened the Friends of Ethiopia-and-Spain, and a campaign was launched to bring the Aframerican minority actively into the ranks of the liberal and radical groups that were aiding the defense of the Republican Loyalists. New slogans were coined: "Fight for Spain to Free Ethiopia"; "A Fascist Spain Will Help Perpetuate a Fascist Ethiopia"; "If Spain Wins Freedom, Ethiopia Will Obtain Liberty"; "Stop the Fascists in Spain and Block Them in Africa."

The propaganda was projected not only for its local but also for its international effect. As native African troops were mustered by the Spanish militarists in their attack upon the Republic and as Aframericans were more or less ideologically grouped with native Africans, it was a thing of international significance to have the Aframericans siding with the Spanish

Republic. But the Hands to Ethiopia had disintegrated, the popular Aframerican leaders, beaten and discouraged, could not be whipped together again into the first line of propaganda activity, and the masses were apathetic. The comrades paraded and slugged their slogans into the air, but the Communist leadership was weak and ineffective without the support of the local leaders.

The leading spirits of the Hands to Ethiopia were still sore and resentful from their skirmish with Maxim Tasan and his tools among the White Friends of Ethiopia. It was Professor Koazhy who started the agitation to oppose the new propaganda of the White Friends among the Aframericans. Koazhy went to see Peixota and asked him to release a public statement that the Hands to Ethiopia was not supporting the Friends of Ethiopia in their campaign for Spain-and-Ethiopia and that the latter organization was not truly representative of the Aframericans.

Peixota demurred at first. He was reluctant to be associated with such a statement, because all his sympathies went to the Loyalists. But he agreed with Koazhy that the Friends of Ethiopia were using defeated Ethiopia for their own purposes. Lij Alamaya supported Koazhy. He considered it a despicable thing that the Friends were dragging the prostrate body of his nation into the campaign for the Spanish Loyalists. To him it was like the defiling of a corpse. He knew that the idea originated in the mind of Maxim Tasan. And he knew that Tasan felt nothing but contempt for Ethiopia. Why should such a vile person be allowed to make a travesty of the misery of Ethiopia? Why should he continue in his attempt to deceive and confuse the Aframericans and the white humanitarians who still believed in human justice? How was it possible that the Maxim Tasans of the world were so agile and adept at changing their colors and jumping from one side to the other at the opportune moment? What was wrong with humanity that it still accepted the leadership of such men? For something *is* wrong; humanity is fatally sick without any principle to guide or morality to sustain it. And the Maxim Tasans are always ahead, outmaneuvering and defeating the honest-minded persons who seek to oppose them.

Persisting in his efforts, Professor Koazhy succeeded in getting the Executive Committee of the remnant of the Hands to Ethiopia to release a statement repudiating the Spain-and-Ethiopia campaign among Aframericans. The statement was prominently featured in Aframerican weeklies, but ignored by the daily press. Indirectly the *Labor Herald* noticed it when its Aframerican writer printed an indictment of reactionary Aframerican leaders who, ignorant of the power politics, were refusing to lead their people onto the international stage of affairs.

Professor Koazhy made sidewalk speeches and collected money, with which he printed the statement of the Hands to Ethiopia leaders in the leaflet form and distributed thousands of copies among the Harlem people.

Meanwhile Maxim Tasan had decided to stage a farewell party in Harlem before sailing away to devote his genius to the cause of the Spanish Republic. Since the defection of Newton Castle, Tasan had found a willing collaborator in Prudhomme Bishop. But actually Tasan despised Bishop and his debased jumbled imitation of the art of elocution, which had imparted a perpetual nauseating sweet expression to his pumpkin-pie face. Tasan's estimate of Prudhomme Bishop was perhaps an indicator of his reaction to the entire Aframerican group. Close contact had filled him with contempt for it. As a man whose life was consecrated to active action by the manipulation of propaganda and intrigue he had discovered the minor theatre of Aframerican life altogether inadequate for his ideas. It was like a tower crowded with somber shadows with a narrow entrance and no exits.

Tasan projected the plan of an all-night fiesta in Harlem for Ethiopia-and-Spain. He confided to Prudhomme Bishop that he was ambitious to put over something unforgettable: something that could assemble a multitude of people and make money. The intake was to be divided between Prudhomme Bishop's Equal Rights Action and the Friends of Ethiopia-and-Spain.

Tasan desired to stage a glorified modernized version of an authentic African pastime. He discussed his conception of it with Prudhomme Bishop. His idea was that as Aframericans were obsessed with synthetic ideas of Africa, with so many pseudo-African societies among them, he would treat them to something genuine.

Tasan was introduced to Diup Wuluff. Diup was a West African who had made several attempts to create an African theatre in Harlem by drawing upon his extensive knowledge of native African amusement patterns. But he had never tasted the sweet fruit of success with any of his ventures. He possessed original ideas of the native African scene but could not develop and clothe them properly to meet the exigencies of the modern American stage. He had staged impressive exhibitions in obscure Harlem places. There were parts that came up heaving like the hulk of an elephant or sharp like the menacing horn of a furious rhinoceros, but they were never expertly welded together to make the whole of the performance a triumph. And apparently Diup could not or would not learn the sophisticated tricks.

When Maxim Tasan made contact with Diup, the latter was destitute and willing to sell his talents for any fee. He supplied Tasan with details of the various native African pastimes. And one above all fascinated Tasan—the Society of African Leopard Men. Tasan thought that nothing could be more original than staging a leopard dance in Harlem. Harlem had witnessed many curiously native African things: dances of African masks, fetishers and medicine men in an orgy of supernatural manifestations,

totem-taboo extravaganzas, festivals of circumcision, and ritu-
als of obscure primitive phallicisms. But Harlem had never had
a leopard dance. And that was Maxim Tasan's choice.

He planned a gala of the Society of Leopard Men with Africans supplemented by Aframericans. Tasan promised to supply
all the skins of the leopards and Diup to find all the men to wear
them. Tasan employed a designer and a decorator to work on
the plan, with Diup furnishing the details. They planned to
erect a kraal in the middle of the hall and create a jungle atmosphere with prowling leopards and the sound of tom-tom.

Tasan gave the requisite publicity to his last gesture in Harlem, and supported by his considerable circle of friends and
their friends, and the followers of Prudhomme Bishop, he had
the assurance of success in the novel venture. He found eager
sponsors among the high lights and big guns of the theatrical
world. Diup Wuluff rounded up all the available African na-
tives in New York, whether they came from the West or the
North or the South or the East—all were partial to the idea of
luxuriating in the skin of the leopard for one night. Diup was
boundlessly enthusiastic. In the dance of the leopard men he
felt the elastic steps leading up the ladder of successful achievement. The white men who Tasan chose to work with him were
extremely tactful. They made him feel that he was the genius of
the grandiose plan and they merely technical assistants to him.

Meanwhile the date of the dance of the Society of Leopard
Men was announced and carried gloriously brightly along on
the crest of the movement to give aid to Republican Spain. But
the real Aframerican friends of Ethiopia in Harlem remained
sullen and unmoved. They agitated against the Communist efforts to recruit Aframerican youth to fight in Spain, citing that
no effort had been made to send a black army to Ethiopia.
They were resentful of the high degree of perfection of the efficiently organized and smoothly running campaign in the hands

of the same whites who had employed every conceivable strata-
gem to handicap the Aframerican Hands to Ethiopia.

A week before the date of the dance, Tasan and Diup were
eating late one evening in the dingy Suckabone Barbecue on
Harlem's Seventh Avenue. Tasan had been attending a Popular
Front meeting whose purpose was to band the matrons of Harlem in a league to work with the special Women's Auxiliary for
Spanish Aid. Now nearly all the assembled Aframerican women
were wives and daughters of doctors and lawyers, schoolteach-
ers and heads of social institutions and stars of the stage. They
had come to the meeting dressed in all the elegance of late-
spring styles, and with an open mind to listen to the words of
their white sisters. But they were affronted by the remarks of
the lady in the chair, who appealed to them to help by saying:
"You can make a very real contribution to the work of helping
Spain. Downtown we have women who have volunteered and
are working in teams knitting socks and sweaters for the brave
Loyalist soldiers, others are busy assorting various articles of
clothing to be dispatched and still others are wrapping up pack-
ages. We want our colored sisters to join us. We all know that
you colored women are the best cooks in the world and we
would like some of you to come downtown to cook some of
your delicious meals for our brave workers."

While the chairman was speaking the expression on the
faces of the Harlem matrons was one of chagrin and hostility.
When she finished there was an unpleasant silence. The chairman stood up again and she said: "The discussion is open and
we would like to have some words of encouragement from our
colored friends."

Finally Mrs. Austinette Burns rose from her seat. She was
tall as a ladder with the aplomb of a mannikin, pale like saw-
dust and haughty like a spirited horse. She was the wife of a
prosperous physician and specialist in kidney diseases and also

the acknowledged social leader of the matrons of Harlem. Mrs. Burns said: "I am so sorry to disappoint the chairman and our downtown friends. But I employ a cook to do my own cooking, I am so busy with more important affairs. Besides, cooking is injurious to my health. I don't know if the chairman employs a cook, but if it is cooks you are looking for you should not have invited us to this meeting. You can find all you need up at the Bronx Slave Market."

Mrs. Burns walked out of the hall and all the other Harlem matrons trooped after her.

Maxim Tasan was extremely irritated by the tactlessness of the lady in the chair. He was leaving the funny little diversion of the Aframerican scene for really big and serious assignments in Spain, and he desired to emphasize the impression externally that the Aframerican people were resigned to linking the fate of Ethiopia with Spain. He wanted to make it appear that the chauvinist-racial and Fascist-motivated policy of the Hands to Ethiopia had bankrupted itself and that the colored folk preferred the Comintern's Friends of Ethiopia operating through the Popular Front. His irritation was increased because earlier in the evening he had espied Professor Koazhy and some of his Senegambians distributing the broadsides against the newly improvised programme of the Friends of Ethiopia-and-Spain.

Diup was long and lanky, and wearing black he made one think more of a hooded serpent than a leopard and leader of leopard men.

Said Tasan to him: "When you stage a carnival of the leopard men in Africa, doesn't something tragic sometimes take place?"

"In Africa, yes," said Diup. "There is always a human victim who is slain to make a sacrifice of blood to the leopards."

"Who does the killing?" asked Tasan.

"One of the leopard men, of course," said Diup.

"And do they merely kill indiscriminately?" asked Tasan. "Just any innocent person?"

"They generally choose a bad person, one who is an evil influence in the community," said Diup.

Tasan remained silent for a while and Diup sucked at his sparerib.

"It would be more exciting if you could put over the real African thing in Harlem," said Tasan, "if you could get away with it as smoothly as they say they do in Africa."

"You mean to have one of the leopards kill somebody," said Diup.

"That's just what I mean," said Tasan. "It would make the affair wonderfully mysterious and reveal the real power of the magic of Africa. I would stand all expenses."

"The killing must be done by a special person," said Diup. "In Africa it is the privilege of certain families. I know only one man in New York who has the right to do it. The mark of it is branded on his arm."

"Would he do it?" Tasan demanded eagerly. "Would he kill a man?"

"Of course he would as part of the performance," said Diup. "He is a real leopard man and if you want the actual thing done as it is done in Africa he will get his victim here just as he would in Africa. But you must have a victim. Who is he?"

"I have a victim in mind," said Tasan, "but can I trust you? Will you swear to keep it a secret?"

"I swear by my mother's head and the leopard's claws to keep the secret," said Diup.

"Whether the victim is killed or not?" said Tasan.

"Whether the victim is killed or not," repeated Diup.

"It is Professor Koazhy," said Tasan.

"Professor Koazhy!" cried Diup, his eyes ablaze like a ferocious wild cat's.

"Sure," said Tasan. "He's a pest in the community and a fakir pretending to know all the mysteries of ancient Africa, all the fetish practices and magic rites. Koazhy is the worst of the fakers in Harlem, thriving on the African racket. It would be appropriate if he were destroyed by the real African magic. If it can be done, it would be a perfect ending."

"It can be done," said Diup, looking steadily down on the floor.

At last it was the exciting day of the leopards' dance for Ethiopia-and-Spain. In the center of the immense Bamboo Hall there was built an impressive kraal, which provided a realistic environment for the performance of the leopard men. Stage and society, literati and sport-lights, Broadway organized a hectic hike to Harlem to enjoy the leopards disporting themselves in their imitation skins.

The well-mixed throng, eager in its expectation of a new thrill of novelty, filled the hall to capacity. Everything was thoroughly prepared, for the comrades of the Comintern excel in promotion and publicity. What other group could assemble such a large and distinctive gathering flavored with ingredients of all strata of society? Among the distinguished Harlemites, Professor Koazhy was conspicuous. He had received a special invitation and unlike Pablo Peixota and Lij Alamaya, who were not present, he was too vain not to accept.

The leopards were corralled, dozens of them herded up by Diup's energy and skill. Brightly spotted with arched tails they plunged in and out of the kraal with regal animal elegance and Maxim Tasan was uplifted with pride in his spotted skin and the whole delightful creation of his imagination. Diup had insisted that Tasan too should be disguised as a leopard with, as a mark of distinction as a special guest, a white plume attached to his tail. Diup informed Tasan that that was the custom in Africa when a white was initiated in the ritual of the black art. Thus the conception and execution of the plan of the leopard dance had projected Tasan into the holy diabolical inner sanctum of black magic.

Director Diup was also distinguished as the leader leopard with two tails. He cracked his long-lashed animal-training whip and the leopard men lined up in ring formation, shaking their paws, shaking their tails, dancing on two feet and dancing on four feet, striding and shaking, leaping and shimmying to the tintamarre of the black orchestra, dominated by the profoundly fatalistic pounding of the tom-tom.

Gorgeously dressed like tropical birds and fascinated by the spotted skins, eagerly the women rushed to find partners among the leopard men. The revelers leaped across the barriers of caste and place and brains, dividing man from man and man from animals, and recklessly gamboled in a whirling orgy of abandon. And Tasan gamboled with them wildly as he never had before. He was intoxicated by the strangeness of his savage role, the sensation of astonishing his illuminated circle with the achievement of possessing the inside knowledge of an initiate of a primitive animistic secret society.

All night the leopards, prompting and leading the dancing, frolicked with their human partners in and out of the kraal. And when dramatically they all collapsed together, exhausted, lying in formation of a semi-circle along the kraal, it seemed as if the performance had reached its climax. But Maxim Tasan could not leave with his departing friends, because for him the greater climax was still to come. At last Diup signaled to him and they disappeared from the scene.

At first, when the plan was worked out, Tasan had expressed his unwillingness to be present at the final denouement of the leopard dance. But Diup had informed him that, according to the African ritual, he had to witness the deed himself, otherwise it could not be executed. Diup and Tasan drove to the corner of a dismal street. They dismissed the taxicab and walked down into the heavy shadows. Diup led Tasan into the damp obscure corridor of an apparently deserted building. Diup instructed Tasan to wait there while he disappeared. Left alone in the jungle of his thoughts, it seemed to Tasan as if he was waiting through the terror of an age. The dreary malodorous corridor of the condemned building in that sinister street was like a cavernous lair of evil spirits who existed upon destruction and death. And for the first time Tasan felt afraid of the hell he had created.

But he was reassured by Diup's appearing with a brother leopard man, the authentic one, who was entitled to do, and capable of executing, the final act of the dance. And now silently, Diup leading the way with Tasan following and the other behind, the three leopard men started to climb the dirty, rank, rubbish-impeded stairs of the humid building.

To Tasan those steps seemed more difficult than the thousands he had negotiated through the intricate years of intrigue. Perhaps he reflected it might have been best if he had not resorted to the exorcism of black magic. It was not as simple as it appeared to the ignorant on the surface. It was satanic, Tasan thought, and from experience he knew what it meant to be an ally of Satan. The night was speeding like a tardy owl winging onward to its hidden rendezvous, but to Tasan it seemed an unending night of nights.

At the top of the last flight of stairs they discovered three other leopards crouching around a man wearing a hideous whitened mask. The man removed the mask and Tasan ejaculated: "Professor Koazhy!"

"Professor Koazhy alive in the flesh," said Koazhy. He said something sharp as the crack of a whip in a phrase unintelligible to Tasan. And Diup answered in another, equally unintelligible.

"What does that mean?" Tasan asked.

"It is the password of Professor Koazhy's Senegambians, of which I am a member," said Diup.

"You a member?" said Tasan.

"Yes, I'm a leading member," said Diup, "and the pledge of

a Senegambian is more sacred than the oath of a member of the Society of Leopard Men."

Koazhy held up his right hand, his crooked fingers making a strange sign. The crouching leopards quickly divested Maxim Tasan of his civilized clothing and left him wrapped in his leopard skin. He tried to protest, but discovered that he was gagged. He was whisked up over the roof to its perilous edge. The street below was deserted and as ominously silent as the jungle of Tasan's imagination.

"Jump!" said Diup. "Do to yourself what you told us to do to Professor Koazhy."

Tasan drew back with a horrible look of fear, turning in an attempt to flee. But the leopard men blocked his way and pressed him back to the edge of the roof.

"Jump!" said Diup, and at his signal the leopards struck their claws into Tasan.

Tasan was shot through with excruciating pain as if a shower of poisoned darts had penetrated his vitals. With the stifled whine of a trapped beast he leaped up and over the roof, his vile body breaking upon and dashing his brains among the garbage of the neglected Harlem pavement.

Explanatory Notes

INTRODUCTION

1   *Habent sua fata libelli:* A Latin phrase meaning "Books have their fates," or, "Books have their own destiny," attributed to Terentianus Maurus, a grammarian from the Mauretania region (now Morocco), who probably lived in 2 AD. The phrase comes from a longer verse, *Pro captu lectoris habent sua fata libelli* (meaning, "According to the capabilities of the reader, books have their destiny," or, "The fate of books depends on the reader's comprehension"), in Terentianus's *De litteris, De syllabis, De Metris*, but has since often been used in its short form as a broad assertion about books. See, for example, Walter Benjamin's "Unpacking My Library" from *Illuminations.*

2   On Roth, see Jay A. Gertzman, *Samuel Roth, Infamous Modernist* (Gainesville: University Press of Florida, 2013); Gertzman, "Not Quite Honest: Samuel Roth's 'Unauthorized' *Ulysses* and the 1927 International Protest," *Joyce Studies Annual* (2009): 34–66; and Paul K. Saint-Amour, "Soliloquy of Samuel Roth: A Paranormal Defense," *James Joyce Quarterly* 37, no. 3 (Spring 2000): 459–77.

3   Vladimir Nabokov, *The Original of Laura*, ed. Dmitri Nabokov (New York: Vintage, 2013); Ralph Ellison, *Three Days Before the Shooting . . .* , ed. John Callahan and Adam Bradley (New York: Modern Library, 2011); Jack Kerouac, *La vie est d'hommage*, ed. Jean-Christophe Cloutier (Montreal: Boréal, 2016); Jack Kerouac, *The Unknown Kerouac: Rare, Unpublished & Newly Translated Writings*, ed. Todd Tietchen (New York: Library of America, 2016); Harper Lee, *Go Set a Watchman* (New York:

Harper Perennial, 2015); David Foster Wallace, *The Pale King* (New York: Little, Brown and Company, 2011).

4 Wayne F. Cooper, *Claude McKay: Rebel Sojourner in the Harlem Renaissance* (Baton Rouge: LSU Press, 1987), 347.

5 See "The Cycle," in McKay, *Complete Poems*, ed. William J. Maxwell (Urbana: University of Illinois Press, 2004), 241–69. McKay's agent Carl Cowl helped arrange the posthumous publication of *Selected Poems of Claude McKay* (1953; repr., New York: Harcourt Brace Jovanovich, 1969). The Jamaican memoir finally appeared nearly three decades later: McKay, *My Green Hills of Jamaica and Five Jamaican Short Stories*, ed. Merwyn Morris (Kingston: Heinemann Educational Book, 1979). Regarding McKay's work on these projects, see Cooper, *Claude McKay*, 363–65.

6 In 1938 and 1939, the literary agent Laurence Roberts wrote McKay regarding the submission of the manuscript of *Harlem Glory* to publishers (he refers to the book both under that title and as "Mellinda and Buster," after the names of two main characters). See Roberts's letters to McKay, 27 July 1938 and 8 February 1939, Folder 177, Claude McKay Collection, Beinecke Rare Book and Manuscript Library, Yale University. The book was published posthumously by McKay's last agent, Carl Cowl, under the title *Harlem Glory: A Fragment of Aframerican Life* (Chicago: Charles H. Kerr, 1990).

7 Carl Cowl, letter to Jean Wagner, 7 February 1970, Box 12, Folder 16, Michel Fabre Collection, Manuscript, Archives, and Rare Book Library, Emory University.

8 See John Macrae, letter to McKay, 7 August 1941, Max Eastman Mss. II, Addition 1, Lilly Library Manuscript Collections, Indiana University. Our thanks to Christoph Irmscher for drawing our attention to this letter and to the other correspondence in this 2017 addition to the Eastman archive. See Christoph Irmscher, *Max Eastman: A Life* (New Haven: Yale University Press, 2017), 305.

9 On McKay's time in Morocco, see Brent Hayes Edwards, "The Taste of the Archive," *Callaloo* 35, no. 4 (2012): 944–72.

10 Wayne Cooper, introduction to *The Passion of Claude McKay: Selected Prose and Poetry, 1912–1948* (New York: Schocken, 1973), 37.

11 For McKay's perspective on the Harlem Artists' Guild, see especially *Harlem: Negro Metropolis* (New York: E. P. Dutton, 1940), 249–51, which introduces a number of concerns that resonate in *Amiable with Big Teeth*, especially in Chapter 20 ("Art and Race").

12 McKay offers a thorough recollection of the Negro Writers' Guild endeavor in the last chapter of *Harlem: Negro Metropolis*, 240–49.

13 Cooper, *Claude McKay*, 311. Cooper does not provide exact dates, but suggests that McKay was hired by the FWP by April 1936. It should go without saying that there were links among these various black intellectual circuits of activity. Ellen Tarry, who would later become one of McKay's closest friends, told an interviewer that it "must have been around 1936" that someone in the Negro Writers' Guild "introduced me to Claude McKay and he asked me to come down and work on the Federal Writers' Project." Ellen Tarry, transcript of interview by W. J. Weatherby, 2 November 1966, WPA History, Reel 5, [Federal] Writers' Program Collection, Schomburg Center for Research in Black Culture, New York Public Library (hereafter NYPL).

14 There are extensive lists of the topics covered and articles produced by the project in Reel 5, [Federal] Writers' Program Collection, Schomburg Center, NYPL.

15 McKay, *Harlem: Negro Metropolis*, 240.

16 On the anti-Italian demonstration at the Bella Restaurant, see "3 Police in Harlem Hurt Fighting Mob," *New York Times* (July 13, 1936): 3. Joseph Fronczak describes a similar protest in the street outside the Italian-operated King Julius General Market in October 1935: see Fronczak, "Local People's Global Politics: A Transnational History of the Hands Off Ethiopia Movement of 1935," *Diplomatic History* 39, no. 2 (2015): 272.

17 The Federal Writers' Project (FWP) included documentation on Gladys Bentley and the Ubangi Club, such as Wilbur Young,

"Gladys Bentley," 28 August 1939, Reel 1, [Federal] Writers' Program Collection, Schomburg Center, NYPL. The description of the Ubangi Club comes from another essay in the FWP: Richard Bruce Nugent, "Gloria Swanson," Reel 1, [Federal] Writers' Program Collection, Schomburg Center, NYPL. For more information on Bentley, see James F. Wilson, "'In My Well of Loneliness': Gladys Bentley's Bulldykin' Blues," in *Bulldaggers, Pansies, and Chocolate Babies: Performance, Race, and Sexuality in the Harlem Renaissance* (Ann Arbor: University of Michigan Press, 2010), 154–91.

18 See, for example, *Harlem: Negro Metropolis*, 175–78, 189, 226. There was extensive newspaper coverage of the Italo-Ethiopian crisis as it unfolded in the fall of 1935 and the spring of 1936. There were also a few important, albeit short, pamphlets on the topic, including the African American roving journalist J. A. Rogers's *The Real Facts About Ethiopia* (1936; repr., Baltimore: Black Classic Press, 1982); and the doctor and Ethiopian envoy Malaku Bayen's *The March of Black Men, Ethiopia Leads: Official Report of the Present State of Affairs and Prospectus: An Authentic Account of the Determined Fight of the Ethiopian People for Their Independence* (New York: Voice of Ethiopia Press, 1939). Another important publication that touches on the crisis, Roi Ottley's book *New World A-Coming: Inside Black America* (1943; repr., New York: Arno Press, 1968), drew extensively on the work of the FWP.

19 For more on the nuances and resonances between *Harlem: Negro Metropolis* and *Amiable with Big Teeth,* see Jean-Christophe Cloutier, "*Amiable with Big Teeth*: The Case of Claude McKay's Last Novel," *Modernism/modernity* 20, no. 3 (September 2013): 557–76.

20 Cooper, introduction to *The Passion of Claude McKay*, 37.

21 John Hope Franklin, *From Slavery to Freedom: A History of African Americans* (1947; repr., New York: Knopf, 1969), 574.

22 Cedric J. Robinson, "The African Diaspora and the Italo-Ethiopian Crisis," *Race & Class* 27, no. 2 (1985): 60.

23 McKay, *Harlem: Negro Metropolis*, 176. This viewpoint was widely shared among African American commentators in the period. For instance, an August 1935 editorial in *Opportunity*

magazine contended that "Ethiopia has become the spiritual fatherland of Negroes throughout the world, and from Bahia to Birmingham, and from New York to Nigeria, peoples of African descent have been stirred to unparalleled unity of thought." "And Ethiopia Shall Stretch Forth Her Arms" [editorial], *Opportunity* 13, no. 8 (August 1935): 230.

24 Ottley, *New World A-Coming*, 109.

25 William R. Scott, *The Sons of Sheba's Race: African-Americans and the Italo-Ethiopian War, 1935–1941* (Bloomington: Indiana University Press, 1993), 210.

26 Robert A. Hill, afterword to *Black Empire*, by George Schuyler, ed. Hill (Boston: Northeastern University Press, 1993), 269.

27 See Hill, "Bibliography: George S. Schuyler's *Pittsburgh Courier* Fiction, 1933–1939," in Schuyler, *Black Empire*, 344. Here is the full bibliographic record: Rachel Call [George S. Schuyler], "Revolt in Ethiopia: A Tale of Black Insurrection Against Italian Imperialism," *Pittsburgh Courier* (July 16, 1938–January 21, 1939). Other examples of Schuyler's black internationalist serial fiction include "The Ethiopian Murder Mystery: A Story of Love and International Intrigue," *Pittsburgh Courier* (October 5, 1935–February 1, 1936); "The Black Internationale: Story of Black Genius Against the World," *Pittsburgh Courier* (November 21, 1936–July 3, 1937); and "Black Empire: An Imaginative Story of a Great New Civilization in Modern Africa," *Pittsburgh Courier* (October 2, 1937–April 16, 1939). A selection of this work is available in *Black Empire* and the follow-up volume *Ethiopian Stories*, ed. Hill (Boston: Northeastern University Press, 1994). On the vindicationist tradition in African American political thought, see especially Wilson Jeremiah Moses, *Afrotopia: The Roots of African American Popular History* (Cambridge, MA: Cambridge University Press, 1998).

28 McKay, letter to Max Eastman, 6 August 1941, Max Eastman Mss. II, Addition 1, Lilly Library Manuscript Collections, Indiana University.

29 McKay, letter to John Macrae, 8 August 1941, Max Eastman Mss. II, Addition 1, Lilly Library Manuscript Collections, Indiana University.

30 For a provocative reflection on the "black impostor" as a political
    actor, see Robert A. Hill's consideration of a number of such
    hoaxes in the period: "King Menelik's Nephew: Prince Thomas
    Mackarooroo, aka Prince Ludwig Menelek of Abyssinia," *Small
    Axe* 26 (June 2008): 15–44; as well as scholarship on the faux
    "African" prophetess Laura Kofey, including Barbara Bair,
    "'Ethiopia Shall Stretch Forth Her Hands unto God': Laura Kofey
    and the Gendered Vision in Redemption in the Garvey Move-
    ment," in *A Mighty Baptism: Race, Gender, and the Creation of
    American Protestantism*, ed. Susan Juster and Lisa MacFarlane
    (Ithaca, NY: Cornell University Press, 1996), 38–63; and Richard
    Newman, "'Warrior Mother of Africa's Warriors of the Most
    High God': Laura Adorkor Kofey and the African Universal
    Church," in *This Far by Faith: Readings in African-American
    Women's Religious Biography*, ed. Judith Weisenfeld and Rich-
    ard Newman (New York: Routledge, 1995), 110–23.

31 Sadie Hall, "Sketches of Colorful Harlem Characters (Chappy Gard-
    ner)," 29 August 1939, Reel 1, [Federal] Writers' Program Collection,
    Schomburg Center, NYPL. On the Princess Tamanya hoax, see
    FWP, *Almanac for New Yorkers, 1938* (New York: Modern Age
    Books, 1937). Even though she was ousted as a fraud, Princess
    Tamanya nevertheless went on tour giving concerts across the
    country between 1935 and 1940. See for example "Tamanya Ap-
    pears with Italian Group," *New York Amsterdam News* (Novem-
    ber 23, 1940): 11.

32 McKay mentions Litvinov's role in international diplomacy
    around the Italo-Ethiopian War in *Harlem: Negro Metropolis*,
    226. For more information on Litvinov's career, see Albert Resis,
    "The Fall of Litvinov: Harbinger of the German-Soviet Non-
    Aggression Pact," *Europe-Asia Studies* 52, no. 1 (2000); Geoffrey
    Roberts, "The Fall of Litvinov: A Revisionist View," *Journal of
    Contemporary History* 27, no. 4 (1992): 639–57.

33 The quotation comes from James W. Ford, "Litvinoff Takes a
    Ride," *Harlem Liberator* (November 25, 1933): 3. William R. Scott
    notes that although the Soviet Union eventually came to protest the
    Italian invasion, Litvinov's initial silence at the League of Nations
    despite the growing tension in the spring of 1935 was taken by
    many African American observers as a premeditated betrayal of
    African sovereignty, and a reneging by the Comintern on its

declared commitment to national self-determination. See Scott, *The Sons of Sheba's Race: African-Americans and the Italo-Ethiopian War, 1935–1941* (Bloomington: Indiana University Press, 1993), 124. Some of the other period coverage in the Communist-affiliated black press includes "Ethiopia and Soviet Russia: Litvinoff, Soviet Diplomat in the 'League' Is Real Thorn in Mussolini's Side," *Negro Liberator* (September 2, 1935): 5; "Soviet Supports Ethiopia," *Negro Liberator* (September 16, 1935): 2; "Maxim Litvinoff Arrives Here," *Harlem Liberator* (November 11, 1933): 1.

34 See Cooper, *Claude McKay*, 297.

35 See Cooper, *Claude McKay*, 298; and Allen Weinstein, *Perjury: The Hiss-Chambers Case* (New York: Knopf, 1978).

36 Cooper, *Claude McKay*, 298.

37 Claude McKay, "Looking Forward—," *New York Amsterdam News* (May 13, 1939): 13.

38 For an extended reading of the ways these sorts of historical transpositions capture the "archival sensibility" of McKay's approach in the novel, see Cloutier, *"Amiable with Big Teeth*: The Case of Claude McKay's Last Novel."

39 On Bayen, see Joseph Harris, *African-American Reactions to the War in Ethiopia, 1936–1941* (Baton Rouge: Louisiana State University Press, 1994), 120.

40 Quoted in William R. Scott, "Malaku E. Bayen: Ethiopian Emissary to Black America, 1936–1941," *Ethiopia Observer* 15, no. 2 (1972). Available online at https://tezetaethiopia.wordpress.com /2005/06/18/malaku-e-bayen-ethiopian-emissary-to-black -america/. Accessed 15 April 2016. See also Harris, *African-American Reactions to the War in Ethiopia*, 122–23.

41 Scott, "Malaku E. Bayen: Ethiopian Emissary to Black America." For more on how some of the Ethiopian aid organizations may have paved the way for the Popular Front in the United States, see Fronczak, "Local People's Global Politics: A Transnational History of the Hands Off Ethiopia Movement of 1935."

42 On the Ethiopian World Federation, see Harris, *African-American Reactions to the War*, 127 ff.; and William A. Shack, "Ethiopia and Afro-Americans: Some Historical Notes, 1920–1970," *Phylon* 35, no. 2 (2nd Quarter, 1974): 149.

43 There is a photograph of Bayen facing page 113 in McKay's *Harlem: Negro Metropolis*, and he is also discussed in the text (pages 176–77). The caption reads: "In 1937 Harlem welcomes Lij Araya Abebe (left) and Dr. Malaku Bayen (right), representatives of Emperor Haile Selassie." The Dutton archive includes a letter from Margaret H. Jacobsen in the editorial department at the publisher E. P. Dutton to Dorothy Bayen at the Ethiopian World Federation, in which Jacobsen requests confirmation that "you have agreed to let him use this picture, and it is our understanding that this is a personal arrangement between you and Mr. McKay and that we are not involved financially in the transaction." Jacobsen, letter to Bayen, 24 July 1940, "Harlem, 1940" Folder, Box 10, E. P. Dutton & Company, Inc. Records, Special Collections Research Center, Syracuse University Library. Bayen replied on 25 July "to confirm that I have agreed to let Mr. McKay use the picture."

44 See Harris, *African-American Reactions to the War*, 79; William R. Scott, *The Sons of Sheba's Race: African-Americans and the Italo-Ethiopian War, 1935–1941* (Bloomington: Indiana University Press, 1993), 117.

45 See "United Ethiopia Council Formed," *New York Amsterdam News* (February 1, 1936): 1; "Zaphiro to Seek Ethiopian Funds: Will Visit 28 Cities in Quest of $500,000," *New York Amsterdam News* (March 14, 1936): 11.

46 Harris, *African-American Reactions to the War in Ethiopia*, 70.

47 Scott, *The Sons of Sheba's Race*, 116; Harris, *African-American Reactions to the War*, 73–74; S. K. B. Asante, "The Afro-American and the Italo-Ethiopian Crisis, 1934–1936," *Race* 15, no. 2 (1973): 173.

48 Scott, 119. See also "Zaphiro Called Back to London," *New York Amsterdam News* (March 21, 1936): 1; "Honors Zaphiro Before Sailing," *New York Amsterdam News* (March 21, 1936): 11.

49 Dan Burley, *Chicago Defender* (January 9, 1937): 26, quoted in Scott, 120.

50 Huggins was the vice chairman of United Aid for Ethiopia. See "United Ethiopia Council Formed," *New York Amsterdam News* (February 1, 1936): 1.

51 On Huggins's role in the 7 March 1935 meeting at the Abyssinian Baptist Church, see Ralph Crowder, "Willis Nathaniel Huggins (1886–1941): Historian, Activist, and Community Mentor," *Afro-Americans in New York Life and History* 30, no. 2 (July 2006): 131; Joseph Fronczak, "Local People's Global Politics: A Transnational History of the Hands Off Ethiopia Movement of 1935," 252; "Ethiopia Unity Rallies Harlem," *Negro Liberator* (March 15, 1935): 1, 2. According to historian William Scott, the speakers included a remarkable array of black intellectual, political, and religious leaders (Huggins, Alfred L. King, Joel A. Rogers, James W. Ford, Arthur Reid, and Adam Clayton Powell Jr.) with affiliations across the political spectrum, from Marcus Garvey's Universal Negro Improvement Association to the Communist Party. See Scott, *The Sons of Sheba's Race*, 110.

52 Scott, *The Sons of Sheba's Race*, 117.

53 "Ethiopian Tragedy to Prove Spur for Negro Unity, Observers Hold," *New York Amsterdam News* (May 9, 1936): 13.

54 Willis N. Huggins, preface to *Introduction to African Civilizations*, by Huggins and John G. Jackson (1937; repr., Baltimore: Black Classic Press, 1999), 15. Huggins writes: "Mr. Claude McKay, the novelist, recently returned from a long stay in North Africa, cleared up many points in regard to that area."

55 "135th Street Library Notes," *New York Amsterdam News* (December 31, 1938): 7.

56 Cooper, *Claude McKay*, 297. On Seifert's life and career, see Elmer W. Dean's odd hagiography, *An Elephant Lives in Harlem* (New York: Ethiopian Press, n.d.); and especially the detailed biographical note on the Barbados-born Seifert's life and career as a Garveyite, bibliophile, and independent historian in *The Marcus Garvey and*

UNIA Papers, Vol 1: 1826–August 1919, ed. Robert A. Hill (Berkeley: University of California Press, 1983), 226 n. 3. Seifert organized his extensive collection of rare books into a research library he named the Ethiopian Research School of History, and also wrote about Ethiopian history: see, for example, Seifert, *The Negro's or Ethiopian's Contribution to Art* (New York: Ethiopian Historical Publishing Co., 1938); Seifert, "Who Are the Ethiopians?," Box 46, Folder 17–18, John Henrik Clarke Papers, Schomburg Center, NYPL.

57   McKay, letter to Max Eastman, 24 August 1934, collected in *The Passion of Claude McKay*, 199.

58   See Robert A. Hill, "On Collectors, Their Contributions to the Documentation of the Black Past," in *Black Bibliophiles and Collectors: Preservers of Black History*, ed. Elinor des Verney Sinnette, W. Paul Coates, and Thomas C. Battle (Washington, DC: Howard University Press, 1990), 47–56.

59   For a discussion of historical reports of "leopard men" across various parts of West Africa in the early twentieth century and a useful discussion of the ways the phenomenon was linked to the "shifting features of the colonial political landscape," see David Pratten, *The Man-Leopard Murders: History and Society in Colonial Nigeria* (London: International African Institute/Edinburgh University Press, 2007), 16.

60   Cooper, *Claude McKay*, 340.

61   Even the titles of his articles and editorials give a sense of the range of his concerns in the late 1930s: McKay, "Dynamite in Africa: Are the 'Popular Fronts' Suppressing Colonial Independence?" *Common Sense* 7 (March 1938): 11; McKay, "Native Liberation Might Have Been Stopped: The Franco Revolt," *New Leader* (February 18, 1939): 2, 5, reprinted in *The Passion of Claude McKay*, 285–89; McKay, "Everybody's Doing It: Anti-Semitic Propaganda Fails to Attract Negroes; Harlemites Face Problems of All Other Slum Dwellers," *New Leader* (May 20, 1939): 5–6; McKay, "Pact Exploded Communist Propaganda Among Negroes," *New Leader* (September 23, 1939): 4–7; McKay, "McKay Urges that New Leader Be Used as War Issues Forum," *New Leader* (October 7, 1939); McKay, "Morocco:

Nerve Center of Nations' Colonial Power Politics," *New Leader* (November 11, 1939): 4; McKay, "Morocco: Duce Uses Anti-Semitism to Win Moslems for Fascism," *New Leader* (November 18, 1939); McKay, "Paul Robeson Backs War on Finns, Ignores Soviet Threat to All Minorities," *New Leader* (January 20, 1940).

62 Cooper, *Claude McKay*, 327–28.

63 McKay, "A Little Lamb to Lead Them: A True Narrative," *The African: Journal of African Affairs* (May–June 1938): 107–8, 112.

64 In the end, McKay and Cullen decided not to take over the editorship. See Cooper, *Claude McKay*, 328. Also see the "Announcement!" under the table of contents in *The African: Journal of African Affairs* (May–June 1938), which reports that "beginning with the next number of THE AFRICAN the editorship will be taken over by Claude McKay, the eminent poet and novelist and former editor of the old LIBERATOR, who will bring to his new work a ripe experience gained from extensive travels and keen observation of social and political movements . . . Mr. McKay will have as his associate, his fellow-craftsman, Countee Cullen, at one time assistant editor of OPPORTUNITY: A JOURNAL OF NEGRO LIFE." In the next issue, there is a small notice explaining that "due to reasons not anticipated, the world renowned post-novelists Claude McKay and Countee Cullen, cannot now serve in the capacities of Editor and Associate Editor respectively as announced in the last issue of THE AFRICAN." *The African: Journal of African Affairs* (July–August 1938): 122. A letter from Cullen to McKay gives us a glimpse into the reasons their editorship takeover fell through: "I am very anxious to know what finally transpired in connection with *The African*. It was a great disappointment to me that we could not make a go of it, but it was impossible to work with such narrow-minded people. They were interested in propaganda only." Cullen, letter to McKay, 24 July 1938, Box 2, Folder 53, Claude McKay Collection, Beinecke Library.

65 McKay, "Pact Exploded Communist Propaganda Among Negroes," *New Leader* (September 23, 1939): 4.

66 McKay, *Harlem: Negro Metropolis*, 188.

67 McKay, "Claude McKay versus Powell," *New York Amsterdam News* (November 6, 1937): 4.

68 "Claude M'Kay, Author, Decries Inroads Made by Communists," *New York Amsterdam News* (September 17, 1938): A3.

69 McKay, *Harlem: Negro Metropolis*, 203. He makes the same point in similar language earlier in the book: the Communists' "primary aim has been radically to exploit the Negro's grievances. Therefore they use their influence to destroy any movement which might make for a practical amelioration of the Negro's problems" (196).

70 McKay, *Harlem: Negro Metropolis*, 259.

71 This common phrase is often traced back to the sermon recounted in Matthew 7:15, in which Jesus says, "Beware of false prophets, which come to you in sheep's clothing, but inwardly they are ravening wolves."

72 McKay, "Pact Exploded Communist Propaganda Among Negroes," *New Leader* (September 23, 1939): 4, 7. He writes: "Two years ago, I voiced the danger of Negroes coming under the control of Moscow dominated Communists exploiting their grievances . . . I thought that the Negro group was being dangerously misled. It profoundly shocked me that a minority group, subject to intolerance and persecution, as the American Negro, should be lured by treacherous propaganda to support and defend one of the most intolerantly tyrannical governments in the world."

73 McKay, *Harlem: Negro Metropolis*, 251.

74 McKay, "Everybody's Doing It: Anti-Semitic Propaganda Fails to Attract Negroes," *New Leader* (May 20, 1939): 5–6.

75 In *Harlem: Negro Metropolis*, McKay describes the gullibility of black intellectuals in language that recalls the title phrase: "While many of their outstanding white colleagues wisely ran to save themselves when the Communists ripped off their masks and flashed daggers, the Negroes stood emotionally fixed like the

boy on the burning deck" (259). Similarly, McKay's 1943 "Cycle" sequence includes a number of poems denouncing what he considered to be attempts by the Communist Party to manipulate black political organizations for propagandistic ends. For example, in poem 26, McKay writes: "Of all the sects I have the Communists, / Who harvest the misery of mankind to build / A new religion, because the ancient mists / Obscure our vision and our eyes are filled! . . . The Communists, blind leaders of the blind, / Manipulating God and politics, / Brazenly hold forth to deceive mankind / With potpourri of clever Marxian tricks . . ." See McKay, "The Cycle," *Complete Poems*, 254. For other poems in the sequence concerning the Communist influence, see 247, 255, 269.

76 Elliott B. Macrae, letter to McKay, 20 January 1941, Box 8, Folder 259, Claude McKay Collection, Beinecke Library.

77 John Macrae, letter to McKay, 7 August 1941, Max Eastman Mss. II, Addition 1, Lilly Library Manuscript Collections, Indiana University.

78 Ledger Book no. 4, May 1939–April 1943, Financial Records, Box 16, E. P. Dutton & Company, Inc. Records, Special Collections Research Center, Syracuse University Library. The ledger (which is a record of Dutton's payments during this period) notes regular payments for $25 to McKay starting on 31 January 1941. The checks are sent first on a weekly basis, then slow to every other week from April to June, and then resume as weekly payments in July. The last payment is dated 25 July 1941. The Claude McKay Collection at the Beinecke also confirms this arrangement, through the preservation of notes that accompanied the payments. In the Beinecke papers, the last trace of this arrangement are notes dated 24 June and 25 June 1941, the first confirming that Dutton would continue advance payments up to $500 (the note says that by the time of this letter, $350 had been paid), and the second addressed to McKay's New York address, asking him to call the office (to confirm whether he was still in Maine or back in New York).

79 McKay, letter to Catherine Latimer, 19 February 1941, Box 1, Folder 4, Acquisitions 1925–1948, Schomburg Center Records, Schomburg Center, NYPL.

80 John Macrae, letter to McKay, 7 August 1941, Max Eastman
    Mss. II, Addition 1, Lilly Library Manuscript Collections, Indi-
    ana University.

81 John Macrae, letter to Max Eastman, 12 February 1941, Box 8,
    Folder 259, Claude McKay Collection, Beinecke Library.

82 McKay, letter to Mr. R. S. Gilmore [marked returned as "un-
    claimed"], 5 March 1941, Box 3, Folder 88, McKay Collection,
    Beinecke Library.

83 A. Philip Randolph, letter to McKay, 4 April 1941, Box 6, Folder
    173, Claude McKay Collection, Beinecke Library. In his biogra-
    phy of McKay, Wayne Cooper quotes the praise of *Harlem: Ne-
    gro Metropolis* in this letter but overlooks the mention of the
    "new book." See Cooper, *Claude McKay*, 345.

84 Carlisle Smyth, letter to McKay, 8 May 1941, Box 6, Folder 195,
    Claude McKay Collection, Beinecke Library.

85 Arcadia Toledano, letter to McKay, 21 May 1941, Box 6, Folder
    202, Claude McKay Collection, Beinecke Library.

86 Johnny Atkinson, letter to McKay, 10 June 1941, Box 1, Folder 1,
    Claude McKay Collection, Beinecke Library.

87 Simon Williamson, letter to McKay, 19 June 1941, Box 1, Folder
    2, Claude McKay Papers (Additions), Schomburg Center, NYPL.

88 McKay, letter to Williamson, 19 May 1941, Box 1, Folder 2,
    Claude McKay Papers (Additions), Schomburg Center, NYPL. In
    fact, the military coup that led to the Spanish Civil War took
    place on 17 July 1936.

89 McKay, letter to Max Eastman, 29 March 1941, McKay Papers,
    Lilly Library Manuscript Collections, Indiana University.

90 Max Eastman, letter to McKay, 20 April 1941, Box 3, Folder 69,
    Claude McKay Collection, Beinecke Library.

91 Max Eastman, letter to McKay, 26 April 1941, Box 3, Folder 69,
    Claude McKay Collection, Beinecke Library.

92 Max Eastman, letter to McKay, 28 May 1941, McKay Papers, Lilly Library Manuscript Collections, Indiana University. The same day, Dutton wrote Eastman to discuss "the necessity of your coming into the office to have a talk with me or with our editor, Mr. Acklom, about the McKay book." Elliott Macrae, letter to Eastman, 28 May 1941, Box 8, Folder 259, Claude McKay Collection, Beinecke Library.

93 Simon Williamson, letter to McKay, 1 June 1941, Box 1, Folder 2, Claude McKay Papers (Additions), Schomburg Center, NYPL.

94 Max Eastman, handwritten note to McKay, n.d., Box 3, Folder 70, Claude McKay Collection, Beinecke Library.

95 John Macrae, letter to McKay, 24 June 1941, Box 8, Folder 259, Claude McKay Collection, Beinecke Library.

96 Ibid.

97 McKay, letter to Carl Van Vechten, 21 July 1941, Carl Van Vechten Papers, Beinecke Library.

98 McKay, letter to Max Eastman, 28 July 1941, McKay Papers, Lilly Library Manuscript Collections, Indiana University.

99 John Macrae, letter to McKay, 7 August 1941, Max Eastman Mss. II, Addition 1, Lilly Library Manuscript Collections, Indiana University.

100 These documents were discovered in Eastman's former residence in Martha's Vineyard by Christoph Irmscher in October 2014 when he was doing research for his biography *Max Eastman: A Life* (New Haven: Yale University Press, 2017). Irmscher cites from these letters in the biography (p. 305), as well as in an online piece titled "Rejecting Claude McKay: An Author's Lost, and Last, Novel," published on the Library of America's website on August 21, 2017 (https://loa.org/news-and-views/1318-rejecting-claude-mckay-an-authors-lost-and-last-novel, accessed 19 October 2017).

101 John Macrae, letter to McKay, 7 August 1941, Max Eastman Mss. II, Addition 1, Lilly Library Manuscript Collections, Indiana University.

102 McKay, letter to John Macrae, 8 August 1941, Max Eastman Mss. II, Addition 1, Lilly Library Manuscript Collections, Indiana University.

103 McKay, letter to Max Eastman, 6 August 1941, Max Eastman Mss. II, Addition 1, Lilly Library Manuscript Collections, Indiana University.

104 Ibid.

105 McKay, letter to John Macrae, 8 August 1941, Max Eastman Mss. II, Addition 1, Lilly Library Manuscript Collections, Indiana University.

106 Ibid.

107 Ibid.

108 Ibid.

109 McKay, letter to Max Eastman, 6 August 1941, Max Eastman Mss. II, Addition 1, Lilly Library Manuscript Collections, Indiana University.

110 Ibid.

111 John Macrae, letter to McKay, 7 August 1941, Max Eastman Mss. II, Addition 1, Lilly Library Manuscript Collections, Indiana University.

112 That is, the inscription in the copy of Roth's *Europe: A Book for America* (New York: Boni and Liveright, 1919) in McKay's papers at the Beinecke Rare Book and Manuscript Library is dated 11 September 1941.

113 McKay, letters to Samuel Roth, 6 October and 8 October 1941, Box 29, Folder 7, Samuel Roth Papers, Rare Book and Manuscript Library, Columbia University.

114 McKay, letter to Samuel Roth, 6 October 1941, Box 36, Folder 26, Samuel Roth Papers, Rare Book and Manuscript Library, Columbia University.

115 McKay, letter to Max Eastman, 30 July 1942, McKay Papers, Lilly Library Manuscript Collections, Indiana University. In this letter, McKay requests a letter of recommendation for his application to the Office of War Information, where he was applying for a position.

116 McKay, letter to Ruth Raphael, 21 January 1942, Box 1, Folder 3, Claude McKay Papers (Additions), Schomburg Center, NYPL.

117 See Cooper, introduction to *The Passion of Claude McKay*, 40; and Ellen Tarry, *The Third Door: The Autobiography of an American Negro Woman* (New York: McKay Co., 1955), 187.

118 McKay, letter to Simon Williamson, n.d. [likely early 1942], Box 1, Folder 2, Claude McKay Papers (Additions), Schomburg Center, NYPL.

119 McKay, letter to Mr. Kohn, 23 March 1942, Box 1, Folder 1, Claude McKay Papers (Additions), Schomburg Center, NYPL.

120 McKay, letter to Catherine Latimer, 19 February 1941, Box 1, Folder 4, Acquisitions 1925–1948, Schomburg Center Records, Schomburg Center, NYPL.

121 McKay, letter to Carl Cowl, 28 July 1947, Box 2, Folder 44, Claude McKay Collection, Beinecke Library.

122 Cooper, *Claude McKay*, 222.

123 McKay, letter to Ivie Jackman, 15 September 1943, Countee Cullen/Harold Jackman Memorial Collection, Robert W. Woodruff Library, Atlanta University.

AMIABLE WITH BIG TEETH

EPIGRAPH

1 **Walter Bagehot (1826–77):** British businessman, essayist, social Darwinist, and journalist. This stanza, suggesting that men

create gods in their own image, appears in Bagehot's essay about religion and morality, "The Ignorance of Man" (1862). Bagehot provides no source for the verse, and it is likely that he composed it himself.

CHAPTER 1

1   ". . . Ethiopia Shall Soon Stretch Out Her Hands to God.": From Psalm 68:31 ("Princes shall come out of Egypt; Ethiopia shall soon stretch out her hands unto God"). Starting in the nineteenth century, many African diasporic theologians and political thinkers interpreted this passage as a prophecy of the coming vindication of the black race.

2   Senegambian Scouts: In the original typescript, McKay had first called the group the "Yoruba Scouts." In revising the manuscript he crossed out "Yoruba" and inserted "Senegambian."

3   Aframericans: In the original typescript, McKay had first used "Afro-American" in this paragraph. He revised the word here (and consistently throughout the rest of the book) to "Aframerican." See the Introduction.

4   The Emperor of Ethiopia: Haile Selassie I (1892–1975) assumed the throne as emperor of Ethiopia in 1930.

5   Back-to-Africa movement: The slogan "Back to Africa" was the phrase most commonly associated with the nationalist movement of the Jamaican Marcus Garvey (1887–1940), the founder of the Universal Negro Improvement Association, which became the largest and most influential popular organization among African Americans in the early 1920s. In the typescript, McKay had originally written "Garvey movement," later revising it to "Back-to-Africa movement."

6   Herodotus, Volney . . . and a hundred more: Herodotus (c. 484–425 BCE), pioneering Greek historian and author of *The Histories* (440 BCE) on the origins of the Greco-Persian Wars; Constantin-François Chassebœuf, comte de Volney (1757–1820), French philosopher, historian, and politician; Jean-François Champollion (1790–1832), French scholar and philologist famous for publishing

the first translation of the Rosetta Stone hieroglyphs; Segismundo Moret (1833–1913), Spanish politician and writer; E. A. Wallis Budge (1857–1934), English orientalist and philologist; Enno Littmann (1875–1958), German orientalist; Leo Frobenius (1873–1938), German archeologist and ethnologist.

CHAPTER 2

1   **in the heyday of the Pan-African movement:** This is an allusion to the "pomp and splendor of titles and uniforms" associated with Marcus Garvey's Universal Negro Improvement Association (see Ch. 1, note 5), rather than to the Pan-African Congresses organized by Garvey's rival, the editor and intellectual W. E. B. Du Bois, in 1919, 1921, 1923, 1927, and 1945.

2   **Harlem Hospital . . . Lincoln Hospital:** Harlem Hospital (founded in 1887) is a teaching hospital on Lenox Avenue and 135th Street in Manhattan; Lincoln Hospital (founded in 1839) is the major medical facility in the South Bronx section of New York City.

3   **"the Ethiopian Lij is the equivalent of the European prince":** The Ethiopian title *Lij* is a Ge'ez word that literally means "child." It is a title issued at birth to sons of members of the *Mesafint*, the hereditary nobility in Ethiopia (in contradistinction to the *Mekwanint*, individuals often of humble origins appointed to specific government or court offices).

4   **the Garvey Pan-African movement:** See Ch. 2, note 1.

5   **"sanctions against Italy":** Italy invaded Ethiopia in October 1935; the following month the League of Nations condemned the aggression and imposed economic sanctions on Italy.

6   **"foul-mouthed Trotskyite":** i.e., a follower of Leon Trotsky (1879–1940), one of the leaders of the Bolshevik Revolution in Russia who, after resisting the rise of Joseph Stalin (1878–1953), was expelled from the Communist Party and then in 1929 exiled from the Soviet Union. Trotsky was assassinated in Mexico in 1940. To an American Communist supporter of the Soviet Union in this period, the charge of being a "Trotskyite" would imply an unconscionable betrayal of the Soviet cause.

CHAPTER 3

1   **the notorious numbers game:** The numbers game or racket (often referred to simply as "the numbers") is an illegal lottery in which the better tries to pick a sequence of three digits to match those picked in a drawing the following day. In the Harlem of the early twentieth century it was largely controlled by organized crime "operators" or bosses. McKay discusses the numbers game in a chapter of his book *Harlem: Negro Metropolis* (1940).

2   **a Mason . . . Colored Elks:** A Mason is a member of a fraternal organization in Freemasonry, a system of affiliation with origins going back to medieval craft guilds in Europe. The Benevolent and Protective Order of Elks is a fraternal order originally founded by Joseph Norcross in New York in 1868.

3   **the Pan-African organization:** See Ch. 2, note 1.

CHAPTER 4

1   **Garveyites:** i.e., followers of Marcus Garvey (see Ch. 1, note 5).

2   **the Emperor's coronation:** Haile Selassie I (1892–1975) assumed the throne as emperor of Ethiopia in 1930. The original typescript of *Amiable with Big Teeth* lists this date erroneously here as 1932 (although the correct date is given later).

CHAPTER 5

1   **the famous 409 Edgecombe Avenue:** The landmark thirteen-story 1917 apartment building overlooking the Harlem River Valley at 154th Street that was one of the most prestigious addresses in the Sugar Hill area of Harlem, with residents including W. E. B. Du Bois, Aaron Douglas, Thurgood Marshall, and Roy Wilkins.

2   **"soon after the Harlem Riots":** On 19 March 1935, after mistaken reports circulated that a police officer had beaten a black teenager accused of stealing a penknife from a store on 125th Street,

thousands participated in street demonstrations that turned vio-lent, resulting in three deaths and extensive property damage. It soon became known as Harlem's first "great" riot.

3   **"Jardin du Ciel of the Plaza Alhambra":** Possibly a reference to the Harlem Alhambra, a large theater on Seventh Avenue at 126th Street that featured vaudeville and later blues and jazz perform-ers, and that included a large glass-covered roof garden. The Sem-inole Cabaret seems to be a fictional establishment.

4   **in Menelik's days:** Menelik II (1844–1913), the Negus ("King") of Shewa from 1866 to 1889 and Negusa Negest ("King of Kings," or emperor) of Ethiopia from 1889 until his death, who, during the 1880s, forcibly expanded the sovereign territory of Ethiopia. In the Battle of Adwa of March 1896, Menelik's forces success-fully repelled the Italian army's attempt to invade Ethiopia.

CHAPTER 6

1   **skillful Tammany politician:** Founded in 1786, Tammany Hall was a political organization associated with the Democratic Party in New York City. The Tammany patronage "machine" orga-nized voting blocks among immigrants in the city and exercised enormous influence over party nominations and local government through the mid-twentieth century.

2   **A Trotskyite group:** See Ch. 2, note 6.

3   **the Savoy:** The famous Harlem ballroom for music and dancing that operated from 1926 to 1948 and was located on Lenox Ave-nue between 140th and 141st Streets.

4   **the Tuskegee Idea of Special Group Development of Aframericans:** Founded in 1881 by Booker T. Washington (1856–1915), the Tuskegee Institute was an African American educational institution focusing on training teachers devoted to Washington's philosophy of "indus-trial education," which emphasized self-reliance and vocational in-struction in agricultural labor.

5   **Stalinites against Trotskyites:** See Ch. 2, note 6.

CHAPTER 7

1   **Apollo Theater:** The legendary music hall founded in 1934 on 125th Street in Harlem.

2   **the flamboyant Aframerican Hubert Fauntleroy Julian:** Hubert Fauntleroy Julian (1897–1983), Trinidad-born African American fighter pilot, parachutist, and adventurer who gained notoriety in the early 1920s performing aerial stunts over Harlem, sometimes at events organized by Marcus Garvey's Universal Negro Improvement Association. Nicknamed "the Black Eagle," Julian traveled independently to Africa during the Italo-Ethiopian War to fight against the Italian invasion; for a time he was even put in command of the Imperial Ethiopian Air Force (which, however, consisted of only three airplanes).

3   **the Rasses, the Queen of Sheba . . . the kind of specie:** *Ras* (which in the Ge'ez language literally means "head") is the highest noble rank in Ethiopia, the rough equivalent of "field marshal" or "duke." The Queen of Sheba is a biblical figure whose visit to King Solomon in Jerusalem is recounted in I Kings 10. "The kind of specie": i.e., the type of coins used as currency in Ethiopia.

4   **the glorious intoxicating era of Prohibition:** Prohibition imposed a ban on the sale, production, and transportation of alcoholic beverages in the Unites States. Enacted with the passage of the Eighteenth Amendment to the US Constitution, it remained in force from 1920 to 1933.

5   **the policy game:** The policy game (or simply "policy") is another name for the illegal lottery called the "numbers." See Ch. 3, note 1.

6   **Lindbergh . . . by immortalizing it in a popular dance:** Charles Augustus Lindbergh (1902–74), American aviator and the first man to successfully cross the Atlantic Ocean by airplane in a single flight. The "Lindy Hop" dance originated in Harlem in the late 1920s. Although it included steps similar to dances that had been popular more than a decade earlier (such as the "Texas Tommy"), it became commonly known as the "Lindbergh Hop" or "Lindy Hop" after Lindbergh's flight (or "hop") across the Atlantic in 1927.

7 **some exciting international signatures in that book:** Most likely a list of names with aristocratic connotations in the period, rather than references to specific historical figures. For example, Duke of Marlborough and Baron Glenconner are titles in the peerage of England; the House of Bourbon-Parme (or *Casa di Borbone di Parma*) is an Italian cadet branch of the French House of Bourbon; the Colonna family is an Italian noble family that had great influence in medieval and Renaissance Rome; the House of Braganza is a Portuguese ducal and later royal house; Hohenlohe is the name of a German princely dynasty; the House of Segur is a family of the French nobility; Bibesco is the name of an aristocratic family in Romania.

8 **Marcel Proust (1871–1922):** Famous French modernist novelist and critic, known for his *À la recherche du temps perdu* (In Search of Lost Time), published in seven parts between 1913 and 1927.

9 **"the Harlem remnant of the lost generation":** Possibly an allusion to the epigraph of Ernest Hemingway's *The Sun Also Rises* (1926), credited to Gertrude Stein ("You are all a lost generation"). The phrase is commonly interpreted as a reference to the directionless hedonism of the American expatriate generation after World War I.

10 **Hitler . . . half apes:** Adolf Hitler's autobiography *Mein Kampf* (My Struggle), in which he first outlined his Nazi political ideology, was published in two volumes in 1925 and 1926.

11 **knobkerry:** An African club or blunt weapon.

12 **Tolstoy, Dostoievsky, Turgenev, Chekhov, Gorky . . . Czarist regime:** Leo Tolstoy (1828–1910), Russian writer best known for the novels *War and Peace* (1869) and *Anna Karenina* (1877); Fyodor Dostoyevsky (1821–81), Russian writer whose major novels include *Crime and Punishment* (1866) and *The Brothers Karamazov* (1880); Ivan Turgenev (1818–83), Russian author whose works include the novel *Fathers and Sons* (1862); Anton Chekhov (1860–1904), Russian playwright and short story writer whose works include the plays *The Seagull* (1896) and *The Cherry Orchard* (1904); and Alexei Maximovich Peshkov, primarily known as Maxim Gorky (1868–1936), Russian socialist realist writer whose works include *The Lower Depths* (1902). The Russian state was ruled by a succession of czars from its consolidation

under Ivan IV in 1547 through its expansion into the Russian Empire under Peter the Great in the seventeenth century, until the Bolshevik Revolution in October 1917, in which the czarist regime was overthrown in favor of a Communist government.

13 **Sugar Hill:** The exclusive area roughly between West 145th Street and West 155th Street in the northern section of Hamilton Heights in Harlem.

CHAPTER 8

1 **what Carl Sandburg dubbed the "hog city":** Most likely an allusion to the poem "Chicago" (1914) by Carl Sandburg (1878–1967), which opens: "Hog Butcher for the World, / Tool Maker, Stacker of Wheat, / Player with Railroads and the Nation's Freight Handler; / Stormy, husky, brawling, / City of the Big Shoulders."

2 **one of the famous Jubilee Singers:** The choral ensemble of the historical black Fisk University in Nashville, Tennessee, the Fisk Jubilee Singers were founded in 1871 to raise money to support the school, and rapidly became famous for their performances of Negro spirituals on tour across the United States and (starting in 1873) in Europe.

3 **a meeting for Scottsboro's boys:** The Scottsboro Boys were nine black teenagers falsely accused of raping two white women in Alabama in 1931. The Communist Party played a key role in appealing the boys' original convictions, although after multiple retrials (during which one of the alleged victims admitted that the rape story was a fabrication), five of them were nonetheless convicted by all-white juries and served significant prison time. Their case incited international indignation as a blatant miscarriage of justice.

4 **at the Savoy dancing palace, the Renaissance, the Witoka:** On the Savoy, see Ch. 6, note 3. Built in 1924, the Renaissance Ballroom was a large ballroom on Seventh Avenue and 139th Street that included a dance hall, a casino, a theater, shops, and restaurants. The Witoka Club was a nightclub located at 222 West 145th Street in Harlem in the 1930s and 1940s.

5 **Father Divine (1876–1965):** An influential and controversial African American spiritual leader and self-proclaimed "deity" who

founded and ran the International Peace Mission movement, with branch communes located around the New York area and eventually internationally. In the early 1930s he held notoriously lavish banquets for as many as three thousand guests at his property in Sayville, New York. McKay includes a chapter on Father Divine in his book *Harlem: Negro Metropolis* (1940).

6   **Grigory Zinoviev (1883–1936):** A Bolshevik revolutionary who in 1917 was one of the seven members of the first politburo in the Soviet Union. He went on to be the head of the Communist International, before being ousted by Stalin from the Soviet leadership in 1926 and executed after a show trial in 1936.

7   **a horde of Union Square comrades and friends:** i.e., sympathizers and fellow travelers from gatherings in Union Square, the park on Broadway at Fourteenth Street in Manhattan that was a historic gathering spot for radical political groups.

8   **"Come on, you Union Square soldiers":** See previous note.

9   **"John Brown's Body":** An American marching song popular among Union soldiers during the Civil War.

10   **American democracy:** In the original typescript, McKay had written: "shirt-sleeve diplomacy was one of the pillars upon which rested American diplomacy." This redundancy appears to be an error, and it seems likely that he meant "American democracy."

CHAPTER 9

1   **Father Divine:** See Ch. 8, note 5.

2   **"the eunuch of the Queen Candace . . . converting the Ethiopians to Christianity":** According to Acts 8:26–40, a eunuch "of great authority under Candace queen of the Ethiopians" came to Jerusalem to worship and was baptized by the apostle Philip. The passage may not refer to a specific historical queen, since in the Meroitic language the word *Candace* means "queen" or "queen mother."

3   **"like Harlequin at a carnival":** Harlequin is a stock character from the Italian *commedia dell'arte* theatrical tradition, an agile and

mischievous servant who competes with Pierrot for the affections of Colombina. Possibly an allusion to the famous painting *Harlequin's Carnival* (1924–25) by Joan Miró, in which the figure of Harlequin appears sorrowful in the midst of Mardi Gras revelry.

CHAPTER 10

1   **Isaiah 53:6:** The fifty-third chapter of the Book of Isaiah describes the sufferings of Christ. In the King James version, Isaiah 53 opens: "Who hath believed our report?" Verses 6–7 read in their entirety: "All we like sheep have gone astray; we have turned every one to his own way; and the Lord hath laid on him the iniquity of us all. He was oppressed, and he was afflicted, yet he opened not his mouth: he is brought as a lamb to the slaughter, and as a sheep before her shearers is dumb, so he openeth not his mouth." Thus the fragment of these verses in the chapter title alludes to the efforts (depicted in the chapter) of Newton Castle and his pro-Soviet followers to discredit Reverend Zebulon Trawl, the Hands to Ethiopia African American aid organization, and by extension the Ethiopian envoy Lij Alamaya. The Harlem protesters are here compared to "sheep" that have been led "astray" by Castle's slander.

2   **Sufi Abdul Hamid** (1903–38): Born Eugene Brown, Hamid was an African American labor leader and a convert to Islam known above all for his role in the boycotts of white-owned Harlem businesses in the 1930s over discriminatory employment practices. Due to his vitriolic criticism of Jewish store owners in particular, he was often accused of anti-Semitism and was sometimes described in the press as the "Black Hitler." McKay devotes a chapter to Hamid and the protests in *Harlem: Negro Metropolis* (1940).

3   **the Pan-African movement:** See Ch. 2, note 1.

CHAPTER 11

1   **Levantine:** i.e., an individual originally of European origin residing in the region bordering the eastern Mediterranean.

2   **sybarite:** A self-indulgent hedonist.

CHAPTER 12

1 **"a sort of Canaan . . . a Zionist streak . . . Back-to-Africa movement . . . Land of Beulah":** Canaan: i.e., the biblical "Promised
Land," specifically the territory promised to Abraham and his descendants in Genesis 17:8. Zionism is the Jewish nationalist and
political movement that supports the reestablishment of a Jewish
homeland in the territory of Canaan. On Marcus Garvey and the
Back-to-Africa movement, see Ch. 1, note 5. Beulah is the metaphor used for the Promised Land or Judea in Isaiah 62:4.

2 **"And Pablo Peixota was a policy king":** See Ch. 7, note 5.

3 **"What's the difference between a policy game . . .":** See previous note.

4 **Father Georgy Gapon (1870–1906):** A Russian Orthodox priest
who led a worker's revolt in St. Petersburg on 22 January 1905.

5 **Father Divine:** See Ch. 8, note 5.

6 **Monk Rasputin:** Father Grigori Rasputin (1869–1916), the infamous Russian mystic known as the "Mad Monk" who was an
adviser to the Romanov family during the reign of Nicholas II, the
last czar of Russia.

CHAPTER 13

1 **he might have been a Ras:** See Ch. 7, note 3.

2 **Central American:** In the original typescript, McKay had written
"Caribbean," later revising it with a handwritten emendation to
"Central American."

3 **known as Honest Peixota in Harlem:** The character Pablo Peixota
seems to be based in part on Casper Holstein, the famous black
"numbers" king in the 1920s. In his book on Harlem, McKay
describes Holstein in a manner that is strikingly reminiscent of
this passage about Peixota. Holstein "was liked, he was respected,
he was trusted. Sometimes faced with the payment of unusually
large sums to winners, some numbers bankers defaulted and fled

Harlem. But Holstein was renowned for his reliability. He paid fully the heaviest winnings." Claude McKay, *Harlem: Negro Metropolis* (New York: E. P. Dutton, 1940), 102–3.

4   **"you abominable bashibazouk"**: An irregular soldier of the Ottoman army; by connotation an adventurer, a mercenary, or an undisciplined and brutal fighter (from the Turkish *basibozuk*, literally "damaged head").

5   **imbibing many rounds of double "shorties" (a Harlem special) of rye**: In the slang of the period, "shorties" were quarter-pint portions of liquor.

6   **Titian-haired**: i.e., with golden-reddish or brownish-orange hair, so named after the hair color of some women in the paintings of the Italian artist Tiziano Vecelli, known as Titian (c. 1488–1576).

CHAPTER 14

1   **". . . lieutenants in the policy game"**: See Ch. 7, note 5.

2   **a Fusion mayor**: The term "electoral fusion" means that a candidate is allowed to appear on a ballot under multiple party lines.

CHAPTER 15

1   **Mr. Secretary Hughes**: Charles Evans Hughes (1862–1948), American politician and statesman. He served as secretary of state from 1921 to 1925.

2   **the Nuremberg decrees**: Anti-Semitic laws the ruling German Nazi Party put into effect in 1935.

3   **"CCC and NLRB . . . and FBI"**: CCC: Civilian Conservation Corps, an American work relief program initiated through the New Deal that ran from 1933 to 1943; NLRB: National Labor Relations Board, formed in 1935; FHA: Federal Housing Administration; AAA: Agricultural Adjustment Act of 1933, a New Deal law designed to reduce surplus and increase the value of crops by paying farmers not to plant on part of their land; TVA: Tennessee Valley Authority,

founded in 1933; NYA: National Youth Administration, a New Deal agency that operated from 1935 to 1939; FBI: Federal Bureau of Investigation, the law-enforcement agency founded in 1908.

4   **"when it withdrew its naval and military forces from Haiti . . . to withdraw from the Philippines":** In July 1915, after years of political instability and violence in Haiti (culminating in the murder of Haitian president Jean Vilbrun Guillaume Sam by a mob), the US president Woodrow Wilson ordered 330 Marines to Port-au-Prince to safeguard American corporate interests there. The US occupation of Haiti lasted until August 1934. Spain ceded the Philippine islands to the United States in 1898 after the Spanish-American War. A US military government ruled the islands until 1901, when the United States withdrew its armed forces and set up the Insular Government of the Philippine Islands, which operated under US supervision until 1935. The Philippines finally gained full sovereignty in 1946.

5   **"the ideal of Collective Security":** A political arrangement that attempts to ensure the security of all states through an agreement that a threat to any individual state is a concern to the entire group. This ideal was a key motivation in the formation of inter-governmental initiatives such as the Inter-Parliamentary Union in 1889, the League of Nations in 1919, and the United Nations in 1945.

CHAPTER 16

1   **the classic grandeur of Duse . . . Josephine Baker:** Eleonora Duse (1858–1924), Italian actress; Josephine Baker (1906–75), American actress, singer, and dancer who became an international star in Paris in the 1920s.

2   *A Song of Lenin:* A tribute made ten years after the death of the Soviet leader Vladimir Lenin, Dziga Vertov's silent documentary film is more commonly known under the title *Three Songs About Lenin* (1934).

3   **Jean Jaurès** (1859–1914): French Socialist Party leader who was attempting to use diplomatic means to prevent the outbreak of war when he was assassinated in July 1914.

4   "the week when the Camelots du Roy spread havoc": The *Fédéra-tion Nationale des Camelots du Roi* (National Federation of the King's Camelots) was the youth organization of the far-right *Ac-tion Française* movement in France; the group played a major role in the violent anti-parliamentary riots that broke out in Paris on 6 February 1934.

CHAPTER 17

1   Gethsemane: The garden at the foot of the Mount of Olives in Jerusalem where Jesus prayed the night before his crucifixion.

2   "since Lenin died": Vladimir Ilyich Ulyanov (1870–1924), Commu-nist revolutionary and political theorist who led the Russian Re-public and later the Soviet Union from the Bolshevik Revolution's overthrow of the czarist regime in 1917 until his death in 1924.

3   "a mad Englishman named Chamberlain and Frenchman called Gobineau": Houston Stewart Chamberlain (1855–1927), a British-German political philosopher whose book *The Foundations of the Nineteenth Century* advocated for the superiority of the Aryan race and influenced the anti-Semitic policies of the National Socialist movement and Nazi regime; Arthur de Gobineau (1816–82), French aristocrat and man of letters who devised the theory of Aryan master race in his book *An Essay on the Inequality of Human Races* (1853–55).

4   Alexander Pushkin (1799–1837): Russian poet, often considered to be the father of modern Russian literature.

CHAPTER 18

1   "Emperor flees Ethiopian Capital": Facing the defeat of the Ethio-pian army by the invading Italian forces, the Emperor Haile Se-lassie left Addis Ababa with his family and fled to Djibouti on 2 May 1936.

CHAPTER 19

1   "the Scottsboro case": See Ch. 8, note 3.

CHAPTER 20

1   **President Hoover:** Herbert Clark Hoover (1874–1964) was the thirty-first president of the United States, serving in office from 1929 to 1933.

2   **"we need Raphaels . . . Gauguins":** Raphael (1483–1520), Italian painter and architect; Jean-François Millet (1814–75), French painter; Paul Gauguin (1848–1903), French Postimpressionist and Symbolist painter, sculptor, ceramist, writer, and printmaker.

3   **such masters as Goya . . . Grosz:** Francisco Goya (1746–1828), Spanish painter and printmaker; Rembrandt (1606–69), Dutch painter and etcher; Frans Hals (1582–1666), Dutch painter; William Hogarth (1697–1764), British painter, engraver, political satirist, and cartoonist; John French Sloan (1871–1961), American painter and realist; and Georg Grosz (1893–1959), German painter and draughtsman.

CHAPTER 21

1   **a W.P.A. teacher:** i.e., a teacher employed by the Works Progress Administration (1935–43), a New Deal initiative headed by Harry Hopkins that provided jobs to many during the Great Depression. See the Introduction.

2   **a perpetual St. Vitus dance:** An allusion to the disease called Sydenham's chorea, a disorder in which the body exhibits rapid, uncoordinated jerking movements.

CHAPTER 22

1   **"We have had the Queen of Romania":** A member of the British royal family, Princess Marie of Edinburgh (1875–1938), or Marie of Romania, was the last queen of Romania as the consort of King Ferdinand I; in the fall of 1926 she visited several cities in the United States, where she was received by enormous crowds.

2   **"the Mosque of Omar":** After the siege of Jerusalem in 637 CE, the Caliph Omar (579–644 CE) came to Jerusalem to accept the

surrender of Patriarch Sophronius. Omar visited the Church of the Holy Sepulchre and was invited to pray there, but declined, so as not to endanger its status as a Christian site. Instead he prayed outside, in the courtyard. The Mosque of Omar was constructed by the Ayyubid Sultan Al-Afdal ibn Salah ad-Din in 1193 in memory of this event.

3 **the Einstein Theory:** i.e., the theory of relativity of physicist Albert Einstein (1879–1955).

4 **"Like Aaron's rod, eh?":** i.e., one of the staves carried by Moses's brother, Aaron, in the Old Testament of the Bible; according to Numbers 17, Aaron's rod was endowed with miraculous power during the Plagues of Egypt.

5 **fellah:** A peasant (Arabic).

6 **Tammany Hall:** See Ch. 6, note 1.

CHAPTER 23

1 **the Spanish Civil War:** This conflict began on 17 July 1936 and ended on 1 April 1939.

Editors' Acknowledgments

The authentication, editing, and publication of Claude Mc-Kay's long-lost novel has been an extremely complex undertaking that, in the nearly eight years since the typescript's discovery, has required at least as much serendipity and sheer perseverance as archival detective work and literary acumen. If the novel offers unexpected revelations into McKay's thinking and writing in his later years, bringing it to print has been an exhaustive lesson in the nuances of copyright and probate. We are extremely grateful to the many colleagues who have assisted us with various aspects of the project.

Hiie Saumaa and Rachel Collins provided research assistance at Columbia and Syracuse, respectively, while Genevieve Deleon transcribed the entire novel from McKay's original typescript. The staff of the Rare Book and Manuscript Library at Columbia University has been instrumental throughout this process; we especially thank Michael Ryan, Sean Quimby, Karla Nielsen, and Alix Ross. In our research into the genesis of *Amiable with Big Teeth* we also drew on the expertise of a number of librarians and archivists at other institutions, including David Frasier at Indiana University; Louise Bernard at Yale University; Randall Burkett and Kevin Young at Emory University; Christopher Harter at Tulane University's Amistad Research Center; and Khalil Muhammad and Diana Lachatanere at the Schomburg Center of the New York Public Library.

This project would simply not have been possible without Diana Lachatanere's support and generosity in particular. Her commitment to McKay's legacy and to the family heirs is extraordinary, and we thank her for everything she has done to help us bring *Amiable with Big Teeth* to readers.

For their invaluable legal advice, we are indebted to Kenneth Crews (the former director of the Copyright Advisory Office in the Columbia University Libraries), Robert Spoo, and especially Alex Chachkes, who was kind enough to represent us pro bono. Jacqueline Bausch of the general counsel's office of the New York Public Library was also helpful during a particularly delicate phase of the legal negotiations. Our agent, Don Fehr of the Trident Media Group, as well as the Faith Childs Agency, which represents the McKay heirs, have been indefatigable in their efforts on behalf of the book. We also thank Elda Rotor of Penguin Classics for her extraordinary patience and steadfast support.

Over the years, a number of colleagues have taken the time to discuss the project with us in depth. Wayne Cooper, Henry Louis Gates Jr., and William Maxwell evaluated our extensive research demonstrating the authenticity of the typescript, and we thank them for their comments and sage counsel. Others who shared their expertise on various topics that have come up during the editorial work—ranging from the history of the Popular Front, to mid-century African American fiction, to the intricacies of copyright law—include Crystal Bartolovich, Mary Britton, Jay Gertzman, Laura Helton, Robert A. Hill, Edward Mendelson, Robert O'Meally, Max Rudin, Paul K. Saint-Amour, and Maura Spiegel. Finally, we thank our families for their patience and encouragement during this novel's peculiar, lengthy, and at times tortuous path to publication.

ALSO AVAILABLE

GEORGE S. SCHUYLER

Black No More

Introduction by Danzy Senna

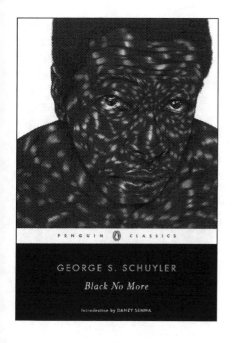

It's 1933 in New York City, and Max Disher, a young black man, decides to undergo a mysterious process that allows people to bleach their skin white—a new way to "solve the American race problem." Lampooning myths of white supremacy and racial purity, *Black No More* is a masterwork of speculative fiction and a hilarious satire of America's obsession with race.

"Schuyler's wild, misanthropic, take-no-prisoners satire of American life seems more relevant than ever."
—Danzy Senna, from the Introduction

 PENGUIN CLASSICS

Ready to find your next great read? Let us help. Visit prh.com/nextread

ALSO AVAILABLE

LANGSTON HUGHES

Not Without Laughter

Introduction by Angela Flournoy

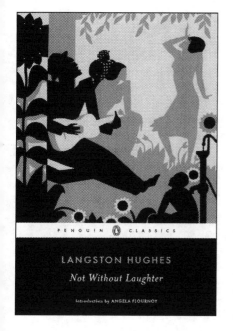

When first published in 1930, *Not Without Laughter* established Langston Hughes as not only a brilliant poet and leading light of the Harlem Renaissance but also a gifted novelist. In telling the story of Sandy Rogers, a young African American boy in small-town Kansas, and of his family, Hughes gives the longings and lineaments of black life in the early twentieth century an important place in the history of racially divided America.

"An eye-opening portrait of the artist as a young black man in the Midwest." –A. Scott Berg, *The New York Times Book Review*

PENGUIN CLASSICS

Ready to find your next great read? Let us help. Visit prh.com/nextread

NELLA LARSEN
PASSING
Introduction by Emily Bernard

Fair, elegant, and ambitious, Clare Kendry is married to a white man unaware of her African American heritage. Clare's childhood friend Irene Redfield, just as light-skinned, has chosen to remain within the black community. A chance encounter forces both to confront the lies they have told—and the fears they have buried within themselves.

WALLACE THURMAN
THE BLACKER THE BERRY . . .
Introduction by Allyson Hobbs

One of the most widely read and controversial works of the Harlem Renaissance, and the first novel to openly address prejudice among black Americans, Wallace Thurman's *The Blacker the Berry . . .* is a book of undiminished power about the invidious role of skin color in American society.

W. E. B. DU BOIS
THE SOULS OF BLACK FOLK
With "The Talented Tenth" and "The Souls of White Folk"
Introduction by Ibram X. Kendi

The landmark book about being black in America, now in an expanded edition commemorating the 150th anniversary of W. E. B. Du Bois's birth and featuring a new introduction by National Book Award–winning author Ibram X. Kendi.

PENGUIN CLASSICS

Ready to find your next great read? Let us help. Visit prh.com/nextread

ALSO AVAILABLE

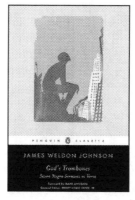
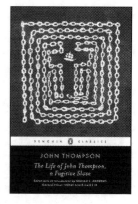

GOD'S TROMBONES
Seven Negro Sermons in Verse
James Weldon Johnson
Foreword by Maya Angelou
General Editor: Henry Louis Gates, Jr.

IOLA LEROY
Frances Ellen Watkins Harper
Introduction by Hollis Robbins
General Editor: Henry Louis Gates, Jr.

**THE LIFE OF JOHN THOMPSON,
A FUGITIVE SLAVE**
John Thompson
Edited with an Introduction
by William L. Andrews
General Editor: Henry Louis Gates, Jr.

THE LIGHT OF TRUTH
Writings of an Anti-Lynching Crusader
Ida B. Wells
Edited with an Introduction
and Notes by Mia Bay
General Editor: Henry Louis Gates, Jr.

**THE PORTABLE CHARLES W.
CHESNUTT**
Charles W. Chesnutt
Edited with an Introduction
by William L. Andrews
General Editor: Henry Louis Gates, Jr.

QUICKSAND
Nella Larsen
Introduction by Thadious M. Davis

TWELVE YEARS A SLAVE
Solomon Northup
Foreword by Steve McQueen
Introduction by Ira Berlin
Afterword by Henry Louis Gates, Jr.
General Editor: Henry Louis Gates, Jr.

(🐧) PENGUIN CLASSICS

Ready to find your next great read? Let us help. Visit prh.com/nextread

Printed in the United States
by Baker & Taylor Publisher Services